I0658589

Side Door

to Heaven

for

Hemingway:

Suicide Barred Him from a Grand Entrance into the Pearly Gates

By: David Wyant

Printed in the United States of America
Wizard of Walloon Press

ISBN 9780990464907

www.wizardofwalloon.com

Table of Contents

4

Dedicated to my father, Julius Amandus Wyant, and Uncle Andrew Wyant for rescuing me from death after drowning and utilizing CPR on my recovery back to life.

Acknowledgements

$\mathcal{T}$ hanks given to God for inspiring this work, and the King James Version of the Bible.

Christel Bassett, trusty, loyal typist, photographer, and editor- in-chief.

Ernest Hemingway Mainland, nephew of Ernest Hemingway, for helpful hints (about his famous Uncle) during lunch at City Park Grill in Petoskey, Michigan.

John Hemingway, son of Gregory Hemingway, grandson of Ernest Hemingway, for the encouraging emails and insights into his troubled father, Gregory Hemingway.

Mariel Hemingway for her encouragement and for all the work she does for suicide prevention. Suicide Hot line 1-800-273-8255 if one is feeling depressed.

All the written Hemingway biographies and sibling biographies for their inspiring information, especially Marcie, Sunny & Leichester's revealing biographies of Ernest.

Petoskey public library, where I researched many times.

James Vol Hartwell of Walloon Lake, for his volumes of information on Prudence Boulton.

Members of the Green Sky Hill Methodist Church for allowing us to visit Prudence's grave-site.

John F. Kennedy Library for the public domain photos of Ernest.

The New York Times and the Key West Citizen, for allowing us to use their headlines.

To all the storytellers of Petoskey, Harbor Springs, Hortons Bay and Lake Walloon, who perpetuated their compelling linguistic phenomenon, and impacted heavily upon young Ernest.

Ernest Hemingway's Funeral, Ketchum, Idaho, July 1961

Chapter 1. July, 1961

After My Apparent Death: Thoughts From the Grave by Hemingway

The Key West Citizen

'PAPA' PASSES

Heyday Of Great Man Remembered

Humor, Vigor Were Memorable Traits

Familiar Figure On Local Scene

Old Pals Hold Fond Memories

Bell Tolls For Writer

Ernest Hemingway Dies Of Gun Shot

2 Are Hurt In Accident

I did all I could to stop them from attaching a name tag to my big toe, but alas it took a number of frustrating days to realize that I was indeed dead. At least my body was in the morgue. Somehow my spirit was still very much alive. Even though I was missing the top of my skull, the other amazing part was that I felt no pain.

What pain eventually arrived was the total lack of interaction I now had with my entire physical world: after yelling as loud as I could, no one could hear me, "I'm alive! I'm alive! You bastards must believe me. I'm still alive, damn it!"

However, all my yelling was in vain for the vocal cords I used to count on for making so many of my best arguments were no longer taking orders from my ever active mind.

It was a grave mistake to think that by destroying my brain, the disturbing and most condemning thoughts would cease, but they still continued, damn it, and that fact disturbed me deeply even more.

Watching my casket being lowered into the Idaho soil, my spirit began to leap from relative to relative trying to console them, "Auntie, I'm fine. I'm okay."

"He was such a nice boy," commented my favorite sister, Ursala. Extreme sadness hovered over everyone gathered around the graveside. Great emotional loss shocked each relative so much so, that Ursala's comments fell empty in a statement that needed no 'amen'.

Ursala's comment ended up merely as an echo, a painful rhetorical comment which generated no reply from the many stunned mourners encircling my grave. Only the wind carried Ursa's statement around the crowd, up and out through the majestic pines that watched the solemn, silent ritual in this cool, clear July 6 morning near Ketchum, Idaho.

During this painful pause, we eventually heard a loud thump as a young altar boy fainted to the ground.

Since I was only a nominal Catholic, I deserved no church high mass funeral, but the Padre did make a grave site interment to set the notion that his ritual might generate prayers to get my sorry ass out of purgatory.

Before the usual ashes to ashes dirt sprinkling, Padre read my favorite Bible passage from the book of Ecclesiastes 1:15, but out of honor to the title, I chose for my last book, the "Sun Also Rises". He failed to, or chose not to, mention that famous phrase. Padre read everything else around it but paused at that part of it.

Immediately, I zoomed over to him to bitch him out, but then he continued with: "A human life without being in Christ is pointless, absurd as the sun, moon, and endless flow of rivers which continue their never ending path across the sky, in pointless pursuit of something, only to return again daily, and repeat the same monotonous cycle day after day, after deadening day.

Those not in Christ die daily due to the absurd redundancy offered by the suns endless pursuit of something that it will never catch. Even during its Asian sojourn at our night, it fails."

Padre made his point off my book title. The irony was deep. Boredom is the year's reward as the sun also rises chasing after an unknown something across the endless sky, and into the eastern hemisphere, and eventually to rise again in our morning dawn only to find another empty cycle of boredom, it never makes any real progress.

The moon too seems to be chasing something across our sky, and our rivers also chase along endlessly in their boring pursuit that only amounts to an empty mind numbing nothing.

Padre continues, "However, the life in Christ never tires of doing good. The sun rising on each new day gives the man in God more time to help others. He searches for the needy who may need only a kind look or a kind word, or a good hug, or a good meal. The sun also rises on those individuals bent only on sense gratification... they are never satisfied and will continually search the world over, thinking life might be better somewhere else, but eventually must come to the realization gained from the continual sunrise, that upon one's life the sun must also set, and conclude the absurd monotony of it all in the end."

The priest really nailed it. At my very own funeral grave talk he called it like it is. He beat me over the head with my very own book title… "...Sun Also Rises."

Well, there ain't nothing I can do about it. Whether Padre knew it or not, I understood this. Throughout my whole body of work this was my main theme. I was trying to point out how hopeless it is to waste one's life in pursuit of hedonism. Yet rather we need to figure out how to return to the garden of Eden, our real home.

My preaching about it I found was a turnoff, so I let my choice of characters tell their story, allowing my readers to make their own conclusions.

Reading every mourner's graveside thoughts, I found they all felt rather comforted by the Padres message. I decided to quit yelling at them.

Someone gave the fallen altar boy a cold canteen of water and he felt better after he was led to a shady spot.

It didn't surprise me that my sister, Sunny, was seeing ghosts, and it didn't surprise me that my widow, my darling wife, Mary, had the thought of all my money on her mind. It was quite a sizable sum... at least three or four million clams, which is why I found the key to my gun case so handy, I guess.

Mary knew I was depressed and had attempted suicide numerous times before, but I always got interrupted by someone, so she will be hard pressed to explain the easy access to my gun rack keys.

My loving wife is going to disappoint me later by making Sunny pay for the Windemere cabin, which I had promised Sunny as an outright gift for her damn good priceless typing job of my manuscripts like "Farewell to Arms."

With me out of the picture now, my dear wife is exhibiting a rather mercenary side and going contrary to my wishes. Seems she had a hidden agenda all along.

Being an educated person, also a writer herself, Mary amazes me, now that I'm dead. For one thing, how come she didn't heed early symptoms of my being suicidal:

1. *Unkempt... disinterest in my personal appearance, evidenced during Lillian Roth's biography.*
2. *Eating and sleeping problems.*
3. *Expressing how I had planned to off myself. I talked of suicide openly.*
4. *Giving away personal possessions, as well as large sums of money often to total strangers.*
5. *I was out of my mind due to my diabetes, my many concussions, and scores of electroshock abuses at the Mayo clinic.*
6. *I needed psychotherapy to nurture my mind back to health, but never got it.*

We could go back to my early teen years and note the early suicidal tendencies exhibited even then, accumulating in my wounding at the Italian front during World War I at Fassalta on the Piave.

That was suicide of the highest magnitude. How else does one explain why an 18-year-old kid rides his bicycle loaded with only chocolate bars and cigarettes onto a battlefield into live trench warfare facing bursting Austrian mortar shells and live enemy machine gun fire.

My risky decision to wander unarmed into the dangerous Italian battlefront, into the jaws of certain death, had to have been generated by none other than suicide of the highest order... A wish for death.

No one in their right mind would have considered throwing caution to the wind and finding themselves walking into the wide-open mouth of instant death, armed with only candy and smokes.

Certainly, it is a fine edge between insanity, heroism, or a strong wish for certain death, yet I, by the grace of God, came out a hero in that scenario during World War I. But now I find myself having a flashback, back to happier times, back to my last summer with all my good friends up in Michigan.

It is with great clarity that I recall that summer of 1917. It was right after high school graduation that all of us who called ourselves Americans felt the strong pull of battle reports of godless Huns who threatened our women, our freedom, and our precious way of life. Young boys had to be 19 in order to sign up for active duty into the war to end all wars.

Many of my close pals lied about their age and a copy of the eye chart circulated between friends, thus ensuring that we would also pass the physical exam.

Father forbid me to go, reminding me of my K.C. Star job in October. Also, I know how bad my eyesight really was, so cheating at the physical exam seemed out of the question.

Strong feelings of guilt followed me down to LaSalle Street railroad station to see our boys off to war without me, their leader. My future had already been decided by Uncle Tylie, who had wrangled a cub reporter position with the Kansas City Star newspaper. I was to report at the newspaper in October, so that left me one last summer to enjoy life up in Michigan with all my lifelong summer friends in Petoskey, Hortons Bay, Charlevoix, Boyne City, and Lake Walloon.

I felt consoled as I anticipated the best summer ever, and come October, I would use my pen to help defeat the godless Huns.

Yet as this drama unfolds, I know you will begin to spot the telltale signs of my courting of disaster at every turn, for even as a kid, I exhibit what seems like I am just accident prone, but it could very well be something much deeper and much more sinister. Be open to the exhibiting of the early signs of my desire to end my very own life by my very own hand.

In fact, our family is a hotbed of self killing, a breeding ground for self annihilation of its members.

My take as to why so many of us choose to bring our precious lives to an end still has to lie with our overly spoiled mother.

She was a frustrated limelight hog, and attention vampire, with an overgrown ability to suck all the energy out of any room she was in This woman felt that all attention, every iota of it, was to be directed toward her. She demanded all our energy and even made us feel guilty if we saved any of it to develop our own private personalities. She felt she owned her children, and she felt she could do whatever she wanted with them. I have a whole lot of rage for that bitch. Brass door knobs lost their luster in her presence, and immediately felt bad for trying to outshine our upstaging mother. That's how bad she was. She made sure that the spotlight always shown on her illustrious image, and if it didn't, she had no qualms about stealing all of it.

Mother is the reason for our suicides. The woman knew no boundaries. Eventually, four of us eight will commit suicide, will take our own lives, so in the Hemingway family each was entertaining dangerous observable factors. Try to spot them.

Psychologists will have a heyday analyzing our regrettable family dynamic.

Yet now somehow the regrets begin again. Sickening voices... subtle now, begin to remind me of my past shortcomings, begin to bitch at me now of my failures in the past, begin to haunt my moments now as soil was ceremoniously tossed upon my shiny bronze casket.

Padre began the soil tossing with the worn out phrase regarding ashes to ashes. The fainted altar boy resumed his duties now, which included handing Padre more gravesite soil soaked in the young lad's teenage tears, which flowed now like a spring which had been tapped within his young heart.

Immediately, my spirit rushed to comfort the lad in order to reassure him that I was all right, "Please don't cry, Larry, I'm okay. I tell you, I'm all right!"

Each family member stepped graveside as the soil tossing ritual continued and not knowing better, my spirit rushed to each one, each sister and nephew, and teary eyed niece, to reassure them also. "Hey, *kid, I'm okay, I'm not in that casket there. I'm here next to you and never felt better. I'm okay I tell you! Okay!"*

But it was no use. They could not hear me.

Sunny one of my favorite sisters brought her son, whom she named after me. "Ernie, my boy, toss this rose. That's it. He loved you you know."

"Yes, Mother... I know."

"I sense his spirit. Can you feel him?"

"Yes, Mother. I mean, no Mother. I feel hungry, can we get an olive burger in this town?"

"Oh, Ernest Hemingway Mainland, now is not a time to be thinking of your stomach!"

Again, the regrets came to mind. I regretted that I had never spent enough time with my nephew, Ernie Mainland, who by this time was in college.

Regrets came flooding into my mind, spoiling a perfectly good funeral. Again, I deeply regretted not being able to silence my conscience with that shotgun blast to my brain. I'd misjudged the function of the brain, and it was adding up to the biggest mistake of my life.

What bothers me most is that Satan played me! And he played me so easily. Satan had tricked me. He had me convinced that the voices in my head would cease after the shotgun blast to the brain, but they now got worse, much worse! A constant barrage of indictments. This is what I can expect for eternity? Constant satanic attacks?

Father Waldmann prayed to God beseeching him to forgive me for taking my own life. Padre also had everyone praying to lift my soul out of purgatory. I likes to hear that.

Hearing my family and friends praying to lift my soul out of purgatory touched me deeply. From my new point of view, I liked the power of prayer, for now I can sense its advantage lies in the faith of the loved one generating the supplications.

When I was in my body, my beliefs were misplaced, for I found myself often knocking on wood, carrying a worn out rabbits foot as well as a horse chestnut in my pockets for good luck. Guess I was superstitious thinking that those items could bring me good luck. I needed to find favor with God in order to have things come my way, and His favor follows a person of strong faith.

Scripture states that without faith, it is impossible to please Him. Therefore, prayers uttered in faith get results. Having read the good book and even memorizing the entire Scripture, I must've missed that vital point.

I regret that I never took any of it seriously, but now I have eternity to regret it.

While I was embodied, God was always willing to give me a second chance, but I missed all the chances I had, and that counts as probably the biggest mistake that I made, for while alive I always had the hope of another chance to become friends with God, and develop a personal relationship with him.

Satan is always hard at work getting us depressed in hopes it will lead to suicide. He and his demons are constantly working hard to talk us into taking our own lives.

Consumption of massive amounts of alcohol played right into their hand for alcohol acts as a depressant on the system. So often I fell into depression, I would pour me a few drinks of gin to act as a pick me up, hoping to counteract the foul mood I was in; however, the drug actually achieved the opposite effect, slamming me further into the depths of deep depression.

Add to that my bad habit of holding a grudge. I regret never forgiving my bitch of a mother. By not forgiving her, I was saddled with having to carry her spoiled diva persona around throughout my entire life.

Those quirky aspects of my personality were caused by my having to see life through her quirky point of view. Had I forgiven her I would've been free to be me.

In my rarefied state of being now out of my body-I see through all of my foolishness. Letting go of past hurts and abuses would have felt good, but I regret… I was too bullheaded in that regard, and during my life I paid for it dearly.

However, if I returned from the grave and started sharing what I now know, who would believe me?!

It's too late now, but now I realize that killing myself actually solved absolutely nothing! It just messed up my back porch, and messed up my hope of ever having a chance for redemption.

Redemption is something that is always available while in the body. Always there for the taking, if one avails themselves of it. Our God is the God of second chances, and no matter how messed up we are, He always offers forgiveness because His Son redeemed us- He paid the price which allowed us to enter His kingdom... As long as we maintain a body!

For some reason that simple truth escaped my scrutiny while memorizing the Bible. Ironic, huh? I missed the main point of the entire Scripture. Of all the books I wrote, I missed the simple message of the best book in the world. Now, what greater tragedy could there be? To miss the chance of free redemption is going to be my everlasting, eternal regret.

Satan tricks me out of my redemption... That's slick talking S.O.B! He actually had me believing that the condemning voices would stop with the blasting away of my brain, so when I easily found the key that unlocked my gun case, grabbed my favorite shotgun, and for the last time fondled the silver inlaid Richardson, double-barreled 12 gauge, Satan knew that he was in the drivers seat. The gun that had ended the lives of so many thousands of innocent wild birds and animals, now ended the life of the intrepid hunter, himself not so innocent.

My thoughts began to drift beyond the dramatic shock of being without my body. My mind drifted toward pleasant times, back to my most idyllic times after high school graduation, back to the beginning of summer vacation.

Signs leading to my suicide were evident then. Carrying guilt about seeing all my pals go off to war always stayed with me. That sad scene on the La Salle Street Railroad platform was forever etched in my mind, mainly because I couldn't go with those unskilled, innocent lads. Being the best shot of all of them was hard to swallow ever after. Why them and not me?

Sure, I had a great opportunity waiting for me in Kansas City, but the scene was so dramatic and so damn tragic that I still have a difficult time clearing my head of those sad images... Well actually, my mind, since my head is gone.

I discovered the hard way that the mind is not housed in the brain from my desperate attempt to silence the nagging mind. I took a shotgun to my brain but still my conscience pestered me.

Chapter 2. June 1917, 44 Years Earlier

Farewell Friends

A WWI Troop Train Departs

Like every 1917 high school graduate, I have a strong urge to enlist in the service of my country, but since Uncle Tyler has so nicely landed me a job reporting for the Kansas City Star newspaper, I am almost compelled to fulfill my obligation to the Star.

Most of my classmates and close pals, however, did enlist, and today got shipped off to boot camp in long passenger trains. Our high school band plays Marshal Music, and friends, as well as family, say their intense farewells on over packed boarding platforms. Our teachers and principal are all here. Tears flow as the trains pull out of Chicago station, jammed with young boys headed straight into the jaws of death. All my closest classmates have that disgusted look, for they really worked on me to join up; even gave me all the eye-chart answers so's I could pass the Army physical.

We all trail along as the train moves slowly at first. Open train windows are filled with the excited faces of future dough boys.

"Hey Hemingstein, we got the eye chart answers here if you change your mind, pal. Give it another thought," yelled Mussie Mussleman.

"Listen Mussy. I'll miss all you great guys but you don't know how bad my eyes are."

"Yeah well, hope you change your mind. Write now, okay?"

"Sure will, pal. Often as I can."

They all know I was the best shot in shooting club, so I can understand their urgings. If there are Krauts to be shot, and there will be, I am the guy who could do the best job and score more kills than any of them, so I know they are feeling like I let them down. I hate that feeling; for I've worked hard to gain their respect and admiration for being a good scout. We've had great times.

"Hey, you birds all know the pen is mightier than the sword. I'll stay state side and kill those Huns with words in the Star."

"Yeah, Hemmie. You give 'em hell, kid!" added Gus Gustavson standing on the platform, the runt of the gang.

"And when you return, we'll all go fishing again," I shouted as the train slowly rumbled past the wooden platform. "Oh God... please watch over those boys. They will need all the help you can give them. Kinda sad huh, Harold, seeing all our gang rolling off to war?"

"Too sad, actually. They will do little to help the war effort. They'll just be fodder for Austrian cannon fire," remarked Harold.

"Ain't it the truth. What a rotten shame."

"Indeed, Austria/Hungary has been busy for years now building up thousands of artillery cannons and battleships, with one goal in mind."

"And what's that Harold?" says I.

"World domination! What else, Hemmie?"

"Yeah, guess you're right. Gosh! I hate to see so many of our pals getting killed or coming back with no arms or legs or messed up inside... ya know, Harold?"

"Just don't you dwell on that too much though, friend. Guilt can eat you up. I feel bad having to go to Harvard, but it's the chance of a lifetime and I can't miss out now."

"Yeah Harold, you'll do well at Harvard. I know you will. Probably be out in three years."

"Two maybe, and Stein, you will be outstanding at the Star."

"Gosh, thanks, pal, for that vote of confidence. Actually kinda looking forward to the challenge; the K.C. Star is one of the best newspapers in America."

"Right, there. I have a feeling you will discover a whole new writing style."

"Really! Now what? Have you become some kinda prophet now?"

"Stein, just common sense. You have your God-given ability to distill everything, like the alchemist which you've become. Newspaper editors like that, you know, brevity, tell the story, but with as few as words possible."

"Okay, got it...like that?"

"Yup," Harold replies.

"Oh, now you're just being funny."

"Nope."

"Come on, Sam," I says.

"Stein, look, don't know exactly where you've picked up your lingo, but you talk and write like no Oak Park chaps. That unique way you phrase a piece is typically you, Hemster. Tell me friend. Where'd you pick that up?"

"Shhh! It's secret. I've been developing this ever since I became editor of the school paper. It's nothing more than Ojibwe gibberish."

"Say, now I get it! Yes! You've become one of them, haven't you?"

"Yup, but don't tell anybody, okay, Samson?"

"Wow! I sniffed out the secret style of the great Hemstein."

"Shhh. Hey pal, seriously, now keep it under your hat, okay?"

"Why, you crafty devil... you became one of the tribe. Now I've met your woodland natives. Heard their brief, short, choppy phraseology, but you...you have synthesized their tongue all together. How'd you do that?"

"Yup, wasn't easy either. It took me several summers, but I've created a whole new form of pidgin English listening to them talk and then transcribing it into an understandable American version."

"Outstanding! You're the Linguist from Walloon!"

"Yup...now, please don't tell that to anyone. White folks hate the Indian, but my best girl, Prudy, is half breed as you know, pal. And hunting, fishing, and trapping with Billy Tabeshaw and Dick Boulton. Hey, through the years it all got under my tongue."

"These indigenous Aborigines have created their own white boy mouthpiece, wow! How incredible, Stein…and only you could have done it."

"Yup. Kinda remarkable, huh? It all hit me one day. Ya see, I kept hearing it. Kept hearing it and thought at first, naw', I thought I was imagining what I heard up in Michigan. But they all talk this way, up in Michigan. Petoskey especially, and they are all story-tellers, story-tellers I tell ya! But now with all the tourists that have discovered the natural beauty in the summer the stories stop. One of these days I will spend a winter up there…in Petoskey…just for the stories, which I'm assuming will start up when tourists vacate the place."

"Remarkable, simply remarkable. So the local story tellers clam up during the arrival of tourists and resorters?"

"Yup…strange phenomenon."

"So why is that, do you suppose?"

"I've speculated on that very question. Uh, here's a nice coffee shop. I'll tell you over a cup a joe."

"Here, Stein, have a seat. Cream? Now where were we? Oh, right, local stories dry up in summer."

"See, now you're talking like them, Sam. Ahh…well sir, I figure the tourists are not there for the stories, just the cool breeze coming off the bay. They sort of snub the locals…arrogance I think…so any self-respecting Petoskeyite naturally shrinks back and sits on all his good stuff…stories…that is."

"So during winter they comes out with the good stuff 'cause they then have a rapt audience, sittin' around the cracker barrel, so to speak," says Harold.

"Now, by June, Watson, you've got it!" I exclaims. "Sugar?"

"Please. So how did you stumble onto this phenom?"

"Samson, just by listening, chum. Listening and more listening. Here's how I got it figured; the Indian speaks very little. They do all their communication thru signing."

"You mean sign language?" Harold questions.

"Yup and gesture and get this…telepathy."

"What!?" exclaims Harold.

"Yeaaah. Not kiddin' you heard right! Telepathy!"

"They can read thoughts?"

"Yup. The humble Redskin is simply amazing. Anglo has no idea, Sam. Now don't get me started on how the English have corrupted vocal communications," I says.

The waitress comes over, "More coffee, sirs?"

"Why yes, waitress. Another round please," says Harold.

"Now there's a good example of good communication. The Native American certainly has perfected code. I wouldn't be surprised one bit if they use their code during the war some day just to confuse the Krauts."

"Great idea, Stein! The Krauts would never figure it out."

"Exactly, but keep that under your lid... also. Don't want the enemy picking up on it to decipher it."

"Yes indeed, spoil everything, 'eh, Stein?"

"Us teens have our own code too, have you noticed?"

"Sort of. I try not to corrupt the Mother tongue."

"See! That's the whole issue here, Samson. The English language has to change. What is needed is an American way of speaking. The Limeys presently have the corner on the market, but in their arrogance, their flowery way of speaking AND their writing has dominated the whole field of literature for centuries. As I see it, that all needs to change. This new century demands it."

"And...correct me if I am wrong...you plan to be the agent for change... right? Ernesto?"

"Bingo, Sherlock! But...lots to do before that, sire."

"Check please," Harold calls.

"Gentlemen, that'll be ten cents," the waitress says. "Thank you."

"So you plan to book for K.C. then?" asks Harold.

"Yup, October," I replies.

"Going back up north then for the summer?"

"Yup. Pops is taking the flivver."

"Brave man," Harold says.

"Yeah. Roads past Grand Rapids are nasty."

To say the least. I hope to hang out at the Midway... do research at University of Chicago. In the fall I'll have all my papers ready. Then three years maximum, I'll have the PhD."

"Mother Grace probably has my whole summer planned in the form of work... do this, dear, do that, darling, and if you have time... do that, my darling boy. She's had another kid, you know?"

Harold asks, "Another one... at her age? Child-bearing years should have been over for her."

"Yeah...go figure. But finally...it's a boy. So she, little Leichester, that's his name, and the four girls will go by lake steamer. Pops the Great Physician, Uncle Tyler and myself will motor up to Uncle George's, who has a nursery in Ironton, Michigan."

"Indeed... I think I recall meeting your Uncle George. He is the gentleman who bailed you out of the blue heron affair, right?"

"Yeah... hey don't spread that around either, okay? I almost shot that useless game warden. Ursula saved me from popping turd-face Evans. Yes indeed. That was quite a summer... that one."

"Well, Hemmingstein. It certainly has been a visit of mixed emotions... saying farewell to all of our classmates. Some we may never see again this side of heaven."

"Yup. Death's gonna have his boney fingers tappin' at our door for all of us, pal."

"Correct again... but I fail to dwell on that very long. Well here's my trolley. Fair thee well. Full stein in every pot...my friend."

"Maybe I'll have you over before you leave for college. Can you still box?"

"Indeed... charming fellow. I owe you a kayo (knock out)."

"Lucky punch that was, Samson."

"Indeed... I rather walked into that one. Well, have a good summer up in Michigan... to coin a phrase. Give my love to your 'twin' sister, Marceline."

"That I will. Study hard at U. of Chicago."

"Go with God, Hemmie."

"Same to you, pal. Drop me a line once in a while."

Chapter 3. Dealing With Guilt

Families say Farewell at a WWI Troop Train Departure

Sister Marcy met me and we caught a train south to Oak Park. Lew Clarahan joined us. During the ride I invited Lew to come up north to Michigan. Lew has a huge crush on Marcy.

"Alright, Lew, then it's settled. You can ride in the flivver with the men," says I.

"Are you kiddin' and leave these pretty ladies unattended and all alone on a big Great Lakes Steamer? I've been up there before and we always had a blast." Lew continued, "Marcy, I'd like to get you on a slow boat to–"

"China?" interrupted Marcy. "And then what?"

"Oh, I don't know. We'll think of something."

"Just what I thought. Spirit is willing, but the creativity is weak," comments Marcy.

"Careful, Lew, Marcy can be a buzzkill," says I.

"Talk about sad. Wasn't it sad seeing all our chums on that jam-packed train?" comments Lew.

"Indeed, Lew. I prayed they all would come back," said Marcy.

I retorted, "But Ivory, you know some are coming back in a box. Harold Samson claims they are all cannon fodder."

Lew commented, "Hey the Krauts can't get all of them! Those are my Pals!"

I tried to be realistic, "Listen, Pilgrims. War is hell, ya know. Millions of boys will be sent to their heavenly rest."

Marcy interjected, "It's none of my business. Lew, but why aren't you enlisting?"

"Hey... let me set the record straight, and it might be your business, Marcy, if you play your cards right. I got accepted to Princeton...dear old Princeton. I start in the fall."

"Yay, isn't that grand, what you say, Ernie?" cheers Marcy.

"Great, but no college for us Hemingway kids. Anyway I nailed down an internship with The Star."

"Kansas City Star? Say, Stein, that's great. I can see you being very successful at it."

"Thanks for those kind words, Lew, but I've had some anxiety about moving out to that wide open town. It's not civilized like O.P."

Lew interjected, "Hey, I thought Wyatt Earp civilized that town long ago?"

Marcy added, "Plus you get to stuff your face with Aunt Arabelle's cooking. I'd call that a good trade...wide-open cow town traded for soothing beef Wellington. Oh, Aunt Arabelle will calm down your anxiety, Oinbones."

"Yeah, I guess you're right, Ivory. I just need more faith," says I.

The conductor yells out, "Oak Park... River Forest."

"Well, here's our stop," Marcy stated.

"Can I walk you home, Marcy?"

"Sure, Lew, see ya, Oinbones."

"Thanks, didn't want to walk with ya anyway, Ivory Tower. I'm going over to see my pal, Frank Lloyd Wright."

I begin to sing to calm my nerves, "Somebody loves me. I wonder who. I wonder who she could be..."

Frank's house is just around the corner from us and he's one my favorite customers on my Oak Leaves paper route. Dandelions were everywhere. Frank was outside sizing up repairs that were needed along the soffits of his house.

"Hi, Mr. Wright, good afternoon to you, sir."

"Good afternoon to you also, my friend, Ernest. What brings you out today?"

"Bunch of us were at the train station today to say goodbye to our friends who are going off to war."

"My goodness, that must have been a sad experience for you?"

"Yeah, it was kinda, actually sad as hell considering most of them will get killed and I'll never see them again."

"Sorry, so sorry for you, my friend. Here's one of my newly designed benches, sit, sit a spell please, won't you, Ernest. Now just let it all out. You must be feeling terrible after saying goodbye to all your dear friends."

"Yeah, Mr. Wright. Just need someone to talk to. Dad's never home, Mother's never got time. She has her music, always. Marcy's with Lewis."

"Well there must be a positive note in there somewhere. You will return once again to Northern Michigan for the summer won't you? That should be fun for you? Right?"

"Well, of course, but...I'll be feelin' guilty havin' fun while my pals are having their butts shot off."

"Well I sure can relate to that alright. Can you think of something positive to cheer you up?"

"Hey, right on! Did I tell you about my new job with Kansas City Star? Internship, starts in October. Got me a reporter's job."

"Well, see. That snapped you right out of that down mood. Say Ernest, I read that nice piece you wrote on my Unitarian Temple project. You captured the essence of my work in a nutshell. Nice job, son."

"Actually, Mr. Wright all the neighborhood watched the temple going up and they thought it looked like a shoebox, but my in depth article revealed your ingenious use of interior space, something that stays hidden until one does an internal search."

"Yes, indeed and because of your wellwritten expose I garnered more home designs in River Forest all on the strength of excellent reporting for the high school newspaper. If ever you should need a letter of recommendation, I would be honored to write one for you."

"Gosh thanks, Mr. Wright. Ya know, I'm glad I stopped in to see you. I was really depressed and didn't know it."

"Can I offer you some libation, lemonade, dandelion wine?"

"What? You have dandy wine? Sput sput!"

"Indeed, let me have my cook pour us a pitcher."

Well, when Frank mentioned dandelion wine I just about jumped in his arms to hug him.

"You know, I surmised you were making something out of all those pesky yellow flowers. They are a curse to every lawn in Oak Park, but not yours."

"Except mine. Most of the plant is edible."

"Yeah, my sister plucks the tender leaves for salad. Up north in Michigan we also collect water cress, burdock root (if boiled) and cat tail, the fluff can even be used as a thickener."

"Ernest, you are just a regular fountain of knowledge when it comes to sharing information. You will have plenty of material for the K.C. Star."

"Gee thanks. Mmmmm, this sure goes down smooth, Mr. Wright. Ahhh."

"Glad you like it Ernest. Cigar? Like Cubans?"

"A stogy? Sure! Please, thank you, Mr. Wright. A Cuban? That's a top of the line smoke. Holy Cow, Gee thanks, sir."

"No problem. Anytime you need a dandelion wine or a nice Cuban cigar you know where to come."

"Mr. Wright, you are gonna spoil me, sir."

"A bit of advice, as your neighbor and friend, Ernest, don't let the turkeys get you down, go fly with the eagles. As artists we have to stick together to support one another. Find a group of artists to hang out with and befriend those who lift up your spirits."

"Gosh, Mr. Wright. Thanks for the treats and friendly advice. I'll remember your kind words. Say is it alright if I write to you?"

"Of course, my lad. Absolutely, Master Hemingway. Now you have a wonderful summer and I'll expect you to stop in before you head out for Kansas."

"Indeed...I certainly will. Thank you. Do you ever get a chance to head north yourself for the hot summer months?"

"Indeed, I have a farm up in Wisconsin. Taliesin it is called."

(Puff, puff) "How nice, sounds Scandinavian. Well tally Ho."

As I skipped back to the Hemingway haunt, my spirits were so high I imagined I should float home I suppose. Frank Lloyd Wright has a way of making a person feel special. Kinda always figured he was encouraging his dandelion crop, while most Oak Parkies tend to rid the yellow blossoms as some kind of scourge.

Wow! Ice cold dandelion wine with a Cuban cigar, the genuine article. Some inner urging prompted me to make a social call on the Wrights and sure enough I hit the jackpot. I'm learning to pay more attention to my intuition, if in fact that's what it is. It could very well be the Holy Spirit using Chicky, the agent of two worlds. This time it was more of any urging rather than an audible voice, so I am being given multiple signals from Above.

What is truly amazing is the impact of a few kind words which I set in motion with my high school paper article about our illustrious architect neighbor Frank Lloyd. It was on the strength of that in depth rendering that I got promoted to editor-in-chief and Mr. Wright got offers for three more architecture contracts. Maybe I should hit up Frank for a whole box of Cubans and a whole jug of wine? Hmmm?

Am I being shown the power of kind words and their respective repercussions? I do think so. Certain words have power.

Ernie Shakes Hands with his Father on Graduation Day

Chapter 4. Ernie Discovers Mother's Scandalous Secret

The Hemingway Family

Upon entering the Hem-Domain our servants were busy taking orders from Mother Grace. Packing her steamer trunks was the grand order of the day.

"Mother, I don't see why you pack all those trunks. They're never touched until we get ready to return for home?"

"Never mind, smarty pants. These are my dresses from Europe."

"Mother, if I may be so bold... that was nineteen years ago and six children ago. Are we being a bit unrealistic? None of them will fit!"

"My dear boy... just wait till your father gets home. You will pay for such impudence. Anyway no more of your nasty lip in front of the help."

"Yeah, right. I need a good strap for not going off to war."

"That will totally be enough now, dear boy."

"Humph... I don't know why good money has to be wasted carting around trunks full of twenty year old dresses that don't fit."

"Just never you mind! Now go straight to your room! Have you been drinking?"

The colored help roll their eyes for they are aware of the waste it is, for they always unpack the steamer trunks unopened upon their return.

My feet just feel like stamping loudly as I make my way to my room upstairs. My war guilt returns as I imagine marching off to fight the Kaiser, boldly tramping shoulder to shoulder with all my high school pals.

I imagine us singing gallant war songs as we all try to march in step.

I imagine myself and my Army buddies sweeping across Europe chasing Kaiser and his turncoat tyrants all the way back to Vienna.

I imagine our triumphant troop returning to our favorite pub and lifting stein after stein in honor of our valor and bravery. More thrilling war songs are sung and friendship is strengthened. That hard-earned camaraderie is what I yearn for... what I miss most from my war torn high school chums.

The separation overwhelms me as I throw myself headfirst onto my bed.

My room starts to spin. That homemade dandelion wine begins its dance within my head urging hundreds of brain cells to give up living and dance themselves to death.

Frank's wonderful Cuban cigar begins to send a message to purge the contents of my stomach, so I roll off my bed and throw up in my wash basin. Looking back on recent occurrences I recall the deliciously buoyant skipping that brought me home, but the toxic encounter with my nemesis, my Mother, sent me regurgitating all and any goodness from my teenage system.

Ah's sick. Ah's depressed. Ah's miserable... again.

As my body shudders after the violent evacuation of any and all things good, I lays on my back staring at the gray ceiling. A faint knock is heard at my door.

"Are you gonna be okay, Wemedge, Hemmie, Big Brother? Can I come in?" My fourteen year old sister Ursula is at my door.

"Yeah... come on in, Littless. It ain't locked. Shouldn't you be practicing your violin?"

"Hey, Pal, I heard Mother chew you out, and then I heard you stomp upstairs, and then I heard you puke, so how's a violin gonna sound with all that crap going on?"

"Good point, Hon. Actually, she makes me feel like crap. Mother Grace is so doggoned out of touch with reality that it turns my friggin' stomach, and I was feeling so darn good comin' from Frank's place."

"If it's any consolation, professor, she engages in these tirades every time we have to pack for our summers up in Michigan."

"But it isn't the packing... cause the colored help does all the packing, the cleaning, the cooking, the baking, the shopping, the washing, the ironing, the child-care... for this she needs a vacation and her very own private stress relief cabin? Naw! Littless, at some point I am gonna get to the bottom of this mystery called Mother Grace."

"Well, good luck, Sherlock. I've been trying to figure her out for years...and I'm as baffled as anyone. So please give me what you've got so far."

"Hon, I can't get a thing out of Pops, but I figure on pumping Uncle Tyler during our flivver trip up north."

"But you will have to get him away from his brother, won't you?"

"Yeah, that will be the tough part, but if we stop at hotels along the way or pitch a tent I can pump Tylie while Pops is off working on the Model T."

"Okay, but what'll be your line of questioning? Wouldn't that depend upon what you are driving at? What you surmise?"

"Right, so what do we surmise, Watson?"

"Gosh, I think she's off her nut...but from what?"

"Been reading a lot of Pop's medical journals and I found some Sigmund."

"Sigmund? You mean Freud? No way."

"Yes way! Here's my plan. According to Freud, the old girl is trying to live through her children. Listen now. Just listen, Littless!"

"Okay. This better be good."

"Grace fails on the operatic stage...okay? Blames the spot lights set off her overly sensitive peepers, right. So she still has that urge to triumph on the operatic stage... but can't for reasons mentioned... so..."

"So? Go ahead, I'm all ears. Make your point."

"So she wants one of us to be her."

"But we're not her. None of us could be a Grace Hemingway. Sorry, I just don't follow you."

"Right... she feels like a failure, tries to create a star through her kids, failure right, so what's left, student, student!"

"Bingo! I get it now. Sherlock, you must be referring to our new nursemaid. Ruth?"

"Yup, Ruthy, but in reality she isn't a nursemaid, only in title alone is she that, because the title is smoke, a cover, a schill."

"A cover, smoke, a schill? For what?"

"Our highly intelligent, overly spoiled, failure of an operatic impresario has cloned herself. Transferred her every emotion, every vocal vibration, every, every...operatic skill..."

"Yes, Big Brother... please go on."

"Every human desire, every carnal desire, every perverted, wanton friggin' naughty desire..."

"Go on...I'm trying to follow."

"Long story short, dear Watson. Grace has transferred herself into Ruth by every means possible, merging all of her will into this young, talented, yet innocent sweetheart of a youth... Ruth Arnold. They are in love."

"Continue – I feel your holding out on me yet."

"Yes...I am, cause the word is too vile for me to say it out loud, but I think you know where this is headed? Littless...I'm sorry, Honey."

"Naw, you don't mean? No, not our dear sweet... butter wouldn't melt in her mouth. Naw...I refuse to...okay...but...in a way it all starts to make sense...the secluded cabin...all the afternoons alone with her. It's the old teacher/student abuse thing, right?"

"Bingo, Watson, now you got it."

"A-a-a-and Ruthie is so naive that she thinks it is part of her lessons, right?"

"Yup!"

"Oh...my...God. Oh...my...Lord. Heaven help her! Big Brother, does Marcy know?"

"Uh-uh, nope! And I would never tell her. It would destroy Marcy if she found out. Ivory is happy in her ignorance, Littless."

"Yeah...as they say, 'Ignorance is bliss'"

"Well I don't think the girl is actually blissful 'cause they do have their run-ins, but Pops... Pops is the guy I'm worried about."

"Oh...my...God! That explains why she paid for his trip to New Orleans. She called it a case of the nerves. Told his friends he was on a study sabbatical. He looked a fright when he returned. Like some wild man."

"Yeah, yeah, now you're gettin' it. So he found out somehow, blew his stack, and she gave him a ticket to cool off."

"Yeah, of all places, the big easy, Sin City Sodom and Gomorrah. New, friggin', Orleans. Yeah, he'd get a good dose of gender-bending down there too, until he got used to it and dealt with it."

"But someone as sanctimonious as he would be snapped... don't you think?"

"Right... so maybe the man did snap."

"Maybe she put him in an asylum until he promised to behave himself. Oh my, poor Father."

"Yeah poor bastard. Poor miserable Pops."

"So while Ruth is around he plays second fiddle."

"Something like that. So he buries himself in his work and..."

"Waits for her to throw him a crumb."

"Something like that."

"So Sunny and Carol and the Baron?"

"They shall never know and that's good."

"Cause ignorance is bliss, huh?"

"Yup...so let's leave it like that, Baby Girl, okay?"

"Oh, Wemedge. Hug me you big, ugly galute. It must have been rough on you to first discover Mother's uh, dalliances?"

"Oh, sure, but I finally got to the bottom of things, and it's Pops who I really worry about."

"Yeah, while she's doing her thing, he has to be the obedient dog waiting..."

"Yeah, waiting for her to throw him a chewed-on bone. Really friggin' God-awfully sad. That's how I sees it."

"Right, me too. What can we do? Now that we know? He's too nice of a guy."

"Not a damn thing, but pray that either she or Ruth comes to their senses...and also pray for Pops to be strong and not go crazy."

"Freud says a guy like Pops needs watching. He may try to self-destruct or make foolish decisions to sabotage her schemes."

"Like give away all his possessions or go to Florida and buy swamp land?"

"Something like that."

Carol, Ernie, Mother Grace, and Leichester

Chapter 5: Tripping on Vile

The Ford Model T

Chicago heat was a scorcher. Cool Northern Michigan was on our minds. Friends with a big buckboard wagon hauled the family steamer trunks down to the docks where they were loaded onto the steamer 'South America'.

Mother's church friends pulled up with a double carriage and team in which to carry all the females, servants, and little Leichester down to the loading dock.

Pops, Uncle Tyler, and I did all we could to gas and oil the Model T. Overnight bags were all we carried, for we figured it to be only a three day trip. Boy were we wrong.

After I cranked the Tin Lizzy a few times she sputtered and Dad set the spark properly so the little four cylinder Ford kicked right in and purred like my pet cat.

The brothers sat in front. I figured I'd let Uncle Tylie be Dad's navigator since he then could chat with his over-worked brother.

"Clarence, we're on our way to a well-deserved vacation. I know I am gonna catch me some nice fish."

"Too bad Arabelle couldn't make the trip."

"Her elderly parents need her care now, but I think we'll have a full house anyway."

"Indeed. Tyler, it's been a while since you and I have fished."

"Des Plains River as I recall. Biggest catfish I've ever seen. Ernie was just a tyke. Remember that, Ernie?"

"Huh? Oh, no sorry, Uncle. What did you use for bait?"

"What was it Clarence?"

"Night crawler."

"I got a letter from Wesley Dilworth. He says walleye are biting on Walloon," says I. "You gentlemen don't mind if I smoke a cigar do you?"

"I mind. Don't want my new auto smelling like a cigar," said Father.

"Oh, silly me, of course. How insensitive of me. Care if I chew tobaccie?" I asked.

"Did you bring a tin can or spittoon?"

"Nope, Pops. Just thought I'd spit out my winder."

"And send streaks of tobaccie juice along me new automobile. Sorry, Ernest."

"Gosh, ah'm sorry. Must've lost my head."

"Here Ernie have some Wrigley chewing gum."

"Don't mind if I do. Thanks, Uncle Tyler. No Dad, I'm not gonna stick a gob under your nice new seats. I'll swallow it before that happens."

"Ernest, you seem to be starting this trip rather testy. Care to talk about it?" asks Tyler.

"Okay...sorry but I been in a rotten mood ever since the train hauled my pals off to war, okay. Guess I have a right to feel some emotion there, right?"

"Why absolutely, son. We all hate to see our young lads march off to an uncertain future," added Pops.

"Harold Samson says they will all be cannon fodder. Millions of boys will never come home. Over half my class enlisted. Now they are marching head on into Kaiser's cut-throat Krauts."

"And you wish you could be with them," says Tyler.

"Actually, yes. Yes I do. We all know I am the best shot in my class," says I.

"That you are, son," added Pops.

"It sounds like you want to be there to protect your pals from invading Huns?" added Tyler.

"Yes sir, Unk. I'll mow down any Krauts who try to injure any of my pals. Those boys are so naïve. Unprepared to fight, I'd have to be training them to shoot and toss grenades and box in hand-to-hand combat. I'd make a heck of a soldier out of them."

Tyler adds, "Well Ernest, as a writer you'll get your chance to stem the tide of this war with your pen."

"Yeah, I know the pen is mightier... But they are all so green, so vulnerable, so untrained, so, so, so killable!" I remarks.

"Calm yourself, son. They will get good drill sergeants to train them to do all that," says Dad.

"But nobody knows them as well as I. I been with them for 17 years, Pop," says I.

"Sounds like you're getting overly sentimental now, Ernest... just stop that," demands Pop.

"Oh Pops... a big part of your son left with those boys yesterday at the train station."

"I understand, son, and you have our sympathy, but just let it ride and focus on doing a good job up in Michigan. There is garden to plant, cabin to get ready, dock to put out, lots of chores, and Mother and I are counting on you to do your part, son. So let's focus on that; not something with which we have no control."

"Your dad's right, Ernie. You're getting all worked up over things beyond your control," Tyler adds.

"God comes to him who waits," added Pops.

"Yeah, well maybe. I need to pee. Can we stop soon, Father? Sign says Hammond, Indiana. I'd hate to decorate the back seat of your new automobile."

"Yes... indeed. I see a filling station just ahead," says Father. Pops added, "Take a peek into that picnic basket, Ernest. I made us a mess of fried chicken last night."

"Wow! Pops, this is great! What are you and Uncle Tyler going to eat? Just kidding."

"Good food can sure change one's mood," said Tyler.

"Hey! Mmm. Pops I found a jar of your sweet pickles."

"Exactly. I canned a batch of those last fall up in Michigan... Grandma Hemingway's recipe."

"Now that woman is a good cook," I stated.

"True words, nephew. Never will you see a skinny Hemingway," commented Tyler, "Thanks to our Mother's fine cooking."

Excitedly, I said, "Hey men! Do you see what I see behind that filling station? An old picnic table. Let's sit down and mow into this fine lunch."

"Here's an old sheet, Ernest. We need a tablecloth. This is a time when Hemingway men come to life."

"I've noticed that, Clarence. Haven't you, Ernie?"

"And what is that, Uncle?" says I.

"That we Hemingway men seem to come alive when food is mentioned," states Tyler.

"Do you mean sort of like Pavlov's dogs?" I says. "Heck I started to drool just at the mention of the phrase 'picnic basket.' Let's see what else you got stashed in here, Father. Wow! Baked beans. And even some old silverware. Thought Mother would've tossed these out along with our pickled snake collection."

"What? Grace tossed out your pickled snakes? Clarence, we started that collection back in grammar school."

"Yup, burned the whole stash along with a lot of other attic keepsakes from Holmes Elementary," I muttered. "Kinda insensitive, wouldn't ya say?"

"Clarence! How could you let her do that?"

"Pops was out of town, right Dad?"

Tyler continued, "And what about our stuffed animals and birds?"

Yup... all burned," I muttered. "But twenty year old dresses from her European sojourn...those she hauls up north and back every dog-gone summer," I stated judgmentally.

"Surely you jest, nephew?" asked Tyler.

"Nope. Pop knows too. It's true...and stop calling me Shirley. Good one, hey Pops? Pops?"

"Why uh, why...Clarence, you're crying. Clarence? My dear sweet brother where are you going? You hardly touched your nice lunch."

"Oh, listen Unk, that's only one small part of things that are going on. Guess he needs to check on the flivver, gas and oil, you know."

"Ernest...I had no idea things were this bad."

"Oh, Unk...you got no idea how bad...you got no idea, no sir, how bad it is."

"If I may ask, son, just how bad? After all he is my brother and we are close."

"Uncle Tyler, God love him, I think he's ready for the rubber room. Yup, indeed, I think Clarence could do something rash."

"Is it Grace?"

"Yup. She's really gone and done it this time, Unk. I'm sitting on some explosive family crap and I don't think Pops can handle it!"

"Hmmm, nice Christian woman like that? Hmm, so when you're ready, Ernie, feel free to tell me. Maybe I can be of help?"

"It's way too much, even for you, Unk. I can't even find the right words, it's so vile!"

"So vile, huh?"

"Yeah...vile!"

"Vile you say? Hmmm. I tell you, Ernie...uh...I can't begin to imagine anything that could be vile. At least not SO vile."

"Yeah I know. Vile isn't it? Uncle Tylie, vile."

"Vile is not a word used very much in our family. Least not on the Hemingway side. Can't imagine anything like vile occurring on the Hall side either? Should we call it vile? Are you sure, Ernie? Vile? Vile, per se?"

"Yeah per se, per se, friggin vile, Unk!"

"Oh my...oh my...oh my, oh my." Uncle Tyler raised his eyes , searching the Hammond, Indiana skies while scratching his thick Hemingway hair. For some reason what was so vile that it didn't need explaining could just be left at that...vile.

Even the degree to which I love gossip and I actually crave it... gossip that is... I felt a heavy weight had been placed upon my gossipy tongue to the point that nothing more could be rung from my poor tongue. Felt like a I had a case of anvil tongue.

"Well, you dear lad. I can see this has given you quite a shock so I will not press you to say anymore about this...this vile...this ...uh....vile. However vile it is, maybe it has to go unsaid and just remain vile."

We finished our lunch. Unk packed it up and placed it into the automobile, while I threw-up behind the filling station.

Tyler put his arm around Clarence's shoulder without saying a word. Pops couldn't lift his head. It looked like it was made of lead as he gazed at the new dusty Ford Model T, and then at his shoes.

"All gassed up? Want me to drive? Okay, I'll drive. Seems like she handles pretty well. Roads are holding up alright. Bet we're getting good gas mileage, huh? Do we need a big jug of water?

Okay Ernie get out front there and crank after I get the spark set right. Probably don't need to choke 'er huh? Should we choke 'er, Clarence? Huh?"

Clarence, my Pops, had been in some kinda freezeup mode just staring at his shoes like he was watching ants crawling out from under his kangaroo leather, ankle top brogans. All he heard was his brother's last sentence regarding a richer gasoline mixture needed to start Henry Ford's new horseless carriage. Finally my Pops blurted out with an emphasis way too much for casual car talk.

"Yes! That's it! Choke the bitch!" Cranking Pop's Model T took a few more than usual turns cause a warm engine never needs choking, but Father's common knowledge of warm engines had been superseded by thoughts of a vile nature which can distract even the calmest of minds.

So what could have been a heck of a tasty picnic lunch, prepared in love, enjoyed by two loving brothers open for a good time, good fellowship, and good food together with me the junior member, all that had been totally decimated by the vile previous actions of one said to be grafted into the family tree, one we all are supposed to love, supposed to trust, supposed to cherish, supposed to think they could never betray that trust. But when betrayal occurs what does one do?

And so our trip continues, but it always is overshadowed by a cloud of the vilest nature, and Father's relationship with his dear wife is now packaged in a wrap of toxin so potent he has to feel like the poisonous rattlesnake which bites his own lip. Life in our family can never be the same for Mother's love has been observed to be nothing more than Mother's love for her career, her image within our community, her projection into the success of her young voice student, and nothing more.

Her close control over husband and children is not for their nurture but rather so they do not damage her almighty reputation.

We have become her trophy family. Clarence has become the trophy husband with the trophy medical practice; our castle-like house stands out as the Kenilworth neighborhood trophy house; and all this for the sake of her self-rationalized, artistic image in hopes that it hides the vile nature of her deepest, selfish routines.

For Father to become accepting of her actions he would have to become just as vile in order to tolerate it, and even if he forgives her and tries to live with her his faith would be terribly at risk.

So it remains to be seen how long the family stays together, or how long I hang around, or how long before Father does something rash.

This summer has all the makings of a drama queen's high-falootin' lesbo fandango. My plan is to work, build up my muscles, and do all my chores, so Pops will be proud of me so that he won't have any stress imposed by my shortcomings. Our existence will be like walking on eggs, but I just want to keep the lid on my rage caused by Mother's well-kept secret and her arrogant dalliance.

I was thinking to myself, Poor Pops, because of his religious nature, and deep seated spirituality, the shocking news that the love of his life has slipped over to the dark side of dangerous dalliances, I just have to offer up a prayer for the old boy, for he suffers so, because it is so unnatural. I bet there is no one in Oak Park who has ever entertained such a thought. We may have to be ostracized to River Forest.

Clarence and Grace Hemingway in Happier Times

Chapter 6. Grand Rapids Breakdown

Grand Rapids, MI, Early 1900s

Tyler states, "Hey folks, you can all take in a nice deep breath now for we are now in beautiful, pristine, clean and green, pure Michigan, home of clean air, clean water, and..."

I blurted, "And Vernors Ginger Ale!"

While Pops said, "Home of the automobile. Home of Kellog's Corn Flakes."

I blurted, "Home of the world's best fishing."

Tyler states, "Home of the Detroit Tigers and Ty Cobb."

I blurted, "Home of Grand Rapids Furniture and Petoskey's Hiawatha Outdoor Theatre, Bay View lecture series, Jesperson's

Restaurant, Hortons Bay, Hortons Crick, and Dilworth chicken dinners."

Tyler commented, "Ernie, take a deep breath. It sounds like you are really looking forward to this summer."

"Yeah, Uncle Tylie. My enthusiasm has returned."

Pop said, "Good driving, Ty. You are making good time. Must we drive through Grand Rapids?"

"Indeed... feels like we need an alignment. That last rut we hit seems to have thrown off the front wheels. Might have sheared a cotter pin?"

Pops said, "I have noticed more filling stations now. Just have to find one with a garage that can do alignments. Keep your eyes peeled, Ernest."

I reply, "Okay Father, but they might be hard to find."

Tyler said, "This bad alignment will slow us down, Clarence. Maybe even ruin a tire."

I state, "Hey Dad, Oak Park has more cars running around than G.R."

Dad replies, "Oak Park is a wealthy community with paved streets."

My reply, "Yup... and G.R. has more dust. You got any goggles... better yet a face mask."

Pop says, "Poor communities have no money to pave their roads so they make do with gravel ones. Sometimes oil is sprayed on the gravel to cut down on the dust. Here Ernest, put my clean handkerchief over your mouth and nose. Too much dust can severely damage one's throat and lungs. You know how sensitive you are in that area."

My reply, "Okay... you dirty rats. This is a stick-up! Hey Uncle, you just passed a garage that does alignments. Check it out."

Ty's reply, "Good, but hang on. I'm stuck in a deep rut before I can turn her around."

I yells, "Holy cow, Unk! The wheel fell off!"

Ty says, "Yeah I was afraid of that deep rut. Wish they'd maintain their roads. Okay everybody out. Let's push 'er along the shoulder, and roll 'er into that garage after I reattach the wheel and secure it with a new cotter pin."

Mechanic greets, "Howdy, Illinois. Gee whiz, youse guys are a long way from home. What can I do ya for?"

Pops says, "Need an alignment. Need my spare up front – passenger side. Then fill 'er up, my good man."

"No problem sir. How far you goin'?"

"Up to God's country... Petoskey."

"Yee-ow! That's a long way in a little flivver. How did you git dis far?"

Tyler says, "Just by the grace of God and fairly decent roads."

"Watch out. I gotta hoist 'er up. It'll be a while. Go ahead, have an ice cold Vernors. Relax, folks. Don't look so worried. Roads are worse where you're headed. Gonna do some fishin? Can't get Vernors in Illinois, can ya! That's Michigan's favorite drink."

I state, "Yup mister, we know. We've been vacationing up here for seventeen years. We're from Oak Park, just south west of Chicago."

Pops states, "We usually take the lake steamer. I had this new Ford Model T so I thought it a novel idea to motor up to Emmet County area. Got a cabin on Lake Walloon."

Mechanic says, "Sir...you do know the roads turn to crap once past G.R.?"

Pop says, "Uh, ah, no. Actually I did not know that, my dear man."

"You'd best spend the night here in G.R. Sir."

"Why is that?"

"Bent spindle. When a wheel flies off like this here all the weight falls right down on that little spindle there. Can't align this rig until I gets a new part. Might take all day tomorrow if I gets lucky."

"Wow. Egad, Godfrey! I never planned on this."

"Yeah. Should always carry extra spindles and cotter keys and spare tires. This here tire is shot. Might have one in back."

As our mechanic gave Pops the bad news and added a demoralizing lecture on back-road emergency repairs, I noticed a familiar face in a Packard which had just pulled up for a fill-up.

I says, "Well, they let anyone buy gasoline here. How the heck are you, Clancy?"

"What the...? Why, I don't believe it! Thought I would never see you again."

"Pops, please come here. Want you to meet the man who saved my life when I ran away from home a few years ago. Ace reporter for the Grand Rapids News... Clancy...my Father."

"Pleasure to meet you. My son never has stopped talking about you, sir. I want to thank you personally for all your healing concern. Truly Ernest might never have pulled through inhaling that hot cinder from the locomotive ordeal without your support."

"Oh shucks, 'twern't nuthin', Doc. Say... looks like every time you hit town ya need help or something. What is it this time?"

"Oh this. Just a bent spindle, but we could use a lift to a good hotel."

"Nice. Hop in. I'm goin' right by the best one in town, the Pick-Nicollete. Nice beds, nice bath and decent prices. I'll get you a reduced rate. Ern's my hero ya' know. Catch ya later, Alfie."

I states, "Clancy, I want you to meet my Pop's brother, Tyler. We're gonna do some fishin' up north."

"Nice to meet ya, Tyler."

Tyler replies, "Ernest tells me you inspired him to become a newspaper man. And I got him an internship with the K.C. Star. Nice to meet you."

"That's great. Keep him under your wing, Uncle, 'cause he's special. We come real close to losin' him, but I kinda tricked him into gettin' well again. He's the real article when it comes to writin'. Ernie's goin' places. Well, here's your hotel. I gotta story to cover, so call me. Maybe we can have coffee before ya' vamooses."

Doc replies, "Thank you so much, Clancy, sir. Have a nice evening."

I comment, "Now brothers, I ask you. What are the odds of that happening? Is someone watching over us? We get Pop's flivver... I mean new automobile... fixed, meet my old pal who just happens to be filling up with gas. Could it be coincidence? I think not! I'd like to think our Good Lord takes a likin' to us. Do I get an Amen?"

"Amen for sure, son. Clancy seemed convinced of your success in the newspaper business."

I replies, "Oh, he's my biggest supporter and to think I met him, Uncle Tylie, after I inhaled a red-hot cinder in a railroad mishap. Whole throat closed up. Terrible, simply terrible."

Hotel clerk asks, "May I help you, gentlemen?"

Pops states, "Indeed, one room with accommodation for three."

I adds, "Good friends of the best newspaper man in G.R."

"Oh... okay. Then you get the Clancy discount. That'll be $7.00. Extra towels are already in your room; complimentary soaps and shampoo also up there. Room service ends at ten o'clock. Here's a brochure of the many attractions in town. A carriage will pick up after breakfast, sirs. Our smoking lounge closes at eleven. Ballroom closes at one; band playing this week is Heydan and his light motif. Tie and jackets of course. May I make reservations for dinner?"

Doc says, "Thank you very much. Yes dinner for three; window table please. Could you send a boy to have our suits cleaned and pressed? Thank you."

I says, "Heck Pops, that's gonna cost ya!"

Doc says, "Think nothing of it. My treat, men. We are going to dine in class tonight! Ahem...if certain others can splurge, so can we, ahem."

I says, "Uh...right! What the heck you say. Say young lady, could you direct me to your smoke shop?"

Clerk responds, "First door on your left, sir. Bell hop wants your bags."

I says, "Very nice spittoons here. Think I'm gonna like this joint, gentlemen. Care to join me for a taste of the Sir Walter Raleigh?"

The brothers went to the room to change out of their dusty road outfits. Me, I was dying for a nice stogy, maybe even an aged French cognac. I snatched my blue legal pad and a sharp pencil in hopes someone might offer me a good story in the bar.

The attendant asks, "What'll it be, sir?"

"Three fat Cubans in your humidor. Would you clip the ends please, Madame?

"Alright. Anything else? Light? Sir?"

"Yeah, where are all the young people?" Puff... puff...

"All gone to fight Kaiser Bill."

"So that means more ladies for me, right?"

"Uh...right...uh, sir."

"And the bar? Which way is dat?" Puff... puff...

"Next door to the right. Thanks for the generous tip, sir."

"Don't mention it, my good woman."

As I opened the door to the bar I could almost hear my Pops lecturing me about the sin of strong drink, but truth be known I've been drinking since age eleven... apple jack, hard cider, and that delightful dandelion wine, but tonight I'm gonna drink a stiff one for all the poor slobs who enlisted to defend our country.

Door-nail-dead is how I describes the ambiance of Pick-Nicolette's bar. The slow-shuffle would be a description of my entrance into the rather bright yet subdued multi-colored lighting that illuminated a bazillion bottles of high priced booze on the wall display. Midwestern jazz was being attempted on the baby grand tucked in one corner. Tickling the 88's was an elderly colored man who smiled only to show off his gold cap teeth.

"Evenin', maestro. Da you know any Chopin?"

"Wha? Who's dat? Dat you, Huckleberry?"

"You bet. An how's my pal Jim tonight, huh?"

The pianist says, "Lord, have mercy! We was on a raft one time."

I answers, "Yup, indeed we was. Jes' floatin' down that big lazy river as easy as ya please. Jes' enjoyin' da scenery and diggin' da darkies banjo music."

"Gosh Huck, where you headin'?"

"No where...and everywhere, ah reckon." Puff, puff. "Care for a smoke, smokey?"

"Heck yes...Thank ya kindly m' lad."

"Light?"

"Uh huh," puff, puff, smack, smack, puff. "Oh, dare she goes. Ummm...real smooth. Tanks, uh, Huck."

"So Jim, dog-gone it. I've heard those riffs back in Chi-town."

"Jim" Playing Piano in the Bar

"Guess some of it rubbed off on my fingers. Tupelo, Mississippi."

Well," puff, "Dat's real nice. Ahm gonna put a dollar in your glass bowl... hear? You keep preachin' to me wif dose ivories." Puff.

"Show-nuff...Huck...an tanks for dat generosity."

"How long you been wifout yo sight, Jim? Seems like forever, huh? Yeah, well, you jus keep up da good work, hear. I likes yo technique?"

As I was done leaning against old Jim's piano I did a slow turn toward the bar and the bar- keep motioned me over for a drink ..on the house."

"What you drinking tonight, Huck?"

"Oh...you must have overheard me jawin' with the piano player?"

"Yes, indeed, Hon. I thought that was some real smooth dialog. Real ethnic. Real snappy wit."

"Thanks," puff puff. "Well tonight is special. I'm drinking cognac. Let's toast to the best bunch of Pals I ever had – going now to be cannon fodder for Kaiser Bill's cannons. Have one yourself. Pip, pip! To half," puff puff, "the graduating class of Oak Park/River Forest whom we sent off on a long gray train. Into the jaws of death rode the one thousand."

Bar-keep asked, "That many, huh?"

"Yup. All good chaps too. Da best," puff, puff.

"That must be sad seeing them go away like that?"

"Yup. Tragic actually. Damn tragic... gee dat's, ahhh, real smooth cognac. Got another one? Yeah I can still see their cherubic faces in the train cars. 'Come on, Hemmie. Come with us. You can shoot better 'n all of us, Stein...Yeah...Hey Hemmie...we got a cheat sheet off the eye-chart. You'll pass da physical, Pal. It's in da bag.'" Puff.

"Must have hurt seeing that train-load of young boys all rolling down to instant death?"

"Oh, heck yeah, hurt me right here. It still hurts. Probably hurt the rest of my life, huh?"

"Yeah, I suppose. That was a rough scene."

"Rough scene. I'll be havin' friggin' nightmares now. Can't hardly sleep now anyway."

"I can relate. That's why I work here. Can't sleep. Husband off to war. At least I get paid for not sleeping. What keeps you from joining all your buddies?"

"Bad eyes. Always bump into things. Irony of it is I can shoot the eyes out of a squirrel at fifty paces. Go figure?"

"Huh? Strange. Wonder what makes that?"

"Hard to explain. Except for my Pops I'm best wingshot when it comes to bird huntin' too. I anticipate where the critter wants to go. It's a Zen thing. Plus Pops trained me by sending me out in the woods with only three shells."

"Ok... I see. Well that'll do it. Darn that cognac goes down real smooth. Have another?"

"Indeed my good lady. Do you smoke cigars?"

"Huh? No. Actually, never tried em."

"Try one of these fat Cubans. Never met a Cuban I didn't like. Something in the way they are cured and then rolled tightly by experts."

Puff... puff. "Hmm." Puff... "Actually, not bad, kid."

"See, I wouldn't steer ya. Most American cigars can't hold a candle to a Cuban, but once in a while a Tampa stogie will taste real good. Enough about stogies. So, sweet-thing, tell me about your husband. You say he is at the front?"

"Actually I just got word he was killed."

"Oh my...I'm so sorry."

"He used to be the bartender here. After our manager got the bad news he thought about it a while then realized I needed a job anyway, so here I am. First female bartender. Actually it's an easy job."

"Well sister, more power to ya. Gosh awful sorry for your loss. When's the funeral?"

"No funeral. He was buried over there. Somewhere on the Western front. I'm still kinda in shock, ya' know?"

"Well that's very understandable. War is hell. Nice girl like you. Gosh, I'm awful sorry. This war is gonna mess up a lot of lives and families too...and it's so senseless."

"Yeah, tell me about it. Just a mixed up mess. Mortar shell got him, so says his C.O. but he was a good soldier. Brave. He told me that Calvin knocked out a couple German machine gun nests single-handed."

"Gosh! No kiddin'?"

"Yes. My husband used to pitch for the Grand Rapids semi-pro baseball team, so he could really wing a grenade. His lieutenant wrote me a nice letter how Cal just out-flanked these German machine gunners and when they wasn't lookin'... plunk! Tossed a perfect strike right in the middle of em. Boom! Guess he took out quite a few machine gun nests. Saved a lot of lives and helped our boys push back the enemy. Yeah, he was not one to sit around in trenches waitin' to get artillery lobbed in on him. Cal and his company are changing the way this war is being fought. Something about mobile flanking units."

"Gosh! Do tell. Mind if I jot this story down?"

"No, go ahead. Are you some kinda writer? Well according to Cal, he used to write a lot, according to him they are trying to fight this war all wrong. Sort of too much like Napoleon times with long lines of rifles all lined up. Then they dug trenches to hide and to avoid getting hit. Well, Cal said they were then like sitting ducks, taking heavy casualties. No way to fight a war. Anyway, long story short, Cal put together fleet-footed athletic units that moved about creating weak spots in these long lines of enemy soldiers."

"Yeah, go on. This is exciting. What's your name?"

"Vera. Anyway, Cal's athletic troop almost single-handedly designed a new form of swift attack force that sought out and created weak spots in enemy lines. Then our boys would storm through these holes along the front, totally surprising the Krauts who thought they could just sit back and lob artillery and mortar shells on our boys in the trenches all day and all night."

"Holy cow! Vera, I am so glad I talked to you. Your husband Calvin might just have shortened this nasty war. Wait 'til I tell my Pals, who are going to be sitting ducks over there."

"Oh yeah. I tell ya...its all in training and getting those legs in shape, and also those arms so they can move fast. That way enemy gunners can't get a good shot 'cause they are moving too fast for enemy rifles to get a bead on them."

"Right. I understand. It takes a good second or two to take aim, but if the target won't stand still a guy's got a chance to sneak along and charge those sectors where the front lines are weak. Hmmm, swift-moving mobile flanking units. Excellent ideas, Vera. You are the greatest! Oh, sorry I completely forgot to introduce myself."

"Yeah, what's your name, stranger?"

"Ernest Hemingway, darlin'. Thank you so much. I'll be writing for the K.C. Star and you've just given me my first big story. Now Vera, do me a big favor."

"Okay, handsome...Ernie."

"Please don't tell anyone the story, okay? Cause this is smashing news! And if Krauts got wind of dis... puff, puff. I gotta wire this off to the K.C. Star right away."

"Hey, where ya' going? You haven't touched your drink!"

"You drink it ,Vera. This is news that has to get written. See the pen will be mightier then the sword...into the jaws of death rode six thousand. Son of a gun...this is gonna be a revolutionary story. Swift-moving mobile-flanking units. Oh boy! That Vera gave me a 64-thousand dollar idea. Gotta call Clancy or someone at the Grand Rapids newspaper. I knew I smelled a story. Hey Pops! Hey Uncle! I just hit pay dirt in the bar here. Got me a story to knock your socks off."

"Come with us, Ernest, we're headed for the dining room."

"Yeah, they roast duck here. Come join us."

"Gee thanks, but I just got me a scoop of the century. Gotta call the newspaper...gotta, gotta."

"Now just you whoa, hold your horses there. It's time to eat. You can do that in the morning. Give yourself a chance to proof-read it tonight in the room."

"Ernest, just calm yourself. Tell us all about this now over dinner. Here's your dinner jacket. Got to wear a jacket. This is fancy dining."

"But Dad, I'm happy being grubby. Besides this story has to go to the newspaper. It is what we call a hot item."

"Oh it is not! Now you've been drinking and you're all upset about the war and you need to just take a deep breath and fill your stomach with nourishment. Relax, son!"

"Oh all right, I guess. You always could calm me down. The story probably is too top secret to let out for all to see. Yeah, phew! Thanks Pops, you may have saved me from a big mistake."

"Here...slip into this nice jacket. Just had it pressed special for you tonight. Did you want me to tie your tie? Okay...uh-uh...there. How does he look, Uncle Tyler?"

"Handsome. I do declare. All the girls in the dining room will catch his eye."

"Yes indeed, the high school graduate/reporter is in the house. Now come on in. You know how much you like roast duck."

"Phew! Must've got carried away there. Phew. Do you really think I'm handsome, Uncle Tylie?"

"Absolutely, Ernest. Must be those dimples or that Charles Atlas physique. Look at those shoulders."

"Uncle, how'd you know I was training with Charles Atlas?"

"Your Mother wrote us."

"Hey, now don't get offended, Father, I got a good joke."

"Okay. Let's sit down and order drinks first. Then you can tell your little humorous piece."

The server came, "Your drinks order, please. My name is Gretchen. I'll be your beverage server."

"I'll have a tall lemonade please with ice," said Pops.

"Same as my brother, please."

"Okay, guess I've had too much alcohol, so okay, ah, I'll have a tall lemonade with ice and a few lemons floating...kinda have them doing the back stroke there, Gretchen, will ya, Honey?"

"Now Ernest please be nice to the young lady. You are not too old for me to spank."

"Yeah, spank him. I want to see that," said Gretchen.

"Now see what you started, Ernie. Ha, ha, ha. Clarence, he's just joshin' with her. Gosh, we're on vacation. Can we loosen up a bit?"

"Ernest, this is a respectable hotel and we'd like to be able to come back here again sometime. Now please be a nice boy. I want you to apologize to Gretchen when she returns with your lemons which are doing the back-stroke," said Pops.

"Ha, ha, ha. Oh...I almost hurt myself. You really had me going there at first, Father. Ha, ha, ha."

"There, now Clarence isn't that better. We don't always have to be so stern."

Gretchen returned, "Okay gentlemen, now here are your drinks. Lemonades all around, and one with floating lemons on top, just what you ordered."

"Oh, oh miss...Gretchen. I want to...uh, a, a, apologize for my earlier comments, okay?"

"Apology accepted, sir."

"Thank you. What I really wanted them lemons doing was the breast stroke. Ha, ha, ha."

"Ha, ha, haaaa. That was very funny...oops...Sorry! Oh! I spilled your drink right in your lap. Excuse me, sir. Please let me wipe it up."

"Well, Ernie, let her wipe it up," said Tyler.

"Ah...ah...uh...no, a, no! That's okay, thanks. Hon, uh, I guess we're ready for our waiter. Harrumph. Time for some food."

"Guess she really got even with you there, Ern," laughed Tyler.

"I ain't talkin' no more. Even my scivies are soaked. Egad, Godfrey! Now a wet lap."

"You deserved that, Ernest," said Pops. "Okay here comes our waiter. So I heard the duck is fabulous here, my good man."

"Indeed, sir. Our chef is at your service, sir."

"That reminds me, son, our fence needs repair. I want to raise ducks again at Longfields. Chickens and pigs also, and geese, too."

"Sure thing, Father."

"Maybe Sumners can give us a hand with hauling some scrap lumber from the saw mill. I'll ask George to give a hand. Would like to spend a night with him when we first arrive up north," said Father.

Duck is probably my family's all time favorite food. The Pick-Nicolette's duck dinner was the best any of us had ever tasted. That evening brought the brothers more together than I have ever seen. Never knew my Father had a sense of humor, but Tyler seemed to have a way of getting him to loosen up enough from his professional image to crack a smile now and then. My lemonade lap dried somewhat, but I still had to walk stiff legged back to our room. In the morning, after a scrumptious breakfast on the hotel's fancy porch, my reporter friend appeared.

"Good mornin', gents. Well I got good news. Your Model T is ready to go. Your new spindle arrived early, and my old pal Alfie got it put back on, so I'd be glad to drive you over. I need gas anyway."

"Tried to reach you last night with a terrific scoop I got on my new war tactics," I said.

"Well great. See you are at it already using your smeller to sniff out a headline. We all knew you would make a great reporter," Clancy replied.

I shared my news with Clancy, but he told me to keep that story under wraps 'cause it would give to much advantage away to the enemy. In his opinion, my scoop was considered Top Secret and would never get printed.

The Model T looked better than ever after her plunge into rut-ville near G.R. I tossed our bags in back and assumed a stoic pose next to them.

Alfie sold Pops extra spindles and a new tire so we could resume our northward sojourn without fear of another breakdown along the way. After all, what else could possibly go wrong?

Pops took the wheel and I never saw him look better. These moments with his dear brother Tyler, then the delightful duck dinner and a few laughs at the expense of my wet lap had buoyed up his spirits, and he was again ready to take command of the journey.

Fixing the Model T

Chapter 7. The Hailstorm from Hell

The Hotel Algonquin

We made good time. By the end of the day we had arrived at a town called Cadillac, named after a famous Indian chief.

That is something one could say about most of these Michigan towns. Petoskey also being named for a colorful chief who maintained a thriving fur trading business.

Roads get continually worse the further north we venture. Father made a profound condemnation of Michigan roads when he stated, "This birthplace of the automobile needs a good spanking if better roads are not built past Grand Rapids!"

Storms came up quickly forcing us to stay put in Cadillac. We pulled into a quaint hotel overlooking Lake Cadillac. Our decision was wise for a violent rain can wash out roads. While trying to navigate during a heavy down pour a whole automobile can slide down an embankment and be swallowed up by a fast flowing river below.

"Hey Pops, you made a wise decision to hole up here in Cadillac."

"Why is that, son?"

"Well take a gander at what's coming off the lake. I'll shut the automobile windows. Those angry black clouds are gonna dump on us very soon."

"Let's get all our gear into our hotel room before it gets soaked," added Uncle Tyler. "Here it comes! Batten down the hatches."

Michigan weather comes up on ya swiftly. Being surrounded by water could account for the state's odd weather patterns and the severity with which it punishes.

This storm was no exception. It seemed to gain momentum and energy as it traveled directly across Lake Cadillac. Then it turned into some kinda not-so-merry merry-go-round dumping sheets of rain and then sucked water up and up into the upper atmosphere thus causing hail, which pummeled Father's new Ford unmercifully. Hail stones the size of ping-pong balls were leaving tiny welts all over Father's new automobile. The Doctor was not happy.

"Hey Pops. Cheer up; that'll buff out," Says I.

Pops ignored that crack the way he has countless times before of other similar situations where I tried to lighten his load with a bit of levity. But for obvious reasons he had identified so heavily with his new Ford automobile that its new pock-marked body struck him like he himself had contracted small pox. That blasted hail unmercifully pelted Father's Model T Ford for about an hour. It seems the storm is circular and keeps returning in various forms depending on the height of its circular clouds. First it is pummeling us like a giant layered doughnut, with lower clouds dumping a torrential downpour of rain sheets, and as the higher clouds rotated our way they let loose with these giant ice balls that hammered little dings onto the shiny new paint job of the Ford. I actually saw it knock birds out of the early summer sky. One moment we had sheets of rain and minutes later devastatingly destructive hail. If this is how it will be going all night, it will be making sleep into a stormy nightmare wondering if Father will snap under the mishaps that have been handed him.

Finally I suggested we check the menu. "Hey Pops, look! Hotel Algonquin is serving fresh caught...walleye!"

Although his spirit is gloomy at the mention of a nice dinner of walleye his countenance lit up like a church afire.

"Brother Tyler, did you hear that? Hotel dining room is serving our favorite fish."

"Well there is only one thing a walleye lover can do at this juncture."

"Put the bib on and start shoveling it in!" I says.

Upon hearing that bit of good news, us three walleye lovers put on ties and dinner jackets knowing this is one meal that definitely uplifts our mood and is going to overcome the slow smoldering rage that was building in Father, and is igniting contagious wildfires of gloom in our entire motor party.

"Clarence, I can't remember the last time I dug into a nice plate of crusty, flaky walleye."

"Me neither. I think it's been a year back when Jim Dilworth had us over for a big fish fry. Is my tie on straight?"

"Indeed," Tyler replies. "Let us see how many fish we can devour. Maybe it'll modify our mood."

"Works for me. Look out chef. Here come the Hemingway men," I says.

"Now Ernie, I'd like to see you much more subdued tonight, okay? Do I have your contract on that tonight? Son?"

"Sure, Pop. My mouth will be so pure if you wring out my tongue Holy Water will pour out."

"Well you don't have to go that far as to insult the Catholic church, but all I ask is to keep it civil. No more lemons doing the back-stroke."

"Okay, okay, Pop. Maybe I'll make it through the evening with a dry lap for a change also, huh?"

"Ha, ha, ha. Hey I wonder if Gretchen is working here tonight?" laughs Tyler.

"If she is, I'll personally give her five bucks to spill more ice water in Ernest's lap."

"Real funny, Father. I think that she would enjoy it. Probably swims in ice water. Little hussy. Last night Gretchen gave me the icy sitz bath of my young life. My voice will be soprano for a few days, I figure."

Our evening spent at the Algonquin was delicious due to the exquisite cuisine (best fish dinner I ever ate) but anytime we took a peek outside at Pop's peppered automobile this feeling of sadness pursues the pit of our respective stomachs. Distraction seems to be what is needed, so I takes it upon myself to entertain the men with my vast array of memorized Longfellow poems.

"Hey men, grab an icy lemonade and pull up a wicker chair whilst I divulges the inner workings of the mind of America's most beloved poet, Longfellow."

"He's a poet and doesn't know it, but his feet show it," remarks Tyler.

"Hey they're Longfellows! Just a little levity going back to when Tyler and I were just lads in the old neighborhood. What are your feet now, size twelves?"Cracked my Uncle.

"Size eleven. Okay Pops. Glad to see you are able to lighten up during probably one of the most frightfully destructive Michigan storms I can remember. Okay, settle down now, boys. Here goes...ahem...

'Under the spreading chestnut tree...'" Well, I proceeded to knock out one good poem after another. My artistic discourse continued for at least two hours when the sound of grown men snoring overpowered my own tonsorial renditions.

Back at our hotel room, I peeled Pop's clothing off down to his skivvies and led him into a big bed of nice clean sheets, tucked him in, said his prayers and the poor man was fast asleep throughout the night even though storms were raging outside on Lake Cadillac and pounding the pampered hood and fenders of his beloved fanciful Ford.

The look on his face in the morning was dreadful so we knew he needed a good Lake Cadillac, Algonquin Hotel breakfast. A gent named Dave Phillips, the chef was not only a good cooker of fresh-caught Walleye, but he was an exceptional artist in his own right when it came to decorative hen-fruit in the morning.

As Pops stumbled into his fresh-cleaned touring outfit (the Algonquin also had a wonderful in-house guest clothing laundering service; something I marveled at being so far from any large metropolis where it is expected),

Uncle Tylie and I each grabbed an arm and quickly, yet judiciously ushered Father past any window viewing his damaged Ford, while aiming him into the hotel kitchen. Uncle and I figured that if Pops woke up to a nice breakfast maybe by the time he eventually would go out to embark on our trip he would feel a whole lot better prepared to face the total destruction of the finish of his new Ford... his precious new Model T Ford.

Breakfast started with Brazilian coffee (they got a lot of coffee in Brazil), prune danish with butter and fresh-squeezed orange juice. Our morning repast continued with Belgium waffles (the ones with deep pockets) filled with strawberries and topped with maple syrup and whipped cream, a side of Plath ham, smoked bacon, and an omelet stuffed with sweet onions, morel mushrooms, spinach and cheddar cheese with a sprig of parsley for a garnish.

"Gentlemen, will there be anything else?" asked the waiter. "Chef Dave Phillips wanted you to have a complimentary bowl of fresh melon balls."

"Oh...my goodness. Thank you ever so much but we must be shoving off now. We're heading up north," replies Clarence.

"Excuse me, gentlemen. My name is Lawrence Fisher. This is my Mother. We're up here vacationing. Whose owns that beat up Ford Model T out there?"

"Well, I brought a new one up here. Are you referring to my new Ford Model T?"says Pops.

"It's the only one in the lot, so it must be yours. Listen I'm in the automobile body business. Mother and I... that is. You know "Body by Fisher." Um, I don't think you've seen what yesterday's storm did to your Ford's body."

"Not exactly, Mr. Fisher. Why, it is real bad?" inquires my nervous Pops.

"What is your name sir?"

"Clarence. Doctor Clarence Hemingway. From Chicago."

"Well, Mr. Hemingway... doctor... ahem...since it was such an act of God-awful- nasty storm and since it was, I say <u>was</u>, a new car, and since it <u>was</u> an act of God, I am prepared to replace that body at no cost to you. In fact I've brought over a factory new one (from a local dealership) the new one now sits next to the battered one of yours out in the parking lot."

"Are you sure? Why thank you, uh... Mr. Fisher...Mrs Fisher...Body by Fisher!"

"Doctor, we can't have you going around driving a new Model T which looks as bad as yours. So if you look outside I've arranged it with our local Ford dealer to replace that terribly hail -pelted one with a...ahem, brand ...ahem...new one. Please come. Please come outside. Come...Look."

Holy cow! I watched my Pops as we all did the surprise shuffle out to the hotel parking lot. The Great Physician's eyes looked like they would pop right out of his skull, for in the bright morning Cadillac sun there next to his multi-pitted wreck of a miserable weather-beaten, pock-marked once new Ford Model T, stood a shiny, mystically glimmering brand new Ford Model T from the local dealership. It appeared like some kind of other worldly vehicle sent from God as it shimmered in the morning mist.

What we had feared a total loss due to the ferocity and finality of yesterday's hail storm was now being replaced by one of the wealthiest, most charitable yet totally unknown automobile moguls and his totally delightful Mother.

"I don't know what to say, sir, uh... Mr. Fisher, Mrs. Fisher. Is this for real? Will I awaken to find it was all only a dream?" uttered our Doc...my totally stunned Dad.

"It is no dream, dear Doctor. Now wouldn't it be the very worst form of advertising if Mother and I allowed you to go on driving around our fair state in a new, terribly beat up Model T that looked like it was in a war zone. That golf ball sized hail made a bazillion small dents all over the outside body of your nice, I mean, once-nice, Ford automobile. So since your misfortune was an act of God, Mother and I thought it only fitting that we replace your nasty one with a shiny new one."

"Praise God! It's a beaut!"exclaimed Doc.

"Only thing we ask, my good Doctor is that you mention our magnanimous exchange here today. Is that a fair deal, sir Doctor? No other strings. Just drive it and smile and be happy, okay and tell 'em where you got it?"advised Mr. Fisher.

"That's a deal. Uh, what was your name again?"asked my Pops thinking it still a dream.

"Lawrence Fisher uh and don't forget Mother Margaret Fisher here...uh okay?"

I interjects: "I had a brainstorm. We all thank you, but since most of us haven't heard of you sir, because you just make the body of the vehicles, your good name is getting lost under the Ford logo here. May I be so bold as to suggest we fashion a placard with your logo on it and place it at the top of the running board. My Pops and I then

The Fisher Family, Famous for their Automobile Bodies

could brag about this wonderful exchange and you can then rivet these little placards on each vehicle as it rolls off the assembly line."

"And what would it say, son?" asks Mrs. Fisher.

"Body by Fisher! Of course! I think you good folks should get some honor. After all it is you and your Mother here who make all these nice bodies, right?"

"That's a splendid idea. What do you think of it, Mother?"

"Oh, by all means. Our name really should get some credit; after all, what would an automobile be without a body? Splendid idea. What's your name?"

"Ernie... Ernest Hemingway. The writer."

So today if you look carefully as you step into a new automobile, at the top of each running board will be found a little plaque giving credit to our generous benefactor Lawrence Fisher and his Mother.

Placing that little logo plate improved the Fisher's name from being an obscure, unknown working behind the scenes name to a big name now in the auto industry. After that plaque improved his popularity he built his Mother a huge mansion along the Detroit River. Personally his gift of a new Model T to Father more than made up for itself in fame and fortune for Lawrence and his Mother.

Father sits up proudly now as I crank the engine.

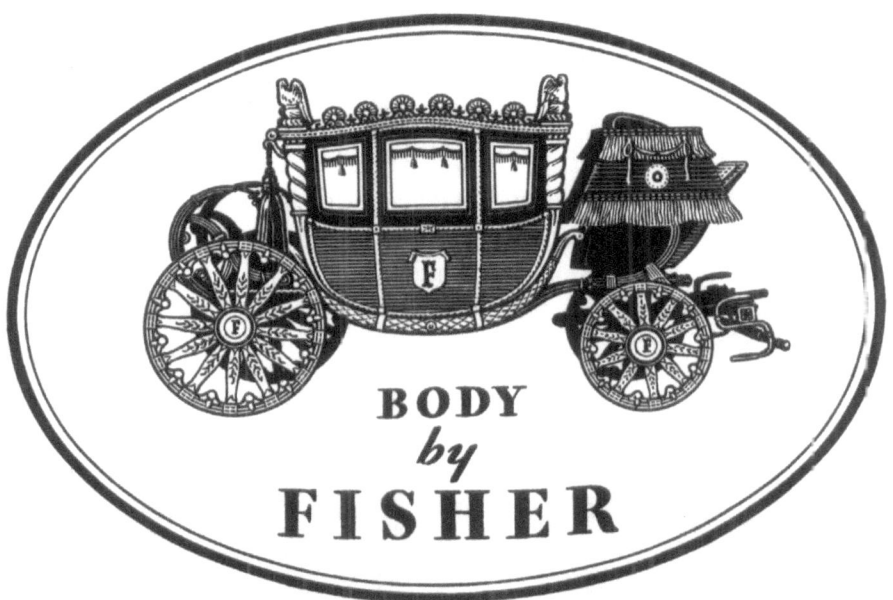

"Switch on?" says I.

"Switch on," replies Pops.

Two firm cranks got that tight little four-banger started and she purred like Bootsie, my six-toed cat, when I scratch behind her ears.

After I hopped into the soft, mohair back seat we slowly rolled over to the old hailstorm victim Model T which now looked like it had chicken pox.

"Well Pops, I don't think we will stop talking about our meeting Lawrence Fisher and his wealthy Mother."

"You can say that again, son. What do you make of all that back there, brother Tyler?"

"Mighty strange and mighty unusual, Clarence."

"You heard that, man," I replies. "It was an act of God and God wanted you to have a new Ford. That is my take on it. That all-night hail storm was sent from God so He could achieve His desire for you, Father. God wants the best for His humble servants. Hey, Father look how He takes care of Uncle Willoughby over there in the jungles of China. I tell ya that brother has told some stories that make your eyes pop. Seriously."

"Hey Pops, why you pulling over? Why are you shaking? Uncle Tyler, you better drive! I think your brother is being overcome with

The Holy Spirit. Drive on, Uncle. This new vehicle is now our fine chariot to the north country."

"Ernest! Just you shush now, hear? Let your Father have his moment in silence. No more pontificating now, okay?"

Father held his head as tears began to flow. I could tell his sobs were coming from a deep emotional space for this stop in Cadillac was truly monumental, very deeply touching.

It's not everyday that one stops at a hotel built for Lawrence Fisher and it's not everyday that one has a new vehicle given to him by that wonderful man. It was no wonder his Mother never let him out of her sight.

Fisher bodies were used exclusively by the early auto industry.

Chapter 8. The Uncles Get Together

The Hemingways and family friends pictured with their Model T.

Our roads were better out of Cadillac, for they were built along parallel to the railroad tracks. Best road beds had to be those that were just an extension of railroad tracks so we had smooth road conditions all the way northward into Boyne Falls.

Pops kinda snapped out of his cryin' jag so we pulled over to see the falls and examine the box lunches that were sent along by Chef Phillips of the Algonquin Hotel.

"Well Pops, shall we see what Chef Phillips fixed for us? That is one terrific chef, I tell ya."

"Thanks Ernest, you really have been doing a good job of trying to lift my spirits along this bouncy, bouncy ride. Tyler too. Uh...a... I have just been dealing with a lot of personal stuff these past few weeks and need to let these woods and rivers and lakes and beautiful scenery also lift my spirits."

"Hey Father...we know. It ain't easy but you can see The Lord is trying to put things right for ya', Pops. Uncle and I are eye witnesses to His goodness."

"Ernest is speaking in The Spirit now, Clarence, and it is true. You are being challenged greatly now and the Lord will see you through your trials. So just open up to the showers of blessing that are coming your way...amen?"

"Amen, brother. You know them?"

"Well yes," replied Tyler. "Isn't it obvious?"

"I guess it doesn't take much for me to notice. Maybe the northwoods living will help us bring all our issues out in the open in order for us to talk them through."

"Good point. We need to talk them through."

"Yeah...talk them through. Pops, I have a feeling you have a volcano's worth of stuff to let loose of. Maybe with your other brother, Uncle George, to help us, you might have an epiphany this summer."

Clarence answers, "Okay, let's stop digging into my personal life."

"Okay, I'm digging into our lunch. Let me see," says Tyler. "Oh boy! Crispy fried Walleye fillets on lettuce with tomato in a sandwich of whole wheat bread with mayo and a side of coleslaw with a handful of bread & butter sweet pickles. Praise the Lord!"

"Pops can I find you a sandwich?"

"Thank you, Ernest, that would be nice of you."

"How about a nice Plath smoked met-wurst on a bed of romaine and dill chip pickles in horsey sauce on pumpernickel? Just what the doctor ordered, right?"

"Right. Please pass it over. Say what do you say we have a walk by the Boyne River to watch the trout rise."

"Now how are you going to get trout to rise in the heat of the day?" asks Tyler.

"Fish have terrific smellers right? Mmmm, this smoked sausage is the best of the wurst. Should smell real tasty to a trout also," replies Pops. "Now watch. Be real still, like a manikin in the windows of Marshall Fields. Now I just bite me off a piece of smoked sausage and toss it deftly by that back wash eddy where trout like to rest. I'm betting he will leave his cool spot in the deep bottom river bed and quickly rise to nail Mr. Plath's finest smoked delight."

"I'll bet you a Vernors," Tyler responds.

"I'll bet you a cigar," I add.

"Quiet...still, real still...here goes...it's in the river now...slowly floating...floating..."

"We win," I says.

"Shhh, quiet," advises Pops. "Shhh...floating...still floating..."

"Surely he has smelled that sausage by now, Clarence. Pay up, please?"

Clarence continues, "...still floating...and...and...and...there! He got it! See, I told you he'd rise. He likes the smell. You owe me, Gentlemen."

"We will have to tell Chef Phillips the news that trout like his food. Have a cigar, Father. Need a light?"

"Oh, keep your cigar, but I will take a Vernors. Let's stroll over to Mill Street Cafe."

"So you think you know your trout, eh?" says Tyler. "Three Vernors please my, good woman. I bet I can get a trout to rise on...on...this bottle cap."

"Oh Ty, don't be polluting this nice stream now," chides Clarence.

"Say...I think I know where your going with this," I says.

"Anything else? We have fresh baked pies," suggests the waitress.

"Looks like you have a train that comes right by here," remarks Tyler.

"Sure does."

"What's it called?"

"The Tuscarora."

"Men, do you realize we could've taken a train up north?" reveals Tyler.

"Yeah," I says.

"Well if it's all the same to you gentlemen, next time I'll take the train. This Model T on these bumpy roads has shook something loose. I may never be the same. Arabelle and I want to have kids."

Uncle George was waiting for us as we sputtered up the two track to his cabin. He embraced his brothers and was absolutely amazed at the fine condition of the Ford.

Pops relayed the adventure and the thrill we had of God replacing the beat up Model T.

"Yes sir, these roads are nothing more than ruts in the ground along a path traveled by the Native American Indian," says George. "Wagons pulled by horses made their imprints as their wheels pressed down vegetation, and before you know it, we gets us a road."

"Gosh! Uncle George. How did the Indians keep from getting lost? They were mostly in moccasins and a few had horses, which really wouldn't press down a good path. Grass grows up."

"Well, good question Ernest. Look closely at some of the trees. What do you see?"

"Why Uncle, I see that some of the trees are bent. Kinda weird looking."

"Yes, indeed, crooked trees deliberately bent by Indians marked the trails down through the years."

"So if we ever find a tree with an unusual bend?" asks Tyler.

"It's probably an old Indian trail. They've got trees, many deformed trees, marking their trails all across the territory. There is a trail going from Mackinaw all the way to Chicago. They call it the grand trunk."

"I get it," I remarks. "The tree trunk is bent in a grand way."

"Right. The trunk gets deformed as a sapling and just keeps growing and growing, getting itself all strange looking." states Uncle George.

Well isn't that grand, but they could've used elephants too, don't ya think?"

"No, Ernest. Elephants need lots of hay to survive. These meager grasses and shrubs up here would never maintain elephants. Oh... now I get it. That was a joke...trunk, ha ha ha ha. I forgot you have a rather dry sense of humor."

"Well isn't that just grand. Thanks for the history of your roads up here, Uncle,"says I.

"My take on future roadwork is that we up north here, will have to wait until this war is over to make any significant improvements," remarks Clarence. "Our war effort takes precedence."

"Indeed," responds Tyler. "I think we are really in for it. The U.S. cannot stay neutral about anything anymore."

"Now don't remind me of seein' all my pals leaving the train station last week," I reminds.

"Yes Ernie," says Uncle George. "Sorry you had to experience that but 'the pen is mightier...'"

"Yeah I know, Uncle, '...is mightier than the sword,' but I have a future ahead of me in journalism since Uncle Tyler landed me an internship with his Kansas City Star. Only future most of those boys have is meeting Saint Peter... I'm afraid."

"Yes...how sad. So all the more reason to maintain a strong military I say...so any tyrants will think twice about trying to dominate the world," responds Uncle George.

"Yeah...one of these days I'm gonna figure out a way to knock out some of their nasty submarines," I replies.

"Good luck with that, Ernest," says Uncle George.

After a brief stay with Uncle George and Aunt Grace, I decided to leave all the brothers in order for them to bond and discuss family issues. Me, I wanted to fish, so I took off on foot to hitchhike into Hortons Bay.

It was a time of lots of horses, and wagons, and occasionally a horseless carriage, which we now call the "car". Warren Sumner gives Ernie a ride into Hortons Bay.

Chapter 9. Hortons Bay Reunion

The Summer Gang: Carl Edgar, Kate Smith, Marcy Hemingway, Bill Horne, Ernest, and Bill Smith.

Before long, Farmer Warren Sumner came by with his buckboard to haul seedling pine trees from Uncle George's who maintained a nursery in Ironton.

"Good to have you back in Michigan again, Ernie. Can I give you a lift over to Hortons?"

"You bet, Mr. Sumner. Want to do some serious fishin'."

"Vollie Fox tells me no one has fished Hortons Crick since you left last fall, Ernie. See?"

"Great! So that means only one thing."

"Giddy up team! Chick, chick. Means only one thing right? See, there will be some good lunker in that magical tributary. They could top five or six pounds, see?"

"Yeah. I see. Are you gonna need help hauling in your hay again this summer?"

"Yup. You bet, Ernie. I see you put on some bulk over last year. You been pumping iron?"

"Not exactly...just Charles. Atlas to be exact. Say, is Beth Dilworth putting together those tasty chicken dinners yet? Are the Bump girls helping again?"

"Hey, only one question at a time. Yes and no. See?"

"No Bump girls?"

"Yes...I mean no. They are on vacation, see. Visiting some relatives over in Minnesota, see, but Bill and Kate Smith are back, Y. K. is back, the rest of your old gang is back, Loomis is back; Grace Quinlan she'll be expecting you to take her fishin, see?"

"I see. I see and uh...I see."

"Yup. That Gracie Q. has blossomed into one young beauty, see? Yeah – filled out in all the right places. See?"

"I can't wait to see, see? Have you ever been out to sea? I have, see. Oh, say can you see? This morning I downed my vitamin C, see? Oh, what the heck, let me guess your favorite letter of the alphabet. Comes after letter B and before letter D, right?"

"Wrong. I always liked letter Z, see?"

"Warren, you're the livin' end. Yikes! Well, here we are, Hortons Bay. Thanks for the lift, Warren."

"Hey, what are neighbors for anyway? Got to get old Dobbin new horse shoes anyway, see?" Mr. Sumner replied. "Hey, village blacksmith, how 'bout some new shoes for old Dobbin here?"

Jim Dilworth's anvil hammering seemed to add a metallic clang to anyone's own heartbeat. His son Wes and I delivered that new anvil a few years ago when I was just a skinny young kid of eleven, or was it twelve? Hauled the metallic monster from Bump Hardware by buckboard. Needed a block and tackle to lift it out of the wagon. It's one heavy anvil. Jim's loud hammering goes on all day permeating the peace and tranquility one should expect from the woods up north here. His rhythmic blows seem to punctuate each whine of the neighborhood hungry saw mill which pontificates an airborne sentence regarding each of its constant gnawing and ripping of the region's tribal hunting grounds.

Clang, clang, whine, whine. Clang, clang, whiiiine. 'Say good bye and farewell to the Indian and his way of life, you all. However Dilworth's anvil also hammers out wrought iron hinges, door latches, fencing, knives, and cutting tools of all kinds. So in the name of progress we must endure a whole cacophony of annoying screeches and clangs, for this new century strongly demands it as it ushers in the westward movement of America in a grand, yet annoying salute.

Figure things this way, sooner or later all the trees will be cut up into lumber and the demand for wrought iron will ease up. Maybe then we will have peace and quiet in Hortons Bay. But for now the racket punctuates the beginning of another busy tourist season for Dilworth's Pine Hurst, Red Fox Inn, the General Store, Jim's Blacksmith shop and a few other businesses which all winter have been waiting for the beginning of this bee-hive of activity.

Not exactly a tourist myself, I provide Beth Dilworth necessary cook-stove fuel, namely chopped wood; I help Sumners haul hay; I instruct guests in the fine art of fishing; give Auntie Charles needed apple picking; Joe Bacon with cow milking, butter churning, ham and bacon smoking; and I also deliver fresh veggies and ice to summer residents of Lake Walloon and fresh fish to hotels.

During my spare time I hunt crows, squirrels, partridge, and pheasant; catch fish; tend garden; keep penned animals like ducks, pigs, and geese in their respective pens until we eats them; and in order to expand my restless mind I read and write poetry or short stories, whichever captures my ever changing teenage moods.

Bay View educational and social functions will take up more of my time this season 'cause I'd like to become a lecturer on the circuit. Also, square dances will be of interest more so than ever.

I walks into Dilworth's Pine Hurst and start to announce my presence. "Hello...anybody here? Is Hortons Bay open for the summer season?"

"Who is there? I'll be right there. Hold on...why young Ernest Hemingway, my goodness, how you have grown! Welcome back, son."

"Hi, Auntie Beth Dilworth. Need any wood chopped?"

"Oh, fiddle sticks with that. Just give me a big bear hug, young-un. So you are all graduated from high school and headed to medical college?"

"Yup, but no college. Going out to Kansas to work on a newspaper, the K. C. Star."

"Well Ernie, isn't that something you've always wanted to do... write?"

"Write? Right! Uncle got me an internship. I start in October. Tyler rode up with us. He and the Doc are at George's in Ironton."

"You rode...up...here? In an automobile? Are you kidding me? Oh my!"

"Hey, it wasn't my idea. Pops went through two cars. He was given a new one in Cadillac on the way up here. It was the craziest thing."

"Well listen, Ernie, I'm glad to see ya son, but I'm awful busy getting those chicken dinners together. My regular help is still on vacation. You remember Marge and Pudge Bump? Well Grace Quinlan's here instead now to lend a hand.

"Yeah I remember Grace Quinlan. Kinda young, kinda tomboy, kinda flat chested?"

"Ernie, you would not know the girl today. Really filled out. A real raven haired beauty."

"Hmm. No kiddin?"

"Hey, Miss Quinlan, would you step out here a minute. Somebody here to say hi. She'll be right out. Just put chicken in the oven."

Grace slips off her apron so's not to hide her new headlights. Casually, as if in slow motion, she slinks out the kitchen screen door to welcome her teenaged friend whom she has not seen since last fall. Grace feels proud to parade in front of men of all ages now to monitor their instant reaction as they gaze at her new bodice, and her other graceful curves. Grace now takes great pleasure in the power that she has discovered, which comes with all her newly-acquired womanly features, and she wonders what might be triggered in the reunion with her old friend, Hemmie.

Our eyes meet and for about ten seconds not a word is spoken. Finally, I feel I should break the delicious silence. "I-i-i-is th-th-that you, Stut? Cripes sake, kid...I-I-heck, I hardly recognize y-y-you. Grace Quinlan, you kinda grew up over night."

"Hi, Hemmie...yeah...I woke up one morning and...and...there they were. It's okay to stare. All the men and boys do it all the time. I'm kinda used to it now."

"C-c-c-could you ...ah...maybe turn around once?"

"Sure...there. What do you think? Huh?"

"Holy cats. Words fail me. I remember last summer you were still a little girl...b-b-but...uh now! You are friggin' gorgeous!"

"Yup. Mother Nature sure was good to me, huh? At first I was kinda frightened, like...they just kept getting b-b-bigger. Each day...bigger and bigger. Seriously, I gotta tell since we is old pals and all."

Words again came to a halt as I become fixated upon young Grace Quinlan's captivating new womanly features, and judging from the way she moved around Dilworth's back porch, I figured she already had learned how to use them. All of a sudden, I discovered that my bad eyesight had somehow corrected itself. In fact, I found that I was now getting x-ray vision, for I systematically could see how her voluptuous body might appear in motion unrestricted by any of her outer or under garments. I completely astounded myself.

As Grace moved to lean her arms on the porch rail, my new found x-ray vision followed her every move. As she paced from rail to rail, at first I noticed her discomfort with my stares, but discomfort eventually shifted to Salome's dance of the seven veils as the temptress in her took over.

I sensed she was using this moment to try new behavior, which first appeared naughty, but eventually settled into a confidently sustained form of naive burlesque. It was hypnotic and I found myself liking it. This newly initiated, young nymph had just succeeded in capturing my total, undivided attention.

My breathing became more labored. My lower extremities received a warmth completely unfamiliar to me up to this point in my young life. With only a few strategic emotionally-charged gestures, young Miss Quinlan had successfully charmed my lower nether-region into complete tumescence.

"Do ya' see what I mean, Hemmie? This new equipment requires some serious personal restraint or else things can get totally out of control."

"Y-y yeahhh! I kinda feel this new equipment should have come with some sort of instruction manual mentioning the dangerous effect it can have upon a guy. What if I now get stuck in the doorway or something? Or get it slammed in a door. Egadd! That could get painful."

"Uh...Hemmie! I'm so sorry. Gosh, I feel so bad now. Am I naughty to find out what these beauties can do?"

"Who can say, kid? How else are you gonna learn, huh? But I will say this... they are spectacular! Just be careful not to be too sporty with them around strangers, okay? They might go off."

"Miss Quinlan, I need a hand in here now, darling!" called Aunty Beth Dilworth. "Say Hemmie, you might try to work that off by chopping some wood for the cook-stove and if it's still a problem after that, I suggest a cool dip in the bay. Good luck. Grace, I will be done around eight o'clock. Isn't puberty wonderful?"

"Huh? Oh, yeah, Auntie Beth. It sure is. I'm gonna chop some wood now."

After an hour of intense wood chopping Beth appears on the porch to notice the huge pile of wood I have split, but the discomfort, for some reason, still gave me hard feelings, so Beth motioned toward the coolness of the bay behind her Bed and Breakfast.

Beth seemed mighty good-natured about my embarrassing ordeal, and as I stripped down and hopped off the end of Dilworth dock, a beautiful sunset gave me a salute and some much needed twilight privacy to hide my cool skinny dip.

With the ever-present bar of soap at the end of each Michigan dock, I laundered my hot sweaty pants and shirt, hanging them to air-dry at the end of Beth's dock.

While scrubbing my underwear in waist high cold water I felt a stabbing pain at the end of my Johnson. I let out one excited yelp. It seems the scrubbing motion during laundry made my willy behave much like something a school of perch or large mouth bass might like to enjoy for their supper. Immediately, I slid my wet (but clean) clothes back on and hopped upon the end of the dock in hopes that all would be air dried when Gracie got off work. Fish nibbling at my manhood began the much needed shrinkage from the stiff condition Grace's seductive dance had caused.

While sitting on the Dilworth's dock at twilight, this whole topic of puberty flashed before me. My own body changes are bad enough to deal with, what with uncontrollable swelling and then aching loins, together with the all consuming urges to fertilize the entire Midwest, but now, to observe my Pal, my playmate with whom I engaged in countless innocent childhood games, all too suddenly show me her new womanly equipment was something now upon which I had to reflect.

There was no easing into adulthood here. No careful period of pubescent education, no purposeful planning to arrive at numerous healthy plateaus of contemplation and Christian mediation along the way. No, we were being bushwhacked, attacked by a full-frontal attack directly in the privates. Our most tender and our most vulnerable of bodily regions had been violated before any kind of wisdom could come into play and rescue us.

For us, the body was willing, dare I say eager, but the mind for some reason had been left out of the equation. My Johnson was saying jump on her and copulate, 'Wham! Bam! Thank you ma'am.' But she, along with all the world's blossoming beauties, was asking for somewhat scientific coital explorations, and I held the test tube, the Bunsen burner, the microscope with which together we could plunge into the deepest of unknown Netherlands of pleasure. Life itself was knocking at the last vestiges of the innocence of childhood, but it snuck-up on me. I was very much not ready to lead my young childhood friend into a labyrinth of untold pubescent confusion, and constant consternation which just the summer before I had encountered with my Indian neighbor, Prudy.

Nah! Tonight will be nothing more than a quiet evening of Hortons Bay fishing, and...if she wants more than that...then she will just have to wait until her wedding night...end of issue.

As I sat on the end of Dilworth's long dock, which jutted out into the cool evening twilight, I splashed my big feet into the lake. Occasionally, a fish would rise to take a nibble on my bare toes. It was then I decided to dig up some worms, bait my hook and surprise young Grace when she finished her kitchen duties.

My thoughts drifted back to when I first met Grace. Her parents, Mr. Thomas Quinlan of Petoskey, and Grace Witherspoon Quinlan of Grand Rapids, were active in Petoskey social circles and in the development of early Petoskey commerce, as were mine. They were wealthy dealers in livestock, and raised their own thoroughbred horses on their 600 acre farm. Grace was about Ursula's age, but even at her young age she had decided to take a risk and ride the adventure train on that of a friendship with an older boy. Her sense of adventure was refreshing to me so I played along with her overly active creativity, 'cause I'm open to new things. Her parents were always present in those days, for any mingling among children usually took place in the parlor where a chaperone was always present. Parlor games, parlor snacks of fireplace popcorn, and cook-stove fudge were an ever-present staple to while away those long summer parlor evenings.

For my own protection from Gracie's feminine beauty and charm, I had to trick myself mentally by considering her my kid sister, and by playing with the names with which I addressed her. She had more affectionate nicknames than any friend. Some days she was: Sister Luke or Stut (the name of a sports-car, Stutz Bearcat), Gee, or G.Q. But today she and her new anatomy had somehow got passed those mental protection devices and was playing with making a visual nerve connection from my eye directly to Mr. Johnson.

No matter how much civility I now brought to bear upon our new relationship, one quick glance at her perky new bodice brought immediate twitches in the nether land of Mr. Johnson. This nerve connection was immediate as if my very own eye had a mind and will power all of its own; a will stronger than any will I could muster to forestall or overcome.

Tonight's evening of your basic Horton's Bay fishing variety was venturing into a time and circumstance never before experienced by a lad of my background. I could feel my whole family tree begin to shudder at the earth-shaking potential and breath-taking possibilities this delightful brunette brought to this summer's magic.

Another part of me informs me that Grace Quinlan is one in a series of ideal, iconic young women who will be coming forward to form a composite from which I will appreciate my ideal, my soul mate, my future wife. This thought, this composite concept, began to soothe my anxious mind. The more I dwell-ed upon it the more my breathing settled into a series of long, deep, cleansing breaths. When I placed Grace Quinlan as one of a number of female friends who would be filling in the blanks of that beautiful puzzle called my future wife, a big load began to lift off my shoulders.

In fact, all women now could qualify for that roll. The truth of that thought caused me to shudder a little, but I let it pass when Mother Grace was also included as one of that number, for she too was actually figuring heavily in the completion of that puzzle, even though we were becoming more at odds with each other. Also, I began to realize I needed to hurry in order to finish my composite woman puzzle; for when it was completed, this mystery women would automatically have to appear and I would recognize her immediately.

This kind of thinking settled me down and gave my future a rosy glow of optimism, which left me feeling thankful the more I meditated on this milestone issue.

That night I failed to remember how many fish we caught for I was busy collecting puzzle pieces, codifying and collating as many aspects of Sister Luke (G.Q...Gee) as I could that night. After I bid her good night, I entered all her exquisite aspects in my journal.

In retrospect, I considered myself blessed for taking time to see how beautiful women began to fit into my life, for it canceled the power that I gave the tantalizing Grace Q. and nullified her stupefying ability.

Grace Quinlan had beauty that set other women talking about her. It would come as no surprise if Petoskey named a street after her. I am willing to bet money someday there will be a Quinlan Street.

As I recollect that super charged day with G.Q., I realize I just saved myself a lot of time and also learned to detour around a lot of trouble; for prior to that realization I spent loads of time acting as the predator, seeking vulnerable girls of whom I could take advantage just for my selfish pleasure. If I were to continue in that mode it would have led to possible STDs or an unwanted pregnancy, both serious life changing events. Things a young single guy like me cannot afford. Also consider the fact that jails are full of lads who get to messin' around with young girls who are minors. A girl of 15 will get you 20. That fact gets a fella keepin' his Mr. Johnson under wraps until the honeymoon, a plan that has the Lord's sanction as well as His blessing.

Now if I can just hold out on that track until the puzzle is done viewing "girl" friends as parts of a composite, I will succeed in speeding up the day in which all my research will pay off big time.

My young life has just taken off in a whole new, totally unexpected, exciting new direction of which I am extremely elated.

Pops asked me to open up the cabin at Walloon, but being that the evening has sneaked up on me, Beth Dilworth has offered sleep-age space above their carriage house. I often crash up there when it's convenient. Wood chopping for her cook-stove or a nice stringer of Hortons Crick trout is considered fare exchange by Auntie Beth.

After I finished entering this stupendous day into my journal, I guess I slipped into dreamland; however, there was a part of me which was aware that I was having a dream. Strangest sensation, I must say. A splinter of my consciousness remained as the observer of the dream and it was a duzie. It was a flash-back of the day's challenges. Grace Quinlan was there in all her pulchritude and the colors were unspeakably beautiful like a painting by Van Gogh, only jacked up 10 octaves.

Music entered the sequence as a band of Celestial Strings, called Saint Peter and His Overcomers, were celebrating my triumphant moments over the trials and temptations presented by the over-developed Miss Quinlan. Thousands of choirs chimed in, offering variations on the theme after which a hundred herald, straight-belled, golden trumpets belted out a brass oratorio loud enough to wake the dead and charm hell out the living.

Saint Peter added what all heavenly hosts were rejoicing about; namely, my successful overcoming of my libido, something I had never before been able to do. "Oh let us honor now one who has come back to the fold, one who finally has allowed the comforter, the Holy Spirit, to enter his heart and mind and together they became overcomers. Hemmie has done it. Finally he has joined the ranks of overcomer! Overcomer, overcomer, overcomer he is, defeating the snares of the evil one."

Well, all the celestial musical and choral groups continued all through what must have been a 2 hour concert that sounded heavenly, hitting unspeakable tones in upper and lower registers. It was a dream like none other. Seeming as if the window to seventh heaven was opened only a crack and for just a while this special program was broadcast right into my dreaming cranium.

A dream like that is unforgettable, in which it is foretelling how righteous actions upon this penultimate earth send wonderful waves which cause celestial reaction up above on the heavenly realms. It is like the angelic multitude are listening to every little thing that occurs on the earthly level and when a soul hits a home-run in terms of overcoming evil with good, it sends them into uncontrollable righteous rejoicing, and for a brief moment, there is a little heaven on earth... a foretaste of things to come... as above, so below, which is what we ask for in the Lord's Prayer, in "thy will be done on earth as it is done in heaven." Herein, we are asking for goodness of the heavenlies to prevail down here on earth, a concept of which I now have intimate knowledge. Through this unusual dream, that point of the two worlds was well driven home and its impact will probably stay with me forever.

The on-going dual nature that occurs daily is alive and well and I certainly acknowledge that anomaly for it is deeply embedded in my awareness now… "as above, so below," now has rich meaning. That's what I would call a milestone dream; some might call it a lucid variety dream, something like I am passing another phase of some kind of initiation, which awakens one into the spiritual aspects which we all can enjoy through meditation.

Sort of like being touched by the work of Bach, Brahms, and Beethoven if one is sensitive enough to the deeper aspects of their work. It seems they had Celestial Music going on inside them continually.

Life is not meaningless nor is it inconsequential, but if you play your cards right, it is our platform from which we can (through faith in Christ) launch ourselves (with aid of the Holy Spirit) into the heavenly home, the happy hunting ground, the born again concept as I see it.

It's hard to believe such a revelation takes place above Dilworth carriage house, which proves the old wake-up call can come anywhere on the road to Damascus, to Emmaus, to a "burning" bush, to Mt. Sinai, anywhere, and nowhere in particular.

Dilworth's "Pinehurst Inn", Hortons Bay, MI

Chapter 10. Chicken Plucking Adventure

Chicken Plucking on the Bacon Farm

Having my senses hyper activated I could actually smell my pal Bill Smith coming across from Red Fox Inn. Taking a few deep breaths and rubbing my eyes, I awaited Bill's arrival which always included the bird mimic whistle of the Bob White. Of course, I answered with a more true to life Bob White call, cause Bill has those thick lips that come from too much trombone playin'.

"Twee-a-wheat, twee-wheat! Thought it wise to announce my presence just in case you might have company up here," states Bill.

"You're too late, scalawag! She just left after chaining me to this bunk and runnin' off with my bag of gold nuggets," I exclaimed.

"Welcome back to God's country, Wemedge, we been expecting you."

"Yup, got in yesterday, Pops drove the flivver."

"He did what?! Oh my God!"

"Yeah, go figure, huh? Big mistake I tell yah, William. We totally trashed one vehicle and some rich automobile mogul gave us a new one coming out of Cadillac. Pops should be coming by soon. "

"Sure been lonesome and boring without yah, pal. Kate will be over joyed to see yah. Odgar's been hangin' around buggin' her again."

"Gosh, he is old enough to be her father, for heaven sake," I stated.

"Yeah.... Don't I know it, wish you would run off with her and elope or somethin'."

"Then I would need a ladder," I smirked.

"True... and the nearest one would be Bump Hardware, all the way over in Petoskey. So cancel that idea for another summer, I guess."

"So, did you get my letter?" I asked.

"Indeed sire, and it was a doozy. That apprenticeship sounds great! Kansas City Star... man! You must be really stoked about that, Wemedge?"

"Oh my gosh, yes! But with mixed emotions creepin' there too... don't yah know?"

"How so?" William asked.

"The war, doofus! I had to ship off a whole trainload of my Oak Park pals the other day. T'was not a pretty sight, I tell, yah, not pretty one friggin' bit. Who's going to protect them? I'm the best shot in the whole outfit. They had the cheat sheet for the damn eye chart so's I could pass the physical that's how great they is, Kingfish. What a great outfit they are. I miss'em already."

"Rest of my graduating class is college bound. Samson... you remember him... he'll be Harvard-bound. He's got ivy growin' out the back of his neck, since he got accepted."

"Yeah... that Samson. Quite the scholar. And Lew Clan-a-ham?"

"Yup... more ivy growing. Coming out of his pants. Lew is Princeton bound."

"Your big sister? Marcy?"

"We don't know. Can't be any coin-age left since Mother Grace spent the family life savings on her second stress-relief cabin across the lake."

"What?! What's with that woman?"

"Oh, tell me about it, but it has acreage for gardens. That made Pops accept it, but Ruth stays over there. Pops banned her from Windemere."

"Mother Grace sure has liberated herself, hasn't she, Wemedge?" states Bill.

"There you go again with the understatement. You know how she chaps my chaps, William! So anyway... have you seen Grace Quinlan lately?"

"Oh that... Kate tells me she got those beauties from Montgomery Wards Catalog."

"Your sister's just plain jealous, son. Can't you see they are real?"

"Hard as hell to tell. Guess there's only one way to find out "

"Yeah... ask her, Billy."

"I was thinking more along the line of an accident... the old bump-and-cop-a-feel routine. Oh excuse me, miss, so sorry, miss, pardon me, miss."

"Awe, come on, Smitty. That's too risky and too risque. A fella could get his face slapped royally... and G.Q., Sister Luke, our Stut... she could do it, Pal. She's the most athletic gal I've ever known. G.Q is built like a Stutz Bearcat... that new sportscar they got out now. She could knock your block off and leave tire tread marks across your forehead."

"Yeah, I suppose you're right, Wemedge."

"You know damn well I am, anyway, I thinks they're... they're the real deal. Hey listen, Stinker, I went fishin' with the girl last night and she's got the headlights. The bonified bosom there with her. She be carryin' the genuine mammarabelia, Mister," says I, trying to sound confident.

"So... I suppose some fish told you?"

"You're a funny little dwarf... so that still leaves us in a pickle, doesn't it. Are they, or aren't they? Real? Or not real? That is the question... somehow I forgot the question. When I first saw them, Mr. Johnson sure thought them to be real," I stated.

"Oh, is that why you was a choppin' all that kindling for Beth Dilworth? Huh?" Bill asked. "Did the heavy physical exertion cool your tool, fool?"

"Uh... not really. Just made Johnson all the more agitated," I counters.

"So, Aunty Beth then suggested a cool dip in Hortons Bay?" says Bill cautiously.

"Hey... yeah! Were you there yesterday? Now that does it. How do you know all this? You were watching my whole ordeal, my whole painful ordeal, weren't you? Now that does it mister smarty pants!"

Guess something just snapped in me and I up and tackled my best friend. Together, we rolled, rough house fashion, down Dilworth's carriage house stairway only to roll at the feet of Aunty Beth Dilworth, who was standing over us.

"Well, for pity sakes. I was just coming to invite you to breakfast, Mr. Hemingway. Is this your new morning workout? Or something?" says she. "Could Grace Quinlan have anything to do with this rough housing? Huh?" she inquires with her hands on her corset-tightened hips.

Bill and I commence to slowly untangle ourselves while brushing dust off each other's rumpled bib overalls. As we both had an arm around the other's shoulder, we slowly rises and begins to follow Aunty Beth to reassure her that we was still the best of pals and that we both had accepted her invite to a steaming hot breakfast of her recent creation.

She states, "Only reason I can think of that wold trigger best friends to lay into each other like that would most definitely have to be a girl. Now you two ruffians wash up a bit at this rain barrel before you come to the back deck where I will serve breakfast. The very idea, well I never... two grown high school graduates wrasslin' each other like a couple of horny white-tail bucks during the rut."

Bill and I seated ourselves at her nicely scrubbed back deck. Gingham covered, home made table cloths lined up against the rough-hewn gopher-wood railing, and jaybirds were calling out among the tall elm trees that trailed down a gentle slope to Dilworth's long, gray dock.

A fine mist still hung along the edges of the bay and fish jumping made fine picturesque splash rings on the flat, dark surface waters.

"Bill, I hope you are proud of yourself, spying on a fellow in tumescent distress."

"Well, Wemedge, it isn't often any of us ever get to place the brunt of a joke on someone as cunning as you. Even Vollie Fox found it exceedingly hilarious."

"What! Even Vollie Fox got to see me with a troubled trouser worm?"

"Yup. We thought it tremendously funny."

"Oh, now doesn't this beat all. You know that after breakfast we must have a duel. I challenge thee to ride the gauntlet for my very own manhood has been besmirched and in front of the entire community."

Bill retorted, "I will grant you that dear fellow, besmirched you are. Irony of it is because of some young filly's padded mail order hormone package. Therein lies the rub. For the source of your swollen obelisk was not even real."

"Oh, now I have got to pound your mousy pea-head into...'"

"Sorry to interrupt your morning joust, my dear knights, but it is time for your porridge," says Grace.

"Well, well, well, and what delicacies doth fair maiden place before all the king's men?" I queried.

"Hear ye, undaunted dusty dimwits. Aunty Beth's exquisite kitchen brings before you Joe Bacon's cherry-wood smoked famous bacon, perfectly fried hash browned, buttered, baby red skinned 'taters, fresh laid country eggs with eyes partially open, and a pile of well stacked buckwheat cakes, smothered in butter and real Michigan maple syrup. Enjoy, gentlemen."

"Did I hear well stacked?" says I.

"You heard right, dark Knight," says Bill.

Grace said, "And here comes now hot beverage, the likes of which often appears on her majesty's breakfast table. Piping hot Michigan chicory with fresh milked Bacon farm cream... not to be confused with Bacons bacon, baking."

"Oh, Miss Quinlan, I must say, you and the fair Miss Dilworth have totally outdone yourselves this morning, since I have only my broad-ax to offer in return."

Says G.Q in return, "Oh, we'll think of something which will even up the barter here at Dilworth's Pinehurst. Aunty Beth will be cut shortly with your orders of the day."

Says I, "G.Q, could you kindly bend low here to pour me a cup of that fine beverage, and find thee a moment to linger by our table in order that you might serve as the garnish which might decorate our delightful plates."

"Gee whiz, Wemedge, you sure have a way with words, but some girls can read between the lines, you know... so... out with it. How come you can't look me in the eye anymore?"

At this very moment, Aunty Beth swings open the screen door and says, "How is breakfast, gentlemen? That bacon is an experiment by Joe Bacon. He wants our opinion, since he's started smoking meats with fruit wood, cherry and apple, using wood from area fruit orchards."

Says I, "Yup, I likes it. Simply divine, Aunty Beth."

Bill adds, "Actually, I'm tasting something in those pancakes, and what would that be?"

Beth says," That light tang? Comes from the buttermilk ala goat. Gives it a little more show. Very good, Master Smith. You've developed a gentleman's higher taste? My chicken eggs? How did you like them? Nice big, orange yolks, eh? Nothing better than a fresh farm chicken egg."

I states, "Yup... my pal Bill and I both agree on that too. That was one heck of a breakfast, Aunty Beth. Kinda liked your garnish, too."

"Garnish, Ernie? Gosh... I forgot a garnish. You're being facetious?"

Says I, "Not at all. Can't take my eyes off her ever since I came into town."

"Oh... you're referring to Grace Quinlan, right? Quite the raven-haired beauty, eh?

At this point, Beth walks over to G.Q. (who was leaning on the rail, staring dreamily across the bay), puts an arm around her shoulder, and states, "Yes, indeed! I agree, Grace certainly has blossomed into one rare, brunette flower, and she has been doing the work of two, since Marge and Pudge are at camp. Grace, you know you have been my right arm since the Bump sisters have gone to Minnesota. I love ya to pieces."

Grace responds, "Gosh, Aunty Beth, I should be thanking you for the experience of learning from the expert person who cooks the famous Dilworth chicken dinners. Your fame as a hostess has spread far and wide."

I adds, "At least as far as Chi-Town, Oak Park anyways. My neighbor Frank Lloyd Wright wants to vacation up here. I been talking his ear off about summers here."

"Well thanks, Master Ernest," Beth says, "Word of mouth is my best advertising, that's for sure. Ahem... now orders for the day. Worthy of breakfast, and if done well, maybe even a chicken dinner."

"Yes, yes, what is it? We'll do anything, won't we, Wemedge," Bill says.

"Huh? Oh yeah, sorry, I was tasting my garnish. Sure is nice scenery you got here," Ernie adds.

"You weren't even listening, were you, Ernest?" Beth asks.

"Uh, Aunty Beth, my attention starts to drift when I see beauty," Ernie answers.

"Well, here's what I need. Joe Bacon has some hens that quit laying and he is selling them to me. So walk over to Bacon's and slaughter me a dozen of those old clucks, pluck them, put them on ice, and haul them back here, okay?"

"Indeed, my Queen. Your wish is my command. May the best man win. He who plucks the most chickens wins the hand of Grace Quinlan for a date," Ernie states.

"You're in the habit of dating my hand? How strange, sire, surely ya' jest," Grace says.

"Now stop calling me Shirley, Stut. Oh, this is gonna be exciting. Grace, start thinkin' about our date, okay?" Ernie says.

"Okay, are you a big spender, 'cause I want to be wined and dined properly like the high class lady that I am."

Ernie grins, "Darn tootin, Gee. Nothin's too good for you... beautiful dish that you are."

"Grace, don't believe him. The evening belongs to us. It was love at first sight, was it not?" Bill asks.

"Okay you two Romeos, go have a chicken plucking good time. Just don't cut yourselves. Anyway, how do you know I am am gonna be available tonight? Have you inquired about being added to my social calendar?" Grace asks.

"Gee whiz, Grace, it's not like you to play hard to get. Pretty please, do what you can to work us in, okay?" Ernie says.

"Well... I'll see what I can do, but I ain't making any promises, boys."

"That is all we can ask, Gracie Q. Come on, Hemstein, we've got a lot of plucking to do. Buck-buck-buguck!" Bill states.

So up the hill we ran, grabbing at each other as we traversed Bacon Road. The morning sun had dried the sand and gravel two-track, which created little dust clouds that floated in the cool Michigan month of June.

Although we were highschool graduates, there was still plenty of kid left in each of us. Bill Smith and I were like the brother neither ever had. I was happy just to hang with Bill in order to create another worthy Hortons Bay adventure. Summers were our time to cut loose. City kids all enjoyed the release that Michigan woodlands offered and we both sensed that our moments with G.Q were gonna be super charged with plenty of high class adventure and high drama as well!

Plenty of new dances were out now that jazz had found it's way up north from Chicago and was now being featured in Petoskey hotels.

My plan for the evening was to allow Bill to win the date with G.Q. And Kate... Bill's gorgeous sister... and I would double date. I happened to know that Cushman House always featured a terrific band and the four of us could cut a rug together.

I wanted to be around to see Bills face when he discovers that Grace Quinlan is all woman, anyway, at least I think she is.

With my arm around Bill's shoulders, we walked up to Bacon farm where Joe had a fire going under a cast iron kettle, full of boiling water.

Morning sun had cleared away the mists from low lying valleys, giving clear blue skies and a light breeze from Walloon Lake.

"Morning Boys," Joe Bacon called. "Glad you could make it. So tell me if'n you never done this before."

"Done what?" Bill asks.

"You know. Butcher chickens," Joe answers.

"Gosh! Heck no! We just got an apple orchard. Hemmie, you?" Bill says.

"Butchered ducks and partridge, and quail and goose... and squirrel too," Ernie answers.

"Well... okay," Joe starts. "Anyway, do you see these here tin funnel things, fastened to this long board. You grabs a hen by the feet and jam the head into the tin funnel until the head sticks out the other end. Then with this sharp knife, you slit her throat, holding onto the feet all the time. Then you cut off her feet, gut her, careful not to puncture intestines, cause oh boy, phew! Just don't, okay! Then, drop her in this cauldron of boiling water and in a few minutes she lets all her feathers go, okay? Feathers go in the barrel here. Tweezers here are for pulling out the pin feathers. So there you go, any questions?"

Bills face looked like he was getting ready to barf. Somehow, in all his existence of seventeen years on the Charles farm, the slaughter of chickens had totally escaped my pal.

"Hey, William," Ernie asks, "Do you want to watch Mr. Bacon do one first?"

"Y-y-y-yeah. I ain't never, you know."

"Okay if Bill watches you do one, Joe?" Ernie asks.

"Course... silly me," Joe states.

Well, it took only three seconds and Joe Bacon had that cluck jammed into a funnel, sliced off her head, laid her on an old kitchen table, removed feet at the joints, opened an incision on her belly, pulled out the innards and dropped her into boiling water.

While the feathers were loosening up, Joe glanced back at his students, only to find me the only one standing. Bill had fainted like a bag of rags and was laid out as if he were watching cloud formations with his eyes closed.

"Some people never get the hang of it," Joe says. "Bill may be one who never gets to try it either. Faints at the sight of blood."

"Yup, Mr. Bacon," Ernie states. "I think he is out for the morning. But I like blood. Like to see it squirt. Gives me the power over life and death. Hey, I figure it this way: if we gonna be carnivores, there's got to be a slaughter somewhere, right, Mr. Bacon? And then there's the skinning, the de-gutting..."

"Good point," Joe says, "Be here this afternoon. We gonna slaughter hogs. I'm gonna smoke the hams and bacon, and pork chops. Ever have smoked chops?"

"Yum! Can't wait. Well, here goes... chicken time. Henny Penny, your time is up," Ernie says. "Speaking of slaughter. You know, Mr. Bacon, I kinda worry about all my pals going off to get slaughtered over in Europe."

"Yeah, I know," Joe says, "Big slaughter there. So many nice young lads... all going off to the war-to-end-all-wars. Tell ya what, Ernest. How 'bout I catch the clucks and you jam them headfirst into the funnels, okay? Here comes Mrs. Bacon. She'll help pluck their feathers. Think she wants to make some pillows. Nothing ever gets wasted here."

"Good morning Mrs. Bacon," says Ernie. "We're having too much fun here, aren't we?"

"Did Bill faint?" Mrs. Bacon asks.

"Yeah, he's one of those... faints at the sight of blood," Joe says.

"He's such a nice boy. Too sensitive. Just not cut out for farmin'," Mrs. Bacon sighs.

"Yeah, but he runs a fine apple orchard. Come here you old cluck," Ernie says.

"Pardon me?" Mrs. Bacon asks.

"Oh, sorry, Mrs. B. I was just talking to this hen here."

"That one there laid a lot of eggs, she did, but her egg factory just gave out. Darndest thing. I raised her from a little chick," Mrs. Bacon said.

"Now, Mrs. Bacon, don't go getting sentimental on me now, or we won't be able to kill our dozen clucks here," Joe states.

"Yeah, Bill and me got a wager goin'. Whomever plucks the most chickens gets a date with Gracie," Ernie says.

"That Quinlan young girl? Pretty girl. But ain't she kinda young for you two ruffians. Thought you had a shine on Bill's sister?"

"Yes... I do, ah..."

"But you haven't seen Gracie lately," Joe states. "She has blossomed into a full grown woman, she has... uh... she has... Mrs. B."

"Uh, I'm sorry, sir," Mrs. Bacon interrupted. "But how would you know all about the maturity of young Miss Quinlan, Mr. Bacon, sir? I'd like an explanation, Father, and it better be good, please."

"Yes, Dear, of course, Dear," Joe stuttered. "It was all in the course of doing business over at Dilworth's lodge. It seems she is Beth Dilworth's summer replacement now that Marge and Pudge are away at camp."

"And?"

"And what?"

"And what. You know what? Mister."

"I'm sorry, Ma'am. I guess I don't follow what you're getting at, Madame Bacon."

"Okay, you two," Ernie butts in. "Just back off 'cause I know where this is gonna lead. Let me say this, okay? What one will notice, having seen Grace. The underdeveloped tomboy shape from last summer and the sudden bodily changes that have taken place in one short year... by that, I mean, she has just blossomed into a regular Venus de Milo. Her female beauty is unmatched by any girl in Michigan. Petoskey will no doubt name a street after her, and laid out Bill here and I are fighting to see who takes her on a date tonight."

Joe Bacon states, "Well put, Ernest. Thanks for bailing me out of that discussion."

"I still have a rolling pin waiting for you, Mr. B," Mrs. Bacon protests.

"Gosh, Mrs. Bacon. You really must gaze at Grace's beauty in order to get the whole picture. You know what they say, "Seeing is believing," and Miss Quinlan is totally transformed by Mother Nature, a sight to behold. Believe me!"

"Hm... I will have to reserve judgment then until I see her myself," Mrs. Bacon answers.

"Good, thank you," Ernie says. "Here's another hen then. Well, look who took a little nap. Good morning, William, did you have a nice rest, 'cause I win the hand of G.Q. Chickens are all plucked and we are ready to pack them in ice."

"Gosh! All I remember was seeing blood and then everything went black. Oddest sensation," Bill states.

"Well, then you better stay out of the field of medicine or chicken slaughter. Just why did you engage in our little wager then, friend?" Ernie asks.

"Believe me, I had no idea. It just snuck up on me. Plus, the very thought of having a date with the beautiful Grace Quinlan. Well, quite honestly, she could launch a thousand ships the way she has grown up. Mother Nature bein' so good to her."

"Thanks, Mr. and Mrs. Bacon. I'll be back for the pig slaughter," Ernie states.

"Okay, Ernest. My best regards to Doctor Clarence and your Mother."

"Sure thing. Pops drove me and Uncle Tyler in the Model T up north this time. Mother and the rest of the family came by boat and train. I got a brother now, you know. Little Leichester."

"It will be a pleasure to see them all again."

Toting six hens wrapped in oil cloth and packed on ice in a rucksack is no easy trick, but Bill and I had a downhill trek, which made our going easy. We had time to reflect along the way.

"Phew, Bill. Thanks for your comments supporting my story regarding G.Q's beauty. I thought Mrs. Bacon was gonna clobber old Joe there with her rolling pin. Jealous for Joe lookin' at Gracie."

"Yeah, look, Pal... have you noticed how uptight everyone is regarding a woman's anatomy? What do you make of that?" Bill asks.

"My friend, just chalk it up to a whole new century. Values are a changing and we're gonna see a whole lot more things a changin' as we claw our way into these new 1900s."

"Some hot day a woman is gonna open her tight collar and expose her neck and loosen her shoes and expose her bare ankles... just to catch a cool breeze... at that moment the whole world of women's fashion is going to change forever... right now that female anatomy is hidden," Billy boy states. "Hey now, listen. Let's us do a double date tonight, okay? I'll take my sister, Kate, and you, if you will, be a pal and let me dance with Grace Quinlan. Is that a deal?"

"I'll have to think about that. After all, we did make a wager and you lost, old boy. Losers weepers, you know."

"Yeah, I acknowledge you won, fair and square alright, but I sure am hoping you will share, like we learned in kindergarten, remember?"

"Gee, Bill, you drives a hard bargain. But you're right. I just might need to dance with my beloved Kate once or twice tonight... uh...But! I need more time to think that over, okay? What else do you bargain with, huh?"

"Alright. I've been holding out on you, Pal. Wanted to surprise you... friend... but look here... I would be willing... to drive us to the Cushman House dance... tonight in... real class! Would you believe in my... new Buick!?"

"Holy cats! Broderick, are you kiddin' me, Godfrey? Honestly, where did you get a Buick? Break your piggy bank? Holy Moley! Okay, now you're talking."

"It's a convertible. Got it from the nutty professor."

"Now you're talking, chum. That in itself would be good for a dance... uno!"

"How about three?"

"Make it two. That's final."

"Okay, two is all I'll need to have her eating out of my hand, thank you, sire."

"That's enthusiastic talk for one who believes in Monkey Wards padding," Ernie smirked.

"I see her beauty in those green pools of hers. Those captivating eyes a fella can get lost within. Ya know, my sister Kate will want more than two dances with you, Wemedge. Get real."

"Ahem... well, lets wait until the time comes for another bargain, okay?"

"Oh, aren't you just being the scheister about this. You are such a dog goned stinker."

"Hey, what's that smell?"

"What smell? Don't smell nothing," Bill says.

"Come on. Let's hurry up there, Romeo. I smells lunch at Dilworth's.

Well, sir. The summer was just getting warmed up and already I could see it was gonna be one to remember. With a good dose of hormones in the mix, a young man's fancy will be well represented, beauty abounds everywhere and now Mr. Buick provides the horseless carriage. Topless none the less.

I was not about to let on to Bill that I was willing to let him win the chicken plucking contest, but who knew he was one who fainted at the first sight of a little blood. Believe me, his sleeping at the slaughter was going to be my big bargaining chip and as you can see, I already started cashing in on it.

Sister Kate is someone I can always schmooze, but this new fully developed filly has taken everyone by storm, even old farmers like Joe Bacon.

If old Joe changes his testimony just one little bit his skull will get a crease in it for ogling a young teen-aged girl.

G.Q has brought out a side in Mrs. Bacon that no one has ever seen before. A good Christian woman like Mrs. B has prejudged her faithful husband, Joe. His many years of loving loyalty could vanish in a micro milli-second. Yes, siree, jealousy was let loose in all the women around the sleepy little hamlet of Hortons Bay, just because one innocent little fair maiden either sent away to Montgomery Wards for some extra fluffy stuffing for her bodice, or merely allowed Mother Nature to be extra good to her in the "Thanks for the Mammaries" Department.

Anyhow, however G.Q's beauty-bumps got there is now a most mute question, isn't it? Everyone will proceed to make mountains out of mole hills anyway, and God help the men who "touch the subject." As for me, I'm just gonna sit back and watch how this kind of contagion can soon spread in a little town still stuck in the Victorian Era.

In all her innocence, Miss Grace Quinlan may just become the patron saint of Hortons Bay, the way she's going, for there are those who love her and those folks who are jealous as heck of her because she is way too beautiful. 'Tis a conundrum, the likes of which I will never understand, but it is a phenomenon which I believe needs a good reporter, so if you don't mind I will keep a record of her adventures, for I personally am fascinated by the way hormones behave.

Chapter 11. The Fire Within

Bill and I and Kate picked up Grace at Dilworth's. She was in all her radiance, decked out in a floor length, lacy, cream colored, mutton chop sleeved Victorian dress complete with parasol. In contrast with her dark tan and dark, almost jet-black, hair and emerald eyes, she could have been a model on the cover of any magazine.

Since I had plucked a dozen hens for her hand, I met Grace Q. at the door and personally escorted her to the open-air Buick.

Bill and Kate sat bug-eyed as she gracefully settled into the back seat. Before I sat next to her I took a moment to gather in the full extent of her glory together with all her feminine pulchritude that she exuded.

"Have a seat, Hemmie, before something happens," she tells me.

"Grace, Sister Luke, I can't take my eyes off you. You are the picture of female femininity. That exquisite outfit is totally divine," I says.

"Welcome aboard, Miss Quinlan," Kate says. "Pay no attention to these oogling young boys. It sure must be unnerving?"

"Oh, contrare. I kinda like all the men giving me the once over. It's exciting. Makes me wanna flaunt it on the dance floor tonight. Gosh what a nice horseless carriage here, Bill."

"Indeed, my good woman and there's more where this comes from. With your obvious beauty as a bargaining chip this maiden voyage should be worth say...a dance with you, maiden?"

"Gosh, absolutely. This here Buick is worth at least..."

"Now, wait a minute," I protest. "Don't mean to interrupt but nice Gracie is my date, William. All negotiations for rug cutting goes through myself here."

"Now you just hold it right there, Hemmie. Let me cut this in the bud, boys. I'm what you calls one of them liberated women, okay? Therefore, no one controls with whom I dance. Ah...that feels good."

"Yeah! You go, girl!" Kate says. "And very soon all of us women will win the right to vote."

"You go, girl! And we both need a cigar, right, Kate?"

"Right you are sister Gee. And as for you, little brother, you got no right to make any women beholdin' to you just 'cause you're sporting a fancy automobile, okay? Gracie and I could get a ride in fancier makes and modes of transport. You dudes should be honored just to be escorting us beautiful women around. Why, I happen to know women who own property even. So there! We dances with whom we ever so pleases and don't you ever forget it."

Silence prevailed after the girls got done putting us boys in our place. I had to acquiesce to their logic and something in their tone made me ask for permission to speak, or maybe roll over and sit up for I have seen dogs treated with more respect.

"Say...ahh...Billy Boy...pull over here so's we can light the ladies a stogie."

"Yeah...sure thing, Hemmie. There."

"Now where's the cigar?" Puff, puff. "How's come it ain't lighting?"

"Suck on it. Suck it good, Sister Luke. There, there, now you got it, Hon. Bill, I never knew watching a lady smoke a stogie could be so down right satisfying."

"Hand me that match, Big Boy," demands Kate. "Bet I can get my cigar started right away." Puff, puff, puff, puff, puff, puff, puff, puff. "Stop staring, Bill, you pervert. There."

"Yeah, look at that nice red tip she gets there, Bill. How's come you ain't lighting up...Bill! Kate, Honey, grab him. I think he wants to faint again. Bill! You're scarin' me."

"Bill, you're scaring me, too!" adds Kate. Slap! Slap! "Snap out of it! You hear, Bill?"

"Huh? Wha... wha... happen?"

"I don't know, Billy. You tell me wha... wha... happened," responds Kate.

"Just was watching you tugging on that cigar with your red lips there and maybe it was the way you was tugging on it. I don't know, all the blood felt like it rushed out of my brain, and...and..."

"And into your other brain?" I asks.

"Yeah... yeah...that's it. Exactly, Hemmie!"

"No hard feelin's chum. How we all doing? These is Cuban smokes. Pretty smooth, eh? Got them from a guy on Halstead Street."

"Bill, are you safe to drive?" Kate asks. "Cuz I can operate dis horseless thing, ya' know."

"Yeah Katie, go ahead. Take over, woman. Wish I could suck a cigar like you, Honey. Take charge Katie; you go, girl. Our driver needs something to wake him up. Here get out of that driver's seat and take a pull on this hip flask I got. Do you like gin? Bill?"

"Leave 'er in neutral, Bill. Keep 'er running!" I says.

"Okay. Thanks, Gracie. Mmm. Nice. Wow! Real smooth, Gracie. Hop in Sister Kate."

"Got it from some girl in Petoskey. Her Dad makes...puff...it in their bathtub. Michigan has been...puff, puff...dry since 1916. Sad eh? A woman can't get a...puff...stiff drink? Puff... Juniper berries...puff...her Pops ferments. Juniper berries. Wow, dis...puff...stuff could get your whole body stiff," Gracie puffs some more.

"Yeah, parts of me are stiff. I know that," I says. "And getting stiffer as we speak. I think it's your perfume...Grace...uh?"

At this point you probably think Bill is getting ready to plant a big, juicy kiss onto Grace Quinlan, since she is, without doubt, the most beautiful young woman in all of Michigan. But as we are finding out, our Bill here is of the sensitive nature. Certain things trigger him like the sight of blood or even the mere mention of the slaughter which brings the image of blood to his mind. Now he's experiencing stiffness. Cigar smoke set him off so he can't drive and he is the only teenager who has an automobile.

This time he fakes a faint, falls back onto the tall grasses growing along the side of the road. Gracie's natural nursing/rescue instincts throw her on his mouth with her plump red lips to administer mouth-to-mouth resuscitation hoping to revive her old friend.

Bill, who is more than conscious, plays along as Grace Q. works her rescue clinic over his trembling, bruised lips. In Bill's mind a rescue kiss is just as good as any kiss, but also in his mind is the fact that he has to expect a slap in the face if G.Q. suspects any amorous intentions.

Meanwhile, Gracie's lit cigar has fallen into a patch of dry, roadside grass. At first it's red glow begins a slow smolder but low moisture and atmospheric conditions around Lake Walloon these past few days soon create ideal conditions for a full-scale, dreaded, forest fire.

Inexperienced Grace, unaware of the dangers of smoking is not aware of the danger caused by discarded cigar butts which are still aglow. Instead she concentrates completely on her patient as the dry grasses around Bill's butt become ignited to match the heat being generated in his young loins.

Both CPR actors are completely unaware of the buildup of flames and smoke encircling Bill's teenaged derriere, but the nose knows. My schnozzola smelled the grass fire, and if left unchecked this fire could level the whole township.

Grasping a blanket from Bill's backseat I sprang off the Buick, threw the blanket over the fire, and pushed Bill (with Grace still attached) into the ditch. Totally surprised, Grace pulls her mouth off Bill's face to observe me stamping out flames.

By this time Kate jumps on me, rolls us up into the blanket and Kate says, "This is the moment pal. Let's make the most of it and the privacy this blanket has to offer us. I've always wanted to roll you into a blanket and make mad, passionate love."

I says, "Oh Kate, those flames were hot, but nothing can compare to the flame you have ignited in my heart! Don't stop, please don't stop. Yes to your strong embrace. Yes, to your cigar breath tongue. Yes to mumph..."

Kate protests, "Shut up you fool, and just love me."

While Kate had me all tangled in the blanket, Grace was still trying CPR on poor fainted Bill, who now had passed out for real after he'd seen hot flames engulf his butt.

Eventually we all came to realize that we had an evening of dance ahead of us in the Cushman House ballroom, and we continued down the roads to Petoskey with Kate behind the wheel of the Buick and me next to her with Grace in the back seat still trying to bring Bill around to consciousness.

Kate parked the Buick in front of McCarthy Barber Shop and band music filtered into the streets from the Cushman House.

"Sounds like my kinda music. Let's get inside and see how many rugs we can cut," Kate exclaims.

Bill loves dancing so at the perfect moment he wakes up so Grace can still take credit for saving him from fainting.

Hotel attendants took our cloaks, brushed us off nicely, and directed us to refreshments spread out on a long table inside the large ballroom.

After we sampled what the hotel had to offer in the way of miniature sandwiches (with the crust missing) and some kinda fruit punch, we commenced to get lost in the wild Chicago rhythms and big band sounds of the all-black ballroom orchestra.

Kate latched onto me like glue. She made the crowd aware that I was her man for the entire evening.

Lucky for me sister Marceline and I had previous formal dance training in Oak Park at the Unitarian Temple, the shoebox-shaped church that Frank Lloyd Write had designed. Our overly religious Father Doc was not keen on the idea of dancing, but for once in her life Mother Grace sided with us kids by allowing it.

G.Q. felt that since Bill finally got resuscitated due to her puffing action into his mouth, she felt obliged to dance with him in order to keep an eye on him. I tell ya, that Bill has now captivated the most beautiful girl in Michigan into watching his every move. How cool is that? It just turned out that way.

Up north here, the barn dance was popular amongst the farmers, but only upper class city folk enjoyed the ballroom variety. Sometimes Bill and I would wear our bib overalls, plaid shirts, and old shoes just to have fun barn dancing. Besides, some of those farm girls are mighty good looking and need good teen male companionship.

Nothing could quite compare to the way Bill worked his way into one whole evening of dances with beautiful Grace Quinlan. His fainting scam got him the best deal I have ever seen since it was only clinical sympathy lip work. It didn't seem to matter much to sly Bill for all he had to do to get a kiss or anything from the most beautiful girl in Michigan was to have a fainting spell.

Just suppose I fainted. Would Gracie give me a little mouth-to-mouth? I kinda doubt it, for Bill seems to have the corner on the market. No one would believe it if such a healthy specimen as I just up and had me a fainting spell.

Now, I wonder just how long this Bill fainting scam is going to work with her.

Since Kate and I had so much success smooching under that fire blanket, she now invites me to walk with a blanket into the woods off Pincherry Road where the Charles farm quietly lays. Someday I'll have to tell you how that is going. But somehow, that night that Bill fainted at the wheel has triggered more interesting patterns for smooching: Gracie Q. now waits for Bill Smith to have a fainting spell and Kate Smith now has a blanket fetish any time she's in an amorous mood. Strange, huh?

In my view, shy Bill has to begin consideration of Gracie when her clinical, sympathy urges begin to wear thin. Hopefully he will figure a well thought out scheme because when she goes amorous the very earth may just start to move and Bill, or whomever she sets her sights on, will be in for one magnificent surprise.

With that thought in mind it just triggered another title for a book: "When G.Q. Makes the Earth Move." That book might be lucky to get a PG rating, when she learns how to use all her newly bestowed gifts from Mother Nature.

Kate now, who has a little more experience mainly because she has had two or three years lead on Grace, can pretty well navigate through the surf of Lake Amorous. She sure is giving me a run for the money just to keep my eye off Grace's figure.

It certainly amazes me how a sleepy, innocently, peaceful, little hamlet such as Hortons Bay has now become a beehive of amorous activity all triggered by a few God given hormones, which seemingly blossomed overnight in one sweet, little, beautiful, young girl named Grace Quinlan. Having a street named in her honor is something which might well happen in Northern Michigan.

At the age of seventeen a young teen's fancy is generally preoccupied with other things... things other than the amorous variety; however, I must have got a good share of it out of my system 'cause Kate was just plain getting me and Mr. Johnson tired out. That fire-blanket evening will forever loom seriously within my memory, and I will think of it and marvel that so much excitement can be packed into one up-north evening.

The Cushman Hotel, Petoskey Michigan.

Chapter 12. An Amorous Wind Blows In

Michigan weather was always unpredictable. One day might start out sunny and mild, only to change and generate winds enough to knock down trees. I have seen horizontal rain up here in Emmet county.

Today started out as one of those days; sunny enough to start planning some outdoor work for Aunty Beth Dilworth, but right after breakfast high winds and rain canceled any projects out of doors.

Bill Smith and I had promised to split wood for Aunty's Kitchen, but our plans took a different twist this day.

"So, Wemedge, there go our plans for outdoor projects, right?" says Bill.

"Yup, for sure, Billy. Just look at the way that northern blow is bending those tall birches," I retort.

"We might be cutting up birches for Aunty's cook-stove. They can't handle being bent like this," remarks Bill.

"A young birch can take enormous bending I have noticed," I reply.

"Guess I was referring to older, more dried out, more bug-infested ones," Bill adds.

"For sure we'll be picking up a lot of dead branches from a variety of trees, William. Speaking of wood, William, how are things going for you with Grace Quinlan?"

"You know better than anyone, Wemedge. She pretty much just wants to play nurse-maid. I have yet to get to first base with her. I've run out of ideas for increased intimacy with her, Chum."

"Yeah, Pal, that can be a real drag, I know. I get that from the Bump girls too. My speculation is girls are too isolated up here. As locals, neither one ever gets a chance to relate with flirty women of the world," says I.

"What do you mean by that, my friend?"

"Well, have you noticed how they are always all business?" I speculate.

"Yeah, right," Bill agrees.

"Now this is just my observation, but maybe these girls up here in the boonies never learn the finer points of flirting. Know what I mean? Your expert city flirts never get up here to show these girls. Plus, they are very socially maladjusted due to all the hard work that is expected of them up here on these farms."

"Ya know, Wemedge, I think you are right. So what is your plan to remedy that?"

"Well, now I'm just goin' on my gut feeling here, but all these girls seem to be starved for affection...Wow look at that! A whole birch just fell over!"

"Yeah, right. How sad. I like birches. So how do you propose we approach these girls to get some affection?"

"Quite honestly I find it will come through... now get this, William 'cause it is genius... through rough housing."

"Huh?"

"Yeah, check it out. While we starts rasslin' with them or tickling them, we just start playing tag or chasing them around and eventually we both falls down and then... bingo... you plants one on her."

"Holy catfish! Do you think it will work?"

"I know it will work. It worked with Prudy," I says.

"Yikes! You think so?" exclaims Bill. "But Prudy is Indian. Does that make a difference?"

"Shouldn't. Now Prudy started it. Threw a biscuit at my nose pimple. It hurt so bad I had to tackle her and before ya' know it we were locked in connubial bliss."

"Well, I'll be darned! I never thought of that before. Doggone, Wemedge, I think you got something there," exclaims Bill.

"Now with your G.Q. here you might have to play her differently, since she could knock you into the next county, but I would start with a little teasing first. Like, when she brings out our breakfast, just yank on her apron strings so she gets the idea you wants to horse-play, okay?"

"Yeah, check."

"Now don't be surprised if she counters. If she counters with a trick of her own, just you be prepared, right?"

"Yeah... I see what you mean. It could escalate and might get out of hand."

"Right, Pal. You got to plan every possible move, like in chess."

"Geez... I see what you mean. So if I yanks on her apron strings she might come back with a spilled glass of water on my lap, right?"

"Right, Pal, but that might work if she tries to mop up your lap with a dishrag. By rubbing your lap, she's signaling that she is is okay with going into your privates."

"My, my, ain't you got all this worked out, Hemmie?" exclaims Bill in astonishment. "But, then what?"

"Then stop right there until another venue allows for more horseplay. Horseplay in a restaurant leaves one rather restricted, know what I mean?"

"Yeah. I get your drift. So maybe out in the woods? Or at a picnic?"

"Righto. You got it, otherwise horseplay in the wrong venue just won't have the proper effect. It could backfire if not done in a cute fashion. And you know G.Q. could open a big can of whoop ass on ya and you would lose out big time, Ralphy. But go ahead with the apron trick. That's good and if she keeps her retaliation cute also, then try something else at another time and place. By Jove, I think he's got it, Watson!"

"Yeah. I need this to get beyond our nursemaid relationship."

"Hey, get creative, Billy. Maybe next time she gives you CPR just grab her and plant a good one her. Would that work? One with some tongue?"

"Gosh, I bet it would, but what if she figures I've been faking the fainting spells and never does CPR again when I do a bona fide pass out?"

"You got something there, Pardner. But I like how you're beginning to think your way out of this."

"Thanks, Hemmie. Your horseplay theory is pure gold. It will work, but not fraught with its own hazards, right?"

"Yeah, but use your intuition. You gotta feel your way through this. You have to leave the impression that it is not intentionally mean-spirited, or nasty, okay. Gotta be playful if you get my drift. Test her reaction. That is critical. If she takes it the wrong way, you're done, Pal, with that gesture. Later then, try something else playful. That's the ticket. It has to always be construed as being playful, but I guarantee it will eventually lead to at least first base with the right jockey with a dry track. Maybe you could steal second."

"Oh that's rich, horseplay...jockey...dry track. Wemedge, you destroy me sometimes with your humor."

"Well, hey look, Pal, we have to keep our sense of humor or we're all done. Might as well cash it in if we take life too seriously, know what I mean?"

"Hemstein, I tell you what, you should write a book on the baseball of courtin'. It would be a smash hit, friend. A home run at the book-stand."

"Oh sure, I'll write lots of books, Pal. Being surrounded by women folk the way I am, I come by their various propensities quite naturally I'd say. I do know how they think. That's half the battle. So once you have that in your bullpen it is easy to pursue women and they don't even know they are putty in your hands."

"Right. Wish I were as confident about girls as you are, Wemedge. I'm too shy."

"William, you will get over it after you try my technique a few times. Soon as I can I will take out a patent on that move. But these are high class dames, ahem, I mean girls... from high class families. Bumps...Quinlans... all very established names in these parts. They are not to be confused with ordinary waitresses who run with a lower class clientele, you understand, Wilhelm?"

"Oh most definitely, most assuredly. Oh you bet, I understand fully."

"Now you take those waitresses in Braun's Beanery there in Petoskey, they need a more direct approach. They would need to be asked right up front, 'Hey, let's go out tonight girl!' See the difference there, Will? No beatin' around the bush with them. Our girls here are not waitresses. They want to be called cooks assistants. G.Q. and our Bump girls, these high class girls, want to be coy, kinda want a guy to sidle up to them. Gives them time to think about it and run some sample movies in their minds. Bill, these girls are like royalty, have to protect the family tree, you know... good breed stock, strong line of family traits, good family tree, you see? One might say they are like Thoroughbreds, beautiful race horses."

"Okay," exclaimed Bill. "Got it."

"Correct. Now would you go out and breed your fine race horse mare here with some old plug off the bone yard?" I demands.

"Neigh, neigh!" says Bill, doing his best horse sounds.

"Right, their offspring would never win the race and royalty now. Would they want to link up with commoners? A commoner would never make it to the throne and neither would their progeny... get it? That's the way these girls think, like royalty, Willy. We gotta understand how these high class fillies think. They are Thoroughbreds, Pal.

"Okay now listen, we have to bus our own plates back to the kitchen and we should volunteer to wash all the family dishes."

"Scrub the floors too Stein, right?"

"Right-o-mundo. Since this weather puts us inside we could at least do these small chores and Beth would be proud and so would G.Q. Get it?"

"Yeah, we have to 'earn our keep,' right, Stein?"

"Now you've got it, Willy Boy, and you'd get to loosen G.Q.'s apron strings too. Go ahead, Pal, try it if she's in a congenial mood."

"Hey! Watch that door to the kitchen. It swings both ways," I caution Bill too late.

"Oops, oh golly gee whiz, Grace! I am so sorry. Let me pick that up please. I got to earn my keep here."

"Gee thanks, Bill. You are a real gentleman. You just went in the 'out' door. Get it? Two swinging doors. But no problem," says Grace Quinlan.

"Say, you got egg down the front of you. Let me wipe it off," offers Bill.

"Sure go ahead this _was_ a clean apron. Gee thanks, Bill. You're so thoughtful. Keep wiping. There's some over here on this side too. You're doing an excellent job. Oops, missed a spot way over here, Bill. Oh, you are so gentle."

"Ahem, excuse me there, Bill, but we've got dishes to wash and floors to scrub. Bill, the girl's apron will be in shreds if you don't cut it out."

Immediately Grace chimes in. "Oh, I don't mind. Egg has got to come out right away or it sets into the fabric. He just went in the 'out' door. No foul. No fault. Thanks, Bill. Looks like you boys have an indoors kind of day. Can I take your order for lunch?"

"Heck yeah. I'll have one of Beth's famous Reubens, easy on the kraut," I states.

"I know we're at war with them...aren't we?" replies G.Q. in a flash. "Do you want one of our famous Reubens too, Bill?..Oh, Bill."

"Huh?" says a thoroughly stunned Bill (still thinking about the egg wiping routine). "Oh yeah. Of course. Bring it on. Easy on the kraut. We are at war with the Krauts."

"Okay, then. See you boys at lunch time," says G.Q.

"Hemstein...I did it! Do you realize? She allowed me to rub them. In fact told me to rub them. This is a major miracle. I got to second base, Pal. I scored a double!"

"Yeah. You sure did, buddy," I answer.

"And they are spectacular!" replies Bill.

"And?" says I.

"And...they most certainly are real, I tell you. Real as real can be!"

"So there you go, Pal. Didn't I tell you? Now do you take back what you said about her visit to Montgomery Wards for padding?" I demand.

"Oh heck yeah, Hemstein. This young filly must've grown up overnight."

"See, my friend. You had it in you all along to ply the trade. I would have to say though that you take a more accidental approach to the technique. It seems to open doors for you, my son."

"Oh, Hemstein! This is going to be one wonderful afternoon."

"Just call me Professor Hemstein, if you don't mind," I reminded rather arrogantly.

"I'm feeling a lot more confident around women now, but I know not all will react the way G.Q. did there, right?"

"Correct, lad. Stut was sympathetic to you from the start. She was in your corner all the way, even though you trashed her nice, clean, white apron. Some other kitchen help would've taken your stupid swinging door routine all the wrong way and maybe cleaned your clock with your own messy food tray," I explained like Charley Chaplin would.

"Yup. I think she likes my touch too. Anyway, it sure seemed that way."

"Willy, you had her purring in your arms. I've never had such a quick-learned student before. You amaze me. Hey, hand me those dish soap powders, will ya? We are gonna have fun today. Too bad the Bump sisters are up in Minnesota; then I would be bustin' my buttons. Hope they gets back to Hortons Bay real soon," I mutter. "Bill, I'll wash so's you don't damage those tender hands of yours. Maybe you'd like to kiss 'em, 'eh? Never wash them for a while, okay?"

Well those Michigan winds blew in some good fortune for us, me and my pal Bill Smith, that is. Doing all her indoor chores established Bill and me as some real handy gents to have around Aunty Beth Dilworth's Pinehurst B&B.

Chapter 13. Gracie's Coming of Age Party

When weather permitted, we cleared the grounds of fallen tree limbs and got ourselves invited to Grace Quinlan's sixteenth birthday party to be held in the fancy garden of the Quinlan home in Petoskey. We both considered that invite to be one heck of an honor since Quinlans are very high society and Bill and I are such a grubby pair of well read woodsy rough necks.

One of our servants had nicely hung my suit in a paper liner filled with mothballs. It fit me like a monkey suit and smelled to high heaven, but heck, I figure after an afternoon in the Michigan breeze, this suit was gonna wow the pants off everyone. Boys would be jealous and all the cute girls will want to hang on each arm of this imported woolen wonder.

Mother had always seen to it that all her children's clothing was nothing but the best. Mine, in this case, was a Brooks Brothers, just about the best there is. It was bought and tailored to fit down on LaSalle Street in Chicago.

My Charles Atlas work outs helped me to really fill out that well tailored suit, thus giving me a strong, manly appearance. Girls love that.

Now Bill's dad was a wealthy college professor and he also saw to it that both Kate and Bill wore only the finest, so as those two arrived in Bill's new Buick, the three of us looked ready for a fashion shoot for G.Q. (Gentlemen's Quarterly).

"Hey, you two. Don't you both look ready to steal the show tonight? I'll just hop in the back seat here. Evening, Miss Kate. You look ravishing, as usual."

"Evenin', Master Hemingway, as do you. Nice suit. What's the gift?"

"Oh, this old thing. Got Gracie some perfume. Imported from Paris, France. From the shape of it, I would say your gift is a new tennis racquet."

"Correct-o-mundo," replies Kate.

"Hey, Wemedge, guess my gift," says Bill.

"Well guessing from the shape...it must be the longest cigar in the world?"

"Nope. Wrong you silly. It's a riding crop. She rides horses you know," says Bill.

"Oh how nice," says Kate. "I think Grace will be pleased. Look, Aunty Charles got her a tin of homemade cookies and a book, *Little Women*. Jim Dilworth forged some spurs and Aunty Beth made her an apple pie and some new aprons," continued Kate. "Oh, and Vollie Fox got her a new fishing reel."

"Gosh kids, we have a Buick full of fancy presents. Young Miss Quinlan will be very pleased," I adds. "And Kate, that pink dress looks very becoming on you. Matches your jet black hair and green eyes."

"Oh this old thing. Dad got me this from a shop in Saint Louis. Thanks for the compliment. I owe you a kiss," counters Kate.

"Can't wait. Say Bill, your Buick sounds like it will make it up the big sand hill on Resort Pike Road."

"Oh yeah. You might have to push, but with the rain we had the sand-hill should be moist enough for good traction. Should I take Eppler maybe?"

"Naw, keep goin'. You're making good time. Ouch! Say, watch those chuck holes. Pal, think I just lost a filling," I remarks.

Kate remarked, "Do you think in our lifetime roads will ever improve up north?"

"Naw. Maybe your grand-kids will have them, but Resort Pike just needs Sandhill removed somehow. Even with a horse and carriage one has to get out to lighten the load in order to crest the top of the rise."

"So maybe you all should hop out until I take a running start at it," says Will.

"Yeah. Good idea, Will," says Kate. "I would hate to get stuck with our good clothes on."

Well, Kate was right. While she and I were locked in fond embrace, brother Bill raced up Sandhill and motioned for us to hop back into the Buick.

"Mmmm, Kate, that was one sweet kiss."

"I just couldn't help myself, Ernest. You look so darn handsome in your suit."

"You sure it's the suit?" I query.

"Well...maybe it's what I feel under the suit," says Kate expanding the idea.

"Making reference to my manly form that is thanks to Charles Atlas, world's most perfectly proportioned man," says I.

"Hey, you two muscle magnets, climb up this blasted hill so we can get to G.Q.'s party. I need some kissing, too," Bill pleads.

"Do you think Grace will let him kiss her?" I ask.

"Well, if she doesn't, she has a whip to use on him. Girls have a rough time getting amorous with the shy guys."

"Yeah, I know. I'm one of those too."

"You most certainly are NOT, Mr. Hemingway!"

"Do you remember our first kiss, Kate?"

"Of course, silly. It was under the apple tree."

"No wrong! It was on the lips."

"Oh, that does it. Last one up the hill is a rotten egg," challenges Kate.

"You're on, your Kate-ness!"

"I won. You're the rotten egg, Wemedge."

"Hey, no fair, I got sand in my shoes. Will you look at that beautiful bay!"

"Yeah, Bill. Can we have a minute to catch our breath?" Kate grabs my arm and we both stare at beautiful Little Traverse Bay below us. We then embrace for a long, extended kiss.

"Hey, now that's it! You two love birds will have to elope tonight. I'll drive you to a good Catholic priest in Petoskey," threatens Bill.

"Okay, okay. You're sure a buzz-kill mentioning marriage. Let me help you in, Kate. There...all in. On Jeeves. On to beautiful Petoskey; on to greener pastures; on to the beautiful lips of Miss Grace Quinlan!" I declare dramatically.

"That ain't all that's beautiful," retorts Bill.

"Will you two boys behave?" shouts Kate.

"Just getting our boy primed here," I states.

Well it was all downhill from there. The crowd was beginning to gather at Quinlans'. Mr. Quinlan had a whole pig roasting on a rotisserie, which was being turned by their hired chef from the Bay View Inn. Another chef from the Perry Hotel was roasting prime rib on a bed of coals. Dozens of dishes filled with delicious vegetables, baked beans, cornbread, biscuits, gravies, and fresh fruits filled two long tables. Mrs. Quinlan was decked out in a sequined dress, greeting all the arrivals. And after Bill parked the Buick we three took the board walk out to the backyard where a string quartet from the symphony was playing background music, making the perfect venue for almost anything romantic to happen. It was the picture perfect summer evening and true to fashion, Petoskey's atmosphere was headed for a dramatic, twilight, outdoor patio birthday party. Piled-high thermal clouds were catching the colors of a setting sun, making the perfect background for Gracie to enter accompanied by her father (Village Planner, Financier, and Livestock Rancher). We gave a standing ovation to which she graciously curtsied and proceeded to greet each of us with hand shakes and more curtsies. Her floor-length dress was cheery, robin egg blue, terraced with horizontal layers of white imported lace, which accented her more than ample bodice.

Bill's eyes were riveted on Grace and totally bedazzled by her stupefying beauty.

I says, "Now, William, don't get cold feet now. Go up to her and plant a kiss on her."

Bill stutters," Duh...duh..do ya think it's appropriate?"

Kate states, "Duh. Yes, of course. Don't get shy now."

"It feels like we could be engaged."

Kate responds, "Don't be silly. It's just a birthday party... a very rich party, but only a party. Now go give her a birthday kiss."

Well Bill got his courage up and slowly shuffled up to Grace, handed her his gift, but stopped and motioned for her to unwrap his gift.

Grace balked and stated, "But we do that, Bill, after I cut the cake."

Bill just shook his head. "N-n-n-no! Open it now. G-G-G-Grace. Please?"

"Okay, but it's...it's...it's...oh, Bill. It's perfect! You shouldn't have! Thank you!" With that outburst of thanks, Grace threw her arms around Bill's neck and gave him a long, passionate kiss. Then with her new jewel-encrusted riding crop, Grace proceeded to whip Bill's buttocks which triggered another passionate five minute kiss.

Well, Grace's mother finally had to pry the two apart and remind her that she had more guests to greet and a whole evening of festivities to attend to.

Spontaneously, all the guests gave a standing ovation, thunderously applauding her spur of the moment riding crop kiss.

Cameras caught that gesture and that most amorous clinch, which to me had to be one of the perfect moments of the summer and of my young teenage years. No doubt about it, the shy guy had seized the moment to plant one on his girl, thus giving her the best birthday Grace Quinlan ever had.

We will have forgot the food, forgot the drinks, forgot the atmosphere, the music, the soft summer breeze off the bay, but etched in our minds forever will be that lusty riding-crop first kiss of Bill Smith and Grace Quinlan.

Years after that perfect kiss, I still try to demystify the whole event and yet all I come up with is some very primal energies of universal significance which were released by my two young, love-starved friends who were way ahead of their Victorian time of life. What remains a mystery is how many couples went home that night and actually tried to recapture that same scene. Harness shops in Petoskey could not keep enough riding crops in stock thereafter, and sales are still brisk to this day as horse populations dwindle; so my guess is Bill and Grace started a whole new amorous movement, by just horsing around. I gave my courtship student Bill an "A" that night and he has been receiving high marks from Grace Quinlan.

Well, this marks a milestone for me, for I know this remarkable summer will more than likely be my last up in Michigan; therefore this acute urgency to make the most of every fun filled moment. What will come to pass will be monumental in the annals of my young life.

It appears to be some kind of chemical, socio-scientific change a youngster undergoes up in Michigan, and it seems to intensify the more one stays up here, and once you realize this you may never return, this whole process intensifies beyond the threshold of human understanding, and it makes the story telling so dad gum believable.

When we know our time together is fast coming to a close, we loosen our guard, we drop certain barriers, and we let go of social blockages that impede the flow of joy and bliss.

Girlfriends learning of a troop's impending ship out will often hurry up and marry their serviceman. Often girls will sacrifice their virginity to a serviceman about to be shipped to the front in harm's way. They will do it for Old Glory. This is what we are fighting for and the enemy can't have it.

It's 1917 and during times of war the people left behind will often do strange things. Things they would never do in peace time. With the U.S. entry into W.W.1 all of us had an uncertain future. I believe that fact played heavily into the unconscious of all party goers that evening all over America. We watched train loads of young Petoskey boys ship out to uncertain death.

Grace Quinlan now has a steady beau. He is none other than my Pal Bill Smith. They have a most unorthodox romance going. As we all know, Bill will faint. Without any warning and for no apparent reason he will just pass out and require mouth to mouth resuscitation. Well Grace is right on spot giving him what he needs to recover; however, now that she has learned that Bill is one heck of a good kisser she is no longer seeing her CPR as a clinical maneuver, but rather a necessary preliminary to an amour-ace recovery. Bill never knows when a fainting spell is about to occur, but if Grace is present he will never have to worry about coming back to waking consciousness, for he's always in his best girl's arms. Kind of a unique situation in which to find himself, I must say, one that he dare not abuse by faking a spell, for the riding crop could be applied to Bill.

Lovers need a lot in common so fainting is just one of many things they both can share. My guess is the birthday party helped cement their relationship and provided the perfect platform in which to launch the ideal rite of passage for my two best friends.

Grace's 16th party will be talked about and discussed by Petoskey townsfolk for many days to come. Also, by her unique reaction to Bill's gift she announces to the whole community her choice in beaus.

Whether Bill planned it that way or not, his good fortune could not have been better, for the result was made in Heaven. Grace is going to bring Bill out of his shyness and Bill can read to her while they tend to Aunty Charles' apple orchard. It's a perfect match.

Chapter 14. Getting Ready for Summer

Hemingway's Windemere Cabin on Walloon Lake

Aunty Beth Dilworth has seen how well Bill and I work together as a team and has contracted us to do repairs in and around her B&B in exchange for bunking above her carriage house anytime I want.

Hortons Bay has become my home away from home as I expand the horizons of my young teenaged life. As a young adult to be able to lead my own life and learn from my own initiative is beginning to feel real good.

Presently the war in Europe hangs heavily over our country, and we feel it up in the boonies of Northern Michigan, where just the other day in Petoskey we said goodbye to dozens of young men who boarded a troop train headed for boot camp.

Many patriotic, under aged boys eager to defend our country find themselves lying about their age. There is nothing more exciting than a good war, but when untrained youngsters jump into the fray, I begin to worry about the wisdom of this decision. In my estimation that's testing one's guardian angel to the limit, and it isn't something one rushes into unless one is suicidal like some of these lads appear to be. But my future feels like a body of work that needs a serious force behind it. Uncharted waters are what is facing me, but my self-confidence is unyielding, like Columbus or Lief Erickson, who bravely set out into dark oceans of the unknown.

Still haunting me are guilt feelings that remain from not leading my classmates off to fight the ungodly horde of Huns in Europe, but I must remain true to my calling "the pen is mightier than the sword."

For years my personal slogan has been "afraid of nothing" so by choosing to stay stateside it appears that I am yellow and chicken livered having gone back on my word. In fact any able bodied, young man staying home is suspect of being un-American, or worse yet, a Kraut sympathizer, or a sissy, or even being mentally ill, or retarded.

Community pressure to give full support to the war effort is immense now, and I feel I may weaken in my personal resolve to focus on journalism. Only time will tell; therefore, I feel I must begin to anticipate an adventure filled experience in Kansas City and think of the positive aspects of the move there, such as Aunt Arabella's fabulous meals. That woman is a veritable wizard in the kitchen. As a reporter for the K.C. Star I will learn valuable experience which will only lead to bigger and better achievements. Plus, the whole country knows the Star to be an outstanding newspaper. My tenure at the Star will open doors anywhere I want to go if I move out of Kansas.

Now, I want this last summer up in Michigan to be the best summer ever. I want to take my mind off the war, my nemesis Mother Grace, and my worry about Pops. I want good times with my friends, and I want to catch a lot of fish.

Aunty Beth Dilworth's B&B was up and running, ready for the influx of summer guests. My Pal Bill Smith and I had the grounds cleared, flower beds were blooming, her wood box was filled, and plenty of logs split, enough to last her a month or so.

"Hey Bill, do you feel up to rowing over to Windemere to help me open up the Hemingway cabin?"

"Sure enough, Wemedge. Looks like perfect weather today... clear blue skies, warm sunshine, and just a slight breeze out of Lake Michigan."

"We might get there just in time to bag us some crows," says I.

"Say, what do you have against crows?"

"Oh, nothing...and everything!" I blurt. "Billy, crows seem to delight in following me around all day. Their nasty caw cawing scares the wild game and puts the fish on edge, but mainly they wake me up way too early when I wants to sleep in every morning. Pops hates them too. Pops delights in my morning crow casualty report."

"No kiddin.' You know the crow is symbolic throughout literature," offers Bill.

"Oh, sure. Who can forget Edgar Allen Poe's *Raven*, huh?" I adds. "Spooky bird."

"The painter Vincent Van Gogh's last landscape, before he killed himself, had a sky full of crows. Harbingers of death. What was the name of that painting? *Corn fields... something.*"

"Yeah, Bill, I think that was it. Hey, here's the rowboat, and oars should be hiding in these bushes. Yup, here they are. Get in, Pal, and I'll shove off. No sense getting your nice shoes wet."

"Cast off, Captain Courageous, sir!" Bill says.

"Yeah, that sure was a good story."

"Yup, the best."

"Hey, did you know I had an uncle who was a ship captain?"

"No kiddin'?" Bill responds.

"Yup, he sailed around the whole Atlantic and Pacific."

"Around the cape?"

"Yup, quite an adventurer he was."

"Wemedge, you have some colorful family, I must say."

"Yup, Civil War hero Grand dad, Uncle Willoughby the missionary in China. Hey! Look at those fish jump, Bill. That one tried to jump into the boat with us."

"He sure did," notes Bill.

"Boy, I can't wait to start catching a bunch of those beauties," I exclaim. "Oh and a Dad who is a famous doctor."

"And an operatic star for a Mother," recalls Bill.

"Oh, yeah...her," I mumble.

"Gosh, Wemedge, did you have another spat with Mother Grace?"

"What a buzz-kill you are today. Yeah Bill, and it's too vile to discuss now, when we're trying our best to have fun," I counter.

"Okay, okay, consider her dropped from discussion. What were we talking about?"

"Oh, I don't know. What do you want to talk about Bill?" says I, trying desperately to change the subject. "Care to share how you came across that nice Buick which you have in your possession?"

"Heck, yeah. That was a guilt payment from the professor, aka, the Nutty Professor," replies Bill.

"Do tell," I demand.

"Yeah. Guess the old boy was feeling guilty about dumping us kids onto Aunty and Uncle Charles every summer, I guess. So one day last month he and an associate rolled up with this nice horseless carriage. They stayed over night and visited, then drove off with his friends' Packard. Guess he was on some research grant. Don't really know what project he was working on but he made it sound very high and mighty. You know how lofty and out of touch he can be. P...H...D...you get my drift?"

"Oh, right, Piled Higher and Deeper. Got it. But he left you a nice vehicle all the same, William," I reassured.

"Indeed, that he did, but I wish he'd spent some time with me, and Kate, and Y.K. He treats us like we're a part of some laboratory experiment," complained Bill.

"Hey, I hear that, Pal. Some parents don't even try to relate to us like persons. They treat us like we are their personal possessions or something. Kids belong to the parents like sheep or cattle. Sometimes I feel like one of her servants."

"Are we back to Mother Grace again?"

"Oh sorry, I tried to avoid that topic, didn't I?" I reply sheepishly.

"I see your cabin, Wemedge. It's still in one piece," Bill shouts.

"Do you see a sandy spot to beach this scow?" says I.

"Yup, to your right a little, Wemedge. Lot of sand here. Looks like that three-day blow washed up a load of fresh beach sand. Lucky you."

"Actually the shore does have a nice place to swim; no steep drop-off. Kinda think that's why this spot was chosen in the first place, Bill. But if it were across the bay I wouldn't have to row every time I wanted to head for Hortons Bay," says I.

"Oh, well. Look how the rowing has built up your biceps, you brute."

"Yeah look at these cannons, 'eh? Although Charles Atlas also had a lot to do with these guns. Your sister Kate sure likes the way they fill out a suit."

"Poor Kate. She sure is stuck on you. I'm afraid she's hopeless."

"Yeah, poor girl, but she must know I belong to the world," I replies.

"I kinda think she is learning that. Slowly, but surely."

"Stop calling me Shirley, will ya? Okay we're here, Bill. Hang on while I give 'er a few stiff oars to beach her. Now hang on while I pull this tub up onto the beach; don't want your nice Thom McCanns to get wet. Okay Bill, I'll hold the bow steady while you jump onto dry land. There, that wasn't so bad." After getting ashore I adds, "By Jove! My man, Friday, I think we are not alone on this island."

"Yeah, but sir, it's actually Monday."

"Oh shut up, Friday!" I says. "That'll be your new name."

"But Who is on second," says Bill.

"Oh don't start with me, Pal. So William, seriously, should we get the cabin opened up...or shall we catch some of those flying fish that tried to swamp our dingy?"

"Such a tough decision, Wemedge. Need you ask? Those fish are powerful... hungry, so let's feed them but with a little extra iron in their diet."

"Yup... I get your drift, and it won't take me but a minute to find my fishin' tackle and then dig us some worms. Can you dig it, William?"

"Indeed I can dig it. Got a shovel?"

"Indeed, Watson. All that rain brought all the worms to the surface so we won't have to dig too deeply. Just got to find the key to the tool shed. There, we're in. Here's a bait bucket, shovel, rods, krill. Oh yeah, we the big fishermen."

"Yeah... we the big fishermen!"

Well, it didn't take long to fill a can with crawlers, grab rods, tackle box, and head back out into Lake Walloon for some outstanding pan fishin'.

Since few cabins had been built and most summer residents had not as yet returned, the lake was teaming with all sorts of fish. Bill and I were feeling nibbles as soon as we cast into the sparkling blue waters.

It was not long before we had a stringer full of perch, bluegill, and sunfish... enough for a full-belly feast.

"Hey, Wemedge, let's stop now. We have enough for our supper."

"Hang on, Bill. I know there has to be a lunker around here with all this feed he's getting, and I bet he's a big-en."

"Okay, but I got to pee...bad."

"Well, stand up in the stern and let fly. The fish might like it."

"B-but w-what if someone sees?"

"Aw... who cares. Fishermen do it all the time," says I.

Well Bill did his job off stern and I felt like a child the night before Christmas. My belief that Santa was gonna deliver the goods kept me sending bait out into Lake Walloon, hoping a big one would strike. Eventually the thought struck me... *if you want to catch the big one, send him big bait, and he will strike!*

"Hey Bill, sorry to make you wait like this but...this fishin' trip goes beyond food on the table. I know there has got to be a big one. The signs are so great that we just can't row back right now without giving it everything we can."

"Yeah... I kinda know that."

"Bill, you can help a lot by chopping up one of those pan fish. I think this lunker is gonna strike on something more tempting than mere crawlers. His lusty gut is waiting for a big mouthful. And if he's sitting on the bottom snoozing I'm gonna set me bobber up another twenty feet, attach a heavier split shot and drop half a tasty, bloody perch right on his big nose."

"Okay Wemedge, here's your new bait."

"All right, Mr. Lunker, here comes your Thanksgiving feast! I'm gonna bet he's over by these reeds...hidin' in all these reeds...just takin' a snooze among all these reeds...hey...I feel a bite."

"Set the hook, Wemedge!"

"Oh... baby! He took it! He was there! Hook, line, and sinker. This guy is full of fight. There he goes. He's runnin' with it."

"Give him line... let him run, Wemedge. Don't let him shake it out."

"He's gonna surface. Look at that, will ya Bill! This is exciting. Did you see him leap? He's a fighter. He's a big-en. Look at that splash. Now he wants to dive. Oh... he's desperate, but he can't shake the hook."

"He's got to be getting tired."

"Do ya think? Nothing doing. He's comin' up again. He's gonna surface. Get a good look at 'em, Bill."

"It's a bass, Wemedge, and a monster."

"He's plunging again. Got to get him away from any snags. Bill, row out into open water. Hurry... before he finds a log to wrap around! Yeah... that's it. Think he's gettin' tired. Grab that landing net, Willy. This big bass is reeling in. Just hope this line doesn't snap under all the strain."

"You hope that old pole doesn't snap."

"Come to Papa...come to Papa...that's it, Mr. Big...just a little bit more...just hold on...just a little bit more." Grunt, grunt. "Okay, Bill. There he is! Get that net under him... quick! You got him. Pull it up... hurry."

"There...there he is, Wemedge. Look at him flop. Still got plenty of fight left."

"Keep the net over him, Bill. He wants to jump out of the boat. Look at him, will ya! Look at the size of this one! That is a trophy, large-mouth bass, Billy Boy."

"Indeed. He's led a long and healthy life with the best of food, but he could not resist that filet of perch when it hit him on the nose."

"Yeah, and after it reached his gullet, he discovered it contained too much iron."

"Ha, ha, ha... right. Poor fella must've had an iron deficiency. Ha, haaa. You should have this bass mounted, Wemedge."

"Of course. I plan on it. Mount him right on my frying pan, with egg wash and corn meal in butter. M-m-m can taste him now. So Bill, aren't you glad we pursued this grand fellow?"

"Indeed, fair Nim Rod. You showed me proud."

"Shall we see if there are any more down in this honey hole?"

"Why not. There's probably one with a larger mouth to coin a new phrase."

"Correct, I get it...small, large...and now larger mouth bass. Oh Bill, you slay me."

Well Bill and I caught three more lunker bass in that hole, mainly because we hid the barb of the hook deeply into the chopped bait allowing it slide along the bottom without getting snagged on weeds. Attaching heavier sinkers, dropped the bait, passed the small pan fish and right under the noses of a school of grand daddy large mouth bass, who were greedy and not used to having door step delivery service directly into their private domain.

It was supper time when we readied the cabin for habitation, and by then we were readied for a healthy meal of fresh, fried fish. We built a fire in the fireplace and fried fish in a fry pan while heating the living room at the same time.

We had already removed the cover of the chimney. One year we failed to remove the cover of the chimney, and back draft smoked us out for a few hours. The cover keeps squirrels out because they can really mess up a cabin if allowed to run free all winter.

"Wemedge, I'm glad we decided to go fishing first."

"Yeah, me too. Man, there is nothin' like a nice mess of fresh fish for supper, and that can of apricots made a perfect dessert. Do you think we'll be able to locate that honey hole again?"

"Yup, I painted an 'X' on the side of the boat," quipped Bill.

"Hey now. That's my joke. You stole my joke. That's alright, I'm too stuffed to argue, Pal. Hey what did you think of that bass?"

"Tasty, my man. Delectable, actually, without the fishy taste. It was simply bass-o-rific, indeed."

"Yeah, it's the cornmeal crust. Luckily we still had a few things to cook with stashed in the cabin pantry."

"So Bill...don't mind me stretchin' out here in front of the fireplace. My bib-overalls got to be opened up a bit. Ahh."

"Never in all my days have I seen a guy so desirous of dining on fish."

"Got to correct you on that, Pal...it's fresh fish. Ain't nuthin' tastier than a fried, fresh caught, pan fish. But that there bass was sent from God. Some dandy treat, huh William? Well you know a fresh trout will turn blue when hits the hot bacon fat."

"M-m-m indeed, my outdoorsy friend. I like an occasional dipping of the fish line, but let's face it, Wemedge, you have got to be addicted to fishing."

"Bill, fishin' to me is a form of the Holy Eucharist. Landing that big large mouth bass today was my personal redemption from my Heavenly Father. He was making a statement to me. Some people think that God only resides in church, but not this kid. He has revealed Himself to me through the beauty of nature."

"My guess is God will follow you to K.C. and bless your writing too, right?"

"Yup... if it is to be. He will no doubt bless all my writing ventures. Wish He would give my poems a little more push, but I continue to hone my skills. Poetry is my first love... you know that?"

"Yeah, you have Longfellow-ed us with untold hours of recitation to the point of auditory fatigue, my friend... no offense."

"Sorry, but I get carried away so. Words have such power. You know that. I'm so fascinated with author word combinations and that Longfellow is best, in my opinion."

"This being our last summer together, do you think we'll go our separate ways?"

"Letter writing will help keep us together."

"Y.K. wants to rent a place in Chicago."

"Well, there ya go. You and Kate can share with Y.K. Cozy set up."

"But...it'll be lonesome there... big city full of strangers and all."

"Look Bill, you're a good writer too. Bet you could find work in advertising like Y.K."

"Yeah, I suppose...but..."

"But what, Pal? Out with it. Billy, what you got stuck in your craw?"

"Ah, ah, uh, well, uh, I'm gonna miss you. That's what I'm trying to say, damn it! Have you got any booze in the cabin?"

"Geez us Bill. Pops would never allow it."

"Promise you'll write me?"

"Oh, hell yeah, Pal. Look are you gonna get all sentimental on me now?"

"Just never mind, okay?"

"Never mind what? Come on Bill, out with it."

"Oh, what the hell, Wemedge. Look, I am afraid I may never see you again if you run off to Kansas. And you'll meet some woman who'll sweep you off your big feet and you'll forget all about the good times we've had and I'll never hear from you again, and...damn it!"

"There, there, now William. It's okay to feel that way. I feel that way too. Like I don't ever want this summer to end. Also...I'm afraid to grow up. That scares the hell out of me...growing up! I kinda never want to grow up. Scares the livin' hell out of me."

"Promise you will write?"

"Yes, I promise. You know that...you know that."

With his head buried in his hands, Bill began to sob, then snort, then shudder all over.

My big hand patted his shoulder, "Look, Billy, you and I will have a terrific summer and we'll meet up in Chicago when I'm in town. You and Kate will move in with Y.K. and Toodles, that new girlfriend of his, and Y.K will find you jobs in advertising which you are good at, and we can party just like at Grace Quinlan's birthday. It will be grand, Pal. Just you see."

"Y-y-yeah...I guess. Just you remember to write, you hear?"

"Promise. Grace Quinlan will write to you too, won't she?"

"Yeah...I suppose."

"And you got your nice Buick."

"Yeah."

"And you and Kate can drive to the beaches and go shopping in The Loop."

"Yeah...I guess."

"And there's all those museums and aquariums and art galleries..."

"Yeah...okay."

"And there's vendors in Lincoln Park where you and Kate can get two big Chicago dogs for a dime...and there is Wrigley Field...and the Cubs will be contenders this year with Zimmer being healed up an' feeling healthy again. Heck Bill, you've got a bright future ahead of you."

"Yeah...I guess so."

"You know I'm right, William. So let me make us a pot of tea. I'll pump some water and put the kettle in the fireplace to get hot. What we need is a nice big pot of some tasty Charlie Grey."

"I think that's Dorian Grey...or maybe Earl Grey? Oh, I don't know."

"Found it. Mother had it stashed way back in the pantry. Good thing I primed our pump. Now to hang this kettle over the fire. Stretch out on some soft pillows there, Bill. Relax. Make yourself at home. That pot will be boiling in no time. Feelin' better already, aren't ya, Willy?"

"Ah, you were right, Wemedge. I just was getting overly sentimental and I got lost in the malaise. Charlie Grey used to pitch for the White Sox, remember? Dorian Grey is some character from a novel."

"Right, Bill. Kinda homo... kinda?"

"I guess. Is that tea ready?"

"Not yet, but she's gettin' there. So Bill, you know you can talk to me about anything, right?"

"Right..."

"So what's Grace Quinlan really like?"

"Huh? Oh... well... she's just peachy."

"Just peachy? What's that mean?"

"Hey you got a Gramaphone. Let's crank it up and listen to records, Wemedge."

"Okay. How 'bout *Buffalo Gals*?"

'Buffalo Gals won't ya' come out tonight, come out tonight, come out tonight.'

"Keep crankin.' She's slowin' down."

"*'Oh... Buffalo Gals won't ya come out tonight a-a-and dance to the light of the moon.'*"

"Hey the kettle's boiling. Let's have a nice cup of Earl May," says I.

"Earl Grey. Earl May used to pitch for the Saint Louis Cardinals," exclaimed Bill.

"Oh yeah. He liked to throw the spitter."

"Put so much spit on the ball Tuggy Tank had to wring it out of his catchers mitt," I says.

"May oh right. He's bounced around the league a lot," says Bill.

"Bill, there is sugar for our tea. Made from Michigan sugar beets. Grown in the thumb area. You know. Around Bad Ax."

"They should call it Bad Ass from Bad Ax."

Says I, "Yeah right. That would sell just swell."

"This tea really hits the spot," announced Bill.

"Did you hit the spot?"

"Huh? What do you mean?"

"You know. With Grace... Gracie Quinlan?"

"Naw. Gee whiz. She's a nice girl. We'd have to be married first," exclaimed Bill.

"But, ya, but, I thought she wanted you at her birthday party. I mean with the riding whip and all?" I muttered.

"Naw... one would think that, but naw. Nothin' like that. She's a heck of a kisser. One heck of a kisser, but time just was not right. Rest of her is spectacular, but lucky the husband on her honeymoon. Say, this tea is delightfully brisk."

"Bill... got to hand it to ya. You really surprise me sometimes. Yup, you are full of surprises. Never thought you'd get to first base with that girl. I figure it must've been the riding whip."

"Yup, that riding crop triggered something in her, or maybe she likes public displays," states Bill.

"That could be it, you know? I bet that's it. I bet there's a part of her that just gets off in public. Oh well, now we know she's got a wild side to her, but it has to be with others watching. Hm... mighty strange."

"Never would have guessed it from her."

"More tea, Bill?"

"Please. Thanks...ahh, still hot. You know, my sister is totally enamored by you. Kate is under your spell. You are all she talks about. She worships you. "

"I know. Kinda hard to take, too."

"Huh? Why would that be a problem? Please tell me," queried Bill. "How would that be hard to take?"

"It just is. She's too easy. She throws herself at me. I guess, I guess a guy wants some mystery, some coyness, some playing hard to get. You know the quarry, the prey, the pursuit?"

"Sort of like hunting? You need the thrill of the chase. Like that?"

"Something like that. Don't get me wrong now, Kate is cute as a bug and smart and a terrific dancer, and just what every guy would ever want, but I need to do the pursuit. I need to initiate the action, the chase."

"I get it. And it's during the buck's season when he is enjoying his rut. He impregnates his does."

"Correct. I think you're almost there."

"And, and after he impregnates his harem, his masculinity is at its peak. He has fought other, lesser males, and bang! Down he goes and we eat his flesh, which is filled with all this maleness. I got it."

"Bingo, Billy, you've got it."

"So that's why people go so darn nuts at Bull fights. Same token. And even run with the bulls."

"Right. To get at that masculine energy, which comes from the pursuit, the subduing, the conquering. Gets the juices flowing. Indians eat the buck's heart for the same feeling of virility, together with the macho image of being big provider for the tribe, then the squaw softens the hide with her teeth, and proudly fashions it into clothes for her man, shoes for his feet, and straps for his leggings."

"Hey, Wemedge, you've got this tribal thing figured out."

"Yup. Wouldn't mind becoming part of the tribe."

"Hey, you could. There's Prudence. She's like the tribal princess and her Father kinda likes you."

"Yeah, I know, but it's too late."

"Why?"

"Their culture is no more. Shot! Capput! Thanks to demon rum."

"Okay, and not to mention the loss of their hunting grounds and decimation... slaughter of the whole native nations and their customs."

"And their buffalo and their fishing streams."

"Huh, how did white man destroy their streams?"

"Logging, silly. Floating all those big logs downstream to the saw mills."

"Oh, I see... logs came by and ripped up the spawning beds. Got it."

"More, tea?"

"Surely, please."

"Don't call me Shirley. I take your scalp."

"No, you don't. You'll have to wrestle me for it."

So, Bill and I did a friendly wrestle in front of the cabin fireplace. Being much stronger than he, I quickly subdued him, but after that, I let him pin me just for the heck of it. Pals often engage in a foolhardy tussle, sometimes to blow off steam. Not to be mean, nor to be injurious.

Even though I am the dominant male, Bill is happy to play a supportive role.

Whenever a group of young, teen boys get together, there will always be one who challenges the others, for the role of leader. It's a tribal... wolf pack kinda, alpha male ritual kind of thing, and today was no exception. I was also thinking how Bill needed to feel included as a vital part of my inner circle of friends. Bill is happy with his supportive role, because he knows I need his input in order to cover my back. He is happy allowing me to lead in our young adventures.

All my young pals who went off to war sensed this leadership quality of mine and they would have fought bravely as a unit... a well functioning team, all trusting my leadership skills. That is what made their departure seem so damn tragic to me. I couldn't go along and lead them. Eventually... somehow, I will get over to that theater of war, and I will do my part to defeat those dastardly forces of evil. That evil Kaiser has got to be stopped and I am going to stop him.

"Gosh, Bill, I'm kinda glad we've had this time together. Do you think you want to give me a hand opening up this cabin for the summer?"

"Sure, Wemedge... just you show me what needs to be done."

So you see? There are leaders and there are followers. Bill is happy being a follower. He would walk over hot coals if he could follow me. He knows I won't let him down. He trusts me and he trusts my ability to make wise choices.

As we examine our own relationships, I have become exceedingly aware of the group dynamics and I have begun to admire certain personalities in this little hamlet up north. From my observation, the region requires a lot of masculine energy.

Humans hard at work have succeeded in carrying out this town and making it hospitable. Tremendous amounts of physical labor cleared the land, laid the railroad, built the roads, bridges, harbors, airfields, and water sewer systems, built the homes, farms, factories, shops and stores. All of these activities are very masculine in nature and anyone engaged in leadership up here gets my admiration for getting the job done.

For some reason, women are attracted to men engaged in exhibiting this masculine energy.

Study of these characters is beginning to fascinate me more and more, together with the women they attract, and the relationship that results.

One day I stood on a railroad platform in Mancelona, Michigan, with a couple prostitutes just to hear from the seamy side of life: resulting conclusion: women are all looking to be swept off their feet by the macho masculine male, who is out there making things happen, whether he is carrying the success of the entire railroad on his shoulders. Women find this fellow attractive and rightfully so. The wild buck who defeats all his challengers gets to impregnate his harem of does for the determining of next year's herd of healthy fawns.

A half-pint imitation of a male just does not cut it with these females. They turn away from such imposters. Women worship the very trousers that cling to the man who is getting things done. He is at home in his body and radiates all the confidences in the world.

Homer wrote about this upon Ulysses's return to Penelope. She had collected a bevy of suitors all clamoring for her affection. Homer was very much aware of how to unravel the ensuing plot to make Ulysses appear as the macho male, rightful mate for her. Since his miraculous journey, Ulysses is now more qualified than ever having endured and survived a series of unspeakable events yet, in disguise, he joins the line of suitors vying for her decision.

Now, along comes this Hemingway kid. Somehow I feel on a similar Odyssey which is more like an invitation unraveling in this Michigan north woods.

I see how this masculine/feminine balance is radically out of whack within the pairing of my very own Mother and Father, and it makes me sick. Mother has de-masculated my Dear Pops and has stolen the reins of leadership from him. Father is nearing the snapping point as a result and needs this summer to regroup and regain his composure. I will do all I can to support my Pops. I will be the model son, planting and tending our big garden, bringing home wild game, fresh milk, eggs, and bacon from the neighboring farms, helping train the girls in the finer points of swimming, fishing, hiking, hunting, tennis, and baseball... basically trying my best to be a good role model.

If the children take after Mother though, and pick up her aggressive ways, that would be most disappointing, but in their worship of her all I can do at this point is pray that it doesn't happen, but underneath all the turmoil, Pops is going to get all my love and support, yes sir."

"Thanks for all your help in bringing this cabin open for the summer season, Bill," I said.

"No problem... after all, what are friends for? Hardest part was getting the dock out and fixing in the pump leather," replied Bill.

"Yeah, well, now a few sprigs of fresh mint down the well should counteract that taste of leather, but my Pops will be proud of me, that's the important thing," I stated.

Bill queried,"He should be proud. But if your Mother poisons his mind against you, what then?"

"What then? I don't know. Just have to hope Father can see through all her bullshit I guess. She's one sweet talking cookie. One day Pops will have to stand up to her. One day."

"Yeah, I wish I would be around when that happens. What would be her reaction, if he finally put his foot down?"

"All hell would cut loose, that's what. She usually throws a tantrum, just like a kid, and since Clarence abhors confrontation, he backs off and gives in to her demands."

"Wow... I can see now what you have to live with, my friend," sympathizes Bill.

"Yeah, and it's no fun seeing my Father after these tirades. He's crushed... simply crushed. A broken and defeated hollow man. He has no comeback for her. Well, I've got plenty on the old girl, but Pops is blinded by love, the poor fool can't see her trickery."

"It probably wouldn't do any good to tell him either. Would it?" asks Bill.

"Nope. He just wouldn't see it, anyway."

"She's pulled the wool far too often."

"And he can't give her the boot?"

"Nope, cause she has all the equity in the place from her Father's estate."

"So Clarence is a kept man?" Bill surmises.

"Yup... sometimes she brings in more than he does. He is that, indeed," says I.

"Holy cow! Wemedge," gasps Bill.

"Yeah, Ursa and I are the only ones who know."

"Well, Wemedge... you certainly have my deepest sympathy," comments Bill.

"My days are numbered around here."

"She knows that, you know?" asks Bill.

"More than likely, Pal. More than likely."

"So she'll make up some excuse to give you the boot?" queries Bill.

"Yup... indeed... give me the boot. That's one way to look at it, Pal," I states.

"But you're only seventeen? She wouldn't?"

"Good Christian that she is... yes she would. Cause I know too much. If I spilled the beans about her and Ruth Arnold, the scandal would ruin her business in Oak Park... conservative O.P, home of the wide lawns."

"...And narrow minds... got it," adds Bill.

"So it is just a matter of time for the good Oak Parkians to wise up that Ruth is more than a protege? That she and your Mom are..."

"Yup!"

"Oh... my... God!" gasps Bill.

"Now you're getting the full impact of it, Pal," I countered.

"This is scandalous" remarks Bill.

I states, "I know of no one who could live with this. Frank Lloyd Wright had to move out of Oak Park because of his dalliances with Mrs. Cheney... went to Europe to live. His scandal killed his business in Oak Park."

Bill counters, "My, oh my... now I see why she wanted that extra cabin built just for her and Ruth."

I adds, "Yeah, because it was on a hill, she claimed the view inspired her music and since the acreage was suitable for gardens, she got Pop's approval for she knows he likes his fresh veggies."

Bill adds, "Pretty dog gone slick of her, my friend, but loaded with duplicity at the same time."

"Very much so," I states. "So there goes college for all the Hemingway kids."

"How selfish, huh?" Bill remarks.

I states, "Yeah, pitiful. Just pitiful. She's so cold butter wouldn't melt in her mouth. But let's turn to happy thoughts."

Bill injects, "Well, we fixed the pump, removed all the shutters from the windows, launched the dock (hope it doesn't float away). What's next, Wemedge?"

I remarks, "Let's fill the wood box. Chopping wood will build up your biceps for the ladies."

Bill replies, "Ha, ha, real funny. Can we use wood knocked down by the wind?"

"Yup, Bill, smaller branches we can use for starter wood. Birch is perfect. Too bad we lost some of our good birches to that three day blow. Must be some bug is boring into them and killing them off."

Bill observes, "Wood box is full, Wemedge. Now what?"

"Let's bust it up and start a pile of logs outside under the eaves. Kinda want it out of the rain. Then I want a tarp over it so's I can keep it dry to split into kindling."

"Gee whiz, Wemedge, then what?"

"Then, Pal, we plants a garden at Longfields. Have to borrow some seed from Earl Bacon. Got to get Sumner's jackasses over there to loosen up the soil... kinda turn it over into long furrows."

"Gosh, you know a lot about farming, don't you?" Bill remarks.

"A little. The guy I admire though, is Jim Dilworth... runs a farm, a blacksmith shop and a bed and breakfast, plus he's a pretty good harness maker. Gets his leather from the Boyne City Tannery. Yeah, I remember when Wes (his son) and I hauled his new anvil from the train station in Walloon. That anvil sure was heavy. Good thing we used a block and tackle that time.

Mother never sees all the work I do around here so she complains I never do anything but lie around in my tent and read.

"So are you planning to pitch the tent again, Wemedge?" asks Bill.

"Heck, yeah. I need my privacy, you know, plus I have to keep pace with our race to read all the great literary works of Kipling, Conrad, and Robert Louis Stevenson. I've got some good books from Oak Park Library. A veritable treasure house I'd say."

Bill suggests, "Hey do you want to do a book swap sometime?"

"Sure, Pal, that way I gets to keep up with you... what are you, some kind of speed reader?"

Bill replies, "I guess. Just hate to put down a good book. If the author keeps me on the edge of my seat, I feel compelled to absorb it all until the end. Like Samuel Clemons."

I interjects, "Some authors I just can't read, but I do find Mark Twain quite enjoyable. Personally, it is my opinion that all American literature will have to go through Huck Finn. He is the American icon, the new standard."

Bill adds, "You know, you might have something there, Wemedge. You just might have something." Bill inquires, "So who is going to tell Kate about Mother Grace?"

Says I, "Better let me tell her. I would prefer that Kate would hear it from me."

Bill states, "Yeah, I don't think I could bring up such a topic with anyone."

"Nope, it's too un-natural, no one should ever have to, I mean, no one period," I demanded. "My Pops really needs this time with his brothers, but I kinda think he should be pulling up here, any minute."

Bill remarks, Great! They will want to fish for their supper once they find out the fish are almost jumping into the boat, today."

I says, "They should see us working. Want to start raking off the grounds?"

"Sure, I'll dig some worms for them," added Bill.

"Rakes are in the back shed. I'll get one for each of us. Pops' flowers will be popping up if we remove all these old leaves and pine needles."

"Your Dad has time to plant flowers?"

"Heck yeah, and he has a knack for it, too. You should see what Uncle George can grow. He owns a nursery in Ironton, Michigan. Uncle also dabbles in real estate."

"You don't say?" said Bill.

"Yup, he's trying to buy the point near Hortons Bay," I pointed out.

"Bet he will. There's some of the best fishing in the area. That uncle is a sharp one."

"Hey Bill."

"Yeah, Wemedge."

"I hate to bring this up, but I really need to get something off my chest," I injected. "Well... my mother had me hating you years ago."

"Oh yeah? How's that?" inquires Bill.

"Because she always compared me to you constantly She used to say, 'Ernest, why can't you be more like Bill Smith? He's such a hard worker, always helping his Aunty Charles. He is so responsible too. Why can't you be more like him?' But that was before I really got to know you, Pal."

"Yeah, I can see how that could happen. But see, now we're best friends. So I can forgive you Wemedge," Bill offered.

"Thanks, Pal. That makes me feel real good," I reminded. "Hey, do you want to help me pitch a tent out on Longfield property?"

"Why, sure enough," replied Bill.

"Cause that way I can tend the garden and be closer to my Pals in Hortons Bay. I can keep the ice house filled with sawdust, too, and trim Pop's fruit trees."

"Gosh, Wemedge. I don't see how your Mother ever thought you to be sluffing off. You are doing more than your share of chores," adds Bill.

"Yeah... go figure. She just loves to hen peck, I think. She's got Pops all riddled with holes."

"Well put, Wemedge. Your poor Pops," consoled Bill.

"Lately now she tries to poison his mind against me," I reveals.

"She might be jealous of your tight relationship with your Pops," conjectures Bill.

"Oh, I know she is. Pops and I go fishin' and shooting together every chance we can. My Father has taught me all the plants, animals, and birds, and lots of stuff about doctoring, too. I know plenty about everything, thanks to Doctor Dad," I observed.

Bill queried, "Do you think there might come a time when you'll know too much?"

"That time has come, Pal. A barmaid laid a heck of a scoop on me, but it'll never be printed cause it's too top secret," I reveals.

"Do you mean...?"

"Yeah... loose lips sink ships. That story will stay sealed in the vault for a long time. If Kaiser's boys got wind of it, the war could drag on for another year," I speculate.

"That big, huh?"

"You bet, Pilgrim. Could get the dough boys out of the trenches and busting through enemy lines. Gosh, I'm itching powerful to post that story! But my reporter friend in G.R. told me to zip my lips.

"Best piece of journalism that never got printed," Bill conjectured.

"Yeah, and my first piece too, dag nab it."

"Wemedge, you'll have plenty of stories to publish over in K.C. Don't you think?" asked Bill. "You bet. Can't wait to get my own column. Phew. Let's take a break from all this raking. Say, Bill, let me get a tin can for all those worms. Dad and Tyler will have plenty of bait there."

Bill Smith and Ernest on Mitchell Street, Downtown, Petoskey.

Chapter 15. Indian Camp Delivery

"Speak of the brothers, is that not the sound of Henry Ford's finest flivver?" asks Bill.

"Well it ain't Turd face Evans 'cause he always slithers out of the bushes... like the slimy snake of a game warden, that he is," I replies.

"Sure enough, here they come in a shiny new flivver. Wait til they see all the worms we have for them," announces Bill.

"Let's hope they have a few moments together to catch us a fish supper. When Mother Grace gets here, he'll be waiting on her hand and foot, and you never know when someone is going to call to have him deliver a baby. Doc has some kinda internal clock... knows when all his pregnant ladies are due, and he's always ready to deliver their babies. Strangest thing. He must know in his bones when Mother will arrive then," I comments.

"So your Father delivers babies?" states a surprised Bill.

"Yup, why does that surprise you?" I retorts.

"Oh, I don't know. He seems so... so... shy, and uncomfortable, and easily embarrassed about women, especially a woman's birth canal," exhorts Bill.

"Yeah? I always wondered about that too, but not after I saw him in operation. Well, here they come. Tell you about that later. Greetings, weary travelers," I shouts.

Aaaauuugaah! Announces the Model T's horn.

"Greetings, son. What a long trip," comments Pops.

"Indeed, are you and Uncle Tyler in for some real good fishing?" I ask.

Tyler shouts, "You bet we are, Ernest!"

"Well, Bill here has all kinds of bait dug up for you men. We fried a belly full of fish yesterday. Meet my Pal, Bill... Bill Smith, my best friend from Hortons Bay summers... my very literary friend, Uncle."

"Ernest tells us all about you, Bill," states Tyler.

"Afternoon, Bill. Good to see you again. Thanks for the worms," says Clarence.

I states, "I took the liberty of getting your rods ready, men. Alls you have to do is loop a worm on. Bill and I caught some of the biggest largemouths over by the edge of the reed patch."

Bill adds, "Take a landing net along. Those bass put up quite a fight. I think you will be pleasantly surprised today."

"Tyler, let's jump out of these dusty suits and into some overalls. I've been waiting for this all year," Clarence declares.

Tyler jokes, "Last one in the boat is a rotten egg."

I reiterates, "Okay, now where were we, Bill, oh, now I remembers, my Pops the baby doctor. So he invites me to tag along with he and Uncle George, rowing across to Indian camp where this squaw is screaming."

"Screaming?" asks Bill.

"Yeah, I mean really letting out with the loud yelps. She was having a rough delivery for some reason," I adds.

"How did he know she was due?"

"Bill, we just went over this. He's got some kind of internal clock, my man, okay? Right... So I'm just a little shaver, maybe seven, right? Or eight, and Pops pulls out his jack knife as calmly as you please. He cuts a slit in her bulging belly and pulled that baby right out of her, right? Then he sews her up with a length of fish line. Perfect, huh? And as we were leaving then, up on the top bunk her husband slits his own throat and bleeds out, right?"

"Oh, for heaven's sake!" Bill remarks shockingly. "That... now that... must have been traumatic for you?"

"Yeah, oh hell yeah! Got me an eye full that day. Had nightmares for many a moon, my Man, many moons, still bothers me."

"Well... why do you suppose Doc took you in the shack to witness all of that? He could've asked you to wait outside, right?"

"Bill... first of all, I worship my Dad, okay? In my eyes, he can do me no wrong, and I guess I always felt it was me. I was to suck it up. I was left having to deal with it, having to deal with watching how the American Native was forced to survive, and I guess he wanted me to see how a doctor delivers a baby. I don't know? It was all so shocking."

"Native Americans sure have a rough time of it all right," agrees Bill.

"Indeed, my friend. Life happens like an iceberg. Only a small piece of it shows, but it may take another lifetime to discover what is underneath. The reasons, the motivation, the moving impulses behind each incident. Life is amazing."

"Pal, at any age, I don't think a person can totally handle seeing another person die."

I speculates, "Now, my Uncle George thought it okay to later hand out cigars."

"Hand out cigars, uhuh? Okay?" utters Bill.

I continues, "Yeah, the custom is when a baby is born the Father...Oh, my God. I just had a weird thought."

Bill adds, "Yeah, me too. Are you thinking what I'm...?"

I continues, "Oh, my God... then Uncle George must have been the father, the f-f-father! Holy crap!"

"See, Wemedge, by talking about that trauma, you have discovered a whole new angle to that incident. Are there any more epiphanies about that? Feel free to go ahead and talk it out."

"Well, sure. Always wondered why the suicide took place, but now that is clearing up too. Being the husband, and being as George was the biological father of his wife's child, her screams made his life unbearable," I surmises.

"Yeah, he's angry, wants to kill George, but fears another race riot or another massacre of his tribe by the white man."

"Well put, Will. Wow! I feel so much better now. Like a whole load has been lifted off my back. I been dragging this around for years. Holy crap!"

As Pops and his brother Tyler cast off in their fishin' boat with high expectations of catching our supper, Bill Smith and I continued our analysis of the Indian "C" section story.

Bill speculates, "So, Wemedge, what we still need to gain an understanding of, is why Doc took you along on that fateful day?"

I states, "As I look back on that whole scene every bit of it scared the shit out of me, but I finally feel we solved the suicide of the husband. Our recent breakthrough certainly makes loads of sense, and with George gesturing with cigar handouts, he sort of gave away his being father of that child. That leaves us still speculating on Pop's motivation for including an eight year old as unwilling witness to some most shocking life episodes."

Bill agrees, "Exactly, Wemedge, just what in the hell did he hope to achieve with your observation of this dramatic happening? Was it some initiation into the misty work of native obstetrics?"

I reply, "Maybe? But Bill, he gave me no recourse, no option to back out. Shouldn't a kid be asked if he wants to view an obstetric operation? If Pops knew the woman was due to deliver, where the hell was his doctor's bag? That too has always baffled me."

Bill suggests, "Maybe the scene was only meant for Uncle George? For his eyes only, and you were supposed to see your Uncle's flippant attitude and unfeeling reaction?"

I reacted thusly, "Now that you mention it, I did wonder about Uncle George's reaction, you know. If he was father of that child, he should've been man enough to care for child and Mother. But he left the cabin puffing on a stogie, and acting totally unconcerned about the whole ordeal, while her husband bled out on the upper bunk."

Bill asked, "Did that strike you in some way?"

I replied, "Hell, yeah. They treated that Indian couple like they were less than human. Pops didn't want to dirty his surgical tools so he whips out his jack knife to perform a C section, then uses old fish line to sew up the incision, yeah, it all makes sense now. They were passive Indian haters."

Bill adds, "Indians, we considered less than human, unworthy of surgical tools, plus proper sanitary means to prevent infection, then to leave the wife with her newborn baby and dead husband. Hell, that whole operation speaks volumes of how the Redman was treated back then. I would not treat a dog like that, William! Yeah, back then a good Indian was a dead Indian. Try to remember that."

I replies, "It looks like it is up to our generation to remedy that. I happen to like my Native American friends, so that's it. Pops must have wanted me to capture all that in hopes that I would change things."

Bill asks, "Hospitals probably refused services to Indians just as common policy? They expected the culture to eventually die out and never be heard from again. Doctor Dad here must have been a rebel. Your average doctor never ever would have entered an Indian dwelling, nor would he have touched one fearing it would make him unclean and contaminated."

I responds, "Right. Guess I forgot my Pops was way ahead of his time in terms of treating Indians. He actually was kinda afraid of some of them, like big Nick Boulton. Pops was intimidated by that big buck. As for me, I respected his woodlands hunting and fishing skills, not to mention my affection for his lovely daughter, Prudence, and her talented brother, Billy. They both were my childhood playmates. Hell, to this day I fashion myself as one of their tribe. Do you know?"

Bill answers, "I kinda knew you had a shine on Prudence, and Billy Tabeshaw, her half brother, is one heck of a deer slayer, and tremendous fisherman, squirrel sharp shooter... he could pop the eye out of a squirrel at 50 paces, your teacher, right?"

My reply, "Indeed, it is necessary to put food on the table. I enjoy bagging wild game for our dinner table. But I'll never forget, one day Pops wanted Nick Boulton to haul one of those deadhead logs that had washed up on our beach up to the cabin, to cut it up for firewood. Nick started in as to the brand on the log... meant it belonged to some lumber company, so Pops backed it off and never pushed the discussion any further. He let big Nick intimidate him. Heck, that loose log was free, finders keepers, ya know?"

Bill inquires, "So how did you feel about that?"

I replies, "I felt Pops should've stood up to that big buck Indian and reminded him of his debt to Pops for unpaid doctor bills. He owed Pops for pumping out his opium and alcohol-filled stomach one time. Saved Nick's life. He almost croaked. So Pops really disappointed me on that showdown."

Bill confides, "Think I would've done the same. It is not easy to encourage confrontation. I always try to avoid it."

I disagree, "Naw, ever since I was a kid, it's been important to me to stand up for my beliefs. Pops could have taken Nick. Pops is strong."

Bill adds, "Yeah, but what if big Nick had a knife, or maybe a tomahawk. Doc played his options and figured the deadhead log might not have been worth it."

I counters, "In my view, Pops just came up looking like a pussy cat."

Bill asks, "Did Nick square things with his doctoring debts?"

I reply, "Eventually he sent his wife Anna over with some nice deerskin moccasins, and a vest, for Pops all hand beaded. Prudence cleans our cabin when she can."

Bill adds, "Well see, he squared it... eventually. They have a sense of honor, but get too goofy when alcohol is around."

"Well, this cabin is looking like it's ready to open for the summer."

I add, "Sure does, my friend. Thanks for helping. Won't you stay for supper?"

Bill remarked, "Thanks, Wemedge, but I should shove off."

I states, "Let's plan on another double date into Petoskey."

"Okay, I'll see if G.Q. and Kate want to date. Give my best regards to your Dad and Uncle. I'll help you pitch that tent on Longfields."

Says I, "Okay, Bill, see ya tomorrow."

Collecting more firewood for the cookstove is my plan in hopes that Pops and Uncle Tyler land a nice stringer of fish for supper.

It's very clear that Mother and the rest of the family got a late start out of Chicago, or might have missed their train out of Harbor Springs, anyway, after the woodbox was filled, I dug worms and tried my luck at dock fishing.

As I reflected on re-living that Indian "C"-section with my pal, Bill, I began to see how important it is to let loose of things stuck in my craw. I value living in the Petoskey area where "talking out" life problems is something we do every day, because this activity is quite prevalent in this community moreso than any area in which I have ever been.

Now I'm having second thoughts about the innocence of Uncle George.

Chapter 16. Skirting the Vile

Petoskey, MI "Dummy Train"

Tyler speaks, "Tell you what, Clarence, you've got yourself a mighty nice place to come and relax. Fish are almost jumping into our boat today."

"Indeed, Dear Brother. Lewis Clarahan will be among us this summer so after we catch a few more perch. They should be arriving by steamer boat."

Tyler remarks, "I declare, brother, you must have a sixth sense if you expect them today yet."

Clarence states, "Why, of course. Just figure. That Chicago lake steamer arrives at Harbor mid afternoon, a train takes them to Petoskey where they catch the dummy train to Walloon. A smaller lake steamer then brings them to here."

Tyler adds, "Let's hope they make all the proper connections on time."

Clarence says, "Two or three more fish and we should see the Walloon Lake steamer chugging up here. It doesn't take E.S.P."

Tyler adds," Okay, but will Ernest have the cabin ready all by himself?"

Clarence states, "Most assuredly, my good man. I have every confidence in the lad."

Tyler agrees, "It looked like he and his chum, Bill have all the grounds raked up nicely."

Clarence nods, "So I noticed. All shutters were off the windows and stored properly. I hope they thought to remove the cover off the chimney. That could be disastrous when we start the fire."

Tyler concludes, "This mess of fish will sure taste good fried in bacon drippings after a good roll in corn meal."

"You still remember our old recipe?" Clarence asks.

"Well that is how we Hemingways have prepared our fish for decades now."

In late afternoon the sun began reflecting off the sparkling blue Walloon Lake water. A few white cumulus clouds continued their thermal build up over the hills leading to Boyne City in the backyard. The two brothers have reeled in a large stringer of pan fish. This is enough for a scrumptious meal for the entire Hemingway family, plus their evening guests, Uncle Tyler and Lewis Clarahan.

From all indications this particular summer seemed a lot like any other vacation up in Michigan, yet an undercurrent of festering repressed emotions was building up in this respectable upper middle class family, and at any moment the lid would come totally off.

"Brother Clarence, your life seems to be so successful; nice family, thriving practice, many talented and handsome children, a talented, loving wife and yet I sense a certain unhappiness with you. You are not the jovial brother I used to know from our youth. At some point, while I am here, I would hope you would feel free to get it off your chest. I'm here for you Clare, you don't need to carry this load all by yourself."

Clare confides, "Indeed Ty, you are touching on a nerve here and asking me to describe what is going on."

Tyler encourages, "Try, my brother.... I know you'll feel..."

Clarence continues, "Look Tyler, you are a sensitive, loving member of the family. I ask you just to be an observer for awhile. Enjoy our company but try to keep an eye out for a most shameful situation that is going on."

Tyler asks, "Shameful?"

Clarence adds, "Yes, shameful, grievously shameful! Uh, Uh... Scandalous too... but beyond that I still haven't found the words in my vocabulary to describe this any more, okay?"

"Must I play twenty questions with you 'cause I hate to see you so distraught, my Brother," counters Tyler.

Clarence suggests, "Right now your prayers would help us immensely."

Tyler still probes, "This isn't about Ernest, is it?"

Clarence answers, "I wish it were, Tyler, but no this does not involve him. He has been my rock lately. Personally, I'm going to miss the lad when he runs off to live with you and Arabelle in Kansas City. Thanks again for landing him that newspaper job. It will do him good to learn the trade. I know you must have pulled some strings with your old college roommate there on the K.C. Star."

Tyler answers, "The newspaper offers intern opportunities throughout the year. Ernest will have to prove himself because there are other qualified college graduates who are waiting in the wings."

Clarence states, "Well, in my view as the president of Oak Park/River Forest School Board, our graduates get about the equivalent of a college course in my humble opinion."

Tyler agrees, "That is a fact. Our Oak Park system is the best in the country, therefore, I have every confidence in my nephew and his journalism ability. This opportunity will give him a good start in his writing career."

"Well we can eliminate any issues, then, with Ernest. I wish you would help me out here, Clare, as to whom this vexing culprit is. You're just going to keep it to yourself?"

Clarence retorts, "Yes indeed, mainly because I wouldn't have the words to sufficiently describe it, and anyway, if and when you find out there is absolutely nothing one can do about it... absolutely... not one dog gone thing."

Tyler comforts, "Well, Brother, I hope just this beating around the bush conversation has helped to diffuse the volatility a bit. Are you feeling anger?"

Clarence replies, "Anger? Tyler I wish it were just anger. No it is out and out rage... white hot rage of the volcanic style! And twice as heated!"

Tyler sympathizes, "Oh, my goodness. My, my goodness, and there is no antidote to this... this white hot style of rage?"

Clarence answers, "None that I know of ... and I don't want to discuss this any further. OKAY. Case closed."

Tyler adds, "If that's the way you want it, that's the way it will be. I guess. Would a little forgiveness help here?"

Clarence shouts, "Ty... I don't want to discuss it any further, Now that's it! End of discussion."

Tyler adds, "Sorry. Obviously, this is a deep seated issue with you so no more talk, end of discussion. I felt the wall go up."

Clarence diverts, "So let us take this nice stringer of fish and start cooking supper."

Tyler still probes, "Shall we talk about this at some other time?"

Clarence reports, "Let's just leave it at that, Dear Brother of mine. You have no idea how vile this is. So drop it. Period!"

Tyler sympathizes, "When you are ready, you know I'm all ears, Clare."

Clarence diverts attention again, "Why, look, here comes Walloon's very own steamer and the rest of the family is on her. Ahoy maties!"

Chapter 17. The Family Arrives for the Summer

Marcy shouts, "Ahoy, maties. We made it. Next time I am taking the Model T!"

Clarence asks, "Here, let me help you with little Leichester. No more Model T trips until Michigan builds better roads. Mercy live."

Marcy adds, "Ever chase a two year old all over the ship and keep him from capsizing the boat?

Phew! Say hi to Daddy, Leichester."

Leichester adds, "Wanna go fishin', go fish!"

Sunny was next to hop off the steamer, then Ursala, little Carol, then Ruth (The children's governess), Mother Grace, then Lewis Clarahan and the the servant girls. A porter dollied all the trunks and boxes leaving a large pile of luggage at the end of Windemere dock. I collared Lewis to help me haul the Hemingway luggage into the cabin.

"Lewis, my Pal, I must say we had the most excellent adventure motoring up here. I got enough material for a whole new chapter in my book. How are things with you, my friend?"

"EGAD, these trunks must have anvils in them, grunt, groan, uh oh, OK I guess. We had an interesting trip. Took longer than I expected though. Storm came up ... grunt, groan ... so we had to pull into harbor town ... ugh, gasp ... kinda forgot the name of it," stated Lewis.

"Out of shape are you, Lew? Did it start with an L?" I queried.

"Ugh ... grunt ... yeah ... think so," replies Lew.

I countered, "Ludington, maybe?"

Lew replies, "Yeah ... ugh, uh, ah ... right that's it. Had to stay over a few days. Big, wild storm – high winds, rain – horizontal rain that is, then hail that is, then hail as big as golf balls."

I concurred, "Yup, we had the same storm hit us in Cadillac. Never seen anything like it, Pal."

Lew adds, "We were making good time, too. That ole steamer she sure was slicing through Lake Michigan. Then all of a sudden we started rocking back and forth. Captain set a course for the nearest refuge that he could. I thought your mother was gonna flip. She yelled that we would miss our train connection to Petoskey and all this. Oh my garsh, these trunks must have lead?"

I queried, "Did she harass the captain, Lew?"

Lewis continued, "Uh, oh yeah. Told him to outrun the storm. Imagine that, Huh? Outrun the dad-gunned- dangerous storm which was churning up Lake Michigan pretty well– 10 foot white caps I'd say."

I commented, "What? She wanted the captain to outrun the storm in that giant bath-tub of a lake steamer. Oh, My God! You saw her in action then. Lew, this is precious. Now you see what I have to deal with .. every friggin' day with that woman."

Lew adds, "Yeah, well instead of huggin' the Baron here – lil Leichester... all of two years of age, guess who she hugged when waves came crashing into the decks?"

I surmise, "Oh, don't tell me. Let me guess. Uh ... was it Mother's music student, the childrens' nurse maid or what-ya-call governess, who is not much older than Marcy?"

Lew states "Yup, that Ruth character ... thought that a bit strange. Know what I mean? Marcy was actually the mother to these little kids. Sunny was huggin' Leichester... the Baron everyone called him... Marcy was hugging the two of them. Ursa was huggin' Carol, and I was left to hug the servant girls... the black housekeeper and cooks. I guess you'd call them. Oh, they were scared! Their eyes were ready to pop out of their heads like they do.

Then all the deck chairs started sliding across the deck, this way and that ... oh it was a harrowing trip, some harrowing trip. Too bad I didn't ride in the flivver with you, Pal."

I concur, "Yeah, but you saw plenty, Lewis, plenty."

After that interchange it hurt me too bad to let on that my Mother had abandoned her family in favor of some outsider waif of a pseudo music student. It hurts too much for Lew to find out the hard way. The situation was so vile that it had its own built in rumor control. No one in Oak Park had ever heard of such scandalous activity, and I sure wasn't going to be the chump who brought shame onto the family name. No sir, not me, and that is why I will never write about the place of my birth, cause I just could never side step that juicy topic of my own Mother's defection over to the other team. Not since Frank Lloyd Wright ran off with Mrs. Cheney. (It was so scandalous that Frank couldn't find a contract again in Oak Park, so they ran off to Europe.) Oak Parkers will have to discover that juicy tid bit all on their own. Case closed.

After helping Lewis Clarahan tote all that heavy luggage and all those steamer trunks into our summer cabin, I decided to help Pops fry the fish and set the table.

I announce, "Now all of you people get settled in and relax. I know it's been a rough ride just to get up here so relax while Father and I prepare your dinner."

Grace says, " Oh Ernest, my sweet boy. I just love it when you take a load off your poor Father."

I surveyed, "Raise your hand if you want fresh-caught fish taken right off our lovely dock? Now raise for roast duck, goose, beef burgundy, beluga caviar, shrimp?"

Marcy jabs, "Oh Ernest, surely you jest? Surely."

I retort, "How many times have I told you to stop calling me Shirley? Do I have a little sibling who would want to set our dining room table? Oh, look at all the eager hands. So hard to choose. Uh, Okay you wore me down... I want to see Beefy and Sunny... front and center, pronto."

Ursa chimes in, "Oh, Oinbones, you're so macho and ah loves that take charge masculinity."

I remind, "Remember, Sunny, forks go to the left."

"Oh, Ursa, Honey, please roll a dozen taters in foil and toss them on the hot coals in our fireplace. We gonna have us a big ole feast tonight."

"Okay Father, I'll dredge the fish in cornmeal, and then drop them into the eggwash while you do your magic in the fry pan."

Grace boasts, "My husband has perfected the Hemingway fish fry. I just can't say enough good things about him, right Uncle Tyler? Hope you enjoy your vacation with us. Ruth, this handsome chap is Clarence's successful brother, Tyler."

Ruth responds, "Charmed I'm sure, Mr. Tyler, sir?"

Grace breaks in, "That's enough, Hon, have a seat next to me at the dining room table, Okay? Now Tyler I want to thank you and Arabelle for taking in my little boy who breaks his Mother's heart to become a newspaper reporter or something."

Tyler counters, "'Twas nothing actually, Grace. When the K.C. Star saw Ernest's resume and read some of his work from Oak Park / River Forest High they were duly impressed. The lad is a natural born and highly trained talent."

Grace sounding surprised, "Oh, … Okay then I … I … I thought he would fit in at the cement plant here in Petoskey. They always need'n help aren't they? Huh! … Okay then. He's such a slouchy, lazy lad, always mooching off his friends. Just want him to find work so he won't be a drain on society. Arabelle is such a good cook. You're a lucky man."

Tyler interrupts, "Yes, indeed, we are so thankful that God has richly blessed all of us … hasn't He …Praise the Lord … Grace."

Tyler a man in whom there is no guile shot a patently religious answer at Mother Grace and then with his enormous brown Hemingway eyes peered right through her, right into her trembling over-spoiled soul.

Eventually Grace replied, "Ty, you can sleep in my bedroom while you're here. Did you know I have my own cabin for my music and my painting, where I teach my students like Ruth Arnold here? Comes from a broken home."

Tyler's retort, "Really. Will there be money for your children to attend college?"

Grace's reply, "Don't really know. We haven't really discussed much college. I think Oak Park / River Forest is their college. Best school in the world, don't you know. My Father was on the school board." Grace excuses herself, "Folks, I have a splitting headache so if you will excuse us, Ruth and I will be rowing over to my art inspiration cabin."

The family replies, "Good night, Mother."

The silence following her exit is so quiet you could cut it with a spatula. Tyler's challenge regarding her reckless spending of her children's college fund had sent her into a tizzy fit and in order to save face in front of everyone whom she had offended, Grace now felt the need for space.

Carol chimed in, "Poor Mommie got a owie. Can I have her fishies?"

Pops answers, "Why of course, fweetie. We'll have plenty of fishies for everyone. Thanks, Tyler. She needed to hear that."

I spouts off, "Yeah, Uncle Ty, you should get the large mouth bass. Here it comes in all its goodness and large mouthiness."

The family cheers, "Pip pip, Hear, hear ... Uncle Tylie ... hear, hear!"

I concur, "God's speaking through Uncle tonight ... shall he ask the Lord's Blessing?"

Tyler prays, "Lord, we just thank you for these lovely fish here which you so abundantly supplied, and we thank you for our lovely children with whom you have showered us with your bounty. Bless this food now to our bodies and us to your service. Amen."

The group adds, "Amen!"

Ursa announces, "Make room for hearth-roasted taters everyone ... pip pip."

The group says, "Hooray for Ursa's taters. Hearth- roasted."

Ursa reminds, "Now these taters are piping hot so, children, be careful, please."

Doc cautions, "Now children, be careful there may be small bones in the fish, so be watching and pulling before eating."

I concur, "Very good, Father. Wise use of gerund phrases."

Marcy adds, "Yes, Father, thanks for the heads up. Now children ... watch for bones and pick them out. I can help if you need it. They can get stuck in your throat and you could choke."

Baron asks, "What are bones?"

I add, "Good one, Baron. Just keep curious throughout you life. Here I'll show you, little Pal. See that little white thing sticking out? Just pluck that out. So simple, bone picking."

Baron adds, "Thanks, Big Brudder. He my Big Brudder."

Meanwhile, Tyler is thinking that he has a bone to pick with his sister-in-law, Grace. So as not to create a scene in front of the children, his discussion regarding the squandering of the childrens college fund needs further analysis. Oh, Tyler would also love to fly in her face about her abandonment of her family and her husband all in the name of music, which includes the romancing of young Ruth Arnold and flaunting it in front of her husband and children. Oh there needs be one gigantic bone picking going on.

Tyler is beginning to see why his brother, Clarence, is so distraught lately, but now he must wait for his chance to pick a bone with Mother Grace. In his mind, he begins rehearsing the key issues of his argument with her... this shameless libertine hussy. If women ever win the right to vote it will mean the destruction of America as we know it, especially if it's women like Grace Hall Hemingway.

Lewis states, " It's exciting coming up to Northern Michigan. There's never a dull moment around here."

Sunny adds, "Yup, that's a fact, Lew. Will you have time to play catch with me? I love baseball."

Ursa states, " Hon, he might have other plans. We're going to have to share Lew aren't we, Marcy?"

Marcy retorts, "You can have him."

Carol jumps in, "He's mine then. Lewis, we can take nature walks and pick pretty flowers and take our shoes off and hunt for Petoskey stones."

Father interjects, "Now girls. It's up to Lewis with whom he spends his time. He is our guest so let's be considerate, okay? Now, who wants more fish? Ernest, please coat some more fish with that delicious corn meal, please, son."

I adds, "Thanks, Father, and thanks for controlling the harem. I think Lew wants to know where our new "Honey hole" is located, right Lewis?'

Lew says, "Oh, you bet, Stein. Fishing is a big part of summer vacation, but I also will make time for all my girls, and even little Leichester. How's that leetle feller?"

Baron states, "Oh goody. Let's make mud pies."

Tyler adds, "Now see what you are in for, Lewis."

Lewis says, "Yeah I knew I was popular, but never this popular. Guess we bonded nicely on that exciting steamboat ride on stormy Lake Michigan."

The call for second helpings prompts Pop and me to fire up the wood burning cook stove. The smell of bacon fat browning a new batch of corn meal encrusted perch and bass filets soon begins to fill the air.

Pops comments, "Ernest, I want to thank you for heading over to the cabin and getting it ready to open for the summer. It gave me time to have a nice reunion in Ironton with Tyler, George, and George's wife, also named Grace. I see you even had time to uncover my crocuses. How nice of you."

I state, "Oh, that. Well, Father, think nothing of it. After all, what are pals for, Huh? I plan to pitch my tent again. Lewis and I will bunk out there and Tyler can use Mother's bedroom since she won't be needing it."

Pops iterates, "It will be a tight squeeze but we'll find sleeping room for everyone, of that I am certain."

I state, "Heck yeah, Father. We could pitch another tent if need be. I'd like to pitch one over at Longfields farm, too, so I can tend to our vegetable garden. How does that sound? After all, you are the boss around here, right?'

Pops adds, "Oh, of course. Sorry I must've drifted off there. Sorry. Oh, surely son."

I add, "Now stop calling me Shirley, Ha ha ha."

"So next time I'm in Bump Hardware I should pick up some canvas tarps," Pops states.

I adds, "Yup, that would be the ticket. We could raise a ton of baking taters, carrots, and all sorts of exotic leaf lettuce, turnips, parsnips... oh, the list goes on and on. I can crate them up in the fall and ship them off by train. Then we could store them in our root cellar in Oak Park. So please pick up seeds, also."

Pops gets sentimental, "Looks like this will be your last summer up north, Ernest. How do you feel about that?"

I continues, "Thanks, Pop. Holy cow! No one has ever asked me how I feel about anything. This is a friggin' first, Father!"

Pops interrupts, "Now take a deep breath, Ernest. Calm thyself."

I stammers, "H- h- how do I feel? Hmm... Sad. That feeling seems to come up first, then excited about the new adventure with that

K. C. Star newspaper... Then sadness again, Father, after saying farewell to so many of my best Pals going off to war, or going off to Harvard and Yale and Princeton, or Illinois... Then rage, that Mother spent my college fund on that damn extra stress relief cabin of hers which we didn't need. So, best way to describe it... How I'm feeling... A great big mixed bag, I guess... Yeah a little sprinkle of sadness, a dash of excitement, and a whole gallon of rage, but having Uncle Tyler in my corner along with Aunt Arabelle and you, Pops-'cause I know you wanted me to partner with you in the doctoring business, so I guess I'm getting ready to make the giant leap into the great unknown, trusting in my writing skills and God given talent."

Pops recaps, "So then sadness, excitement, and a whole lot of rage. That's quite the recipe. Oh, shucks, here I go almost burning the fish. Ouch!"

I announces, "Okay gentlemen and ladies, now who wanted filet of sole? Lobster? Can't have any, but we do have fresh caught panfish right out of beautiful Walloon to quote a song written by somebody who will remain nameless."

Marcy says, "I do. I wants fresh fish from Loona."

Ursa asks, "Balloona Walloona for moi?"

Lewis answers, "Plain fish for me, Chef."

Carol wonders, "Can I have cotton candy?"

Tyler reminds, "Carol, you'll have to visit River View off Belmont for that... in Chicago."

Carol revises, "Okay, give me liberty or..."

Sunny adds, "Give me death... Patrick Henry."

Ursa questioned, "What's for dessert?"

Baron states, "I smelled apple pie."

Pops adds, "Bingo, Baron. You win, little buddy."

Baron reminds, "Me not little. Me big boy."

Pops returns from the kitchen. "Well, big boys and girls, here's dessert. Tyler gets the first piece. You know why?"

Carol interjects, "' Cause Uncle Tylie is our guest."

Pops adds, "That's right, Beefy. We show respect and honor for our guests by letting them go first, or have the first piece in this case."

Baron states, "Unka Tylie, will you leave some for me?"

Tyler replies, "Yes, big boy. That I will. Apple pie is everyone's favorite. All of us Hemingways anyways. Thank you, brother Clarence."

Ursa asks, "So, Uncle Tyler, how do you like fishing in our nice lake Walloon?"

Tyler replies, "Ursula, I like it a lot. You must have these fish trained. They almost want to jump right into the boat. Why, within an hour, your father and I had caught enough for supper."

Sunny adds, "Did you remember to set the hook?"

Tyler states, "No doubt, Sunny, but after I lost a few fish, I made sure that hook was set real good."

Sunny makes a jerking motion, mimicking how she sets the hook. Soon Ursula is making a similar motion. Eventually Baron tries his hand at a similar, but exaggerated jerking motion.

Pops reminds, "Careful there, Leichester, you might spill your water glass, or fall out of your high chair."

Carol pipes in, "Daddy, when you going to take me fishing?"

Pops replies, "Well, Beefy, when you learn to bait your own hook, then you can come fishing with us."

Carol responds, "Eww! Do you mean jam a poor, slimy, filthy, dirty worm onto a sharp hook? Yuck!"

Pops adds, "That's right, Hon. Those are the facts of life... I mean, fishing. This summer, I really would like you to bait your own hook. Could you try real hard to do that?"

Ursula adds, "Yeah, Beefy, we all had to go through this when we were your age. Think of it as your initiation into the Hemingway clan of outdoor naturalists. Plus, it feels so good when you can eat those fishes. It's all about eating: fish eats your worm, gets hooked, gets reeled in, ends up in the fry pan, and onto your little plate. Then you eat him or her. Got it?"

Carol asks, "Then, that makes me a member of your club?"

Ursula replies, "Yeah, kinda, but putting the worm on the hook is the initiation ritual to see if you have the toughness that all us Hemingways possess, got it?"

Sunny adds, "Granted, Beefy, it is kinda disgusting, but initiation's are like that, Hon. That is if you want to join our club? Baiting a hook isn't any worse than making... Mud pies, or picking used gum off the bedpost... And I know how you like to do those things."

Carol pauses, then states, "Hey, you know... I'll give it a try. How do you know I chew old gum?"

I adds, "Atta big girl, Beefy, 'cause this summer no one is going to put your worm on. You get that, right? You're on your own this year."

Carol says, "Harrumph... okay, okay, quit picking on me. Gee whiz, I'll do it already. No big deal!"

Marcy answers, "Atta girl! That's our Beefy! Pip, Pip for Beefy."

Everyone chorused, "Pip, Pip for Beefy!"

Tyler says, "I think Carol should get the next piece of apple pie. Here you go, Hon."

Carol answers, "Oh, goody. Thanks. You are my favorite uncle. Yes, mmm, Uncle Tylie, dish me in please. You're my all time favorite Uncle. Unkie, mmm. Thanks, thank you."

Marcy adds, "Now, Beefy, if I find a sturdy box or crate for you to stand on, we'd like you to join us in the dishwashing club."

Ursa adds, "Yeah, we need one more member in our dishwashing club."

Carol answers, "Gee whiz, I got all these clubs to join. This is exciting, folks. Let me know if I qualify for any more clubs. But it's those initiations I have to watch."

Ursa comments, "This kid is smarter than you think."

Pops states, "Isn't that true about a lot of things in life? Just one challenge after another and one more initiation fee to come up with."

I says, "So true. I bet they have initiations at the K. C. Star, too."

Tyler adds, "As far as I know they will expect you to hang around police stations and hospitals getting the scoop, and your initiation would be... To sacrifice normal sleeping hours."

Pops adds, "Indeed, you will work the graveyard shift, 'cause nobody else wants to. Interns can count on very little sleep in most any profession, don't you think, Ty?"

Tyler comments, "That is true and you'll be asked to do the crummy jobs nobody else wants."

I inject, "Well, I'm not emptying garbage or taking out the trash."

Tyler states, "Now don't be surprised if they ask you to sharpen everyone's pencils. You could do that, right?"

I reports, "Hey, I come from lumbering country. I can handle sharpening a few pencils, but if I have to draw a line... Don't think I want to do obituaries."

Tyler adds, "Oh, of course. You are meant for bigger stuff. Stiffer competition."

Pops comments, "Oh, Tyler. Aren't you the punster? More pie anyone? Okay girls, dishwashing club is now in session. Here's a potato crate for Beefy to stand on."

We all chant, "Hemingway summer camp is now officially open."

Opening of the Hemingway summer cabin went along as smoothly as it could. My sisters giggled and tossed soap bubbles at each other, Pops unpacked a few steamer trunks and suitcases, while Uncle Tyler, Lewis Clarahan, and I stepped out back for a stogie and story swapping.

I remarked, "No, Lew, you don't inhale those smokes or you will lose your dinner. Trust me."

Tyler says, "Say, wasn't that little Leichester, The Baron running to the outhouse?"

I adds, "Yeah, he probably has to pee, but he has a box to stand on in the house of hemlock. Just hope his aim is exceptional."

Lew adds, "I hope his aim is impeccable, puff, puff. Baron and I bonded on the boat ride up here. Puff, he sure is a ball of energy, kept everyone antsy trying to keep him out of trouble."

I remarks, "Hold my cigar, Lewis, please. I'd better help him unbutton his pants. He still has trouble with buttons. Well, that's a big boy. You just drop your trousers. Good, all done. Okay, all tucked in nicely. Now, run back into the kitchen. They need you to untie their aprons."

Tyler cracks, "Ernest, now don't teach him new tricks."

I replies, "Aww, I just wanted him into the house so the girls can keep an eye on him. He's learning so many new things; however, his sisters don't let him pull pranks. Puff, puff."

Tyler comments, "This would be the time for a good governess, don't you think?"

I confess, "Yeah, one would think so, but Mother calls the shots for Ruth's opera career too."

Tyler cracks, "Oh... Yeah... How stupid of me... Of course. Silly me? Opera before family."

Lewis adds, "Right, the show must go on. Puff, Puff. I learned a lot on that boat ride up here."

I states, "Yeah, I bet you did, Lew. Bet you did. Well, while there is still...Puff, Puff... Plenty of daylight... Puff... Lew, can you help me pitch our tent?"

Lew says, "Certainly, Stein. Let's do this. I need to get horizontal."

I remarks, "Not going to have an accident now are you, Lew?"

Lewis responds, "No, just very worn out from the wild boat ride, the trains, and the high drama."

Says I, "Yeah, well, welcome to Windemere, magical land of enchantment, and beautiful Walloona."

Tyler asks, "Where do you get this Walloona phrase?"

I replied, "Oh, I'm being sarcastic. It's from a song Mother Grace wrote called, Beautiful Walloona. It never caught on. Now, you both know my Mother okay, so I'm in a good mood. Now, why spoil it… Thanks."

Tyler remarks, "If I know my brother, he will have hot tea on the porch facing the sunset."

I reply, "Thanks, Uncle. Main thing is, that we support my Dad, and thanks for your kind words."

Lew remarks, "Nice man, your Uncle."

Says I, "Yup, peach of a… Puff, Puff… Man. I owe him, all right, Lewis, could you run the end of this rope over to that birch tree, there? Now wrap her around a couple times and tie it off. There now, we drape my canvas over this taut rope and stake 'er down. I have folding cots in the shed for our sleeping arrangements."

Lewis adds, "That looks real comfy, Stein. Thanks."

I remarks, "You know me, Lew, right? So what's missing?"

Lew says, "A lamp, for reading books at night."

I adds, "Yup, you got that right, Pal… Now what else?"

Lew says, "Uh…hmm… Oh, I got it! Jug of hard cider."

States I, "Bingo, you know me too well. Here she is."

"Nice, Stein. Are we going to imbibe?"

"Sure, here take a pull. No backwash though. Got this beauty from my apple fanatic friend, Sir William Smith! The apple of Aunty Charles' eye. Hey! Please, I beg of you. No backwash, please. So? How is it?"

Lew answers, "Smooth. Real appley and like silk. My compliments to the brewmaster. This delicate palette of mine has never tasted better… Ever. Now, is this the same Bill I met over in Hortons?"

"One in the same. Literary gentleman. Got himself a new Buick from Daddy. Drink up, Lew."

"How sweet."

"Speaking of sweet, wait till you meets his girlfriend, Grace Quinlan. Oh, my God."

"Exciting."

"Exciting! You don't know the meaning."

"Okay. I am prepared to rename it."

"Add voluptuous, and a bazillion adjectives. The girl grew up rather righteously over the winter. Got herself some mean set of perfectly formed... Curvaceous... hormones, Lew, serious. We'll go fishing in Hortons creek one day, and I'll let you see her at Aunty Beth's."

"You got a lot of Aunts here, Stein?"

"Yeah, well it's only affectionate names. She prepares some of the world's finest dinners."

"Think we ate there a couple years ago."

"That's right. Back when you were a skinny punk of a kid. Still in knickers."

"And you were too. Then, somehow you had that growth spurt and then Mr. Atlas came to visit."

"Right, I remember now. Say, Lew, I brought my boxing gloves. Want to go a few rounds with Ye Olde Brute?"

"Sure, I owe you a shiner and a knockout, which I never forgot, but maybe tomorrow after I loosen up, okay?"

"Okay, the world needs a new bobble head doll, I figures. Ha ha Ha."

"Oh! Real funny coming from a true canvas back. Okay, enough smack. Tomorrow, Pal. You can give me two shiners. Deal?"

"Deal. So, Stein, shall we assemble the library? I'm itching to see your new collection."

"Got Kipling, Conrad, R. L. Stevenson, Mark Twain, you name it. Here, set up these potato crates. Stack them, that's it."

"Gee, Stein, this is going to be a swell summer."

"You bet it is, Lewis, and I want you to propose to my big sister, too."

"Yeah, well please put in a good word for me."

"But you'll be hopping the ivy train to Princeton."

"Okay, but still, there's a lot her brother can do in the way of encouragement, right?"

"So, you're really enamored of the old Ivory Tower."

"That be truth, Stein, my main man, and with your wordage, I know I could win her."

"So, you don't plan on meeting some college, raven haired beauty, swinging from the ivy?"

"Well, as of this minute, I wear my heart on my sleeve for your beauteous sister, Marcy."

"Being as we're Pals I have no other desire but to unite you with said sister. In fact, we could triple date with Bill Smith, who owns a classy horseless Buick Mobile."

"What could be more perfect? We could go to Bay View dances and parties, square dancing too. Yahoo! Stein, you just made my day."

That glorious day finally wore down to a dying ember. The kids made popcorn in the fireplace, sharing ghost stories. Lewis and I read by lantern until our eyelids got heavy, we turned off the lantern, and we both slipped off to dreamland.

As I lay on my bunk, reflecting on family dynamics, and my covey of friends still somewhat loyal to my thoughts, I couldn't help but dwell upon what they had picked up on the lifestyle of my Mother.

What would profit anyone to learn that she has been hitting on her precious student? Would it profit anyone if someone confronted the old girl on her irresponsible behavior? So far, Ursula and I are the only kids who know. We made a pact not to tell anyone, but I cannot condone Mother's activity any longer. Our relationship is strained enough already with her lack of understanding of me, and my desire to be a writer.

Mother has to be worried about the scandal this story would cause in Oak Park and it appears to be only a matter of time before she will be history in that fair city.

Mafia crooks live in River Forest so my guess is, she'll eventually head there with Ruth, meanwhile my thoughts drift to the reaction of my Pops. Dear old Father, dear sensitive hard working, Dr. Dad.

Religious fanatic that he is, he must be experiencing some kind of personal hell.

My future will soon have me escaping the high drama of it all, but as I leave for Kansas, I fear for my Pop's sanity. I also fear for Ursula's well being because Mother, with her well tooled radar, will eventually sense that her son knows of her intimate involvement with Ruth.

All in all, Mother Grace is a hard pill to swallow for anybody, Ruth or no Ruth, but with the appearance of this new viler-than-vile intimacy, the thought of being a Hemingway needs a powerful antidote, and from the looks of it, that antidote is me. As far as observers know, Father is developing a nervous condition, but I go one step further, to the cause of that nervousness, and it has to be the relationship between Mother Grace and young Ruth Arnold.

Mother Grace's Cottage at Longfields

Walloon Lake View from Longfields

Chapter 18. A New Dawn, with a New Perspective

Processing the aforementioned challenge, I am brought back to tent awareness. Lew's snoring indicates I needs be quiet, as I slip outside to examine the sunrise brightly peeking through the pines and birches surrounding Windmere.

After a quick trip to Hemlock Haven for a pee, being myself a creature of habit, I find myself standing in the misty Walloon morning, holding my trustee .22, loaded with three short rifle shells. After a few deep inhalations of the pine scented light breeze, a pair of noisy crows head their way to our fresh compost pile.

When the pair came within range, I taught them both... Pop, pop... No more crows.

"What the...?" Asked Lewis. "Aren't you up too early? The sun was just coming up!"

Says I, "Yup, best time to pop crows."

Lew remarks, "E Gad! Now I've seen everything."

I reply, "No big deal. Just about all summer long my morning ritual is... Shoot crows."

Lew asks, "Let me climb into my shoes. Okay, now that I've been rudely awakened, I suppose we cook crow stew?"

I retorts, "No... Can't eat these black critters. They eat carrion... Rotting flesh."

Lew adds, "Oh, well excuse me. Thought we always ate everything we pop."

I follows, "Crow is one exception, and skunk another. Woodchuck too, according to Harold Samson. He shot one, and Dad made us cook it. Tasted like yesterdays inner tube."

Lew continues, "And coyote?"

I reply, "Why? They keep down the rabbit population. If it weren't for animals of prey, we'd be overrun. They balances each other out."

Lew reacts, "Yeah, yeah okay, save me the lecture, let me visit Hemlock Haven. I gotta pee so bad." Upon Lew's return, he asks, "What's for breakfast?"

I state, "We hike for that. Over to the Joe Bacon Farm. He supplies us with bacon, ham, eggs, butter, and milk. So let's go, Lewis, and sometimes Mrs. B sends us her latest jams or jellies. When our garden ripens, we barter with our veggies. When Pop's fruit trees mature, we'll have fruit with which to barter."

Lew states, "Bartering... You like that sort of exchange?"

I adds, "Yup, saves on cash flow, and taxes, and record keeping. These farm folks up north have a lot of self-respect, good fresh eats, but nothing more than that in the name of cash. Very self-sufficient. They have to be, living so far away... In the boonies I say."

Lew queries, "When you Hemingways moved here, you brought art, music, doctoring... A whole lot of culture too, I'd say."

I answers, "Yeah... Guess you could say that. Mother gets together with Mrs. Bacon to draw and paint with oil paints on canvas."

Lew guesses, "That Bay View lecture circuit community brings a lot of culture up here too, I bet."

I replied, "You bet. All of us go there for the whole day. Marcy plays violin in the Symphony. Mother takes painting class. Ursa and Sunny take drama classes, too, and tennis, boating, archery, you name it, they've got it. Famous lecturers visit here too. William Jennings Bryan once spoke here. He delivered his famous, controversial "Cross of Gold" lecture which catapulted him into the Democratic Presidential nomination. As a part of the newsworthy Chautauqua series of lecture houses, Bay View has become the most prestigious arena in Northern Michigan."

Lew states, "What an ideal place for a kid to spend his summers."

I concur, "Yup, I just love it up here. This wilderness living gets me nice and centered and into nature. Having Native American kids as next-door neighbors is teaching me plenty about survival also. Well, here's the path which I takes over to the Joe Bacon Farm. Notice the bent tree branches? That's a signpost left by our Ottawa Pals. Pretty neat, huh, Lew?"

Lew asks, "How far does this trail take us?"

I responds, "All the way to Chi-town."

Lew, surprised, answers "No shit? Wow! And they just followed this series of crooked trunks. Now that is simply amazing."

I adds, "Hell yeah, but one has to have a pretty good pair of moccasins to do <u>that</u> trip. See that root sticking up?"

Lew states, "Uhuh. What about it, Stein?"

I confess, "As a kid, going for our families milk, I tripped on that damned root and run a sharp stick down my throat. Hurt like hell, but Dr. Dad cauterized it and it healed up. Still get bad throat infections as a carryover of that accident."

Lew asks, "Did you spill the milk?"

I recalls, "No, but I just spilled the beans, ha ha."

"Oh, aren't you the funny man today? Say, Stein, after breakfast, how about we get these black squirrels with our .22s?"

I adds, "Absolutely, Pal. Ain't nothing better eating then squirrel stew. Throw in some carrots, 'taters, and maybe a parsnip, or a nice rutabaga, an onion, and little salt and pepper… Smack, smack… Then you got yourself some good… Oh… And a side of hot buttermilk biscuits with a dab of butter melting. That's what I call heavenly. You know, my little sis, Sunny, is good at hunting squirrel. Takes a lot of stealth and teamwork."

Lew asks, "So, Stein, what did you do with this morning's crows?"

I reply, "Buried them black rascals under the birches. Fertilizer, you know. That's about all they're good for."

Lew queries, "Why do you hate crows so much? Stein?"

I reply, "My Pops and I both hate crows equally, probably because they make such a racket every morning and it disturbs our sleep. Neither of us sleeps very well anyway, also, shooting crow is good practice for pheasant and partridge season. My Dad is the best wing shot. They also raid songbird nests and eat other nestling eggs."

Lew states, "Is that Joe Bacon's farm up ahead?"

I answers, "That it is, and good thing we brought rucksacks because these people will load them up with some awesome goodies.

Lew states, "Look at all those cows!"

I adds, "Well said, city lad. Can you tell me what breed of cattle Bacon's have?"

Lew guesses, "Indeed, my good tutor, sir. My guess is that all these girls are none other than Holsteins."

I answers, "You are correct, and why the Holstein variety?"

Lew guesses, "Well if I had eighty some tits to pull twice a day, I'd need lots of milk for my efforts, so I'd say because of volume."

I replies, "Nailed it! Holsteins provide Farmer Bacon with an enormous amount, which they pour into large milk cans. We get 2 gallons every other day. Here you go, Lew. Will you need a yoke for the shoulder carry?"

Lew replies, "Okay, hang those milk cans."

I says, "Now, here comes that busy man. Greetings, Mr. Bacon. We are finally up here for the summer."

Joe salutes, "Morning, Ernest. And this must be Lewis? Welcome back. Could you use some smoked bacon, ham, eggs, and butter? Just slide them in that rucksack. Here comes the Mrs."

Mrs. Bacon exclaims, "Welcome back, Ernest. Here, take some currant jelly and canned apricots. I know how you like them. Here's a couple loaves of fresh bread, too. I guess Mother Grace will be teaching oil painting again, right?"

I answer, "Oh, you bet, if we ever get unpacked."

Mrs. Bacon adds, "Brought too much stuff again, huh?"

Says I, "Oh, you know Mother. She never does travel light. I got all your goodies in these rucksacks. Sure do thank you for feeding us so well. You remember Lewis Clarahan?"

Mrs. Bacon answers, "I sure do. You boys staying out of trouble?"

Lewis replies, "Oh, yes ma'am. But we do plan on helping you bring in hay again this year. And I want to learn how to milk cows."

Says Mrs. Bacon, "Oh, don't be silly. Our cows are all milked before you boys wake up. Anyway, why would a city boy want to be doing a thing like that?"

I states, "Lew is just making small talk, but we always enjoy putting up your hay. Did you plant a big garden again? Well, we got a ways to haul all this, so thanks again. Can the good doctor stop in and give you your yearly physicals?"

Mrs. Bacon replies, "Oh, absolutely, and if you need seeds for your garden, we have extra."

I says, "Thank you kindly, Mrs. Bacon. We gotta be shoving off now."

Mrs. Bacon adds, "God bless you, boys."

Chapter 19. That Magical Hamlet, Hortons Bay

Horton's Bay, Mich. P.O. Boyne City, Mich.

Keeping a journal in these activities up in Northern Michigan seems like the job of a good newspaper man, like me. For someday, someone will read it and love it. Being this is such a small five-building burg, one would think that if every citizen kept busy and minded their own business there would be very little to write about. But human nature being what it is, lying within every person that lives here is a whole exciting storybook going on in life and the Hamlet of Hortons Bay is far from dull, since few citizens can mind their own business.

Yours truly, being wide-eyed and ever alert to things going on around him continues a daily vigil practicing writing journals of the highest order on ordinary life in an extraordinary microcosm called Hortons Bay.

Let us focus on the name of this community, Hortons Bay.

Legend has it that in the 1850s Hortons and his wife traveled north from Toledo, Ohio headed for Canada and settled here instead because of the outrageous beauty of the region. Fish were abundant in the Lake, then called Bear Lake, as well as in the spring fed stream which he called Hortons Creek. Game was also abundant.

Native Americans were a friendly tribe from Canada called the Ottawa, which means *'The Astonishing'*. The original tribes ran off to Canada to escape the white's wrath due to the Fort Michilimackinac massacre. Folks make the mistake of calling this place Horton or Horton's, but the couple who first settled here was the Hortons, spelled with an "s."

Virgin pine were thick, so tree clearing at first produced some nice log cabins for the Hortons family and also a few brave settlers who bought land from Mr. Hortons.

Farming crops and apple orchards as well as other fruit trees were soon planted. Our very productive sawmill made its presence. A blacksmith shop, a general store, and a small resort called Pinehurst, with a few cabins. The kitchen was next to spring up.

Developing this area was not easy since all work was done by backbreaking labor using horses and oxen and mules. My Uncle George and Aunt Grace were the first of the Hemingway's to make it up north here. They bought land called The Point which juts out into Lake Charlevoix, as Pine Lake soon was called. Must've been a lot of Frenchmen around then, I figure to come up with that name.

Uncle George tried his hand at growing trees, plants, shrubs, and flowers in a nursery which he started in Ironton. Soon all the Hemingway brothers (Aside from Willoughby, a missionary doctor in China), Tyler and my Pops, Clarence, the doctor, found refuge up here away from the summer city heat of Chicago. When the 20th century arrived, I was only one, yet I had my very first glimpse of this wonderland. My parents booked a few weeks at the Walloon Hotel.

When money was tight, we stayed with Uncle George and Aunt Grace, but eventually Mr. Morford agreed to build us a cozy little cabin at waters edge right off of Resort Pike. As a builder, Mr. M. was an expert, logging all the nearby hardwoods, hauling them out with his excellent team of horses and shaping them by hand with crosscut saw and broad ax.

Morford bought land around our place and continues to provide families with great homes along Morford Road.

Resort Pike remains the main access for the summer people who are buying up the waterfront land for summer cabins. Playing with the white newcomers children was okay, but for some reason the Indian Redskin children were my friends of choice. At an early age, an Indian kid learned to survive out in the wild forests and I wanted to learn all I could about subsisting off the land outside.

Aunt Arabella sewed me an Indian outfit with fringes along the edge of the legs and sleeves. That suit was my main covering all summer long. Wearing that fringed outfit made me feel like I was no longer a white kid with British ancestry, for while I wore that fringed outfit I felt like an integral, important member of the tribe as they taught me to fish and hunt and gather wild edible plants for our dinner table. My beaded leather belt held a tomahawk, a knife, and a pouch to store things like frogs and snakes.

My first crush was on a young Redskin girl called Prudy Boulton. She was the sister of my best Indian pal called Billy Tabeshaw, his father, big Nick Boulton, and mother Anna Tabeshaw did odd jobs for us.

Making money for the tribe was a tough job. The Redskin found they could sell bark from the hemlock tree. Hemlock bark was needed across the Lake where a leather tanning business was started in Boyne City.

Hand-operated spoke-shaves, a two handled sharp draw blade, peels the bark which is piled and stacked into a hay wagon.

When the wagon can't hold anymore, it is dumped into a flat car, perched on a narrow gauge railroad that rolls downhill to a long dock where a barge is waiting to float it over to Boyne City tannery.

Fascinated area kids always wanted to be on time the day all the hemlock bark got hauled away. The process required hard work but it is one of the number one ways the tribe takes in money.

Handmade basket selling is another form of income. This is done by the tribal mothers who visit wealthy tourists while they sit on the rocking chairs of hotel porches.

So here I am trying to paint a picture of my favorite little town Hortons Bay, and I would be remiss if I didn't mention Vollie Fox of Red Fox Inn. Vollie saw all the tourists filling Auntie Beth's Pinehurst Inn, therefore, he added more bedrooms to his house across the street and even started cooking chicken dinners. He survives on housing the overflow in town, but can't compete with Beth's chicken dinners.

Our general store supplies everything else you may need while in town. They sell a wide variety of dry goods, hardware, yard goods, dairy items, candy, soda pop, coffee and tea, (and before prohibition, which started early in Michigan, 1916, they sold beer and wine) and now that a few horseless carriages make it up here, the general store will be selling oil and gasoline from big drums outside.

As small as it is, Hortons Bay has just about got it all-anything a guy could want. We even have a blacksmith shop and a livery stable where you could rent a horse and carriage or stable your horse.

Jim Dilworth has recently expanded his blacksmith business to also include harnesses making and wagon repair.

Recently, a group of Methodists have decided that we need a bigger church, so work has begun laying the foundation for expansion of our little chapel along with the parsonage to house the minister and his family. Maybe one day I'll be married there. You never know.

Once Fourth of July rolls around this little Burg goes all out. We have a parade with floats. Civil War veterans polish their brass and try their darndest to squeeze into their faded blues in order to march in step. We hear speeches and then dig into some of the best eats afterward. At dark somebody always shoots up rockets and lights firecrackers. Horses and carriages get decorated. Sometimes we have horse races. Kids decorate their dogs and cats and haul them around on their bicycles. We have the usual foot races, tugs of wars, pie eating contests, boat races, and colorful ribbons are given out for dozens of contests. Pies, cakes, and pickles are judged with always the same people winning every year. Barbershop quartets stroll the streets, amazing us with their close harmonies and male companionship.

Men have to be in contests, arm wrestling, and bareknuckle boxing, logrolling and log tossing. Orations and poetry reading go on all day. Joe Bacon always roasts a steer or ox on a spit where everyone takes a turn with cranking the critter over the hot coals. This feature attracts people from miles around when the wind is right.

This July, our village parade will have a shortage of young men for every able bodied fella is off fighting in Europe.

During poetry reading I usually recite "The Charge of the Light Brigade" and Longfellow's "Under the Spreading Chestnut…" Afterwards I haul Jim Dilworth on stage to get applause. He comes up and flexes his muscles. Then everyone whistles and hoots until he announces Beth will have a chicken wing eating contest on the back porch of Pinehurst.

It might surprise a few people but one year my little sister, Sunny, won that contest eating 22 wings. We followed her around with a bucket, expecting her to eventually toss those 22 wings, but the kid never did, plus to our surprise later in the day she ate a big dinner. Kids! Go figure? My guess is she's going through a growth spurt.

Chicken wings are not eaten by high class people. The neck and giblets are not usually relished by the upper crust either. My family eats everything, so I guess we are not to be considered upper-middle-class or just one big hungry bunch.

Every July when my birthday rolls along, I put in my order for a duck dinner. My Pops raises domestic ducks in a pen around the back of our cabin. He fixes half a dozen and invites all the relatives. That Pops really likes his duck and since they are the domestic kind they can be enjoyed all year long.

My love for Hortons Bay includes a lot of things but mainly comes down to the love that we share for each other. It needs to be mentioned that this mutual affection which we have for each other has created a bubble of protection in the wilderness, a veritable refuge for creativity in all areas of life. With me of course is the fishing. Jim shows his love through blacksmithing, his wife Beth shows her love through her cooking. Vollie Fox shows his love with his hospitality at Red Fox Inn, and everyone else shows their love by going out of their way to make residents and visitors feel at home here. Anyone in search of the good life would eventually have to end their search once they pull into intoxicating Hortons Bay. Stop... go no further.

Wander over to Auntie Charles' Apple Orchard for the true taste of apples like they were meant to taste. No doubt her nephew Bill might be found up a tree pruning or plucking, just doing his loving of good healthy Michigan heirloom apples. His perky sister, Kate, will probably be hanging laundry on the line to dry. We might say she is the apple of my eye.

The best butter, milk, eggs, chickens, smoked bacon, and ham can be found at the Joe Bacon Dairy Farm. Other farms worthy of note are Kotesky's, Johnychecks's, and Martinchek's.

Can you guess which farmer came from Canada and which came from Bohemia?

All these thoughts run through the fertile mind of a good newspapermen such as myself. Someone other than me would be missing the finer nuances of observation with which a good reporter is born.

Thoughts like these I maintain out of necessity, arrogant as they may sound, for if my mind were to wander and start worrying about all my pals headed over to fight the hordes of Huns in Kaiser's evil army, I would slip into a tearjerker stage of sentimentalism from which I may never recover.

The last words I shouted to the passenger cars full of their innocent round pie-faces as the troop train dreadfully rolled out of LaSalle Station were, "You all know I would love to go with you boys to pop some Krauts, but I must stay here to write, for the pen is mightier than the sword."

Part of me still wants to charge a machine gun nest full of Krauts in order to toss in a well-placed grenade. Part of me wants to see a flaming Kraut stagger out, all colored red and blackened, crimson, now silence making it safe for my pals to move on to capture more Kraut strongholds.

But since my bad eyes keep me out of the regular service, I often pray that God will find me another agency in which to serve my country; meanwhile, I take pencil in hand and mumble the mantra that pens are mightier.

But through the simple act of writing down my troubles, I have discovered a little relief. Using my friends as sounding boards often works if they are willing to sit through my extended rants. Sometimes they go on into the wee hours. Bill, Kate, and YK have heard enough to fill volumes, so if I run out of paper and my friends ready ears, then I turn to boxing. Striking a punching bag provides temporary relief somehow, and if a sparring partner or punching bag is not available, I punch the air. It's called shadowboxing.

Boxing at shadows has been occupying much of my time lately, for I have much rage to neutralize and if I ever connect with one he'll be out for the count. During the school year back in Oak Park, Illinois, often my pals will come over to my place and we put on the big gloves to go a few rounds right in mother's big music room. It is indescribable, the feeling I get when my glove cleanly connects with the guys face. Sounds like I enjoy inflicting pain on people, but there's a part of me that actually is quite sensitive and gentle, so I guess I'm not a true sadist, am I? Women will never receive my punches, for I have had it ingrained in me that a guy never strikes a woman for no reason, absolutely not. Having witnessed it myself, I know some women who push their luck on this issue. In my neighborhood, folks are specially aghast to hear of the lad who struck a girl. It's just one of those unwritten rules of our society, especially in conservative Oak Park. The guilty lad would be ostracized and forever thought of as one strange cookie. When teams are chosen the kid who hit the girl will always be chosen last, another unwritten law-kinda like shunning that is practiced among the Amish sects.

So that brings us back to the tranquility which I experience every summer up in Michigan. Strolling through the forests makes me vulnerable, so that I feel connected with the universe.

Feeling cool pine needles under my bare feet, moist spruce, scented breezes gently drifting by my blissful face, humbled by giant over towering white pines would send along a patchwork of light and shadow patterns on the forest floor, I pass through my virgin Michigan trail and feel centered.

Jaybird's sharp call announces my coming as black squirrel chases his mate around the massive trunk of majestic oaks, as if they ignore my entrance. Chipmunks scurry, quickly seeking cover under overhanging ferns. Mr. Robin, who I think should be named the Michigan state bird, cocks his head and listens to hear earthworms tunneling just beneath his bony feet. As I continue my measured steps along the multi pattern floor, numerous, unnoticed beady eyes follow my footfalls, but due to their expert coloring they blend totally into their natural surroundings.

Dropping to a yoga formation, I use a tall pine as a backrest and my first inclination is to inhale all the intoxicating smells of spruce, balsam, and Cedar.

Challenging me continually is probably the issue facing every writer and that is to convey exactly what I see in a way that captures my true feelings while expressing it like no other writer has done before. Daily, this challenge crosses my mind and forces me to familiarize myself with all the greats of literature. Often I parodied his work just to prove to myself that I can meet their style, but even if I do succeed the winning efforts are shallow, since I then must go beyond to create a style which is uniquely my own, all the while being mindful of my readers and their developing state of mind, which is constantly reacting to the internal impact of each well chosen word.

What do I want to say, and can I say it so it will impact the reader, so he will think he is having my same experience?

My desire is to have the reader become so immersed in my images, subject matter, feelings of atmosphere, and internal conditions, that he gets hooked to want to know the content of the next page and eventually the next book.

I will know that I have arrived when my choice of words will put the reader on the edge of his seat.

Techniques I plan to use for doing this will include description of atmospheric conditions, thereby letting readers learn of the weather, the wind, the temperature, the sky, the sun, if rain or snow and sleet are expected. Building a world around the reader creates a framework on which to place each character as he enters the scene and slips himself into the plot. In a sense, if written properly the reader will wear the plot. Readers get further led into the story by skillful use of dialogue which is crisp, logical, thought provoking, and utilizes colloquial language to make the reader settle into the feeling that he is personally partaking in the unfolding of their drama.

Entertaining thoughts such as these continue throughout the hours when I meditate on the direction my life and career are headed. Mother says I need to be more responsible yet she has no idea my responsibilities lay with the readers of the world. A writer like me belongs to the world. Mother's got her music, so God bless her, she has absolutely no way to come close to understanding of what a good writer has on his mind. It really bothers met that my Mother never takes the time to understand me or my Pops. She's in her own little world as I sees it.

Grace Hemingway with 6 week old Ernest, sitting on the site of their not-yet-built cabin at Windemere.

Chapter 20. An Intimate Glimpse into the Hemingway Family

    The rhythm of the raindrops did finally lull me to sleep. An all night rain will give the garden a good soak... and also keep Mother home to relate to her kids, husband, and brother-in-law, Tyler. Pops slept on the floor, but was nicely cushioned by a soft feather-bed left by Grandmother Hemingway, so he slept better than all of us, even though he sacrificed his bed to his brother, Tyler.

At dawn, good old Pops was up before all of us frying bacon and whipping up a batch of his famous buckwheat pancakes. As I opened the kitchen door, the intoxicating aroma of Joe Bacon's smoked bacon frying on the stove intoxicated my smeller. It was heavenly.

    Pops greets, "Morning Ernest and Lewis. Did you boys sleep well? I pumped a basin full of water, so wash up. Breakfast will soon be served."

Two-year-old Leichester came bounding into the kitchen along with Carol, Sunny, and Ursula, who held up his arms like a circus trapeze artist.

Leichester says, "Look Daddy, me in circus."

Clarence says, "Well, you little monkey, go get washed up and hop into your high chair. Breakfast is almost ready. Hi girls. Sleep well?"

Sunny answers, "Yes, Daddy. The raindrops put me to sleep last night, they did."

Ursa adds, "That's funny, Sunny. How's come you aren't wet?"

Marcy enters, "Yes, Sunny, was it a dry rain?"

Sunny adds, "Oh, real funny. You know what I meant. Daddy, they are picking on me again."

Clarence says, "Now girls, try to be civil with each other."

Carol asks, "Like the Civil War, Daddy?"

Marcy says, "There was nothing civil about that, Dad."

Daddy says, "Okay then, try to be nice, okay?"

Ursula says, "Nice big bow in your hair, Sunny. Did you need a crane to get that up there?"

Clarence states, "Now Ursa, that was uncalled for."

Ursa says, "Well, I used the word nice."

Clarence says, "Yes, you did at that, but Sunny likes big bows."

Ruth says, "Mother Grace is ready to take sustenance."

Clarence states, "Tray is ready. It's over there. Help yourself... Ahem... Sigh..."

Tyler enters, "Morning Hemingway's. I trust you all slept well."

All in a chorus the kids answer, "Morning, Uncle Tylie."

I ask, "Okay Leichester, are you ready to fly, fly, up in the air and down on your throne?"

Leichester says, "Oh, Ernie you so strong big brudder. Me king now. Me on him thrown."

I add, "But Daddy is king. What if we dub you... Baron?"

Leichester answers, "Okay- me Baron. What does a Baron do?"

I adds, "Absolutely nothing. That's why you are are Baron. Sound good?"

Leichester says, "Yeah! Me Baron."

Clarence says, "Okay, places everyone. Tyler, prayer please."

Tyler says, "Please bless us thy gifts from your bountiful goodness. Through Jesus, amen."

Pops adds, "Now, pass to the left. Bacon fried to perfection, fluffy pancakes-, eggs scrambled perfectly.

Tyler adds, "Syrup... Mapled to perfection."

Carol states, "Oh, that was sweet, Uncle. Got any more like that? Sweet."

Tyler says, "Not eggs-actly."

Ursa answers, "Oh, that one hurt, Uncle."

Sunny answers, "But the yolks on you, Ursa."

Ursa says, "Eww. Help Daddy. Sunny made me a funny."

Lewis asks, "Could a chicken lay a square egg?"

Clarence answers, "I suppose, if she got cornered too many times. Eight times to be exact."

Lewis says, "But that would be a stretch."

Marcy answers, "Ha, ha, haaaa... too funny, Lewis."

Lewis says, "Could Mr. Sanford top that?"

Sanford was a young man who Marcy had met at Bay View Sunday school classes. She later married him.

Marcy says, "Oh... um... sure. Many times over."

Sunny interrupts, "But this rain will mean the fish will be biting. Who wants to go out today and wash some worms?"

Leichester states, "Me, me want to fish... too."

I state, "Barons don't fish. Remember, they don't do anything, Baron."

Leichester says, "Me don't want to be Baron anymore."

Clarence says, "Good idea. I have a taste for fish. My brother always has, right, Tyler?"

Tyler says, "You got that right Clarence. There should be plenty of worms all around."

Sunny states, "Yup, worms could drown during a rain if'n they didn't crawl to the surface."

Carol asks, "So why are they called night crawlers?"

Lew says, "I know. 'Cause the sun hurts their eyes."

Sunny says, "Worms don't have eyes, silly."

Lew says, "Only when they vote. Then the ayes have it."

I add, "Oh, that one hurt my brain."

Marcy asks, "What brain?"

Ursa adds, "The one he uses for a hat rack."

Clarence says, "Okay children, this is getting out of hand. Raise of hands for seconds, and as if Maple syrup wasn't enough, I broke open a jar of Grandmother Hemingway's orange marmalade."

Tyler remarks, "You saved the best until last. Oh boy, Clare."

Clarence says, "Yes, and she is still going strong. Got a letter just yesterday, children. She wants us all to enjoy ourselves on beautiful Walloona, hugs all around, and a special tweak on the cheek for big boy Leichester. Arabella's helping her with her smaller house."

Leichester asks, "She give me a tweak on me cheek?"

Clarence says, "Yes, and everybody... let's give big boy tweak on him cheek. Oh, and Ernest your grandmother wishes you success in Kansas City, and hopes you don't get tired of Aunt Arabella's cooking. And girls, she wants you to catch lots of fish up North this summer."

I suggest, "Thanks, Father for that news from Oak Park. Now back to the cookstove. Here, let me give you a hand with that. Show me how you mix that delicious buckwheat batter. Lew, come learn how the master does it."

Tyler interjects, "Hey kids, did you know that buckwheat really isn't a member of the wheat family? Surprise... it's related to rhubarb. Is that strange?"

Marcy adds, "Now Uncle Tyler, don't try to sour us on our buckwheat cakes.

Sunny says, "Oh that pun left a sour taste in my brain."

Carol says, "What brain?"

Marcy says, "Now, Sunny is right. I learned that we eat with our brain. Pavlov's dogs eventually began to salivate at the ringing of the bell."

Ursula says, "Okay, let's try it. Everybody think... Bacon... Oh my... I'm drooling already."

Sunny says, "Me too."

Leichester answers, "Too me. Ha ha ha. Me two gonna be three ha ha ha."

Carol says, "For a Baron, you really crack me up."

Tyler calls into the kitchen, "Clarence, guess you'd better fry up some more bacon. My brain needs it."

Sunny adds, "Yeah my brain needs it too."

Ursa says, "Yeah, but my brain could eat your brain."

Sunny says, "Oh yeah?"

Ursula answers, "Yeah... Burp!"

Marcy says, "That was quick."

Ursa adds, "Not much there. Ha ha ha. I ate Sunny's brain and I'm still hungry... burp."

Leichester asks, "Eat my brain, sister?"

Ursa says, "Oh, no, then your bonnet will fall off."

Leichester says, "Me don't wear bonnets. Me a boy."

Tyler interrupts, "Okay, okay, that's enough. Here's a riddle for you. What's black and white and read all over?"

Carol says, "Oh… I know this one… Think, think."

Marcy answers, "It's a trick question. Don't trouble your brain."

Sunny asks, "What brain? She just ate mine."

Tyler asks, "Give up?"

Marcy answers, "Yup our brains are all busy eating. Ha ha ha."

Tyler answers, "A newspaper."

Sunny says, "Oh, right. Red and read, to read. Shucks. My brain was still chewing on bacon."

Marcy says, "I got one. What train eats gum?"

Ursa answers, "That's easy, Chattanooga Choo Choo. Ha ha."

Tyler says, "Oh, you children are too smart for me."

Tyler states, "*As poetic as can be. Tyler's soliloquy.*

Who has more fun than us Hemingway's?

Who can chew the way we do?

Who can play with words as we have on this happy day?

Soon life will send us on our separate ways, yet we will cherish these fun memories. Yes, in memory thus fondly tucked away in a place called Windemere.

When we are gone what gaiety will echo here off these walls? Whose voice and when will often sit on hand hewn oaken beams as these save junior generations be in strong branches of our blessed family tree.

So cherish we this moment of the eternal now.

And pledged to years that follow next our progeny do show, what love and cheer our garden plow for others for to hear.

For love goes on and never ends

then sow your garden dear.

Lift nectar of the apricot

In solemn voice awhile

PIP PIP to the Hemingway's

Click glasses to us now."

Everyone says, "PIP PIP-to us Hemingway's."

I add, "Gosh Uncle Ty... That was simply beautiful."

Clarence says, "Hear, hear! To Tyler... fairest of the fair. PIP PIP to Tyler. He's our man. Fairest of our clan. Seconds now on buckwheat cakes and on bacon... Into the Grandmother's orange marmalade. Dig in... all of you. She loves us all."

Marcy says, "PIP PIP to Grandmother Hemingway, I can taste the love."

Tyler says, "I drink to that. Apricot juice all around."

Festivities of this grand summer morning eventually die down. The girls joyfully wash dishes. Ruth rowed Mother across the lake to her music lesson, and we men dug worms and cast off our boat for a morning fish.

Marcy and the rest cast off later and joined us at the edge of the reeds. A light breeze still drifted down from the north, but skies were clear and temperatures were still cool as the sun began to climb up into the Michigan sky. It gave the promise of a perfect, yet cool day.

Clarence says, "Fish like these cool days right after a good rain."

Tyler adds, "Indeed... must be because krill or shrimp that get circulated and dropped during a downpour. They snap at anything."

I spout, "Hey Unc... you've got a nibble. Look!"

Clarence says, "Let him take a good bite first, then set the hook."

Tyler says, "Ernest, get the landing net ready. I've got a feisty bass and he's trying to shake that hook. Clarence, could you row away from the reeds, please?"

Clarence says, "Oh yes, indeed, of course. He might wrap around a reed and pull free. Steady as she goes, men. He wants to surface. Look at the size of him... a veritable monster!"

I states, "He's a good 5 pounds if'n he's an ounce, right Father?"

Clarence says, "At least five, if not more, Son. He's full of scrap isn't he, Tyler? Easy now, brother."

Tyler states, "Hope this bamboo pole holds up. Steady now, Mister."

Lewis adds, "Wow.. it's a wide mouth, uh... I mean a large mouth."

I remark, "Tyler, your pole might snap. Could you pull him in by hand? Got gloves?"

Tyler says, "Got to try. This pole is gonna crack if I don't do something... Steady now... Steady."

Clarence says, "Anybody got gloves? Gloves anybody?"

I comment, "Nope, gotta haul him in by your bare hands Uncle."

Tyler says, dropping his pole, "I'm going after this lunker by hand. Ernest, get that net ready, young man. He's cutting into my hands."

Clarence says, "Tyler. Don't give up."

Tyler answers, "He...he's full of fight. God, help me! I want him."

Lew says, "Stay with him, Uncle. You've almost got him. Get that net under him, Stein, all of him!"

I remark, "Oh, Uncle, he's a beaut! But just look at your palms."

Tyler says, "Wow... never did that before. Look at him fight for his life...sliced up my palms pretty good."

I remark, "I'll stick him with my knife."

Tyler answers, "Good idea. He's still flopping. Stick'm again! Get his brain."

I comment, "This must be a catfish, men."

Tyler asks, "Why?"

I says, "He's got nine lives."

Tyler says, "Ha ha ha... so funny. Oh, oh, oh, my poor hands...all sliced up by that line."

I add, "Hey, I've stabbed him in the brain and he's still flopping. Look, my knife is in his friggin' brain and still he flops around. Go figure, men."

Clarence says, "My guess is he'll be flopping as we fry him in the frying pan. Ty, in my tackle box is a bottle of iodine. Dab your hands."

I comment, "Hey, this bass might be a world record. Shoot, he's way over 10 pounds. Look, Pop's!"

During that magical day we reeled in our limit of pan fish but there was something about watching my Uncle Tyler valiantly fighting that whopper of a bass, that stuck in my mind. I was fascinated as he grabbed that taught fishing line with bare hands, determined to land that lunker even at the cost of his pretty pink palms. This really intrigued me and I locked it in my memory to be used at a later time.

His stern, square jawed resolve registered deeply in my young sight. Thinking to myself, I begin to plan a gut wrenching, blockbuster novel about his exploits.

Being more than an ordinary fish story, my Uncle's expressions and attitude will surely come into play. I'd like to capture in words something about his risk taking and courage, and the giving of all that he had within him, to the point of complete exhaustion. A fishing story like that would be fascinating to read.

He talked to the fish, and I like that. I like how he mentioned how good his fishy flesh would taste on the family supper table sort of talked that big fish into surrendering up his life as a fish to become a part of our human bodies and a part of our nice family. That Uncle Tyler was a fabulous inspiration for me today. Not only does he find me an exciting newspaper job with the best paper in America, but the guy triggers ideas in my head for a knockout novel.

Sure looking forward to living with him and Aunt Arabella in Kansas City. Hope his sliced up palms heal up fast so we can venture out again on our lake for more exciting adventures. I am beginning to see Uncle as an angel sent by God to minister to my stressed out father and take me under his wing as I starts out on my new writing career. When the girls bring in their limit of fish together with ours we'll have , heap big Hemingway fish fry.

One would think that all we do is fish up in Michigan. Even though that takes up a good godly portion of our days, we also attend dances whenever we can. This summer is no exception as I look forward to our attendance at Bay View dances.

Carol and Sunny are still too young, and too much like tomboys to enter into enjoyment of the opposite sex. If a boy absently stepped on their toes, I do believe they'd haul off and deck the poor lad, but, Ursula (Ursa, or Littless as she is called) has developed a certain mystical charm her own feminine mystique... a grace and poise about her that has captivated certain vulnerable yet observant young lads of her age. Curious how hormones work?

Michigan sun has tanned Ursa's olive skin to the darkness of the proverbial coffee bean, and when she flashes her dark brown Hemingway eyes coupled with our patented dimples and white toothed smile, there isn't a brother more proud to whirl her around the dance floor than I.

Of course, Ursa, hates to share me with Kate, but to keep peace I occasionally let other boys give her a twirl. I must say... now that Marcy has jilted him, my good pal Lewis Clarahan also finds Ursa attractive. Hey, who can blame him? He came up here from Chicago to see Marcy, and she dropped him from her Ivory Tower. My nickname for her, or I.T.or just plain Ivory, due to her arrogance and lack of compassion for the commoners around her.

Winds are now shifting out of the south, so tomorrow will be much warmer. It might be a good day to row over to Longfields and weed the garden.

Rains will cause weeds to shoot up overnight. After that, I will disturb Mother and Ruth just to say I forgive them. That should make her hit high C on the musical scale.

After that I'll walk down to Pinehurst in Hortons Bay, pick up windfall limbs, rake the grass, chop cookstove wood, and invite Kate to a chicken dinner at Aunty Beth Dilworth's place, that venerable lodge of culinary luxury, and if Sir William, her estranged brother, is pruning apple trees, he shall be my guest also. Life could not get much sweeter, I must say. I love this place, my summer place. How could life be any better someplace else?

One could travel the world over to England or France, Antarctica or Africa perchance. One could search Europe, Italy, Asia, or India. China or Spain, and then back again only to find it's all right here, in homey, humble, little Hortons Bay.

This place is enchanted like magical Brigadoon, like London at midnight, or Paris at noon, but one town outshines them in every which way for I've made my mind up, it's my Hortons Bay.

Down town Hortons Bay, Michigan

Chapter 21. Ernie's Stress Relief Plan

Marcy and Ernie, High School Graduation Oak Park/River Forest , Illinois, 1917

Yesterday, Uncle Tyler hopped a train for Chicago to visit Grandmother Hemingway for a while to see if her life could be made more comfortable, and then he plans to railroad out to Kansas with Aunt Arabella, who spent some time in Oak Park helping grandma move into a smaller house.

Mother Grace had her eye on the departed Anson Hemingway mansion, but Dad's brothers aced her out of that, since Grandmother still owns it.

In October, Pops wants to take me to the train station when I return from Michigan. He says he wants to give me a good send off to Kansas, so I'll save money on train fare. Sometimes I consider myself the closest friend he has, but he's afraid to get *too* close, for it might ruin his dignity if we were to be Pals.

Wish he would use me to unload his burdens, but he shoulders them all, every little issue that arises in our big family.

Marcy wants to attend Oberlin, but she'll need a job to pay her way. Often I wish we hadn't been so darned competitive in school, especially with the high school newspaper. It's my fault. I know it is. Marcy and I could be a lot closer.

Trying to ace people out in order to be tops of everything is my undoing, but this summer I promise to work through that malady. Maybe with Marcy's help we can rescue our relationship to some degree.

People don't see it, but I've got a lot of insecurities. Having a Mother who has no understanding of me probably has a lot to do with it.

Having a mother who has no support for my chosen career of writing makes it doubly difficult to succeed. Writers have so many things to keep in mind, so many thoughts to juggle, so many words to consider, and so many words and phrases to cut out which probably is the hardest part.

Cutting a passage down to its simplest form and still getting the point across has become my main issue. My teachers in high school did their best, and I admire them for their terrific efforts. They helped me mold myself, and ready me for this reporter's job, and I'm sure Uncle Tyler's Pal at The Star will take me under his wing, but I'm still developing my special style, my unique imprint, my voice which will make me stand out from all other writers. Hopefully, the Star style will give me an adventure because it will make me impact the printed page in such a way that readers won't want to put my stories down. It'll be fresh, surprising, captivating, as well as rewarding.

I am looking forward to that first day in Kansas, but I'm a little scared at the same time for its all new to me. The city is new, being on my own is new, meeting news deadlines is new, the Star's style is new to me, and the faces will all be new.

Except for Aunt Arabelle and Uncle Tyler's face's, I will have the challenge of meeting new friends and hopefully establishing at least one good friend. Maybe even discovering me a new Pal, a good pal like Lew and Bill and Harold.

As far as girls go, I might not have the time for girls at first. A girl tends to be a distraction for me. Settling into a whole new life will keep me too busy at first, plus living with Aunt and Uncle would be awkward for dating. I'm thinking I'll lay low until I have the privacy of my own apartment. Yeah, that's the ticket, get me my own apartment and then start the dating scene.

Being that is a long way off, I shouldn't spoil it by thinking too much about it. My brain hurts when I think too much. Coach thinks I could have a concussion from too much football, plus I promised myself never to let my future get in the way of the present, but I have no clue as to how to stop guilty feelings about my past, so I write about it in hopes of getting clear of bad memories. Most of the time my journal writing helps, but not always.

My Pals Lew, and Harold, and Bill let me talk through my personal issues, and that's what I will miss when I'm separated from them. Pals let you talk about any darn thing. My buried bad memories concern me, because I forget what it was I buried only to find later, that certain moments will trigger them, and then I slips into a black ass funk ...totally out of control, and it's unexplainable and troubling to my spirits.

Pals like Lew are far and few. For after our discussion I felt so much better. Pops lets me slip into his office library to read the latest medical findings and lately I've been fascinated by the work of Sigmund Freud. Study of the mind is most fascinating and I plan to master my mind, which is why I stay away from my past and refuse to conjecture about the future, yet guilt still perplexes me. I often bully friends if they get too close to touching insecurities of mine, which is merely a defense mechanism and nothing actually meant to be malicious.

Folks are puzzled by my shadowboxing. Out of force of habit I will just start punching the air. Why? Just another defense mechanism-a way of intimidating others I guess. It's an unconscious habit of mine-probably meant to dominate others or attract attention. It keeps people off balance. I might be taunting them. I like to keep them guessing-gets them worried. Gets them thinking that I'm crazy and might do anything. I never really analyzed it, but it's my way of funnin' with people, and maybe I'll grow up someday and get tired of it.

Boxing was intriguing to me in high school. I traveled to downtown Chicago to train with the best pugilists of the day thinking that one day I could be a contender...a champ, but alas my trainer said that I was strong as a bull, packed a mean wallop of a punch, threw nice combinations, but lacked speedy footwork. Reason, my feet are too darned big and they slow me down and make me clumsy. Boxing requires dancing like a ballet dancer, so all I've got left is to spar with, are my pals and this foolish habit of shadowboxing to pass the time. Easy habit I'd say, but due to force of habit, now it has become something I do when I catch myself trying to think too much. A good boxer doesn't think about it, he just comes by it naturally, like hitting a baseball or riding a bike.

I have found that thinking takes me out of the present... haunts me with the past, or frightens me of the future. I'm learning to love the Eternal Now.

Boxing, camping, shooting, fishing, and journal writing have become my main outlets for relieving stress, and I stumble upon them quite naturally, yet somewhat accidental. They all make me feel good.

Of all these avenues, journal writing seems the safest and most effective, the most stress specific. If issues come up, I simply take pencil and notepad and jot them down. As soon as they collect on paper, I seem to be released from their troubling power, due to the fact that I gets them away from me, and on paper, out of mind, gone. This process has been my mainstay through the years, and I find threads of them can be woven into good storylines, thus giving myself release from their psychic irritation, as well as offering good, marketable story content.

However much I enjoy utilizing my favorite stress relief activities, none of them have been able to touch the guilt. This one issue always remains... festering... untouched, and it bothers me.

Throughout this summer I'll keep this challenge on the back of my bucket list: things to do this summer; namely, how to rid myself of guilt.

Having religious fanatics as parents has done a number on me in this department. As Congregationalists, they can lay a lot of law on a guy, yet they have no sure-fire vehicle in their religion that absolves a guy from guilt.

From my observation, this factor tends to put the priest in the drivers seat, for it keeps the sinners always wondering if they measure up by doing penances. It causes the sinner to keep coming back to church for answers-answers that for me have not been forthcoming. Plain grape juice and bread and a remembrance ritual just aren't potent enough for me these days either. That or my sins are unforgivable. That's a heck of a note. This guilt from the law and not knowing if I have finally done enough penances gets me real frustrated and I hate it. I hate church because of it. Priests have too much power and the poor guilt- ridden laity are left in the dark having to figure things out, decipher the theology and deep mysteries of God for themselves.

Lately, I've been using alcohol to numb my mind of guilt. Drinking booze helps me forget temporarily, but then next morning I gots me a doozy of a headache and a very upset stomach.

Prohibition came early for Michigan. This state banned booze and strong drink around 1916, so my pals and I concoct applejack by placing a jug of cider and raisins on a steam radiator where it ferments in a few days.

Dandelion wine is also around, actually, any fruit can be made into wine, or distilled over heat, and its vapors condense into brandy along a series of coils.

Strong drink is a fascinating subject for me and I've made myself well- educated on the subject. Now since the whole country is forbidden to drink it, again, due to the action of some more religious fanatics, we want to drink it all the more, even women who used to be more responsible about it are sporting hip flasks fastened to their stocking garters.

Chapter 22. Ernie Opens Up to the Holy Spirit

Tell someone they are banned from doing something, and out of spite folks will go ahead and do just the opposite. Case in point, Garden of Eden and the forbidden fruit. Eve lost it due to that beguiling serpent. She ate of it, gave it to Adam, and now we're trying to return to that closeness with God which we lost through Adam and Eve's stupid mistake

However, when the proper time was right, Jesus paid the ransom for us at the price of His own death, and after three days in the grave, He returned triumphant. That's what we call the Gospel. That is what we believe. We believe that our mistakes are covered with the blood of Jesus the Christ. We have faith that He will also lift us triumphantly from the grave in like manner.

Through Adam's mistake, death and a whole lot of misery was brought into the world and through Jesus, the second Adam, death was overcome. The ransom was paid.

When it finally hit me that no matter what I did in terms of keeping the law perfectly, it was never going to happen, (No one can keep the Law perfectly), so I shifted my awareness to the fact that I already was cleared through Christ's suffering and death. (The Supreme Sacrifice)

Simplistic as it sounds...having nothing to do on my part except having this faith that all my mistakes were already covered... has been sounding way too simple.

Accepting this concept has been a stumbling block for me. Accepting it was most difficult for me to do mainly because it just seemed way too simple and I was sure there was something else I must do. My Pal, Lew, assures me many folks are stymied by it, just like me. It just seems way too simple.

That night in our tent Lewis and I could be heard discussing this very topic.

I revealed, "But Lew, my Pal, I still feel obligated to do something to earn salvation. Come on, there has to be some catch to this - it can't be only through faith. In my estimation, that is way too easy - way too effortless. Shouldn't there be some kind of effort involved? I find it too simple to believe."

Lew answers, "Stein, that is where the third member of the Trinity comes in. The Holy Spirit - when asked – He will come into your heart and cause faith to happen. By ourselves alone we cannot achieve belief in this...the Gospel, but the invited Holy Spirit sets up shop in our hearts and helps us to make sense of all of this.

When Jesus left the earth He did not abandon us to figure out how to accept all this on our own. He sent The Comforter, the Holy Spirit. I'm surprised your church did not inform you about this?"

I answer, "Pal, you know, they just might have told me but maybe I fell asleep around that time, or this concept could've made no sense to me at the time, quite possibly I was angry with my parents for making me sit through all those long services. To me, their theology sounded like blah, blah, blah... Furthermore, blah, blah, blah. And then some more blah, blah, blah, because all the while my mind was dreaming about fishing."

Lew responds, "Okay, okay, Stein, if you were forced to attend along with them. I can see you may have felt no need to understand."

I suggest, "Hey, mind if I open these tent flaps a bit? I feel a bit heated up here tonight. Maybe the Holy Spirit will be able to enter if we make Him an opening."

We had a huge full moon that evening, so the open tent let in moonlight as well as a gentle summer breeze drifting across the surface of our shimmering Lake Walloon, thus rendering an auspicious atmosphere that anything we wanted to happen could very well occur.

A symphony of spring peepers were chiming in, echoing a note of clarity to this evening while a mysterious whippoorwill could be heard near the edge of the forest. Eventually, I felt I had to add some words to this picturesque scene.

I noted, "Now, Lewis, if the Holy Spirit wants to come and surprise us....uh... I see no reason for Him to not give us a little visit."

Lew adds, "If'n he thinks your heart is ready... you've cleaned up a little spot for Him to sit down, you know, Stein, this would be the perfect time and place for Him to make His entrance... so... you are a man of words, say something... something that will indicate your heart is contrite and sincere... surely you can charm Him in here, Pal."

For the first time in my life I was speechless...even after Lew had called me Shirley.

With so much pressure on me to invite this powerful person of the divine Trinity into me, I clammed up. Nothing came out of my mouth save a few guttural squawks, like a giant, dumbfounded awkward awk might make.

Lewis sat on the edge of his bunk and had presence of mind to hand me his canteen.

Lewis offers, "Maybe a swig of well water will clear your throat, huh? Here, take a pull on this and remember He is a person. He is The Comforter, and Jesus sent Him here to answer any questions we have and help us to make sense of the Gospel... So, just talk to Him like you would to your pals. He loves you and it is His desire to abide with you and generate faith. You need Him, Stein, to make your life worth living. So... go ahead... do it."

Spring peepers stopped their busy, sharp- toned symphony making it a silent moonlit night and that shocked me. The mysterious call of the dark forest whippoorwill ceased also, as if he sensed something of a Holy Wind had entered his domain. All the young, immature, green, tree leaves that were half ventured out as if testing the cold Michigan spring nights began to flutter and flap up and down and around, indicating a mysterious spiral shaped mini cyclone had just moved through the forest and was hovering, just hovering in our vicinity and was waiting for an invitation, any invitation, mainly my verbal invitation which now seemed to stick in my shy and very nervous throat.

Lew stated, "Gee, what was that, Stein?"

I remarked, "God, I don't know, L-L-Lew. All of a sudden everything got real quiet. too quiet!"

Lew states, "See, you can talk... So I'll shut up and just let you find the words to welcome in The Holy Spirit, okay? Go ahead."

I added, "Yeah... okay... th-th-thanks...L-L-Lewis."

At that point my thoughts were firing like a Thompson Tommy gun, thinking about how unworthy I was to approach the third person of the Trinity. My past mistakes flashed by me as if on review , for me to acknowledge and say goodbye to them forever, then my future sins flashed before me, especially my favorite passions: like lusting after shapely women and overindulging in alcohol, and overeating and killing defenseless animals. All this material flashed through my mind before I said my invitation because I knew I still would not be perfect. When it comes to my favorite sins I felt I had no power to control myself.

Lew interrupted, "Go ahead, Stein. He's here. Can't you feel Him?"

I muttered, "Oh yeah... But I ain't quite ready, okay? I'm worried I might have to give up my favorite sins."

Lew says, "Listen, Stein. There is now no condemnation. Remember from our Bible study? No condemnation... get it? Just do it! Say something, Pal!"

In my memory I found in Romans 8:1, 'Therefore, there is now no condemnation for those who are in Christ Jesus .' Memorizing the Bible I recall that powerful tidbit. After Lewis mentioned that wonderful phrase 'no condemnation', I felt I now was ready to say my invitation. That little tidbit of information was giving me courage.

I began, "Ahem... Dear Holy Spirit...uh... please come into my trembling heart this night and clear up any doubts, or fears, and give me the faith needed to receive the Gospel. I need Your comfort. I need Your wisdom. I need the peace that passes all understanding..."

He could not wait... for before I could finish that last sentence the tent began to bulge, the flaps began to flutter and my heart seemed to enlarge. He was in!

He ...The Holy Spirit Himself ...had entered my trembling heart.

Immediately, I hopped off my bunk and yelled at the spring peepers to resume their evening symphony. My feet could not sit still. Dancing around the tent and out to the main road I told the lonely whippoorwill he could again continue his mystic call.

Lew yells, "Hey, Stein, get back here. You'll wake up everybody."

Being as I now had the Spirit, I could feel everything else which had His spirit.

Bushes even responded to me, birds awoke from their nighttime roost in the taller trees. All my senses were amplified to the point where I could hear earthworms burrowing beneath the soil, rabbits breathing in the bush. Bats could be heard nervously dashing about during the bright moonlit evening, sending out their radar tones in search of flying insects.

My own blood squishing through its myriad network of arteries became audible deep within my body. Also heightened is my smeller. Granted, my tribal friends had already taught me to smell game, but now, in my accelerated state, I was able to smell various soils, and squirrels sound asleep in their treetop nests. It's weird. Cedars and spruce some 30 yards away smelled like expensive French perfume.

I heard chipmunks snoring and having chipmunk dreams in their burrows. Ever heard a chipmunk snore?.

As I quickly scampered about on this bright, moonlit night, it becomes vividly apparent that my new friend the Holy Spirit is giving me a crash course in how Adam must have communed with all life in the Garden of Eden.

Squatting down on an old stump I finally sat quietly, trying to gain composure in order to process all of this. So much was happening so rapidly that I needed time to process these rarefied new facilities that all my sense organs were experiencing.

Knowing Lewis was worried about my whereabouts, I sent him a telepathic message not to come look. Time alone in which to process what it means to now be possessed of the Holy Spirit seems to be most expedient.

By closing my eyes, my attention was drawn to the connection between the rate of my breathing and the reaction from all other surrounding organs. It had now become apparent that all organs were taking their cue from my lungs and my carefully controlled rhythmic breathing.

Wanting to rise up and rush into the cabin to tell Doctor Dad, I immediately felt my butt glued down to the stump as if I needed to sit in order to experience more revealing phenomenon.

Continuing to monitor internal organ reactions to my controlled breathing revealed that I eventually could slow down my own heart rate... slowly bringing it down to a restful pulsation. In turn all other surrounding organs began to respond in kind, all taking their cue from my intentional expansion and contraction of the air sacs called my lungs of which I now had conscious control.

Immediately the thought was given to me that after His Baptism, Jesus underwent similar training, only He had 40 days of it in the wilderness of Jerusalem, followed by three temptations by Satan himself - kind of a final testing before His ministry began.

Wishing that I had 40 days in which to train with the Holy Spirit the word was given me to return to my tent and wait for further clues. A series of deeper encounters similar to this evening's lessons would soon follow.

Chapter 23. The Hemingway Holy Spirit Experience

Hemingway Point on Lake Charlevoix

As I rested in the misty twilight, seated upon that rough hewn tree stump, my invitation to the Holy Spirit began to create wonderful sensations within my body. The spirit proceeded to put on a demonstration aimed at showing me what each of my senses were really supposed to be doing when operating in a rarefied fashion.

An interchange with Him began unfolding, revealing the wisdom that each sense organ also had an upgraded usage, all which utilized touching into a universal network similar to an emerald spiderweb which connected me to the matrix of life... an interconnectedness with all living things.

Carl Jung hinted at this, calling it the collective unconscious, but the Spirit brought about further proof of this through a hook up with the matrix which allowed that all life was collecting data into a universal pool.

The Spirit then gave me access to anything on this platform simply by calling out its name, something like system analysis of the unit's collection was being summoned for my personal asking.

Immediately, I was humbled at the breakthrough possibilities which this network allowed me. It was like God's feedback device.

Simply by calling a name I was able to do a scan of that person's body to feel and to touch into their thoughts and even monitor what they had for breakfast.

First name which came to mind was Uncle Willoughby out in China where he was trying to convert the Chinese natives into becoming Christians.

To my surprise, I instantly learned what he had for breakfast, and that he had also picked up malaria, and they soon would be headed stateside for his treatment or retirement.

Distant viewing of this nature continued first with family and then with my Pals in boot camp.

Finally, dehydration began to set in meaning we'd have to call a halt to this exhibition in order to get a drink of pump water. Remembering my canteen was waiting in my tent, I pulled back the tent flap, sat on my bunk, and took a long pull from the cool contents of my canteen.

Lewis says, "I was wondering if you'd come back. How's it going?"

I offered a breathless reply, "Lewis... my Pal...you have no idea ...what just happened out there ...this evening."

Lewis says, "Oh yeah, try me."

I say, "No words come to me as yet. Still trying to integrate all that went on, but picked up on Uncle Will way over in China. Poor guy has Malaria. All our Pals at boot camp are well. Except for Mussie Mussleman who needs kosher food."

Lewis says, "Poor Mussie needs kosher. Mess halls are never gonna feature kosher anything. ...I see you like playing 'I peek'?"

I reply, "Hey, it's not a game, Lew, but pick a name - any name and I'll tell you what I pick up."

Lew says, "Okay, um, how about Marcy Hemingway?"

I reply, "That's easy. Here it is ... now strictly clinical, okay...she's overly conscious about her height, feels she's too tall, and has totally fallen for this Sanford guy. Wants to build a cabin next to this one, will write a book about life with the family...uh...and will live to a ripe old age, 90 something."

Lewis says, "Holy cow. You got all that?"

I states, "Yup and I could go on..."

Lewis asks, "Can you do horse races?"

I state, "Why not. Let's give it a try."

Clarence yells, "It's time you boys drifted off to sleep now, hear?"

I reply, "Okay, Father. We will. Uncle Will is coming home." I shouted.

Clarence says, "Yes, I know, he contracted malaria. Got a letter yesterday. Now get to sleep."

I reply, "See Lew. I told you. This Holy Spirit really works. Distant viewing is a blast! How can I get to sleep knowing I can tap into the whole telephone directory without a telephone-egad, Mr. Godfrey!"

Lew says, "Yeah - just the big telephone in the sky. Tomorrow we visit the racetrack. Oh boy."

Eventually we both dropped off to dreamland, but only after a lot of tossing and turning.

The next morning at breakfast, it was easy to sidestep Pop's questioning of how I knew about uncle Willoughby's return. I simply told him a little birdie told me, but now he thinks I read his mail. Being psychic isn't gonna be easy. First, I must curb my enthusiasm. Going through old tribunes in a box by the cook-stove revealed a fairly recent race from Arlington Raceway out in Palatine. Eager to read it in private, Lewis and I snatched it and headed outside for the privacy and stillness of my tent.

I states, "Okay, Lew, here's how we figure this. I'll go through and pick the winners and then we'll get the Tribune from the following day to see if they won."

Lewis says, "That makes sense. So do you need time to meditate? Good luck, Stein."

I say, "Yeah... give me a minute. I'm kinda new at this you know. Let me study the race form."

Lewis stepped out to visit the house of Hemlock, our outhouse, which gave me time to pencil in the winning horses. Winners of each race had a nice golden glow around their names, so immediately I penciled a big circle around them. With Lew gone, I also decided to close my eyes and picture each of the winners in my mind.

A horse named Lucky Duck came into view as being from one stable that needs watching.

During my distant viewing, the Holy Spirit did not let me down in this regard, for I saw his handlers drugging their horse. I kinda wondered if my powers were to be used for personal gain, and my answer came in the form of a reporters exposé. Spirit wanted me to expose the rotten crews that were doping their horses for illegal winnings.

Lewis says, "Well, Pal, got all the winners circled?"

I state, "Huh? Oh yeah, that. Uh, yeah, got all the winners all right, but…"

Lewis says, "But what? Come on tell, what's up?"

I answer, "Well, Lew, we got a problem. Not only did I pick the winners but Spirit also reveals their handlers are pumping them all full of drugs in order to win."

Lew says, "Huh? Wow! You got a big scoop there, Stein. You will be an ace reporter? Are you gonna write something?"

I says, "Listen kid, I don't think we're supposed to gain from this by personal betting, but I got one heck of a story out of it."

Lew says, "Gosh, Stein. At least that's something, huh?"

I add, "Yeah, and I can help Dr. Dad diagnose with his patients too."

Lewis says, "That is if he will allow it, right?"

I add, "Yeah, I'll have to figure out that part of it, but heck, I can get inside a patient and tell him what's wrong with them."

Lewis says, "Wow Stein, that's just awesome. How can you do that?"

I retort, "It's not me, Lewis. It's Him. He lets me see what He wants me to see. The Spirit is still in charge here, my friend. As a reporter I can present the whole truth about a story when He lets me see the heart of the matter."

Lewis says, "Wow! This skill derived from Spirit's visits comes in perfect timing with your new Kansas City job. What a boon for you, huh?"

I add, "Yes, indeed. With His help I'll always be at the right place…

Lewis interrupts, "…and at the right time. That's awesome. You will have the inside dope on everything. The mark of a good newsman."

I add, "Yeah, I'll be able to do in depth reporting. This racetrack story is already taking shape because this dope is the real dope."

After chopping extra cook stove wood for the day we realized we had time to visit someone.

Lewis says, "So what's on your agenda today, Stein?"

I reply, "Well, it's for sure we have to hike over to Hortons Bay to tell Bill Smith."

Lew says, "And hope he doesn't faint."

I add, "Right, but his girl will be there to bring him around. I figured she would do a good mouth to mouth on our boy."

Upon arrival across the Bay, I hid the oars in a nearby juniper bush and my Pal Lewis Clarahan and I made the 3 mile trek to that magical Hamlet of Hortons Bay. I liked the feeling of pine needles on my bare feet.

Lew says, "Call this a foolish question if you will, but will we do any fishing while we're here?"

I reply, "Yeah, that's a foolish question, Lewis. I got a taste for some rainbow trout and I bet Auntie Beth will buy some too."

It's cool and skies were cloudy today which makes for good trout fishing. They get real finicky if they see lots of shadows, but first we must share the good news with Bill Smith.

As usual Bill was up an apple tree hard at work grafting a sweet strain of apple to Auntie Charles' old heirloom apple trees.

I call out, "Ahoy matey. spot any whales yet?"

Bill says, "Well I'll be, Ernest Hemingway. Where you been? Oh. thar she blows."

I retort, "She blows all right, Pal. You remember my Oak Park friend Lewis of the Clarahan clan?"

Bill adds, "Indeed. Welcome. Just let me seal up this new graft with tar and tape and I'll jump right down. Auntie is gonna have a nice crop of good, sweet, eating apples this fall."

I report, "Lots of nice young buds appearing as far as the eye can see. Would you have time in your busy calendar to join us in a fish-off at Hortons crick?"

Lew adds, "Nice, cool, cloudy day. Trout should be biting nicely."

Bill states, "Let's hope they are, Wemedge. There...now I'll have five different varieties of apples growing on this tree."

I add, "William, if I didn't know you came from St. Louis, Chicago would be first in my mind."

Bill asks, "Why is that, Wemedge...why Chi Town?"

I retort, "Because of all the graft involved."

Bill laughs, "Ha ha ha... good one, Wemedge. So look out below. There, now what's got you smiling so?

I replied, "Sit down, Billy Boy."

Lew asks, "Bill... ask Stein to guess what you had for breakfast."

Bill adds, "Huh? That's a strange request. Okay, friend. What did I have for breakfast?"

I add, "Okay... promise you won't faint alright?"

Bill says, "Promise."

I state, "Here goes...not your usual bacon and eggs, right?"

Bill says, "Right, so far you're right on. Please continue."

I add, "This morning was unusual. I am getting that it was a birthday."

Bill says, "Yeah. Go on."

I add, "This morning was so unusual that Aunty made Belgian waffles, and she ain't even from Belgium."

Bill says, "So far so good. Please go on Hemstein"

I add, "Uh... and she served them with butter, strawberry jam, and fresh whipping cream, topped with cinnamon maple sprinkles, plus fresh, hot chicory with cream (because coffee is too hard to get now that we're at war)."

Bill answers, "Holy crap! How did you do that?"

Lew says, "Not bad, Bill, huh? The kid's got a gift."

Bill says, "Right to a T. Even to the chicory. Gee whiz! I'm impressed, sir. Holy crap! Now what gives? What's the trick? Fill me in. This'll be good. I got a feeling. Oh, by the way, it was Auntie Charles' birthday."

I state, "Last night was a very special night. Ummm...I asked the Holy Spirit into my heart, and now... I'm kinda psychic. That's it."

Lew adds, "Right, and Spirit has already given him a story for the newspaper and his Uncle in China has malaria."

Bill asks, "You can diagnose disease?"

I add, "Yup. Kinda humbling isn't it, William. But I can't gamble with this gift."

Bill says, "Of course. It has to be used for the benefit of mankind, right?"

I add, "Right. Rather sobering too. It's not a parlor trick. It's all Spirit led... for... the greater good of mankind."

Lew says, "Yeah, we have to give honor to God. God gets all the credit, but there is more."

I state, "It's called distant viewing. I travel along an Emerald Web which connects all living things and at the mention of a name it all comes to me."

Bill adds, "Even what they ate for breakfast. Well, that comes just in time for this newspaper gig in Kansas. Perfect timing."

Lew adds, "That's what I said...perfect. Perfect timing for our boy."

Bill says, "With this new gift your confidence level should feel pretty good."

I report, "Indeed, William. Bring it on. I can handle the toughest assignment."

Lew says, "That's the spirit, Stein. You now have your very own crap- sorter, ha ha ha....sort of. You'll have an edge over all the other reporters."

I add, "That's one way to look at it."

Bill adds, "Yeah you will be an asset to that K.C. Star newspaper. Good reporting is always appreciated and your readers will be eager to read your in depth articles wondering what you'll dream up next."

Lew adds, "Yeah, you've got two avid readers right here already, Stein."

I retort, "Thanks for your support, gentleman."

Bill says, "Now... how much trouble are you in... since your new gift has arrived?"

I asked, "Huh? Oh...right. Ah… Father thinks I been snooping in his mail. Marcy thinks I have x-ray vision since I commented on her padded bra."

Bill says, "I figured you couldn't keep a lid on hot news like that. So now you know everything, but have to stay silent. That'll be a tough assignment for you, Pal."

I reply, "Yeah, so I guess I'll have to write it all down from now on."

Bill says, "Oh - by the way - my breakfast had strawberry preserves, not jam as you reported."

I retort, "So - what's the diff?"

Bill says, "Preserves leave the berry more intact, I guess, but all the rest was right. Well done, Wemedge. So have you considered testing G.Q.?"

I add, "Are you kidding? That girl scares me. I always think she wants to knock my block off."

Bill says, "Aw, not so. I've managed to tame that filly."

I state, "If it's all the same with you, let's test my E.S.P. on someone else, not G.Q."

Bill says, "Okay-man, she's got you fooled."

Lew interjects, "Got it. Predict how many fish I will catch today."

I add, "Good one. Do I have any bets? Five trout."

Lew asks, "Five trout? Now if I catch 6 or 4 you owe me a dollar... right?"

I state, "Yup. Wanna bet?"

Lew asks, "Um. Okay. It's a bet. Let's get our gear from behind Red Fox Inn."

Vollie Fox asks, "Gentlemen, are we going fishing? Auntie Beth will buy all you boys catch."

I add, "See! What did I tell you? I just knew."

Bill says, "Lovely guess. So tell Vollie what he had for breakfast then."

Vollie asks, "Are we taking bets again on my eating habits?"

I add, "Yeah. One buck says I can guess what Vollie ate this morning gents."

Vollie says, "Now that's confidence, Ernest. You're on."

I state, "Okay, give me a second...it's coming to me now. Um... Um... Cream of wheat with brown sugar, hot chicory and cream... No... Milk, with cinnamon toast... Yeah that's it... uhhh... And you slurp-drink from your saucer. There... that's it, gentleman. Now you pay me."

Bill asks, "Was that right, Vollie?"

Vollie says, "You was peeking through our kitchen winder, eh, Mister. Yeah, he is right on the money, I even sips my hot drinks from my saucer, I does."

I state, "Pay me, boys. Now, did I make believers out of you all? Anymore tests of my psychic ability?"

Lew says, "Here's your money, mister. Now let's catch us some trout."

Bill says, "Yes indeed. Let's catch us some trout."

Vollie says, "Say Ernest, how did you do that?"

I reply, "It's a gift of the Spirit. Ever since I invited Him into my heart He lets me see things. Simple as that."

Vollie asks, "Mind if'n I join you men. I got to learn more about this...this... the Spirit. Sips chicory from a saucer - well I'll be."

As we all strolled toward Hortons Crick I cautions the boys to find a deep hole in the river, stand still like a statue, be quiet, and drop the worm on the trout's nose.

Before the afternoon was over, we all had five trout each.

Bill states, "Well I'll be... Five trout apiece, and they are all beauties. That makes 20 trout and all good sized ones, some as long as your arm!"

Lew says, "Stein predicted I would land five. Oh my goodness. Here's another buck I owe. He just made another three bucks."

Vollie says, "Auntie Beth sees us coming. She has a gunnysack with ice and she's behind the bushes so Mr. Evans can't see."

I add, "She won't be foolish enough to pay us today, would she?"

Bill says, "Right, but she'll just slip it in your pay envelope for chopping firewood tomorrow."

Lewis adds, "Smart lady. It's against the law to buy sport fish for a restaurant."

Vollie says, "20 good sized trout. Now that's a mess of fish for Pinehurst Inn. Now can we ...can we find what she had for breakfast?"

I state, "Don't be silly, Vollie. Everyone knows she had pancakes, hash browns, bacon, and two eggs... sunny side up."

Bill says, "Now stop that, Wemedge. You're gonna make me faint."

I ask, "Promise, Billy?"

Vollie says, "Well, Aunty Beth. Here is that mess of trout you ordered."

Aunt Beth says, "Thanks, gentleman. Haven't seen Evans around have you?"

Vollie answers, "Nope. Didn't even smell him..that rotten turd of a Game Warden."

Aunt Beth winks, "Well you boys know the drill. Come payday, come see me, okay?"

Guests of Pinehurst Inn got dined well tonight, for there isn't anything tastier on God's green earth than bacon fried trout, fresh from the cool, clear Hortons Crick and served up with mashed taters, fresh asparagus which grows mysteriously under Beth's romantic lilac tree, green beans, and buttermilk biscuits with fresh-churned butter

Auntie Beth could get at least two dollars a plate for such a doggone dandy meal like that. Her high end gentlemen boarders will tip her mighty well too. Best tip they could give is to tell other wealthy businessman in Chicago where to spend a vacation...at enchanted Hortons Bay. That's the finest tip ever.

My ESP was beginning to finally pay off. I made about five bucks today guessing breakfasts and the number of fish taken from the creek; however, my Pal the Holy Spirit will not tolerate much more of my abuse of His gift through gambling.

Meditation on the proper use of the psychic gifts and distant viewing has become my number one goal now, for using the gift for the greater good of mankind will ensure that it will not depart. That's my take on the issue anyway.

My own insecurities and this need I have to be noticed gets me in trouble with my new gifts.

Spirit is reminding me that ESP is like having the mind of God, and to use it for personal gain is degrading to the gift, so I should definitely not play "I peek" with it.

Now I have to remind all my friends, but it's so hard for me to wipe the smirk off my face when we are together for they know I can read their thoughts.

With Kate, it is always easy to read her for she has a one track mind... get me under a blanket.

Soon I realize having ESP is more of a burden since I'm losing friends. I guess having their thoughts probed is like an invasion of privacy, so those friends with things to hide seem to shy away. Finally, I made a deal with Spirit to pop in when needed so's I can have a fairly normal life.

During prayer I find that Spirit visits and helps me connect nicely with folks at a distance, thus making for some very effective results. Just this morning I prayed that Uncle Willoughby would be healed of malaria and he was. Now he can stay in China and continue his valuable medical missionary work.

ESP can let me ask instantly during prayer, thus giving me a very effective prayer life utilizing healing at a distance.

Not to be trifled with, this gift cannot be wasted on parlor games. Mother Grace has always been interested in Spiritism much to the dismay of Father who is as mainstream religion as one gets. I hate to admit it but Mother Grace has her footprints all over my young malleable brain,

Who has not read the works of Mary Baker Eddy, Madam Blavatsky, and others whose radical Spiritist treaties jam the headlines of today's 1917 newspapers.

But a most unlikely candidate would have to be me, Ernie Hemingway, whose rough and tumble, devil may care outer demeanor betrays a sensitive caring inner life devoted to love of God and his fellow man, and woman.

Just goes to show that God works in mysterious ways when he up and taps the most unlikely characters to further his kingdom. Like for instance, Moses, Gideon, or David, or Saul of Tarsus, or the fishermen/disciples of Jesus, all common uneducated men, yet devoted in the Lord to do miraculous deeds. All of them most unlikely, yet they became transformed to do the will of God through the Holy Spirit. Moses was reluctant at first, but he ended up talking to a burning bush...a most unusual convincer wouldn't you say?

This fact gives hope to the common uneducated citizen like me. All what is needed is a little willingness and God comes in and provides the rest.

Not college bound, no real stand out in school, no outstanding athlete, nothing that would turn heads in fabulous Oak Park or anywhere else, yet in the Misty twilight behind Windemere cabin in the summer of 1917, American literature was about to become transformed through the reunion of a humble devotee namely, myself, and our omniscient Holy Spirit.

With the indwelling of the Holy Spirit, the printed page would drastically change and never look back... and I am just the bold and brash kid that can do it. My plan is to bring fallen man back to the Garden of Eden through a series of breakout books which will show the way. Following the lives of most common downtrodden characters available, my readers will be riveted chapter after chapter as to how God moves in one's life.

Readers will be spellbound at my shocking character development who will reveal their plight through crisp and common street dialogue.

Scene after adventurous scene, readers will vicariously emerge and arrive at an unstated submerged truth. I call it my iceberg theory. That will leave them shocked, surprised, and lead them to get inspired to not waste this God given thing called life. My work will have allegory-earthly stories with heavenly meaning...thus exposing possibly every sin, every item revealing the modern day prejudice and pitfall possible for the American reader. Yet my work will not be limited to America alone, for my theme will be Universal Truth, as applicable as the Bible, (which I have memorized, by the way).

At the risk of sounding boastful, be assured I yield to the guiding of the Holy Spirit who provides me with what to say throughout each series. I pursue His direction through daily meditation. I humble myself to His leadership as a sheep of his flock, His Rod and His staff they urge me daily in the right direction. His gentle urgings are a result of an intimacy which has been cultivated since this summer's first invitation in the misty twilight at the stump in my Windemere backyard. Spirit craves intimacy and desires being allowed access to all the minute (seemingly insignificant) details of my day.

Converts to his authenticity now are growing which include Lew, Bill, and Vollie Fox, who still slurps his hot chicory from a saucer in bafflement, yet believes, for only the Spirit would have known the menu on that cool summer Hortons Bay morning.

Folks would refer to this spiritual experience as the born again moment referred to in the Bible, and I must admit I have emerged a totally new creation with a totally new sense of appreciation for how Spirit moves.

Credit for the most amazing awareness will always belong to the Lord without any claim of worthiness on my part other than to maintain in meager willingness which I can muster for certain.

So for the payoff I have a reassurance that all my needs are met, but from force of habit, just like my Pops, I continually have money worries. With more faith I hope that someday those concerns would dissipate as I have more important issues to pursue.

I am off on the most magnificent adventure, the wildest ride of my young life with the Holy Spirit in the lead. These are certainly tumultuous times with radical changes all around me. (Invention of the automobile, air travel, telephone, lightbulb, radio, and the list goes on. I'm privy to the latest developments in medicine because I sneak into my dad's office and read all the medical journals.) I have decided to become the jawbone of my generation to reflect and expose the undercurrent of these radical times. I will be the original "shock-jock" of the 20th century, and people can't wait to read my stuff.

Ernie fishing Horton's Crick

Chapter 24. Sharing the Epiphany

Warren Sumner and Ernie

Meanwhile, behind Pinehurst in Hortons Bay:

Kate says, "So Wemedge, Dear boy. I hear tell of this new skill that has the whole town talking? I'm most anxious to hear about it."

I remark, "Oh Kate my pet you startled me. Let me just stack this cookstove wood here behind Aunty Beth's kitchen. Be right with you, my flower."

Kate says, "Can you tell me what I ate for lunch?"

I answer, "No can do, my pet."

Kate asks, "Oh, why not? You did all our friends... I'm miffed. Harumph!"

I retort, "Kate, my pet. I vowed to myself not to make a parlor game of it. You know...it's much too serious ... this gift I have. Please try to understand, Darling."

Kate answers, "Oh ... all right, but, but... Wemedge."

I respond, "No buts, now try to be serious and no, I can't kiss you out here in public."

Kate says, "What? It's true! You can read minds!"

I say, "Of, course I can, and tonight under the blanket, just you and me and sandwiches, make three."

Kate says, "Holy cow! You are remarkable …"

I add, "Summer sausage, mustard, and pickles. Please pardon the interruption, now I must stack this kindling wood for Liz's kitchen."

Kate says, "Oh, I can't wait to…"

I interrupt, "Yes, you can wait for you are ovulating right now, girlfriend."

Kate says, "Huh? This guy is remarkable! He is!"

I add, "You know, my love for you, but marriage? Not quite... you know I'm too young."

Kate says, "Now you just stop this invasion of my private thoughts. How dare you!"

I add, "Well… That's what you were thinking… Right?"

Kate says, "I ... I ... okay. You were right. It's, it's, it's... what I was thinking, all right; however, now I'm afraid to think. Oh, Wemedge, I feel so strange."

I say, "I'm so sorry, Kate. Sorry. Please let me go in now. Its payday. Please… Your green eyes are sparkling again, thanks."

Kate says, "Here let me get the door."

I state, "Hi, Auntie Beth. More wood for your cook stove."

Beth says, "Just stack it in there behind my stove. And this envelope is for you. Hush now, hear? Thank you, my dear boy."

Kate says, "Wemedge, let's head for the general store, we need an ice cold ginger ale. Don't you think?"

I reply "Indeed, we do. Oh, Kate, this is so exciting. I must share it with you."

Kate says, "Here, lets sit behind Vollie Fox's place. Drink that cold ginger brew. It tickle's my nose, you? Now, Dear boy, tell your Dear Kate all about it."

I adds "Oh Kate, you know our love is unquenchable."

Kate says, "Come on now. No poetry okay. Just the facts, if you please."

I add, "Okay... okay... just the facts. So last night, Lewis challenged me to ask the Holy Spirit into my heart…"

Kate says, "Aha, aha… go on… and?"

I explain, "So... I did... and He, the Holy Spirit that is, came in and... and now, I am psychic."

Kate asks, "And that's it? That's the big deal?"

I add, "Long story short, honest Injun."

Kate says, "Well I'll be darned. So now you gonna be one of them religious fanatics?"

I answer, "Oh no! You know me, Stutt... Mr. Practical. No "Holy-Roller" stuff for me. Spirit helps me to see the truth in things - like horse racing. I got a whole scoop story about drugs they use to dope racehorses. He's gonna make an ace reporter out of me...He is."

Kate says, "Well-well-well. I'm happy for you, my love."

I reply, "Thanks. You'll see. I gotta use the gift wisely though, even though I know what you had for breakfast. What matters is the more important stuff, like...healing Uncle Willoughby of malaria."

Kate asks, "What? You can do that? Holy cow, Wemedge, get outta here!"

I add, "Yeah, like right now He wants to know what you are gonna do with your life?"

Kate says, "Wow! Give me a minute... Okay? Gee whiz, I need some time. Hold your horses...what if I'm having too much fun right now? Does He need an answer right now? Or w-was that a rhetorical question? Egad!"

I reply, "Calm yourself, woman. It's just the way He is. He is blunt as heck. Be thinking about it though because a human life is precious, and it's time for us to ponder where we are all headed. That question is a big'un."

Kate says, "Oh, my God. Hug me, Wemedge. It's just that no one has ever got into my case like that before. Phew! Listen, the Madam, Auntie Charles, is having us throw her gentry self, a surprise birthday party this afternoon. Want to come join us for cake and, uh, chicory? Coffee is scarce you know."

I reply, "Heck yeah. I'll be there. I'm acquiring a taste for chicory, then your sweet pillow lips also...your sweet pouty, pillowy lips."

Kate says, "Oh, go ahead. Break a girl's heart. (Smack) you know I loves you, but you're too darn young to marry."

I answer, "I love your rosy, pillow lips and adventuresome tongue. Time for my 2 o'clock swim out Pinehurst back. Oh come on now, Stut. You've given me hard feelings."

Kate says, "Go then, sir plunge- a- lot. Let the large mouth Bass take care of that tumescent lance."

I add, "Oh, aren't you the funny one. See you at three then?"

Kate says, "Sounds like a plan. Bring Ursa and Sunny if they likes. Marcy is a buzz kill."

I reply, "Will do my best. Fare thee well... oh, and you had waffles and strawberry preserves with whipped cream, complete with cinnamon maple sprinkles."

Kate says, "Oh shut up and jump in the lake while you're at it. Please, I need my privacy!"

I add, "Yes, my sugarplum. Of course, my pet. As you wish. No more invasions."

Kate says, "Go cool your tool, fool. Before I kick your breeches."

Well, I learned that Kate hates to have her mind invaded and she's definitely not ready for any serious self examination either. So I'll just let it ride with her on the ESP issue. I love her and respect her too much to spoil things with her this summer. My last summer with her must be special... free from strife at any cost. We will always love each other, but not enough to go scampering down the aisle. End of episode, and end of delusion. I like that about Kate. Her brother, Bill, is my best pal, and her brother Y.K. is great also. The Charles family and I are the summer people, along with our supporting cast of Hortons Bay citizens, and also a goodly amount of Petoskey-ites, like Marge and Pudge Bump and Grace Quinlan. We are tight.

If and when I do meet Miss Right, we will be wed in that little trick church up the road and all my friends will be invited, yes indeed ,,, all of them.

Nothing like a nice cool dip in Lake Charlevoix to calm a man down and gain a proper perspective, ahhh... indeed...yes, indeed.

Ouch these fish sure like to nibble on worms... Eegad! Now stop that! I need that to have children. Now, let's see how far I can swim underwater without coming up for air.

Madame Charles's birthday party was a smashing success. Kate had baked a two layer, molten lava, chocolate variety cake with cream cheese filling topped with strawberry preserves.

Most of the summer people were there to see and wish the elder gentry lady another healthy year. She amazes our citizens at the way she handles her team of prancers and sporty carriage. No one can get them to prance to town like the Madame Charles.

As we all related her extra special gifts and skills which she most graciously shares with our little community, her nephews Y.K. and William took turns hand- cranking the oaken ice cream churn which was jammed around a tightly packed arrangement of chipped ice covered with rock salt. The two lads expended copious amounts of elbow grease just so Kate's molten lava cake could be complete. When the dessert duo finished their diligent cranking, a cheer went up for the frigid delight at the same time that the Madame blew out the candles on her cake.

A traditional celebration such as this included various games after consumption of that fabulous cake and thick creamy ice cream.

Being staunch Republicans, we rather enjoyed playing pin the tail the donkey. We viewed the family Charles stere-optic machine and cranked up their elaborate Victrola which played all of Madame's favorite songs.

All the men engaged in arm wrestling which Jim Dilworth, our village blacksmith, who always seems to dominate the event. With his narrow shoulders and scrawny arms one would never guess him to be so tough to beat, but pounding iron all day has given him tremendous endurance, a quality greatly needed to tire each individual challenger at the manly sport of arm wrestling.

With everyone needing a break from the games, I invited folks to grab a glass of cider and sit down to listen as I recited poetry. My extensive memory of Longfellow entertained our party goers the rest of the evening. Guests eventually filed out the door as I continued my long poetry oration. Finally, Kate comes out and gently tugs at my arm to give my vocal cords a rest.

Kate says, "Hey, Henry Wadsworth...give it a rest, Pal. All the guests are gone, Aunty has retired to her room, and out of respect for our appreciation of all those fine rhymes and couplets let's just call it an evening, okay?"

I answer, "All right then, but I'm just getting to the good part."

Kate says, "Hold that thought, sire… To be continued, I'm sure, old sport. Maybe tomorrow when you take me… On a picnic, where we can hear the rest of Wadsworth."

I replied, "Great idea. Will there be sandwiches?"

Kate says, "Ham for the ham, right from Joe Bacon's smokehouse, on the homemade rye which I baked along with the cake."

I added, "With dill pickles...big fat dill pickles?"

Kate says, "Yes of course - with dill pickles, why of course, with big, fat dill pickles, why not dill pickles?"

I add, "And mustard? Gotta have mustard."

Kate says, "The Bard will get his mustard, but you should've known that, for you are the one with ESP."

I report, "Remember, Stut, I don't use it around you. I can't play 'I peek' around you. So do I get an onion sandwich too?"

Kate says, "Yes, you big man, you'll get your onion sandwich too. Anything else? Only guy I know who eats onion sandwiches. Gee whiz... don't your parents feed you?"

I add, "Gotta have a big slice of Bermuda onion, yes, indeed, then I can dip the whole thing in the creek."

Kate says, "Oh, for heaven's sake. Now cut that out. You're getting me all moist, you rascal. You are bringing the sausage Mister, a big long smoked bratwurst if I have anything to say about this picnic lunch."

I retort, "Now who is using ESP, huh? Who's the rascal?"

Kate says, "Hug me, Wemedge. Now go home."

I report, "Did you hear the one about the blonde?"

Kate says, "Yeah, yeah, got her tongue caught in the toaster trying to make French toast. Maybe you can bunk above Liz Dilworth's carriage house tonight, Wemedge."

I say, "That's what I'm thinking. Too far and too late to trek all the way back to Windemere."

Kate says, "Good night, you big lunk. Come over about three when I finish laundry. You'll see me hanging it out to dry."

I add, "Hang yourself out to dry."

Kate says, "Oh shut up. Now shoo. You hear?"

I state, "Okay. My ESP says I'm not wanted."

Kate says, "Now stop that, Wemedge."

Long shadows had faded away by now. Evening dew had settled in already as I shuffled down Pin Cherry Road making my way toward Dilworth's. Twilight was winning its battle with the last days of this beautiful enchanted birthday bash at the Madame's, and a whippoorwill was calling his mate to roost for the evening at the edge of the swamp. The familiar squeak of the horse- barn door announced that Jim Dilworth had just finished bedding down Sea Biscuit in his stall as I approached."

I state, "Sure was a nice birthday party for the Madame, right Jim?"

Jim says, "Oh, sure was. Sorry we had to slip out on your poetry recitation, Ernest. Want to bunk up above for the night?"

I reply, "Yeah, if I could. It's a long, dark walk back to Walloon."

Jim says, "Sure. Maybe chop some wood for the Mrs. in the morning. I think your toothbrush is still up there. Okay?"

I chuckle, "Yeah. Ha ha. Thanks Jim. You're a pal. Well good night, Jim."

Jim says, "You're invited for breakfast in the morning."

I add, "Thanks Jim. I know. Fresh smoked Joe Bacon ham, right?"

Jim asks, "Why yes. How did you know?"

I add, "A little birdie told me."

Jim says, "Well Ernest, see you in the A.M...sleep well."

I add, "Yeah, thanks Jim. Same to you... Hey, Sea Biscuit, want to hear some poetry?"

Sea Biscuit says, "Snort, chortle, snort!"

I add, "Look I can take a hint. Maybe tomorrow. But I can guess what you had for supper, hay, right?"

Sea Biscuit says, "Snort, chortle."

I say, "Just horsing around with you, Pal. Good night, Sea Biscuit."

Symphonic crickets and a swamp full of spring peepers slowly lulled me to sleep as I stretched out on the comfortable Dilworth carriage house accommodations.

My evening prayers had to include a big thank you for the priceless Madame Charles birthday party with all of its fine refreshments, the bevy of loyal summer friends, and the close knit friendliness of Hortons Bay locals. This last summer up in Michigan is already shaping up to being my best ever, summer vacation.

With a spirit of gratitude to Holy Spirit and thankfulness for my lovely location, dreamland took me voluntarily and I awoke feeling most rested.

Descending the rough, squeaky, loft stairs, I filled Sea Biscuit's feed trough with oats and alfalfa and strolled over to the village blacksmith shop where I chop some wood for Jim's forge. Liz's wood pile was next and I chopped a nice cord, enough to keep her cook-stove going all week.

Liz says, "My goodness, Ernest, you must've worked up a good appetite this morning. Please join us for breakfast out on the porch after your bath in our Lake."

I reply, "Thank you ma'am. Lake sure is getting warm. May I trouble you for a clean towel?"

Liz says, "I'll send Grace Quinlan down when you finish bathing."

Bathing in Lake Charlevoix is not uncommon, for a bar of homemade laundry soap always can be found on the dock. Since GQ would be bringing down a clean towel, I lathered up with clothes on, taking care of two jobs at once.

Grace says, "I do declare, Master Ernest, I was hoping to glimpse your new manly physique with the fetch of this clean towel. I is so disappointed, I'll have you know."

I retort, "Sorry to short you on the visuals there, GQ. I have a Charles Atlas brochure you can peruse at home."

Grace says, "This morning sun should dry your brand-name duds in a hurry. Abercrombie and Fitch, sire?"

I add, "Oh, but of course. Mother insists her family be clothed properly. Came right over from the Madame's party."

GQ says, "But won't your parents wonder where you were last night?"

I add, "Look GQ, when you reach 17 and get yourself graduated from high school, they pretty much are done worrying and prefer a permanent move out."

GQ asks, "Do you fear an ouster soon?"

I add, "Oh yeah. It's in the air... Because I know too much."

GQ asks, "And...?"

I say, "They are afraid I'll contaminate the minds of the younger sibs, know what I mean?"

GQ says, "Sort of... Daddy wants me to train horses, says I got a knack for it with our stables... Don't forget to dry behind your ears."

I add, "Real funny. Interesting... Still wet behind the ears refers to a state of juvenalia. Hmm... Curious."

GQ states, "It's true, Ernie. Don't ever grow up. Your youthful spirit is refreshing."

I reply, "Why thank you, young Grace. Believe me it is no conscious effort on my part. I'm a little sweet potato who says, "I yam what I yam.""

GQ says, "Ha, ha - good one. Got to remember that. We are gonna miss you next summer though when you are off writing copy for Kansas."

I reply, "Oh, well, you'll have all your friends here, the Bumps: Marge and Pudge, and Ursa and Sunny Hemingstein."

GQ says, "True… But no one's as funny as you, Ernie. You are the spark plug of the area. Promise you will write to me?"

I add, "Count on it, my friend. You will be another sister for me. I'd love to write letters to you, Grace Quinlan. There, all clean. Just have to let the warm air dry everything and hope these duds don't shrink. Hon, you've got two more years of high school. Anything can happen during that time. You might change your mind. I might come back and carry you off to my… my castle in Bavaria."

Grace asks, "Aren't we at war with them?"

I retort, "Naw... it's Austria and Hungary."

GQ says, "A lot of your pals lied about their age and volunteered to fight them didn't they?"

I answer, "Yes, indeed. I was one, but I flunked the eye exam. Got my Mothers bad eyes; however, we saw them all off at the railway station in Chicago."

GQ says, "That... that must have been sad for you?"

I reply, "The saddest day of my life. The absolute saddest, Gee, absolutely the most sad, good Godfrey."

GQ says, "Many of them won't be coming back."

I reply, "Yup, can we change the subject, please?"

GQ answers, "Sure, sorry, how insensitive of me, so sorry. Well, you're gonna enjoy today's breakfast."

I reply, "Now you're talkin'. Let me guess: ham from Bacons, um… um… Belgian waffles with strawberry preserves, with cream, um… and American fried potatoes, and coffee mixed with chicory, served with a sprig of mint."

GQ says, "Incredible, how did you do that?"

I retort, "Never mind. It's a long story. Help, give me a hand up to the dock. Hope my trousers don't split."

GQ says, "And what would you do if they did?"

I reply, "Guess I'd have to wear your apron to breakfast. Ha ha ha."

GQ answers, "Oh, you are too much, Stein."

Liz announces, "Ding, ding, ding, breakfast is served."

GQ says, "Don't tell us. Ernie's already guessed it."

Liz adds, "Bet he can make it disappear too. Come on, sit down, Houdini. You clean up well, young man."

I say, "Gosh, I'm famished, Auntie Beth. Hi, Jim. Hi, Wesley. How's life under the spreading chestnut tree?"

Wes says, "Welcome back for the summer, Ernie."

Jim adds, "Let us pray: Father, for these gifts let us be ever thankful. Through Jesus Christ. Amen."

Everyone answers, "Amen."

I state, "How can you make Belgian waffles, Auntie, when you're not even from Belgium?"

Beth says, "Yeah, I know... it isn't easy. But I'm getting 'batter' at it."

Wes says, "Oh that was a good comeback, Mother. Hey, Ernie, we all enjoyed your poetry at the Madame's birthday party... And wasn't that some nice cake that Kate baked?"

I reply, "Thanks, Wes. Yeah, all that poetry... that was Longfellow. Folks tell me I'm to be a good poet."

Wes asks, "Why?"

I retort, "Because my big feet show it... long fellows."

Liz groans, "Now, don't spoil their appetites, Ernest. That was a bad one."

Wes says, "Yeah. Two thirds of a pun... P - U!"

Jim says, "Okay boys, just eat. Save the BS for your garden."

Liz says, "Boys, the coffee has been supplemented a bit with chicory. Hope you like it."

Jim says, "Yup, since the war we've cut way back in order to send it overseas for our troops."

Wes says, "Mother, I like it. I don't mind the sacrifice if our boys are getting a good hot cuppa Joe."

GQ adds, "Ernie tried to volunteer."

I adds "Yeah, but my bad eyes kept me out."

Jim says "Well, Ernie, at least you made the attempt, but you're only 17? 19 is the cut off."

I reply, "Yeah, we all lied about our age just to get overseas and pop us some Austrians. I really wanted to fly. I think that would be exciting."

Jim says, "Ernie, you'd be a sitting duck up there. Some of Kaiser's boys would part you hair with a long gun, like a Mauser."

I reply, "Yeah, I know. But hair grows back."

Wes says, "Depending on how short it got."

Liz says, "Now, you men change the subject. How do you like the waffles? More ham?"

GQ asks, "More coffee? Let me jump up and bring more of everything out here. Gosh, isn't it a beautiful morning? Doesn't Ernie look handsome without his bib overalls?"

Wes answers, "Yeah, Ernie... you been working out haven't you? Those are some big guns there for farming."

I say, "Yup. I can pitch hay with the best of men. Thanks to Charles Atlas."

Wes says, "And it's good protection I bet. We got a letter from Grace Hemingway stating that you've been training in boxing over in Chicago. Now I call that exciting."

Jim says, "Yeah, Ernie... bet you can teach us all how to box... wouldn't that bring in the tourists to Hortons Bay. Say... I'm sorry. I beat all you boys in arm wrestling last night. Does your arm hurt today?"

Wes says, "Oh Dad, you know we just let you win so's you wouldn't whine about us cheating."

Jim answers, "Yeah, I know you guys cheat all the time. But come over and slam a 10 pound sledgehammer all day and see if you can cheat on that."

Lew says, "Yes, Wesley, your father works hard all day long. When will you be able to keep up?

Wes answers, "Hey, I just need more experience. Are you saying I'm a slacker?"

Liz says, "No, it's just that when we need some work done around here, you are nowhere to be found."

Wes says, "Okay, Mother. Make me a list and I'll do it... I see it as a failure to communicate, that's all."

I add, "Wes, I can help, too, if you need me."

Wes says, "Mother, you know I help out at Earl Sumner's, and Joe Bacon's, and the O'Donnell's, and the Charles'. They all need help. But in exchange I get eggs, chicken, ham, bacon, butter, milk, cream, feed for Sea Biscuit..."

Liz answers, "Of course, Wesley. I forgot. It's just been a lot of strain and not having the Bump girls here this summer, and Father takes on more than he can handle. Now he's also a farrier, or fixing horse shoes, and trimming hooves. There's not time enough within a day for all of it to get done."

I add, "Hey, count me in. If you need help, Auntie Beth. Wes and I can relieve you a lot of stress. After breakfast we can sit down and make up a list so's Wes and I can get started on what needs doing."

After we made a list, Wesley Dilworth and I teamed up to build and repair, paint and varnish numerous items around Pinehurst B&B. It looks spiffy just in time for Beth's northbound guests.

Opening up communications between Wes and his mother just made everything around Hortons Bay a lot happier. I am looking forward to trying this list idea with Mother Grace… that is…if she'll listen?

Well, I made big strides today overcoming the need to be noticed for my ESP skills. My dog gone insecurities force me to overcome by entertaining others. Reciting Longfellow at Madame's party for two hours was a start in the right direction, also, becoming an expert in everything wastes a lot of my time and energy, but when I start pontificating on the subjects near and dear, people sit up and take notice, hoping to learn something. The ESP aspect of the 'I Peek Game' accomplishes none of that, plus it only pads my ego, giving no glory to God who provides the gift.

Furthermore, ESP could be cultivated by most anyone with the desire to develop intuition. My internal wisdom tells me to savor my ESP desires for the journalism challenge that awaits me in Kansas and Spirit will probably reveal plenty and any number of topics of interest to my readers.

Helping Wes Dilworth finish his list of chores is getting him in good with Auntie Beth, his dear mother, and is putting me in good stead with him too, which means good eats and the use of a crashpad when I need to escape the tyrant of Windemere, Mother Grace.

I state, "Thanks, Wesley for letting me help around this place. It s good experience for me. Oh, and thanks for the use of your bib overalls. Saves my new fancy duds for more casual activity like this afternoon's picnic with Miss Kate."

Wes says, "You are right welcome, Ernest. Many hands make light work, they say. I owe you for rescuing me from Mother who thinks I can read her mind regarding labor that needs to be done."

I add, "Trust me, Wesley, Pal, you sure don't need to read people's minds to get along. Just keep open lines of communication allowing both of you to openly share your needs. Aunty Beth used my invitation to sit down and lay her needs on paper...simple as that. I think she was tired of playing the martyr... reluctant Messiah game. I doubt if she really wanted to nag you there at breakfast, but asking her for a list of jobs was better than pouting and feeling hurt. Don't you think?"

Wes answers, "Yeah... say, Ernest, that shows great insight into family dynamics. I'm proud of you, Pal. How do you do that?"

I explain, "Oh, I tell you, Wes. I have this new friend who I allowed to enter my heart. It was just the other night when I invited the Holy Spirit into my heart. He has opened up a whole new world for me. One that I never knew existed."

Wes interrupts, "Do tell... I'm all ears."

I add, "Allow me to back up a bit for now I recall it was my high school charming friend, Lewis Clarahan who suggested it."

Wes says, "No kidding... I remember Lew... nice kid."

I add, "Priceless friend... best in all the world, part of the crew who all took the Bible reading contest. Harold Samson read it twice to our once. Morris Mussleman was allowed to skip the New Testament."

Wes says, "Because he's Jewish."

I add, "Right, you remember I had him up here fishing one summer. His Pop's tinkers in their garage... invented the coaster brake for bicycles, also invented the pneumatic tire."

Wes says, "That really helped the airline industry. Landing a plane is now much softer."

I add, "Right you are, Wes. So anyway back to Lewis...his Pops is a postal inspector, very sharp man, anyway, after I went one step beyond Bible reading to go one step further than all my pals, I memorized the whole Bible. Competitive old me. Wes, I go ahead and memorize the whole of Scripture."

Wes says "Yes, yes, go on. I sense we're almost getting to your point."

I say, "Sorry if I digress, but I needed that prelude to lead into the best part. So Lew, knowing my Herculean task of memorizing the whole Bible, the cocky kid asked me if I ever internalized it."

Wes says, "Huh?"

I add, "You know. Did I ever take any of it to heart? You know, it knocked me off my ass. Actually, after showing off by speed reading it and then memorizing all scriptures in order to brag about it. I actually had not taken any of it to my heart."

Wes says, "Go on, please, go on."

I said, "All right, all right, don't rush me, okay, so that night after Lew gave me the challenge, I slipped out of our tent into the evening air, sat on an old stump, and there got quiet and prayerful and meditative."

Wes says, "Go on, holy Moses, please finish."

I add, "Well, to make a long story short, I asked the Holy Spirit into my heart."

Wes says, "Holy Moses!

I say, "No, Holy Spirit, Wes."

Wes says, "Okay, okay, and, and…"

I said, "Well… He did."

Wes says, "He did what?"

I said, "He came into my heart, silly."

Wes asks, "And?"

I say, "And I've never been the same since! And all at peace with the world, not a care in the world. All my senses were heightened so's I could hear chipmunks snoring, and He revealed the Emerald Web… the universal matrix… upon which all life forms belonged, and this allowed me to travel to China, to visit uncle Willoughby and discovered he contracted malaria, and now I got ESP so's I can tell what folks ate for breakfast. Cool, huh?"

Wes says, "Holy Moses, Ernest. That's the best yarn you've told yet. I've been simply spellbound hearing you retell that fabulous night."

I said, "Well, Wes, it actually happened that way. I never hide anything from you, as we're best pals and everything. And now you've never known me to stretch the truth, right?"

Wes says, "Holy… Moses. I'm flabbergasted, my young friend. Let me sit down. Chipmunks can snore?"

I add, "Heck yeah. Like robins can hear worms burrowing beneath the soil. Yup, all my senses were upped an octave or more. I can do distant healing too… actually prayed for Uncle Will and instantly the malaria left."

Wes says, "Well, well, what about predicting horse races? What about that? Huh?"

I add, "Not a chance… Oh, I can do it. But He doesn't like it."

Wes asks, "Who doesn't?"

I add, "Holy Spirit. Nothing for personal gain. It has to benefit all mankind and I have to give full credit always to Him."

Wes says, "My goodness, well... Isn't this a remarkable occurrence. Well, I'll be! Ernest, holy Moses. You have to be the most unlikely person to be gifted in this fashion."

I add, "Yeah, but don't you see, that's the whole point of it all. God anoints common, ordinary flunkies...always. Take Jesus' first disciples..."

Wes says, "Yup, I know, just ordinary fishermen."

I said, "And me?"

Wes says, "Just an ordinary fisherman?"

I say, "Yes, indeed. Who would've guessed at that? And I kinda got a whole line of novels lined up now which will lead us back to the Garden of Eden."

Wes asks, "No kidding? Well, Ernest Hemingway, that will be quite an ambition, I do declare, if you can do that... wow!"

I say, "Yup, He revealed it all to me... book titles will come from Scripture themes, and will release people from fear and guilt."

Wes says, "I thought Jesus did that."

I say, "Well, He did, but my work will cover areas of a deep-seated nature which Jesus couldn't have time to cover."

Wes says, "Like what, pray tell?"

I say, "Kinky stuff. What people are too ashamed to discuss... gender bending."

Wes asks, "You're losing me pal... what?"

I say, "Ever want to wear women's underwear? Allow the wife to play the man in bed? Cut a woman's hair real short? Role play? Interview prostitutes? Homosexuals? What makes the dark side tick? It was all revealed as to themes I need to illuminate."

Wes says, "Do you mean Sodom and Gomorrah stuff?"

I say, "Well, sort of. As much as censors will allow of course."

Wes says, "Hey, if you do it right, you would be the only one to bring it off. Yup, you clever Ernest Hemingway. Thanks for sharing that with me. Very interesting. And you think there'll be a market for this kinky material?"

I say, "Indeed, just look at how popular Sigmund is these days."

Wes asks, "Sigmund? Oh... You mean Freud...yeah...oh yeah...he lectures to packed halls all over France and the United States."

I say, "But first I want to write all about my summer here in Hortons Bay."

Wes says, "More power to you, Pal. We got lots of characters here for sure. Just don't mention my name, okay? Nothing too shocking, okay? Holy Moses!"

I say, "Deal. Well, Wes, there you go. I just outlined the next 10 years of my writing career for you. Think you will remember me when you go into a bookstore?"

Wes says, "I'll remember, Master Ernest. I will, oh yeah. Your work will be hard to put down for you sure do tell a right remarkable yarn. Yes, indeed. Quite the remarkable storyteller you are, indeed... And to think I watched you grow up every summer right here in little Hortons Bay. Holy Moses!"

I state, "Here's my whole point, Wesley. Shoot, Sodom and Gomorrah were evil, deranged towns... so evil that God decided to punish the whole town wipe them all out with fire and brimstone, but now... Now, He can't do that see, because since Jesus' sacrifice of life, and death, and resurrection, the Father can't condemn sinners anymore - can't do it. Now, therefore, there is no more condemnation. Jesus has changed the heart of God... because a sinner is still as evil as Sodom and Gomorrah, worse, there is a real chance that he will hear about Jesus and believe the good gospel message, for God would have no man to perish. I've seen the connection of all life, like Paul of Tarsus."

Wes says, "Wow... you got all this when you invited the Holy Spirit into your heart? Back there in the woods of Walloon?"

I say, "Yup... yes indeed, my good man. The Scriptures being made clear now due to the urgings of Spirit. He helps me to decode the mysteries of the ages, and it is wonderful, Wes. Simply wonderful, pal. Mine eyes are opened. I've been to the mountaintop."

Wes says, "Holy Moses! Well Ernest, you have certainly given me plenty to consider. Sleep may not come easy for me tonight with all you've given me to ponder... And I will take a very close look at all what you've shared. I'm honored to hear your testimony."

I add, "Wes, the Holy Spirit is always at work planting seeds. With me, His seeds took root, grew up, and He harvested His crop out behind Windemere the other night. You've done some farming and gardening. You know about germination and all that. You get baptized. Hear the gospel as the seed... you hear it and it takes root in your heart and mind. As you read Scripture you water it and fertilize that germinating seed. Over time, given all the proper watering and fertilizing, eventually faith takes root, sprouts, and grows due to Bible study, and serving, listening, praying, walking the talk and before long you find yourself inviting Him in and you have an epiphany experience similar, if not more spectacular, than mine... which I shared."

Wes says, "Holy Moses! That sure is clear enough. I mean the way you explain it all is okay... And stuff."

When Wes said 'and stuff', something told me he was putting me off in order to get me off his case. My words had been enough and he was on overload tilt, to be continued. He will follow the dramatic change in me and in the back of his mind my testimony is stored and he has to mull a few things over in his life circumstances. Maybe his future wife will be the spark that he needs to move up in consciousness. Maybe he needs a few more Holy Moly experiences, or a few more Holy Moses life happenings for him to commit consciously, and invite the Spirit into his heart. Or maybe he'll find a friend like Lew Clarahan who will challenge him to invite Him in like he did to me. Whatever the case, only time will tell. Yes sir, only time will tell, and out here in Hortons Bay anything can happen... anything.

Ernie catches a big trout!

Chapter 25. Kate Finds Her Bliss and Then Loses It

Kate says, "Afternoon, big man. Ready for a rip snorting picnic?"

I said, "You bet, my pet, most ready. I is the pic of picnic snack."

Kate says, "Well spoken. I'm sure, Lord Sandwich."

I replied, "Such crust, my dear."

Kate adds, "You seem to know where your bread is buttered."

I quipped, "And that's no baloney. Now hand me some of your load and let's trek into yonder forest."

Kate says, "You sure have a way with words, Chump."

I retort, "The better to while and woo you."

Kate says, "Funny, I didn't feel anything like while, or for that matter woo, either."

I ask, "Do I smell what I smell wafting from yonder basket o' picnic?"

Kate answers, "Your bugle does not betray you, sire. Rubens on marble rye with horsin' around sauce and dilly of a pickle on the side."

I reply, "The heck you say?"

Kate says, "Yup... heck... there, I said it. Now can you guess the beverage of choice?"

I answers, "Indeed, my pet, with a capital 'V', for Detroit's drink, later called Michigan's drink, ice cold Vernors ginger ale. That pale amber elixir aged four long years in oaken barrels by nifty gnomes."

Kate asks, "And?"

I add, "Lava chocolate cake leftover from yesterday's priceless party. Holy cow, Kate, I could kiss you."

Kate asks, "Well?"

I say, "Oh baby...smooch!, Your hair smells divine... like... er... sauerkraut."

Kate adds, "Imported, nonetheless."

I ask, "From?"

Kate says, "From Madame Charles's crock, where else? She's always got something fermenting in the basement. Plus, not one but two stout blankets to wrestle in."

I add, "Oh Darling, Kate. That does it! Let's run off and find a woodchuck who will marry us right now, for I am in love. Struck by your green eyed beauty and raven hair and of course your choice of picnic fare."

Kate says, "You're on, my prince, to the nearest overstuffed rodent that resembles a wood chuck for instant wedlock."

I state, "Onward and upward, my ready babe-in-the-woods. How's this hearty growth of hemlocks?"

Kate answers, "Nope, onward...no privacy....plus Hemlock's poison."

I add, "Yeah, you're right. Look at what one glass did to poor... poor... Pythias."

Kate says, "No silly, it weren't Pythias. It was the Scarlet Pumpernickel."

I retort, "No it wasn't pumpernickel precious... It was... Rumpelstiltskin."

Kate adds, "No, it was Rumpled Foreskin wasn't it?"

I add, "No, that was his rabbi, from my latest tip."

Kate says, "Nay, nay, you knave, it was rumpled one eye of trouser worm on Avon."

I say, "Yikes! What felony a philosopher of fame was felt by a flask of Hemlock, pray tell?"

Kate says, "It'll come to me, halt, steady thy steed, Sedgwick. By Jove and I think we found our private spot. It is here beneath these towering cedars, which will provide soft bows on which to slide my frantically thrusting gluteus maximus."

I add, "How utterly romantic of you, my Queen. Drop your blankets here, my Dear, and spread your moistened gear. This sojourn hath found us our love nest, I fears."

Kate says, "Pithy, dear Heathclift, but enough of enchantment for my aphrodisiac ears."

I add, "You can say that again."

Kate says, "Come lie with me this mercurial moment, my liege, for alas, I see the monument for me rearing his helmeted head 'neath thine quivering kilt."

I add, "Alas, you drive a stiff bargain, my scullery maid, now leaps he from his uncomforted cod piece, framed phelial by thy red-pillow lips."

Kate says, "Mmm, blimey what briny bastions protrude midst thy bad boy loins."

I add, "The better to plow your furrowed fields, my feverish filly. Now, bare your blushing bodice to match thy blanched buttocks which do skid amid these softened cedars."

Kate says, "Your ribald romantic gymnastics do stretch my pouting internal target to it's max amid your mangling mandrakes, my man. Now mum's the word as I work this whiley owl's release, as your rising pulse doth climax reveal."

I interject, "Foresooth and forthwith doth your internal foncling befroth mine tumescent manhood. Would you catch it or shall I let it fly?"

Kate says, "Give it flight, fare Dinkum for I fear your flashtail flagellum far too fertile are, and you and I are far too young to propagate new progeny on this God-forsaken planet at this time."

I add, "Ah, just let my quaking torso rest upon your rotund rump a while, til moving earth doth calm itself, and my spent testes also, only moreso."

Food revived our love spent bodies as we tore into our delicious picnic lunch. Kate had that satisfied look as her drooping eyelids also indicated a well satiated appetite for good food and good lovin'.

I state, "Some day they'll build a shrine here for us."

Kate asks, "Do ya think so, Wemedge?"

I state, "I do. Our sweet lovin' has charged the very air in each corner of this grove of cedars. There is bound to be at least a church goes up here some fine day."

Kate sighs, "How nice of you to say, Wemedge. Just look how the trees seem to lean over to watch us put a show on for them."

I observe, "These cedars are mating even as we speak. Don't kid yourself. All of nature is having sex."

Kate asks, "Oh yeah?"

I add, "Uhuh. Look, the trees release pollen and a good wind comes along and spreads it to the neighboring trees. Bees and butterflies and birds get into the act. They all help the trees and flowers propagate... birds and squirrels nest and have sex right in these very trees."

Kate says, "Boy, if trees could talk, eh?"

I said, "Oh, I'm sure they would have plenty to say. Jesus talked to a fig tree once."

Kate adds, "No kidding."

I say, "Darn tootin'. It got lazy, I guess. Produced plenty of nice leaves but held off producing it's nice figs, so Jesus looked for some figs... guess He liked figs... maybe had a taste for figs or something, and bingo, Jesus cursed that doggone lazy fig tree."

Kate adds, "Okay, and...?"

I add, "And the disciples strolled by the next day for example. That same tree was all shriveled up and was dead as hell."

Kate asks, "No kidding?"

I says, "No kidding, kid. Jesus nailed that lazy fig tree, dead as heck in one day."

Kate says, "Good lesson for us to produce... be fruitful..."

I add, "Yeah... produce... Or else. So I've already written a few good poems and short stories."

Kate adds, "Yeah, I know, Wemedge. They're really good."

I say, "Thanks, Kate, that means a lot to me. Now if I can get some support from the fam, especially Mother, that would be nice."

Kate says, "Don't hold your breath, hon. That woman is in her own little world and there is room for no one else, but maybe that... Ruth Arnold character."

I ask, "You noticed, huh?"

Kate answers, "Hey, the whole town wonders about her. The scandal will really hit hard in Oak Park. My guess is she leaves for neighboring River Forest...seriously."

I add, "She's ruining the Hemingway name."

Kate says, "Yup. So guess what, big man?"

I ask, "What?"

Kate continues, "You are gonna have to make a big name for yourself to make up for the damage. Got it?"

I add, "Got it. Wow... Am I ever stuffed. Say, Kate, thanks for fixing that nice lunch. And thanks for fixing that nice lovin'."

Kate says, "The pleasure was partly yours."

I state, "Sure, it was. Super! We'll have to do this again sometime."

Kate agrees, "Well, love, it's getting late. Shadows are getting long, and you haven't been home in two days. Maybe you want to check in with them, huh?"

I reply, "Yeah. I suppose so. Not that I relish the idea. She's gonna kick me out anyway. My guess is Mother is drafting an eviction letter as we speak."

Kate says, "Just go face the music... And if she gets too busy, just blast her about her sleazy relationship with that Ruth character. It must drive your father nuts."

I add, "Yeah... Kate... I love how you love me. But you have no idea what an emotional stranglehold she has on everyone, especially Pops. She'll be the death of him. You just watch and see."

Kate exclaims, "Oh, look what's in the ice chest. A Vernors ginger ale. Oh boy."

I say, "Hey, hon, let's celebrate. To a successful summer."

Kate, agrees, "Pip Pip, hooray. Drink up, all that passion has made me thirsty. What a delightful afternoon, thanks, my man."

I state, "Pleasure was all mine. How was it for you?"

Kate answers, "Delightful, you are my perfect lover. Was I better than Prudence?"

I state, "Now let's not start comparing, please."

Kate continues, "Well how can I compete with her long brown legs? Her pitch black hair? Her tight..."

I state, "Don't go there! Oh, just stop it, Kate. You're trying to ruin a perfect day. Now change the subject right now, please Kate. I'm getting embarrassed."

Kate says, "Okay... I'm... Sorry... Wemedge... guess I just want to know where I stand with you. That's all."

I add, "I know. You're too insecure. Listen...You are tops in my book."

Kate asks, "And Grace Quinlan?"

I state, "Oh come on... She's only 16!"

Kate continues, "But you would do her, right? Her parents are wealthy you know. They could slam your ass in Jackson prison, you know."

I state, "Please Kate... please. Stop it!"

Kate continues, "And Marge Bump? You want to do her. And Pudge Bump. You'd like to bump both of them from the rump. Like bookends, right?"

I say, "Calm yourself now, Kate. Well this is going nowhere. Stop it, I say. Oh let's just go now. I got everything collected. Gosh that was good cake."

Kate continues, "You'd bang all of them at once. Orgy style, wouldn't you?"

I add, "And those Reubens were so delightful."

Kate adds, "You'd nail..."

I add, "Say, wasn't that Vernors just the best thirst quencher. Thanks again for that."

Kate stops, "Yeah. Let's get the hell out of here. Holy shit, it's starting to rain."

I state, "Welcome to Michigan. You never know what kind of weather to expect. Here, put this blanket over your head. It'll be good fishing tonight. Let's run to that big maple tree to keep dry. Your hair smells intoxicating, kid. Kinda like sweat and steam and sauerkraut."

After the rains let up, Kate and I made our way back to Hortons Bay. All along the cool, wet, path I couldn't help thinking about Kate trying to ruin all that good picnic and good lovemaking laid out in this blissful natural setting up on a bed of sweet smelling cedar boughs. She went from high ecstasy down to the basement of depravity in an instant to thoughts about my previous girlfriends. Jealousy was the evil tripwire. Call it her insecurity or whatever, she just couldn't maintain her bliss and then the notion struck me as she needs to invite Spirit into her life also. Spirit would have helped her maintain her bliss.

Spirit gives us this peace that passes all understanding... it gives the sky, and faith to trust all that is well with the world. Spirit was the difference this afternoon and from that understanding I determine to pray that Kate would accept the Lord as her own personal savior and invite Spirit into her heart. She then would be beautiful inside and out. Right now her beauty is only of the outer variety.

I asked, "So Kate, my sweet, what are your plans at summer's end, college, job, marriage to Edgar... what?"

Kate answers, "Probably an advertising job in Chicago. YK and Doodles have this huge place in the north side of Chicago, and they have room for Bill and I. As for Edgar, that poor creature just comes around here mourning for a date with me, but, but... I don't know. He's such a slug... you know? Just not my idea of Mr. Excitement. I mean, he's nice and all... rich too... but not social... a doofus. Do you follow me?"

I reply, "Yeah, he sure is stuck by you though. But who needs a charity case, I follow you."

Kate continues, "YK has some connection in the world of advertising, so Bill and I are considering taking him up on that. Pay is decent. You might like writing good advertising."

I add, "Let's see if this Kansas job pans out for me. Well kid, here we are back in the metropolis. Guess I'll head over to Windemere to face the music. No pun intended. Give my love to the Madame and your brilliant brother, Bill. Think I'll hang this wet blanket on Auntie Beth's clothes line to dry. She won't mind."

Kate says, "Just make sure you wash off all your boys there. Good night, Wemedge."

Since the afternoon rain had started to clear, I decided to venture the three mile trek back home.

I yell, "Auntie Beth. I'll be heading over to Windemere now, so... Thanks a bunch for lodging and feeding me, you hear?"

Beth says, "Pleasure, Master Ernest. Please give my best to your parents. Looking forward to seeing them real soon. I'll take care of that wet blanket for you."

Kate Smith, front and center, and Ernie with the hat, all taking a swim at Hortons Bay.

Chapter 26. Ernie's Big Breakthrough

The walk seems longer than usual. Maybe it was the soggy ground which slid out from under my bare feet, or maybe it was the thought of having to explain my two day absence to Mother who was gonna bitch lecture me about Christian responsibility.

I figure she'll nag me for half an hour. I'd sooner take an Austrian bullet in the ass than have to cower to Mother Grace's self righteous barrage. Suddenly I imagine Krauts were crouching behind every bush and tree all along the soggy path toward home. With that thought, my lucky walking stick instantly became a sniper rifle which I popped off a few rounds at those ominous Austrian bastards, and my heart began to ache for all of my Pals heading into harms way over in Europe, throwing their innocent youth away to Kaiser's cutthroat's... the lads were falling left and right, helplessly untrained and ill-equipped in a war which was hopeless and useless. Spirit then gave me a heads up that I was slipping dangerously into an unwanted depression, and a song came to mind...

I sing, "*Onward Christian soldiers. Marching off to war, with the cross of Jesus going on before... Marching into battle, knocking off our foe...*"

Eventually I made up my own words and soon my spirits began to lift out of the funk I had been in.

My weary walk toward Windemere became uplifted to plateau on which I was ready and competent to face anything... Kaiser's awful enemy or even the nasty jaws of my menacing Mother.

Suddenly it dawned on me that my very own Mother had not accepted Spirit into her heart. Sure, she talked a good game using jargon which church people use, but she just did not exhibit the qualities of one who'd been born again.

What an epiphany! The paragon of virtue, the self righteous, pompous, religious fanatic of a Mother Grace had been lowered down with this new realization. Spirit within me had shown me that this quick to judgment Jezebel was needing to get off her high horse and humble herself enough to ask Spirit into her own black heart. Oh what a relief it is to have Spirit on my side whispering words of hope into my trembling heart.

Of course! It all becomes clear to me. In her self seeking spoiled state of mind she has no clue as to the pain she is causing my Pops with her dastardly dalliances with intern Ruth. By her refusal to become domestic in the kitchen and in the broom closet she has put untold strain on us all.

Why that sanctimonious, judgmental monster! She has been using sentimental blackmail on all of us for years hiding behind the mantle of motherhood in order to carry on her nefarious schemes.

She has diluted the whole community with the arts... utilizing music to provide a mask for her real intentions, and using my Father's social standing to bilk these backwoods bumpkins into submission to her every whim.

Oh boy... now ain't that the scoop of the century. My very own Mother has now become nothing more than just another servant of Satan, who stands in need of acceptance of the Gospel into her very own dark heart.

After this remarkable breakthrough my mood became one of victory and rejoicing with my slow, reluctant steps lifting into the skipping cadence, followed by a joy filled mad dash to witness to my family, especially my needy Mother.

At every step I had to marvel at the emotional transformation my track had undergone, and I let out a yelp thanking the Holy Spirit for transforming my attitude and for helping me to see the needs of my mother. As my rowboat approached Windemere property, my attitude became one of thankfulness and blessing, for I especially want to thank Lew Clarahan for his support in my accepting the Holy Spirit.

This young lads intervention has made all the difference in the world, and I must express my gratitude toward him before he hops a train back to Chicago.

I states, "Hey, Lewis, my good pal and buddy. Old friend and confident."

Lew says, "Howdy, stranger. I had the tent all to myself last night as well as the night before."

I say, "Yeah, well I had business in the big city of Hortons Bay. Is Mother upset?"

Lew answers, "My pal... You know, I think she figured you were on to some new adventure. but I did my best to cover for you...

chopped firewood, raked the grounds, shot some crows, caught some nice crappies and dug a new hole for garbage. Your Pops got a telegram that Uncle Willoughby won't be coming back from China after all. Seems he had a miraculous healing of his malaria. My guess is you already knew that though... Right?"

I reply, "Ha ha... Oh yeah, Spirit took care of Uncle through prayer. So thanks for covering my back, Lewis... And thanks for turning me onto Spirit, especially. Sorry things went downhill for you with Marcy, but this frees you up now to find some nice Oak Park girl, or heck, maybe you'll meet one on the train back home."

Lew says, "Thanks for putting me up, and for putting up with my antics. You certainly have a beautiful spot up here, but Oak Park is calling me back to get ready for Princeton."

I reply, "Yeah... good luck this fall. You'll do well, I'm sure. It's Princeton's gain, and our loss seeing you leave, Lew. But imagine all those good looking coeds enrolled there. If I know you, you'll be a professor at that college."

Sad to describe seeing Lewis back to the city. Glad is knowing he will do well at Princeton.

Starting our motor launch I boated Lew and his gear over to Walloon village where he would catch the train. Watching the train leave the village station, I felt the vacancy of his leaving. More than any other friend Lew was the brother I needed while in school. Spirit was ready to reassure me that I will make good friends in Kansas, so I looked forward to my Kansas adventure.

My biological brother, Leichester, (aka Baron), is only two, and 15 years younger. He is my dear Pal, but having one my own age is most beneficial to me now during these tumultuous times in which we live.

My Spirit Pal, of course, is always there to reassure, comfort, and guide. Don't get me wrong but having a best friend your own age, that's priceless.

Mother Grace thinks I spend too much time away from my own home... to the neglect of my precious chores; however, the friendships that I am cultivating each summer are people who will support me throughout my adult life.

**Lewis Clarahan and Ernie, summer 1916 when they hiked
from Oak Park, Illinois to Petoskey, Michigan.**

Chapter 27. Clarence Darrow to the Rescue

When July 4 rolls around the little town of Hortons Bay, totally transforms itself.

Every citizen, big and little, does his or her very best to decorate anything and everything that can take a strip of bunting or banner, or Stars & Stripes, the Old Glory, or red, white and blue fabric. Each storefront or town shop gets hung heavily with patriotic decoration.

A review stand gets built where judges and town dignitaries all sit to assess the floats and various entries that will parade by.

Children get into decorating also, as they are found wrapping crêpe paper in a festive manner around the tricycles, bicycles, scooters, and wagons. Even the family pets get wrapped in patriotic colors, since numerous prizes can be won on that most nationalistic of days in our little Hamlet.

For a Hortons Bay kid to sit out the parade on the sidelines, it would certainly warp the child for life.

A soft, westerly breeze was bringing in moist, pine scented July air from Little Traverse Bay.

I was sitting on the rough front porch of Red Fox Inn whittling a stick. Bill Smith and I contemplated the coming event.

"So, Sir William, what will you decorate for an entry in the forthcoming parade?"

"Gonna enter my Buick, yes siree, Stein. Want to help me hang crêpe paper on the old girl?"

"Why certainly, Pal. I'm an old crêpe paper hanger, from way back. Can we get our gals involved, maybe?"

"By Jove, I think they'd be delighted, old chap. Let's bring the Buick around behind Vollie Fox's Red Fox Inn to get everyone involved... make it a community project."

"I like how you think, William. This is an historic vehicle."

"Yes, indeed, Stein. No doubt the first vehicle of its kind in a Fourth of July parade... Up north anyway."

"Do you think my Pops would want his Tin Lizzy entered?"

"Stein, knowing him, I kinda doubt it. Too much exposure for a shy guy like him."

"Yeah, you're so right. At least we finally got the pollen problem solved. No more pines."

"Yeah, that forest fire took out all the pine trees around your homestead."

"Who told you that?"

"Turdface, the local Game Warden, was around town yesterday, making sure all the Indians have fishing licenses."

"Huh? He's gonna get himself killed! That crazy bastard has gone too far! After we take their hunting grounds away, he can't expect those poor creatures to buy fishing licenses on top of that. Oh, some of them will pop him one of these days."

"Yeah, like Nick Boulton."

"Exactly. All it would take is a little firewater to get big Nick riled up and he'll go after Turdface Evans."

"Yup, he could snap the Game Warden's scrawny pencil neck, he could. Gee, how does a man like Mr. Evans get to be so hated in a community?"

"I'll tell you why!"

"Hey, Vollie Fox. Why you old son of a preacher man. You scared us."

"Well boys, how did you manage to stay out of jail this time? Game Warden been looking for you."

"We were just discussing his useless hide. Now what did we do, Vollie?"

"It has come to our attention you was trapping the state animal: namely, the wolverine. That's a protected species in Michigan, you know."

"Oh for pity's sake! Are you kidding me? Sunny and I found that wolverine caught in somebody else's friggin' bear trap is what we did. We don't set traps. No, Sir. That was someone else. Not us. No, Sir!"

"Now, now, calm yourself, Ernest. I know that. Bill knows that. We all know that, but our illustrious Game Warden has been after you, I guess... For some unknown reason."

"Indian lover. That's it. I be fraternizing with the enemy. That's got to be it."

"Oh... Yeah. He's quite the white supremacist, that dad blamed game Warden."

"Plus, he has the bad habit of building a case on hearsay only."

"Yup, his scrawny, ugly son runs back home to report and squeal like a pig to Mr. Evans... the original Turdface himself."

"Oh, yeah, I remember that blue heron incident, Ernest."

"Right, Vollie, all hearsay. But I paid a hefty fine, I did, to the judge in Boyne City. A whopping $15. Wes Dilworth and Uncle George talked me into turning myself in."

"Laid yourself on the mercy of the court, did you?"

"Exactly... why fight it? He had no proof. Turdface never saw me shoot it."

"But he had the dead heron."

"Yeah, sure, he had the heron, but he never saw me kill it."

"But his son saw you shoot it."

"… Right. So why drag it into court and waste the county's money, so I paid the fine... up front to spare a lengthy, expensive court battle, and that's what the Game Warden counts on, that the hicks up here can't afford a lawyer, and can't afford a lengthy courtroom battle... so they settle out of court and pay the fine. Mother took after him with a shotgun. Ran them off our property, she did."

"Yeah, good old Mother Grace. So now I am a fugitive from the law, I suppose, is that right Bill?"

"I guess… You know Mr. Evans."

"Maybe I better lay low for a while, huh, Bill?"

"No. He has no proof. Where's the wolverine? Can he prove the trap is yours, Wemedge? How can he prove the trap is yours?"

"He doesn't need proof. Not Mr. Evans. Not Turdface Evans. Does he ever need proof? That guy oversteps his bounds every day around here. He would arrest his own grandmother and throw her in the slammer just on a whim."

"Shit, this means you won't be riding the Buick in the Fourth of July parade, Wemedge."

"Probably not. What's the fine, Billy, for killing a wolverine out of season?"

"Oh, I bet it's quite steep since they are protected, and plus they are the state animal. You'll probably get some jail time on top of it. Maybe 1000 clams. What say, Vollie?"

"Bill, I'd say you are pretty darn close."

"Oh great. Now I'm a jailbird. Holy shit, you guys. Give me some wiggle room here. Vollie, what the hell."

"Hey. I've got it. Ernie, have no fear when your pal, old Vollie Fox, is here."

"Why?"

"Cause… Clarence Darrow is here."

"What? The world famous Scopes lawyer? Defender of little Bobby Franks murderers... Leopold and Loeb of Charlevoix?"

"Yes… Indeed. He is my cousin and he's coming up for vacation. Staying at Red Fox Inn, just like he usually does."

"No kidding, boy, Vollie, you have saved the day. Better yet, you have saved my ass. Get me an appointment with him. Would you please? I'll give you my new shotgun. Please, Vollie."

"Oh, now, none of that, my young friend. Mr. Darrow is well aware of Mr. Evans disregard for the law up north… And he's been waiting for a chance to get him fired or at least transferred...or jailed."

"Gee, Wemedge, I can see the headlines now: Petoskey News Press... Clarence Darrow here to defend young Ernie Hemingstein, killer of wild wolverines."

"Hell, yeah, let's fight this crooked Mr. Evans. Thanks, Vollie. You have given me hope. Say, Mr. Fox, can I buy you a cold Vernors Ginger Ale?"

"You bet, and I happen to have a couple fresh Cubans here."

"All right! Let's celebrate. May I light that stogie for you, Sire? And Bill, it looks like I'll be riding with you in the Fourth of July parade after all. I've changed my mind. I'll have the country's best lawyer on my case."

"Okay, that's the spirit, Wemedge!"

"To victory!"

"To victory! This cold Vernors tastes great on a hot summer day, Wemedge."

Bill says, "You can say that (puff puff), again. And a smooth stogie tastes great on any day."

Someday I'll travel to Cuba. Maybe settle down there, maybe write me a few novels, maybe design me a nice fishing boat. Maybe write me the greatest fishin' story in the world. Maybe?

Well that night I could hardly sleep. I kept mulling over and over the killing of that wolverine and how Mr. Clarence Darrow, the famous American lawyer, was gonna get me freed. In my mind, I was gathering evidence for the defense, but then I had this chilling thought.

Oh my goodness gracious, Pops has stuffed that Wolverine and Ursa had removed the claws, and it is in my possession and, and… holy shit! I am sunk!

Then I thought, but somehow that famous lawyer that he is, Mr. Clarence Darrow, will get the evidence necessary to clear me and maybe even find the jerk who laid that bear trap. He's the one we need to clear me. The real ownership of that trap will put me in the clear. Soon it became clear that we need to set a trap for the trapper and subpoena him to testify in court that someone else is the rightful owner of the trap, which killed our wolverine in question. It all comes clear to me now.

So early the next morning as the light of dawn peeked through the thick tree line, there I was crouched behind a bush at the location of the bear trap.

Whomever set that heavy metal device will be back if only to check the condition of the bait. Packing two onion on rye sandwiches, I could stay out here all day. I settled in, crouching on cedar boughs and well hidden behind dense bushes of elderberry.

Hours slipped by. My presence was duly noted by chickadees, chipmunks, squirrels, and mosquitoes alike, but no sign of my trap setter. After downing both my onion sandwiches, I was beginning to think my bear trap vigil was wasted. Just as I was expecting this day to be a total loss, and as my eyes closed in nap mode, I heard a twig snap and then two or three more snaps in succession, and the hunched over figure of an elderly man appeared to check the trap. My heart raced.

How do I approach him?

Carefully, the man placed both feet up on the edge of the trap and added fresh bait while recharging the powerful spring mechanism. He went about his business, methodically, as he had obviously done many times before.

As he turned to walk away he stood up and sniffed the air stating, "Do I smell onions?"

Thinking this was the appropriate time to introduce myself, I walked out from behind the bushes. "It's just me, sir, Ernie Hemingway."

"Well I'll be darned. Doc Hemingway's son. Hi, Ernie. I'm Judge Jennings. What brings you out this way?"

"What a pleasant surprise, Judge. I'll tell you why I'm here."

After relating the wolverine story to Judge, he rolled his eyes and said, "Young Hemingway, you have no worries. You did the right thing by putting that creature out of his misery. Now let's set a trap for Mr. Evans... our overzealous game Warden. If and when he files a case against you for killing protected species, we will file a counter suit against him for unlawful arrest, and we can sue him for damages, and pain, and suffering."

"Holy cow. Is that a fact?"

"Yes, indeed it is. This Evans character has been abusing folks long enough and I will put a stop to his trumped up charges and insensitive abuse, and assault as well, of the downtrodden Native

Americans. He could start another Indian uprising if left to operate unchecked. This bully has been filing trumped up charges against locals for years, just to Lord it over our innocent hunters and fisherman."

"Right on, Judge, he is a local tyrant we now can stop, can't we?"

"I will do everything in my power to nail that evil man."

"Most hated man in Emmet County. Say, Judge… Ah, did you know Clarence Darrow is coming up for vacation?"

"No, I hadn't heard a thing, been busy setting traps and setting my docket."

"Yeah, Vollie Fox always puts him up at Red Fox Inn. He's some shirt tail relative or something."

"I had heard he had family up here. Thought it was with the Bumps over at the hardware."

"Well… that could be, too. So together we could… me and you, that is… we could put him away… Turdface, that is… Mr. Evans, that is."

"Indeed, we could young man. I like the way you think. Well, if he is after you for killing a wolverine, the trap is set."

"Yeah, and I guess I am the bait."

"Yes indeed, you are the bait, but be strong in your conviction and I will eventually claim ownership of the trap. You had mercy on that poor unfortunate wolverine critter… put him out of his misery."

"Yeah, he's gonna put me in ownership of that trap and later if you

Clarence Darrow in Action, during the Leopold and Loeb murder trial. Leopold and Loeb were from Charlevoix Loeb Farms which is now Castle Farms.

claim it, he can be counter sued for false arrest, right?"

"Oh yes, yes indeed. But I think a class-action suit from all of us will put him behind bars or cost him his job for misuse of his office. Lansing would then remove him from his post."

"Gee, you really know your law."

"Well, I've been judge now for 10 years in Michigan... used to be a lawless area... people then took the law into their own hands and that promotes innocents being abused."

"Yeah, must've been a wild time for you?"

"Indeed it was, but the railroad changed all that. Well, I must check my other traps and then get back to the office. Pleasure meeting you now, Hemingway."

"Same here, judge. Please keep in touch. You just made my day."

"Thanks. Glad to help. The onions gave you away, you know. Just onions, no meat, no lettuce, no tomato?"

"Yup... just onions, right."

"Well I'll be. Gotta try that."

"Oh, and sometimes I dip it, if'n it's too dry."

"Dip it? In what? You got no gravy?"

"The lake or river... Just a quick one."

"Never heard of it."

"Try it. You'll like it. Oh... and caraway seeds. The rye has to have them little caraway seeds. Makes all the difference in the world."

"I declare," said judge, scratching his head.

"Gotta get me a haircut, judge. Probably see you at McCarthy's barbershop in Petoskey, I must look my best in court."

"Yes, indeed. McCarthy will fill you in on all the news in town. His shop is the hub for anything happening."

"There, my trap's baited with fresh meat. Bears love elderberry so that's why I figure I'll catch one at this spot. Don't quite know how a wolverine came about these parts? Must've got lost."

"Sure was nice chatting with you, Judge. Gotta run now."

"Good show. See you in court, Ernest."

"Yup, see you in court, Judge."

Well that certainly was an unexpected event. Never in my days have I ever expected to get a surprise like that. A guy can't make up these stories, imagine that? The very judge who will try my case turns out is the owner of the trap that caught my wolverine, which means I am off the hook and in like Flynn, and with Clarence Darrow as my defense... How can I lose, huh? Oh, better not say that. Gotta think positive... I am a winnin' this case. When I inform my Pops, he will be flabbergasted. He will probably say, "Divine Providence, my boy. God is actively at work here today."

Now I'm hoping to also nail Turdface Evans, so we can get him out of the Game Warden business, permanent like.

Judge Jennings has hatched a plan. Don't know exactly what he has in mind, but it sure sounded good and I hope it traps Evans and puts him away for good.

I like that Judge. Never liked paying a $15 fine to the judge in Boyne City, but that blue heron killing taught me a lesson, and talking to this Judge Jennings has won me over to liking judges. Yes siree, I am liking judges once again.

Being hauled into court by Game Warden Turdface Evans will be a real treat, and I ain't scared one bit. With Judge Jennings presiding, and Clarence Darrow defending, that day will be monumental, since I happen to know Turdface is walking into the trap of his own making.

Skies were cloudy and wind was blowing oak tree blossoms across the road when I decided to hike over to Hortons Bay to meet Mr. Darrow. Being excited to meet him, I even forgot my morning crow hunt. All my chores were done. Plenty of wood was split for our cook stove, and I had dug a new pit for the morning moving of our outhouse, AKA Hemlock Haven.

Pops and Marcy will have to help me move it now. I covered the old pit so's no one can accidentally tumble into it... what a mess that would be, huh?

Walking the 3 miles to Hortons Crick across pine needles... felt good on my bare feet. My bib overalls were clean and my slouch hat cocked to one side made me look real dapper for a meeting with the world famous lawyer.

When I strolled into Hortons Bay, I noticed John Kotesky's model T was parked by Auntie Beth's Pinehurst, so I figured he had transported Mr. Darrow over here from Walloon train station. John has himself a nice little business going back and forth providing a much-needed taxi service up here in the boonies.

Eating home cooked breakfast after a long train ride would be first on the agenda for my famous lawyer. At least, that is what I expected, but lately nothing has been as I expected, for when I threw open the door to Pinehurst, there sat John, Vollie, and Clarence Darrow waiting to down the big Pinehurst breakfast.

Vollie had the biggest smile, and he surprised me by inviting me, "Ernie, my Pal, please join us. Won't you pull up a chair and meet my cousin, Clarence Darrow, and have breakfast?"

"Oh please. Don't get up. I would be honored, of course. Mr. Darrow, I'm so glad to finally meet you."

"Okay, Ernest, what'll you have?" Auntie Beth inquired.

"Oh... I... uh, the usual, Auntie Beth. Thanks. So, good trip so far?"

Darrow says, "Nice to meet you, Ernest. Your name just came up as one who could show me how to fish Hortons Creek."

"I most solemnly swear, uh, I mean of course, Mr. Darrow. Hortons Creek is under my spell."

"Your modesty must be matched by an equally abundant catch. Would you be available today for a fishing lesson?"

"Why, of course. Fishing would be first on the docket, Mr. Darrow."

"I like this lad. He's quick. Well then, cousin Vollie, let's have a good breakfast, grab some fishing gear, and then try our luck. That sound like a plan?"

"Sure sounds like a plan. Might be just what the doctor ordered to unwind you from your busy Chicago courtroom scene. Not to mention, the lovely train ride."

"Well, like I said, Ernie, here is one of our best fisherman. Yesterday he hauled out nine trout as long as your arm, he did. We may dine on them for dinner if you find the food acceptable here."

At that moment, Grace Quinlan entered. "Gentlemen, your breakfast. We serve family style off this cute little wagon, and if you ever need help, please ring this little dingaling."

Grace was dressed in a formfitting, red, gingham patterned dress, which matched her hat, and the tablecloth, and the drapes. Her white starched apron accented the entire outfit. As she walked out through the swinging doors toward the kitchen, all eyes were on her backside which appeared as two cub bears caught in a gunnysack.

"Hey, it ain't illegal to watch a lady walk away, is it?" remarks Vollie.

"Heck, I sure hope not, or I am guilty as charged," replied Mr. Darrow.

"Now men, she is only 16," I stated.

"Right, and 16 will get you twenty in Joliet. Ha, ha, ha, come on," says Darrow. "Us lawyers have to remind ourselves of that statute every day."

Having a very special guest for breakfast brought Auntie Beth out of the kitchen to explain that no waitress would be available since food was served family style and was stacked on fancy wooden carts brought out by Miss Quinlan.

"So it's our special honor to have you today, Mr. Darrow. As you can see, you just help yourself from this big serving bowl on the cart. Today we have farm fresh scrambled eggs with diced Plath smoked ham, Plath smoked bacon, sweet buttermilk pancakes with fresh blueberries, corned beef hash, wheat toast, butter, Madame Charles's homemade orange marmalade, fresh orange juice, and fresh ground Italian roast coffee blended with chicory 'cause of the war. Enjoy, and if you run out of anything, just ring that ornate brass bell and my assistant will come out. Dinner is served at 5 o'clock sharp. This evening fresh caught trout is the main course. Any questions? -Well then, enjoy."

"Simply beautiful, the food I mean," remarks Darrow.

Vollie Fox commented, "Yup, we get this every day here. And we bask in the skills of one remarkable woman. Plus, she runs the resort too. Wealthy businessman come from Chicago and stay for weeks on end... they do this every summer... word of mouth... And she is always full... never a vacancy. Simply remarkable."

"And one can fish off the dock?" asks Darrow."

"Yes sir, but if you are hankering for trout, Hortons Crick is just a short walk up the road toward the 'Voix... uh, I mean Charlevoix," I explained.

Vollie adds, "Fish off the dock if'n you want small pan fish like; perch, bluegill, sunfish and the like... And once in a while a walleye gets lost. If you dangle your bare feet they'll nibble at your toes, right Ernie?"

"Ahem... Right. Let's just leave it at that. Please pass the flapjacks," I said.

"Oh, boy, these eggs are simply superb don't you think, cousin Vollie?"

"No doubt... laid early this morning right across the street and over the hill at Joe Bacon farm. We used to raise chickens but the roosters disturbed our guests who wanted to sleep in every morning."

"Oh is that so?" Darrow inquired.

"Yup, you know, cock a doodle doo. Roosters think it's their job to crow up the sun at early dawn. Crazy creatures, huh?"

"Mmm. This bacon is simply divine...nice and crunchy. Beth mentioned who smokes it. Who did she say?" asks Darrow.

"Oh, uh, Emile Plath from Rogers City. Old German recipe he brought over from the Fatherland... Best sausage in the world. His smoked pork chops are out of this world, answered Vollie Fox."

I add, "Plath's 'wurst is the best."

"Oh, that was a rich one, Ernest," replied Darrow.

"Hey, I'm only a kid. I couldn't resist."

"Okay, Ernie, we know. You missed the old grind. Quit fooling around," remarks Darrow. " Coffee anyone?"

"Please cousin."

"Me too, Mr. Darrow, thanks." I said, "Think I'll grab some more bacon and eggs too."

"Well Ernie, I can't wait to catch these trout I've heard so much about."

"Hmm... sorry... got my mouth full. Oh yeah, sir, uh, they are tricky to catch but you've got to out think them."

"Indeed... isn't that true, even in the courts... just got to out think them... the prosecution that is."

"You know Judge Jennings, sir?"

"Why yes, we went to law school together."

"You mean you're Pals?"

"Oh yes, I've known Jim Jennings for at least 30 years."

"So what I tell you won't shock you?"

"Ernie, it takes a lot to shock this old lawyer, but go ahead, try to shock me."

"Okay, here goes... I , I... I need you to... To put away the G-G-Game Warden."

"All right, just take a deep breath and calm yourself, Ernie. And what was that? Say that again, please."

"Yeah, Mr. Evans a.k.a. Turdface Evans is gunning for me. He claims I killed a wolverine out of season."

"Well, first of all, there never is a season for hunting wolverine. They are protected... they are the state animal, scary as heck, but go on, please... I'm here to hear it ...see if you have a case?"

"Well, my sister Sunny and I was out plinking with our .22 rifles as we usually do... crow hunting, you know, uh, and we comes across this male wolverine stuck in your pal's bear trap. Oh, he was angry, tried to chew his own leg off, so Sunny put him out of his misery ... plugged him through an eye with her .22."

"Any witnesses?"

"Not that I know of."

"Then he has no case."

"Now, his jerk son, he shadows me, see... all over the place... spying on me, see... he may be his only witness. He got me for shooting a blue heron off season, once."

"Let's get it straight, there is no season on blue heron, son. So you're saying the Game Warden's son may be his witness to this wolverine killing?"

"Exactly. I don't know that for certain, but the trap was set by Judge Jennings, your pal."

"Wow! How intriguing. I'll take the case, Ernie. You got me so interested in this, I've got to see that this goes to trial."

"Oh, swell, Mr. Darrow! I'm so glad."

Darrow added, "With Jim Jennings sitting at the bench, this sounds like a slam dunk. I've heard stories about this Evans. He arrests people on hearsay, hauls them in on trumped up charges... oh yeah we've got to stop this one."

"Exactly! You know his pattern?"

"Yes indeed, a blatant misuse of power. Excuse me, do we need more coffee, gents?"

"No, let's get you some fishing gear and head out there, on to Hortons Creek with Vollie Fox."

Beyond my wildest expectations would best describe my feelings that morning. Clarence was a quick study during our hours along the creek. He learned to avoid the quicksand, quietly stayed in the cool shadows, and cast nicely into deep cool eddies where the lunkers were hiding. He placed his hook through the bottom lip of his grasshopper, and managed to entice a few big brookies to surface.

Vollie brought out his longhandled landing net, which makes hauling in these muscular scrappers a lot easier.

When we had caught enough for our supper, I hauled a stringer full back to Pinehurst kitchen.

Darrow asked, "Tell me, Ernest, why did you toss the fish guts along the edge of the creek like that? I would've tossed them into the creek?"

I replied, "Oh... force of habit, I guess. It feeds the mink and otter well who survive along the creek edge. Why pollute a nice clear springfed stream like this natural gem?"

"I find you to be the natural gem, Ernest."

"Oh gosh, Mr. Darrow."

"No seriously... You should write a book."

"Gosh, do you really think so?"

"Yes, indeed. You know all the finer points of trout fishing, plus you showed me many pointers on how to fine tune my casting, and use my visual awareness. You are the indisputable master of the sport."

Hortons Creek at Hortons Bay, Michigan

"Well sir you were a quick study...but SPORT? Never thought of it as a sport. Up here we fish to survive.... fishing as a sport?...... You know, Mr. Darrow, I think you might have something there... I ain't never thought of it like that before, fishing as a sport... I always think of fishing as more of...a... a... a... a religion more than anything."

"Well Ernest, whatever way you look at it, the fact remains that you seem to have a very good handle on the subject, and I want to thank you, young man, for showing me the ropes and the finer points to fishing on this stream here."

"My pleasure, to be sure, Mr. Darrow, and my thanks to you for volunteering your lawyering skills on my wolverine predicament here. I started to go into shock again over Game Warden Evans."

"Don't you worry, I'll get together with Judge Jennings and we will plot a course for you to win in court, and we will put that rascal Evans away for good," reassured Darrow.

Overburdened with about nine good-sized trout we moseyed over to Pinehurst where Auntie Beth thanked us for the nice stringer of fresh fish. She gave me a wink which meant there would be a little extra in my pay this week. As she handed the fish to Gracie Quinlan she added, "You know, Master Hemingway, that look on your face tells me our famous lawyer visitor taught you more about the law than you taught him about fish? Thanks Gracie. Please scale and put these nice trout on ice for tonight's fish fry."

"Yes'm, Aunty Beth," was Grace's reply.

"Thank you, then we roll the fish in flour, dip them in egg wash, then breadcrumb, and then into a hot buttered iron skillet."

"Yes'm, Aunty. So that's your secret... flour first, then egg wash," affirmed Gracie.

"Exactly, flour dusting first, otherwise the egg will simply slide off the slippery skin of the trout. Hemingways all use cornmeal, but I like flour with my special seasoning at the end. My way adds more flavor."

"Will you ever reveal your special seasoning?" asked Gracie.

"Maybe at your wedding, young lady."

"Roll some of those trout in cornmeal just for me, okay?"

"Don't you worry none now, Master Ernest. I'll make sure you get plenty of cornmeal sautéed trout. I must say, young man, you sure supplied us with a fine mess of fish. We'll be out of luck when you run off into the wicked world of Kansas City. Please stay and help Miss Quinlan batter the fish for frying. I'm sure she would like some company?"

"Sure will. Thanks for those kind words, Aunty, but Vollie Fox can get pretty good fish. He says he taught me how to fish."

"Students often surpass the teacher, and I think that is true in your case," provided Beth.

"I agree," added Gracie, "No one can catch fish like you, Ernie. I'm gonna really miss you when you're gone. Promise you'll write me?"

"Hey, why so glum? I ain't leaving 'til October. Heck, we got a whole summer to enjoy... So let's live it up, Gracie."

"Of course, we enjoy your fish, but I'm hoping there's more than that between us. I just can't put my finger on it, but, when you come on the scene... Ernie... The whole world lights up. It's like us making one of those new picture shows together and each of us is in your picture... Ernie... It feels like you are the director and you bring out the best in us, the actors, me and Bill and Kate and Oddgar, and Vollie, and Jim, and Auntie Beth, and Wesley. Hortons Bay residents are actors in your movie."

"Wow, that was really beautiful, Gracie. You really mean that? How long have you known this?"

"Oh, I don't know. I guess for some time now. Last summer... when all the summer people made it up here and we were all together, you were a leader and we took all our cues from you."

"Gee... no kidding?"

"Yes, and... and most days it was a comedy... you would see to that... And... And then some days you would go within yourself and we knew we had to wait."

"Go on, wait for what?"

"Oh, I don't know... As I recall you first had to go kill something... Yeah that's it, you had to kill something, and then. and then everything would go back to normal again. You were never without a rifle, your shoulder pistol, or your knife, or your slingshot... always with some kind of weapon."

"Yes, you're right, but please go on."

"And then, and then, after you killed some crows or some squirrels or some partridges or some ducks or mourning doves, you would gather us around and delight us with your stories about the hunt."

"This is exciting. Go on please, Gracie."

"Yeah... And we, like dummies, let you pontificate along for hours and it was like, you had this ability to create movies in our heads. You had this mass hypnosis ability. Ernie, I couldn't pull away. I was mesmerized and I would glance around at the others and they were caught in your spell also."

"Yes, yes, go on. This is intriguing."

"Well, I guess you are so caught up in every little detail... That's what hooks us, and pretty soon you've sucked us into your world, and we saved ourselves $.17 and a nickel popcorn, the total cost of the picture show."

"Gosh Gracie... I was not aware... That was most eloquent. No one has ever said it better. You pay me a most high complement... uh... I feel I'm tapping into some pretty profound awareness, but from a humble perspective it's not so much me, Dearie, it's the Holy Spirit, actually."

"I thought so. Nobody could do that on their own. Well I'll be! When did this happen? I mean you and He? I mean you invited Him in... right?"

"It all happened the night my pal Lew Clarahan challenged me to accept Him. Oh, that was a night to remember. For I had no idea what to expect, for I thought I had a whole lot more sinning to do... Why favorites, you know, like my cussin' and drinking hooch, and getting to second base with the girls, you know, and stealing cherries and pulling pranks on folks, you know, and leering at French postcards."

"Yeah, Ernie, I know all that too well, go on."

"Well long story short, I invited Him... the Holy Spirit... in... into my heart, like I wanted to have a devoted close friend or something, a special friend who would not desert me, or stab me in the back, betray me or talk about me when I wasn't around, like when my back was turned, or distort what I say to make me appear stupid to my other pals. You know what I mean?"

"Oh, Ernie, do I ever! Please continue."

"Anyway, Gracie, once I opened up for Him, he opened up many secrets of the universe to me. All my senses were upped an octave. My eyes were super sensitive to light and sound and I can read minds ... pick out thoughts floating. Next there was telling people what they had for breakfast."

"My goodness that must've freaked people out?"

"Oh, yeah. It did, so... since then I have tamed down my behavior... a lot. Gracie, that fish needs flour. You accidentally dropped him right into the egg wash."

"Oh yeah, silly me, huh? Guess I got distracted by your powerful story, Ernie."

"Thanks, anyway I have tempered my topics quite a bit when I share with these folks."

"Most folks don't like you peeking into their private lives... not even what they eat for breakfast."

Auntie Beth appeared at the kitchen sink to survey our fish preparation.

"Mighty nice coating on them fish you know. Now stick around, Ernie, as we sauté these beauties in butter - put on an apron if 'n you don't mind."

"Oh, sure, why not. This looks like fun."

So Gracie Quinlan and I fried those beautiful trout while Auntie made coleslaw and potato salad.

"Ernie, you're helping me with dinner makes it quicker to get these things ready for our distinguished guest, Mr. Darrow. For a city feller, he sure can eat. Well, Ernie, you got a hearty appetite too."

"Auntie, I get that from my Pops, the great physician. We Hemingway's like nothing better than fresh caught trout....fresher the better, by golly."

"Well, Vollie Fox just brought in his stringer of trout, so we'll add them to what we have here. Looks like no one will go hungry tonight. I sure hope Mr. Darrow likes my cooking."

"Oh, I'm sure he will, Aunty Beth," said Grace Quinlan, trying to reassure Beth.

"By golly, I think I'll make a batch of Hush Puppies too," said Beth.

"Oh, that would be divine," added Grace.

"Ernie, if I mix a big bowl of batter, could you drop the balls in the hot oil?"

"Never made hush puppies before, but hey Auntie, I'm game for anything tonight.

"Cooking is easy and fun if you know what you're doing, right, Auntie Beth?"

"Darn tootin', Gracie, and you are a big part of my success here at Pinehurst."Ernie - here is an ice cream scoop for you. It makes perfect hush puppies. Makes them all uniform in size."

"Ernie - most men would never don an apron to help out in the kitchen. They would stay away, saying that's woman's work," commented Gracie Quinlan.

"At home, my Pops does all the cooking. My mother never sets foot in our kitchen. She ain't never learned to cook," Ernie says as he coats the scoop in bacon grease so it will release the hush puppy batter.

"Up in these parts that is mighty strange. Men and women have to both work hard to make a living," commented Beth.

I added, "She hires colored folk for our cooking and cleaning, and even child rearing."

Auntie Beth's Buttermilk Hushpuppy Recipe

1 quart vegetable oil for frying, or as needed
1 cup buttermilk
1/4 cup vegetable oil
2 eggs, room temperature
1 cup cornmeal
1 cup all-purpose flour
1/4 cup white sugar (optional)
1/2 teaspoon baking soda
1/2 teaspoon salt
1/2 cup minced onion
4 green onions, minced

Heat 1 quart vegetable oil in a deep-fryer or large saucepan to 365 degrees F (185 degrees C). Preheat oven to 200 degrees F (95 degrees C).Whisk buttermilk, 1/4 cup vegetable oil, and eggs in a bowl. Combine cornmeal, flour, sugar, baking soda, and salt in a separate bowl. Fold buttermilk mixture, onion, and green onions into cornmeal mixture until just mixed. Drop 6 to 8 tablespoon-sized balls of batter into the hot oil; fry until each hush puppy is golden brown, turning the hush puppies to cook evenly, 6 to 10 minutes. Remove hush puppies with a slotted spoon and place on brown paper bags to drain. Repeat with any remaining batter. Transfer hush puppies to a baking sheet and keep warm in the preheated oven until ready to serve.

"Now that ain't right. I'm sorry, Ernest, but that would not fly up North here, maybe in Oak Park, Illinois, but not up here... no way."

"Not to change the subject, Beth, but how am I doing with these hush puppies?"

"Ernie, oh they're gonna turn out perfect. Dip them out when they get brown."

About this time the Madame Aunty Charles appears at the kitchen door...

"Elizabeth, look, I baked a blackberry cobbler. Do you think Clarence Darrow would like this for dessert? I'm so excited to have him in our little town for vacation."

"Oh, Mrs. Charles, how neighborly of you. What a pleasant surprise. I was needing a dessert and here you bring it. Thank you so very much. I love your cobbler."

"You need extra hands tonight? Ernest, you amaze me. Ah do declare, you look so handsome in that white apron."

"Thanks, Aunty Charles. We got us a good fish fry. Hope Mr. Darrow enjoys it?" I replied excitedly

"This is so exciting. It's not everyday a famous lawyer like he comes to Hortons Bay."

"And he won't eat good like this every day either. Ernie, could you run out and cut off some nice fresh asparagus that grows under my lilac tree?"

"Yes'm, it would be a pleasure. Hush puppies are ready... be back in a flash."

As the screen door slammed behind me, Madame Charles started in about me.

"Now that Ernie Hemingway's gonna make some girl a nice husband."

"Yeah isn't he dreamy... he is so handsome, so witty, so charming, and he writes... and he caught most of these fish today."

"Well, Gracie, if I were you, I'd set my sights on this young man. He's going places, ah do declare. You mark my word. Well, I better get back to the farm. Nice seeing you all again."

While picking asparagus behind Pinehurst, I heard the Madame's team prancing back to the Charles Apple Orchard. I like the way she puts those prancers through their paces. Most folks think she abuses them due to the way she whips them to perform, but I think they like being encouraged to do their utmost and gallop to the max. It's what they were bred to do. Prance. I can't fault the woman for wanting to get the most from her horses. It's just unusual for a mature gentry lady like her.

Beth's mysterious patch of asparagus was going strong under the shade of her lilac tree, and I was able to cut about 5 pounds of the succulent green stalks. Heaven knows why this tender veggie decided to grow here, since Beth never planted it here. Because her husband proposed marriage to her under this tree when lilacs were at the most fragrant, I guess. The asparagus appear each year without planting, as God's way of commemorating that auspicious event.

The romantic ways of Beth and Jim Dilworth seem to perpetuate the enchantment one feels around this unique town of Hortons Bay, as he happily pounds out a nice living as town blacksmith and horse farrier, while his bride happily cooks the world famous chicken dinners of Pinehurst B&B.

Love seems to find a way of expression beyond kisses and hugs. Persons in love will manifest love in whatever they do, whatever the shape that may take, whether it be classic cooking, baking, or the mundane metallic clang of a sledge hammer shaping a red, hot horseshoe.

After unloading my apron full of asparagus in the kitchen sink I guess my curiosity got the best of me so I asked Auntie Beth, "So Auntie Beth, when did all that asparagus start growing all by itself?"

"Ernie, it started out all by itself right after my Jim asked for my hand in marriage, back when we were courting, there was nothing... just grass... that's all that was growing there."

"It just self, generated itself right after your Jim popped the question, right under the lilac tree?"

"Yup... and then appeared like overnight, like them fairy-ring mushrooms do, just as green as God's green apples, Ernie. Darndest thing you ever did see, and they appear there every year."

"Love!" exclaimed Gracie. "Now when I eat your asparagus, Auntie, I'll be eating love."

"Well, uh, yeah, I guess you could say that, Gracie. Never thought of it quite like that, but yes indeedy. You go right ahead and imagine that, girl."

"Maybe Jim had an asparagus seed stuck in the knee of his bib overalls and they stuck to the soil as he got down and proposed."

"Oh golly Gee… I don't know… You two kids are reading way too much into this patch of asparagus. I have work to do. Now, after you wash that pile of asparagus, we're gonna steam them and then sauté them in a frying pan with butter, kosher salt, and fresh cracked pepper. Seeds on his knees...well, now, I've heard everything young'n… Jim with seeds on his knees...what will you youngsters dream up next?"

"Oh, I don't know, but give us time and we'll come up with something, Aunty?

Now, on her own volition, the most voluptuously beautiful girl in all of Michigan, Gracie Quinlan... on impulse... just grabbed my arm, pulled my face down, and planted a juicy kiss on my cheek.

Out of reflex I turned, pulled her face, which smelled now of fried fish, right up to mine and pressed her mouth against my sweaty lips.

Auntie Beth yelled, "Cut that out, you two. We got a big dinner to put on. I said, cut that… Oh shucks all anyway."

Gracie said, "Aren't hormones wonderful, Ernie?

"Um… They sure are. Especially on you, for you wear them so nicely."

Last few days God gave me some mighty nice unexpected happenings. First, there was discovering that Judge Jennings was the owner of the trap which caught my wolverine, next was the news that Clarence Darrow, America's most popular lawyer, was staying in Hortons Bay, next is teaching him to fish Hortons Crick, and that he wants to represent me if and when game Warden Evans arrests me for killing the rare state animal.

Now, Gracie Quinlan wants a piece of me. As if kitchen work is not hot enough. How fortunate is that? And all that unexpected. God sure is full of surprises. When I least expect it, He comes through for me in very profound ways.

A guy can't make up this stuff for the way things play themselves out, it has to be like my Pops would say, indeed, simply Divine Providence, my son.

If game Warden Evans name used to get mentioned, my usual reaction was to go into panic mode and my stomach felt like it would get twisted into great gnarly knots, but not anymore. These latest experiences have given me confidence and certainly a great inner peace.

From now on, that evil nemesis of mine, Turd Face Evans, can't touch me. I am a Mr. Sturdy Ernie, with Judge Jennings and Clarence Darrow on my side. I figure it this way: if a guy can have a few good friends, he should let them be a judge and a lawyer, and maybe an auto mechanic. With friends like these, most of life's problems are solved.

John Koteskey's model T was heard at Pinehurst front door. Aunty Beth flew into high gear making last-minute touches to her big fish fry.

"Gracie, make sure that everyone has a napkin, Dearie. Straighten your apron please. Ernie, you want to sit next to Mr. Darrow. Any second now they'll be coming through that doorway."

Eating together with Clarence Darrow would be my grandest moment. I only want to pick his brain as to how we should go about putting away our out of control Game Warden, Mr. Evans.

My heart was racing as the heavy door swung open and three figures appeared in Beth's dining room.

"Welcome, gentleman. Welcome to my humble establishment. Dinner is ready. Ernie, could you seat our special guests?" Announced a nervous Beth Dilworth.

As I took the jackets, to my surprise, the one extra gentleman was none other than Judge Jennings. Mr. Darrow and Vollie Fox handed me their hats and I commented on Mr. Darrow's hat. "Good evening gentlemen, Judge, Your Honor. Nice Stetson, Mr. Darrow."

"Thank you, Ernie. Just bought that in Petoskey at Kotwicki's Haberdashery. You remember Judge Jennings?"

"Well, that's just perfect having us all together like this. May I adjust your chairs? Mr. Fox, evening."

"Water for everyone?" Asked Grace Quinlan.

"Now remember, Sirs, we serve family style. I will be wheeling the serving cart out here after we serve you your drinks. Your Honor, what can I get you from the bar?"

"Well thank you, young lady. My how you've grown. I remember you as a little girl running around the country club. Oh, of course, make mine a glass of Chardonnay."

"Mr. Darrow?"

"I'll have a Maker's Mark with a beer chaser."

"Mr. Fox? Please. You're gawking, Vollie."

"Oh, uh, yes Gracie, make mine a Kimmel."

"Mr. Hemingway?"

… "The usual please, Gracie."

"Vernors ginger ale?"

"Correct, thank you. Can't get that at Oak Park, can we?"

"Want that with ice?"

"Please," I answered.

"Remember now gentlemen, I'm not a waitress. Please consider me the chef's assistant. Must've been a dusty trip coming from Petoskey? I'll get those drinks now, thank you."

Vollie said, "Thank you, Grace. Dusty is right. Plus the roads up here are terrible. Any news on when they'll be fixed?"

Judge Jennings replied, "When the war ends, maybe we'll have extra money for infrastructure repairs."

"My Pops made the mistake of driving his model T up here from Oak Park. What a harrowing adventure that was," I added.

"That's why I always take the train up here from Chicago," Commented Darrow.

Vollie Fox added, "Yes, the Indiana Railroad now has three passenger trains into Petoskey every day, even on Sunday."

"Even on Sunday? Now that's progress," commented Judge Jennings. "Churches must be packed then?"

I remarked, "Well, uh... not exactly, Judge. They flock up to see that outdoor Theatre called Hiawatha. Have you seen it yet?"

"Now all you locals have seen it, but I haven't," stated Clarence Darrow.

"The Indian Chief comes to our place on Lake Walloon. I'll take you, Mr. Darrow," I volunteered. "Yeah, the Chief is the star of the show. He showed me how to make a birchbark canoe....fragile craft,had to part my hair down the middle to keep it from tipping over."

Everyone laughed, "Ha ha ha... that's hilarious, Ernie."

"Okay gentlemen, here come your drinks, enjoy," said Gracie. "I'll have to head back to help Auntie Beth now…saluto..." declared young Gracie Quinlan upon her return from the bar.

Judge remarked, "Thanks, Grace, my, my, how that girl has grown."

I added, "Yeah, and in all the right places."

Darrow injected, "Yeah, Judge... as you know 16 will get you 20."

Judge lifted his glass in toast, "Well boys… Here's to a short war".

"Hear, hear!" Vollie said. "Down the hatch."

"Cheers! Real smooth," commented Darrow.

"Yes, indeed. Someday Vernors will be available in Illinois. I can't wait. Can't wait to get into the war...pop me some Krauts," I stated mindlessly searching for a lead-in to discuss my wolverine case with the judge and Darrow.

"That's a noble thought, Ernie, but you are not 19 as yet?" replied Vollie Fox.

"Oh... Never thought of that," I stated.

"Okay, gentlemen. Here's to dinner: fresh caught trout with all the trimmings, all for your dining pleasure. Ring the bell if you need more," announced Aunty Beth Dilworth, as she wheeled in her handy two shelf, high wheeled dinner cart, loaded down with trout, hush puppies, asparagus, tater salad, coleslaw, kosher salt and peppercorn grinding mills, and a bottle of malt vinegar .

"The Madame Charles baked you gents a nice blackberry cobbler for dessert, so I must return to my kitchen to make some whipped cream, enjoy."

So without discussion, I hopped up to the food cart and began passing, serving bowls... main entrées first.

"Auntie Beth drafted me to help prepare all this good dinner, men," I said.

"Did you learn all her secrets, Ernie?"

"Vollie, matter of fact I learned a lot, but when it came to adding herbs and spices to the batter on which we dip the fish, she left the room... so that is still secret. Oh, and the potato salad is secret. I wish I knew how she gets the texture so buttery without using butter?"

"Young Mr. Hemingway and I caught most of these nice trout this morning after breakfast," said a proud Clarence Darrow.

"Take as much as you want, cousin, cause Ernie and I can always get our fill any day of the week," stated Vollie.

I quickly interjected, "I wish you hadn't said that, Vollie. Now the judge will think we are big violators."

Vollie added, "Oh... Of course, I mean anytime they are in season of course, ahem."

"We are all law abiding citizens here, aren't we, judge?" replies Darrow.

"Ahem, before he became judge..."

Judge quipped, "Just never mind, Clarence. No need to be telling stories out of school. That was when we were young and frivolous."

Clarence added, "Oh... ahem, right... young and frivolous."

Now is my chance to bring up the Wolverine killing, but I couldn't think of a good way to lead into it.

Vollie said, "Ernie, you look like you might have a fish bone stuck in your throat. Here, eat some bread, it might help?"

No, "Actually... I was just wondering how long Judge Jennings has been trapping, that's all."

"Well, good question... Guess it started back when I was your age, Ernie. Started out with small game and then worked my way up to big game like black bear. You found my trap."

"Yup... sure did, Judge. But you got yourself a wolverine though, Judge. My sister and I stumbled onto him. She popped him in the brain. Had to put him out of his misery. So there. Now you know the truth, and nothing but the truth, so help me, God."

Mr. Darrow mentioned, "And now your overzealous game Warden wants your hide for that mercy killing. Is that the scenario here?"

Vollie Fox concurred, "Yes, that's right. He was around just the other day looking for poor Ernie."

Clarence asked, "Evidence... now what kind of evidence does Evans have?"

"None that we know of, Sir. My Pops went ahead and gutted the poor thing. We gave his heart to the Indians (heap big medicine you know). Pops likes to stuff animals for our museum back in Oak Park, so the poor critter gets stuffed."

"Circumstantial," stated Clarence.

"Yes, purely circumstantial,"concurred Judge. Won't carry much weight in the poaching case... one nondescript stuffed wolverine in your father's possession. Could be any Wolverine. There's no telling how it got there... No bullet wounds... No puncture of hide... Could've died of natural causes."

Clarence added, "Indeed... very flimsy case in which to arrest anyone... Hearsay alone. I could sue for fake arrest and get you restitution for damages too. You could walk away a wealthy man, Ernie."

Vollie added, "Yes, the newspapers will make a big deal about this... Nasty Game Warden Pinches 17-year-old Child for Fake Killing State Animal... Ends Up in Slammer for False Arrest... and Child

Abuse. Oh, this would not go good with Lansing officials either. No, no, they don't like being embarrassed. Evans could get recalled. Not to mention, child abuse since Ernie is only 17. Evans could lose his retirement."

Clarence says, "Right, the age of majority is 18. Something we need to also consider. Good thinking, cousin."

Judge says, "Clearly, Mr. Darrow and I need to research other counter-charges we could bring to this most interesting of cases. This will be one for the juris-prudence record book."

Clearly Auntie Beth must've been eavesdropping, for just at the right moment she sprang through the swinging doors from the kitchen with another wagon full of the evening desserts with whipped cream and cinnamon Maple sprinkles.

"Surprise! Earlier I was promoting the Madame's cobbler... Well looky here, Mother Bacon from over the hill, just sent over a fresh blueberry pie. Hope you gentlemen don't mind also having another dessert, and not to be outdone, my able son, Wesley, volunteered to crank you a whole bucket of fresh, creamy, vanilla ice cream."

About this time, Gracie Quinlan pushed through the swinging doors and announced another surprise: "Gentlemen, the Bump sisters are back from camp way up in Minnesota, and they have worked out a routine of song and dance while you eat your dessert. Nothing like a little first class entertainment imported right from the land of sky blue waters. Marge...Pudge...hit it!"

The swinging door opened again as the cutest young, innocent girls danced into the dining room floor, dressed as German beer garden girls, tap dancing and singing the Schnitzel Bank song. Marge and Pudge, aged 16 and 15 danced and sang a half dozen comedy songs which poked fun at Austrians with whom we are presently at war.

After we had finished our bounty of desserts, the Bump sisters gave a final encore bowing their way backwards to the swinging kitchen doors.

Vollie Fox had this to say, "Anyone care for a nice Cuban?"

"Cigars! What could be more fitting, cousin," replied Clarence reaching for matches.

Just as we all had started having a good pull on our first-class smokes, imported from Cuba, and certain that we had enjoyed all the possible homespun surprises man could ever imagine, Aunty Beth waltzed in with the dramatic flair of arms and swirling petticoats: "Gentlemen, I know you are going to wonder how we could possibly top such a meal as you enjoyed here tonight, but I want to invite you to dinner tomorrow, for I'll be barbecuing my famous chicken dinners."

Words stuck in my throat due to all the love and support I felt this night, but shaking hands I said, "Well Judge, John Koteskey is outside waiting to drive you back to Petoskey, so I'll say my goodbyes now and thanks so much for coming to my rescue in this wolverine issue."

"Ernie... you're a good kid. I love your undying sense of adventure, and your ability to always be at the center of the action. Please give my best to your father and mother, and rest assured, me and my friend Darrow, will make sure justice is served and Evans is put where he belongs."

Darrow added, "Ernie, that was the best fish dinner I have ever eaten. Thanks for the fishing lessons and rest easy, Judge and I will make this wolverine case a study in jurisprudence. Textbooks will include what we will reveal on this case. Have faith and don't let this Game Warden intimidate you, okay? His goose is cooked."

"Thanks, Mr. Darrow. I may be only 17, but if we can put this slime away, I'm going for it, and with your help, together we can stand up to him and make it happen. This thug has been bothering Emmet County for far too long."

The back deck of Auntie Beth's "Pinehurst" in Hortons Bay.

Chapter 28. I Take Gracie for a Test Drive

"Psst... Hey Ernie," came a voice from the swinging door, which leads to the kitchen. "It's me, Grace. Hey, hon, do you want to walk in the moonlight?"

"Hi, Gracie, heck yeah. What a romantic idea. I like the way you think, sweetie. Let's go. Hang up that apron. Take my hand."

Grace said, "Guess where I'd like to walk tonight?"

"Well, I know the spot, but go ahead with your idea. It's hard for me to think right now."

"Good idea. Let's not talk, or think, just soak up the moonlight and the twilight's misty atmosphere," said Grace.

To tell me to stop talking is like asking Niagara Falls to flow backward. This evening's excitement has me more charged up than ever in my life, but in order to honor Gracie and the full moon, I bit my lip as we slid along the dew covered path, watching lightning bugs flashing messages in the twilight.

Waiting for Gracie to break the silence took a while, but as the hand holding needed to shift to a more comfortable position, she whispered seductively, "Hold me, Ernie. Oh, how I've longed for your firm...manly... touch."

So there it is... me and Grace Quinlan, without argue, the most beautiful girl in all of Michigan, embracing under a bright, full moon. An artist couldn't paint a better picture as the light evening breeze brought with it the intoxicating odor of lilac, spruce, and cedar, and the smell of fried fish, which still lingered in her auburn curls.

Her cool, milky skin pressed lightly against my face, as her breathing turned to a faster pace, now intermixed with occasional light, drawn out moans, which came from deep within her psyche.

"Oh... Ernie... please, kiss me."

At that request, my fingers slid up the nape of her neck and snagged a handful of that nice, auburn hair. Then, I pressed her puffy, moist mouth against my waiting lips, just like I saw done in a movie once.

After a prolonged minute or so, she pushed away to catch her breath. Her mouth tasted salty with a hint of blueberry pie, and whipped cream. I liked that kind of kiss.

Our arms locked around each other into a tight embrace, until she tilted back her head and said, "Kiss me again, you Brute."

Her lips quivered and moved in a passionate wave, like motion, never once injecting her pretty pink tongue like the French are prone to do, but this time she applied more pressure until the sweet, delicate touch of her puffy lips moved into pushy cadences of deliberate fluttering arpeggios across her perfect teeth.

Had I been a trumpet player, my lips would have let her continue, but my embouchure was flabby and I did a moan as if in slight pain, and she backed off again, thrusting her head into my well muscled chest using a rather squirming motion, exploring to see if the contours of our bodies could fit, coupled with more of her tantalizing moans.

At this moment, I realized this was her very first experience of heavy petting, and Gracie had saved herself for this special moment in which to awaken her new, ample, female equipment.

"Oh, Ernie, no one has ever kissed me like that. You are fantastic... Let's do that again... p-p-p-please?"

"Okay, Gracie, but you are right. Let's cut the talking. I think it kinda diminishes the lovey feeling."

Feeling her legs buckle, I gently allowed her overly developed young frame to slide onto the moist shoreline grasses. I liked it when her pendulous breasts flattened over her young chest as she nestled her back into the cool grass.

I liked it when she drew me on top of her in order to be stimulated by my weight. I liked it when I felt the heaving of her every breath and heard it echo instantly, into the caverns of my curious, sensitive ears. With our next kiss, I felt her relinquish control and allow me to explore inside her open mouth, with my plunging tongue. She gently sucked on it... in an in and out fashion.

"Oh, Ernie... I'm glad you go to the movies. You learned a lot about loving."

"Mmm... yes, and that's only the coming attractions."

After that witty crack, along with my well placed knee working her groin, I felt her whole body get the shakes as if some mystic bow was playing her like a Stradivarius violin. Those vibrations were now involuntary, and danced across her entire firm, young body.

I liked it when she allowed her body to take over. She was out of control, like the Titanic ship captain who calls to abandon the ship, and then rides it down... she was surrendering to her new found womanhood, while I was triggering all the right buttons, and we were gamely dumbfounded by our own unbridled, God given passions.

We had become a sensational lovemaking machine that was totally triggered, and now set on automatic... beyond the point of no return, and we both liked it.

We had unknowingly thrown all the switches, and had worked ourselves into an oily shipwreck of lathered up passions, and we were plunging into the bottom, caught in life's most tempting whirlpool, yes, sucked down by that old proverbial maelstrom of carnality, which every young teenage couple must ride, just this side of copulation. The verifiable sirens of desire were calling us... the beautiful Gracie Quinlan and I, the ship of young fools without a compass, totally rudderless, and going down, down, down, gamely riding the "Wild Thing", the "Demi-Death," and too young and too inexperienced to know where it would lead, even if it was a trip to the moon on gossamer wings.

All of a sudden a rogue rainstorm moved through Hortons Bay, giving us the cold shower that we most certainly needed to cool off our mutual ardor.

Gracie and I made a mad dash toward a grove of nearby maple trees, where we rode out the swift moving, summer downpour. Under the umbrella of maples, she and I became chatty...

"I like the smell of your wet hair, Grace."

"Ernie, are you sorry that the rains came?"

"Auburn hair is attractive on you."

"Did you like the way I kiss?"

"I'm gonna marry some woman, but she has to have auburn hair."

"Do you like my figure? Like my butt? Wonder what short hair would look like? I think I'm fat. You think I'm fat, Ernie?"

"That's it! She'd have auburn hair, but then she'd cut it short, just for me."

"Men stare at me... makes me happy, yet nervous at the same time. I'm so confused."

"Short auburn hair won't be around for quite a while though."

"You summer people were surprised to see my big growth spurt, when you returned, weren't you? Hormones are wonderful, aren't they? Do you think Mother Nature was good to me?"

"Grace... How long will it take before women will be comfortable wearing their hair short?"

"I had a great time tonight, Ernie. Should we do it again?"

"Well, Grace, the rain stopped. I'd better get you back to Pinehurst. Aunty Beth won't be doing all those dishes by herself."

"Yeah, Ernie, I guess you're right. Let's head back. Rain clouds now cover our nice moon anyway. I hate clouds. Clouds are not romantic. That's where Jim proposed to Aunty Beth..."

"Bill Smith is entering his Buick in the fourth of July parade. You want to ride with us? I have to keep an eye peeled for Mr. Evans, that bastard wants to arrest me. Maybe I should lay low."

As I recall the heavy petting incident, that unexpected rainstorm actually saved us both... Gracie and me... 'cause even though it was painful to call a halt to the loveplay, neither one of us was prepared to venture beyond what bliss we had already experienced. Besides that, the guilt of smooching Bill's girl and trying to explain it to him and Kate would've been too much for me.

God's timing in sending that rogue rainstorm was perfect, for had we continued our escalation course in love making 101, neither of us was aware of the consequences that could have occurred, and we were too young for the life changing events if a pregnancy occurred.

Gracie and I later made a pact not to blab to anyone about the incident, but to cherish it as one of those most memorable experiences, the skills of which could be saved and savored for the wedding night.

Mind you now, I am not one to advocate for unprotected premarital relations, but there comes in life certain moments called teachable moments, and that soiree between Gracie and me ranks right up there as one of my most intimately memorable moments ever. When asked to go to my "happy place" now, I'll know where I go... to love session 101, with Grace Quinlan... just before the rain.

Now, I know you're thinking me a cad for exploiting a young, defenseless, innocent, but oh contrary, Gracie herself initiated the entire incident, inviting me as catalyst to test drive her new equipment. Just like those young thoroughbred race horses, which finally mature enough to compete on the racetrack. Their owners are eager to see what they are capable of doing, so what do the owners do? They hire a professional jockey to ride the youngster to reveal her capabilities.

Same situation with Gracie and me. As I see it, she wanted me to give her new equipment a test drive, a shake down cruise, so to speak, so she could see what her new God given stuff was capable of, when she was put through her paces by an expert.

Mind you, I ain't no expert, but in Gracie's eyes, I would do, and after our short test drive, I think she was very satisfied, anyway, I almost heard no complaints.

Plus, from my point of view, we diffused the annoying sexual tension that always existed between us.

As her rider during the test drive, I can report a very successful shake-down, test ride.

The thoroughbred performs admirably well and had plenty more to give in the stretch. That's my impartial opinion.

Bill and Kate never caught on to GQ and I later, but I think they both wondered why Gracie and I acted so friendly thereafter. Kate, being a woman of the world, picked up on it, but she never let on, which is very uncharacteristic for Kate. I surmise she was comfortably content and very satisfied that I used techniques on her which I learned from Gracie.

My only caveat would be to say that this is a most isolated incident, Gracie and I, so rest assured that not many girls are gonna throw themselves at you for test purposes only, so don't wait around hoping it will happen to you, dear boy, because chances are it won't. Nor am I advocating it, cause I did feel guilty afterwards.

Truth be known, I was always a bit afraid of Gracie's athleticism. She was a jockey of unparalleled reputation...her dad owning a large stable of fine stock and all... that's why her snap decision to let me press all her buttons came as quite a shock to me and no boasting of it will ever come out of me, because I fear Gracie's right cross. Even sharing this unusual incident could still put me on her hit list, so please keep this under your hat.

Chapter 29. A Fourth of July to Forget

Fourth of July came early to citizens of Hortons Bay this year since we were obsessed with schmoozing our famous pal, Clarence Darrow, but Bill Smith and I started draping red and white crêpe paper around his blue Buick convertible. Early morning dew made the decoration sag and stretch quite a lot. Kate and Gracie Quinlan joined us later in the morning with chicken salad sandwiches on whole wheat, plus a cold jug of lemonade which they made at Pinehurst.

"Should you be laying low for a while, Wemedge?" says Kate.

"Yeah, Stein, old Mr. Evans, our esteemed Game Warden is gunning for you," added Bill.

Gracie said, "Yeah Ernie, aren't you worried a little?"

"No, let's face it, I can't hide forever from him. Ursa and I tried that once and believe me, it was a friggin' nightmare slogging through the swamps for a week."

Bill remarked, "Actually, it was more like two."

"Was it that long? Bill, this damn crepe paper is sagging so... I'm getting frustrated," I complained.

"Don't worry, Stein. Late morning sun will tighten it up, and then the girls can help us hang some more. Aunty, the Madame, will hitch up her prancers soon, so we'll have to help her decorate them and her carriage also."

"Hope we don't run out of decorations?" Gracie queried.

"Oh... don't worry, Vollie Fox always gets in the spirit and sends away for cases of decorations. He gets done hanging bunting all over Red Fox Inn, then he'll bring out his stash for the rest of town," I reported.

"Oh yeah, I plum forgot how patriotic he gets every Fourth of July," added Grace.

Soon, parade goers started arriving in horsedrawn wagons, carts, carriages, bicycles, tricycles, unicycles, high wheel cycles, and John Kotesky pulled up with his model T taxi, Bill pulled right behind, and the girls and I hopped in to proudly represent the horseless carriage great brigade of which there were only two.

Half a dozen Civil War veterans led the parade sporting Old Glory in their full dress woolen uniforms, followed by our community band, a barbershop quartet, DAR (Daughters of the American Revolution), the Knights of Columbus, and then municipal horsedrawn wagons for obvious reasons, followed by a couple of clowns, working brooms and wheelbarrows to deposit road apples, then ours... the motorized vehicle division followed by all the bicycle and foot powered vehicles, children with wagons, pets, and various marching clubs and organizations, women's voting rights and alcohol prohibition made up the rear.

This motley crew slowly marched down the highway toward Charlevoix, passing in front of the review stand inhabited by four of Hortons Bay dignitaries.

As Bill's Buick slowly inched in front of the review stands, a tall, strange, mustached uniform man with a Winchester 30/30 ran out in front of us demanding that we halt.

"Now hold it right there, mister! I'm here to arrest Ernest Hemingway. Step down and deliver... now!"

"What? Are you kidding? This is the Fourth of July. This is the parade," commented Kate Smith.

"Never you mind, miss. I am law enforcement here. Now Hemingway, step down and put your hands behind you... you violater!"

"But, but, what's the charge that is so important to halt the Fourth of July parade?" I countered.

"You know darn well, you poacher!"

I wasn't going to argue with Winchester, so out of shocking humility, I reluctantly obeyed orders only to see Game Warden Evans pull up with his team pulling a wagon decked out with Game Warden markings.

"So it is you, Evans! Must you stop the Fourth of July parade to make your silly arrest?" I yelled in complete astonishment.

Evans yelled, "When there are lawbreakers present, nothing is sacred. Now climb in. You are going to jail, you ruffian. Put the cuffs on him, Cousteau."

Passing the reviewing stand, all faces of society's finest stared, aghast at what had transpired. What had just agonizingly occurred seemed more bizarre than their wildest nightmares, and I, Doc Hemingway's pride and joy, seems to be the cause of it.

Nowhere in the annals of parades worldwide had anything so goshe, so utterly grotesque, so absolutely, inhumanely heinous, ever appeared on record."

Shocked to the marrow, all parade participants and viewers alike fled to the safety of their respective domiciles. Abandoned bunting and patriotic streamers littered the empty streets, and occasionally rolled down empty streets as if teased by some unseen demons which now roamed the vacant review stand.

Instead of the rousing sound of Marshall music, and triumphant military marching boots, all that one heard was the sound of heavy doors swiftly slamming, metal, and deadbolts clacking briskly.

Instead of the innocent sounds of excited children eagerly awaiting their awards for best decorated bike, all one heard was the whimper of confused mourning doves echoing down empty and lonely parade routes, forever silent until next year.

Traditional group gaiety and remembered national purpose, had gone with the wind and had totally disappeared along with the tantalizing smell of warm hotdogs laden with mustard and steaming sauerkraut.

So stunning was the Game Warden's brutal arrest upon this gentle little Hamlet of Hortons Bay that it brought all Fourth of July festivities to an abrupt halt, as I sadly rode toward jail in total disbelief and overwhelming despair.

Slamming wrought iron jail doors soon announced a freedom-lost reality to my sensitive nervous system. A cold, hard, flea infested muslin mattress was my only comfort in this gray, dingy, decor from Hades.

"Hey, Mr. Evans, what's the charge? Shouldn't a guy be told why he's being arrested?"

"Listen, you young hooligan, you know perfectly well. I've been trying to nab you for years, so shut up and take your punishment."

"Sure wish I knew. Say, doesn't a guy get a phone call?"

"Nope, not the likes of you!"

An episode like this was never expected.

Having a personal vendetta against me, and my friendship with the Native Americans, Game Warden Evans made numerous legal errors in my arrest.

Letting his emotions overrule his sense of proper protocol, the legal errors began to mount. As I made note of each of Evans legal mistakes, I began to see him falling deeper and deeper into a trap of his own making.

His ignoring prisoner rights for so many years has clouded his rational mind until he no longer has a handle on the proper way to make an arrest. Because few arrests are ever challenged in court, intimidated citizens ignorant of their rights during arrest simply pay the fines and are released without taking Evans on in a court of law.

With Judge Jennings and Clarence Darrow backing me, we will have plenty against Evans, enough to reverse the roles and put him behind bars instead of me.

After hearing of my arrest, Darrow hailed John Kotesky's taxi and rushed to the Petoskey jailhouse, pronto.

Haggling with Evans, Darrow finally sprung me from jail, so I did not have to spend another night on that mangy mattress.

Darrow stated, "Aren't you the lucky chap having a smart lawyer available to spring you from that unsanitary cell?"

"Gosh, Mr. Darrow, thanks a million. I was getting the willies in that filthy pen."

Clarence commented, "Hey, this guy Evans is a piece of work."

I countered, "You noticed?"

"Indeed, Ernie, he really has it in for you, for some reason. I was lucky to get you released. What a hard head he is."

I added, "Oh, I have a huge list of infractions I noted in the mishandling of my arrest, alone. Imagine how many other errors we will find."

"Ernie, when I get him in the courtroom, Judge Jennings and I will spring the trap. And then we will throw the book at him."

I add, "Can't wait to see his ugly face when he realizes he is the one being on trial."

"Well, Ernie, the Kotesky taxi is waiting, so let me drop you off somewhere."

"Thanks, Mr. Darrow, but I itch all over. I think I'll take a soak with a bar of pine tar soap, and wash up in Lake Michigan, then over to McCarthy Barber shop for a shave and a haircut, and to catch up on all the gossip. Tell Judge I said, 'hey'."

"Right-good idea. You will look nice in the courtroom. Going over to Judge's office right now to file grievances."

Clouds filled the skies over Little Traverse Bay, but water temps for July 5 were warm. A warm, moist breeze was drifting up from the southeast, giving lumber schooners of full sail off Petoskey municipal docks.

Work boats, fishing boats, and fishnet drying racks dotted the harbor as I soaped up, including my clothes, which also need disinfecting due to my brief stay in the infected Petoskey slammer. After scrubbing and soaking in the Bay, my stomach told me it was hungry, so I headed for Jesperson's restaurant for sustenance.

Wolfing down a ham on rye, and a bowl of their famous vegetable soup, followed by a delightful piece of their famous banana cream pie, I realized I needed a haircut.

My clothes smelled like pine tar when I shuffled into McCarthy Barber shop.

"Hey, Ernie, long time no see. How you been? Your dad?"

McCarthy Barbershop in Downtown Petoskey, where Ernie got his haircuts and got updated on all the local gossip.

"Oh, good... good. Thanks for asking! Just a little off the top and trim the sides, so I look good in court, Mr. McCarthy."

"Yeah, heard all about your arrest. Totally stopped the Hortons Bay Parade. Brought the whole show to a screaming halt. Man, that Game Warden is such a brute."

"Wow! News travels fast around here. A guy can't keep any secrets, that's for sure."

"Small towns... you know."

"Everything happens to me. I guess I'm just a fool."

"Well, that's part of being a teenager."

"But why does life have to be so complicated?"

"You just wait. It'll get more so."

"Ever spend the night in our delightful jail?"

"Can't say that I have. How does this length feel to you, yes?"

"Cut a little more off the top, please. Lop off those sideburns too. Looks too shabby."

"Won't be long, I'll have you looking like a clean cut All American boy."

"I sure hope so, Mr. McCarthy. My reputation got somewhat tarnished yesterday right in the middle of that big parade."

"So I heard. How's that now? Short enough for you?"

"Let me see… You know... I think you got it, Mr. McCarthy. I likes it."

"Good, now for the hot towel. Ready?"

"Ready, Ah, that feels good. I might fall asleep on the best hot towel."

"Not much sleep in jail, huh?"

"Nope. It sure was a far cry from the Cushman Hotel next door. This jails a doggone dump!"

"Hey, Ernie, take a little snooze if you want. I gotta sharpen this razor on my leather strop. Then I have to whip up a good lather for your shave. Ernie, I'll never forget when your Pops brought you in here for your first shave. You ended up looking like a million bucks."

"Felt like it too. I skipped all the way to the library, I recall."

As McCarthy had my whole head wrapped in a steaming hot towel, I drifted off to the rhythm of McCarthy honing his razor on the long, leather strop. I dreamed of my upcoming courtroom scene and the feeling of victory, as I walked out a free man in my imagination. Then I saw myself strut out to the courtroom steps where all my girlfriends lined up to cheer my success.

"Wake up, Ernie... you slept right through my best shave. Now a splash of Bay rum and another look like a million bucks. What does the magic mirror say?"

"You outdid yourself, Mr. McCarthy, I look halfway human again... And you got rid of that smell of pine tar."

McCarthy did his usual towel snap and whisk room dusting of my semi dry clothing as I dreamily rose from his magical new hydraulic barber chair.

"Here's two bits, my good man. With a transformation like this, my case will be a shoe in success."

"No doubt, Ernie, you look a winner."

"Hey, there's my ride home. Thanks, Mr. McCarthy."

My luck was getting better, for as I glanced out the barber shop open door, there came Wes Dilworth driving his buckboard wagon."

"Wes! How about lift?"

"Of course, Ernie. Hop in. You look like a million bucks."

"So, lucky me, huh? What brings you to Teposkey?"

"Thought you were in jail, so folks in Hortons Bay sent me to spring you loose."

"Well, my good man, thanks, my lawyer sprung me after a night in the local hoozgow."

"My, yes that was our famous visitor, Clarence Darrow, right?"

"Right, but after a night of darkest misery, I had to freshen up with a dip in Lake Michigan, with a bar of pine tar soap, and a new facelift from McCarthy."

"Well hop in, pal. The whole town is still in shock from that arrest which halted our Fourth of July."

"What! No fireworks either?"

"Nope... yesterday the tyrant Evans scared away the festivities of the whole day... caused a small riot."

"Yeah... well no one was more shocked than I, dear boy. He must've been hiding behind the reviewing stand, he and his hired gun. What a huge rifle!"

"Yup... then all the kids screamed and women folk rushed them home for cover. You never know with that Evans. In a matter of minutes the streets were totally empty, my man. What a panic. I never seen the likes of it... ever. Place is still a ghost town."

"Well, I'll have to make an appearance over there so folks will know all is well, and they can feel safe walking the street once again."

"You need anything from Bump Hardware, while I'm in town?"

"Matter of fact, I do. Mind if I pick up a box of .22 shorts? Crows are getting out of hand around Windemere cabin. Oh... And I'm needing my own library card so I'll run up the street."

"You mean your Pops has been making you use his library card all these years?"

"Yup, so he can control what us kids read. No steamy John Steinbeck. Mother hates Steinbeck, but heck, I am 17... a high school graduate... I should be able to have my own library card."

"Heck yeah, Ernie. It's time you assert yourself. You're a big boy now."

"What they don't know is that I've been using my grandma's card anyway."

"You rascal, you. Well, make it snappy, I'll be at the hardware. Jim needs iron for horseshoes and harness fasteners. Did you know Jim now makes harnesses?"

"Your Pops is an artist, well, you know that, right. Okay, I'll be right back. Just so darn glad you came to get me."

The cranky old librarian gave me the fisheye about getting my own library card. Later, I met up with Wes Dilworth and bought a box of shells. Soon we were on our way back to Hortons Bay.

Ernie's Nemesis: Game Warden Evans

Chapter 30. Juvenile Justice for Hortons Bay

Waving to me were all my pals in Hortons Bay.

Remnants of the abandoned Fourth of July parade still fluttered along the edges of the streets. Loose strands of red, white, and blue crêpe paper caught the cool breeze on this warm summer afternoon, and patriotic bunting still hung as if it didn't get enough show on the fourth.

Jim waved a horseshoe at me from his anvil at the blacksmith shop, as Wes tied the team up to a hitching post near the watering trough.

"Think I'll pop in and say hello to your mother. Thanks for the ride, Wes."

My fear was that some town folks would blame me for the interruption of their July fourth plans, being as Mr. Evans arrested me and shut down the entire day's festivities.

"Afternoon, Auntie Beth," I stated.

"Well look who's here, gosh, Ernest, sure is good to see you. Here's a box full of blue ribbons for you to hand out. President of the festivities committee left these, and the list of folks who should receive an award. She thought it fitting that you should present them personally, so everyone will know you haven't been executed. Since everyone fears Turdface Evans, and since it was his arrest of you at gunpoint that quelled the festivities of the fourth, Madame Charles thought it fitting that you finish the job so the children will know you are alive and well, and it will make the kids feel good to get their ribbons."

"Well, that's awful nice of her. I like kids. Have you seen Bill and Kate around?"

"Probably at the Charles farm. Folks are bit shy about coming downtown out of fear of that fanatic Game Warden. He really slipped his nut yesterday. The nerves that idiot had, coming out during the Independence Day parade with a godforsaken shotgun and waving it at everyone. That man is nuts, I tell you. Are you all right, son?"

"Spent a dismal night in that dismal jail, which I don't want to do again. Clarence Darrow sprung me though."

"Good, I see you got a nice haircut and shave. How are the McCarthy's?"

"Oh fine, I guess. I fell asleep in the barber chair."

"Okay, well you run along now and hand out those nice ribbons, and then come back for a nice chicken dinner. You must be starved!"

"Yeah, I really am. Had a bite at Jesperson's, but now I'm ready for chicken."

"Put a saddle on Seabiscuit if you want."

"Gee, that'd be great. You know how I love that guy."

"Yeah, and he loves you too."

"I noticed. Seabiscuit is my all time favorite horse, and I try to ride him every chance I get. Children of the community will be thrilled to see me ride up with shining ribbons for them."

As I settled the handsome Palomino, I realized most of the town's children would be attending Vacation Bible school at the Methodist Church, so I directed Seabiscuit up the hill to the church.

After a slow, deliberate canter, we arrived at the church. Seabiscuit announced his presence with a loud whinny, followed by a very audible snort.

All the children were enjoying a little snack when we arrived, so it was no disturbance to dismount with my box of surprise ribbons and state the purpose of my visit.

"Gee, Ernie, we thought you were dead or executed by the Game Warden."

"Well, I'm very much alive and I've brought your awards for entering in the Fourth of July parade. That Game Warden may soon be gone if all goes well. Okay, for best decorated bikes the award goes to…"

Handing out the ribbons was a perfect way for me to reenter society after my agonizing overnight lockup. Even with America's best lawyer on my side, while in jail I still took the whole dramatic ordeal personally. Guess my faith is weak, or Mad Dog Evans is much too convincing. His ferocity had quite an impact on the sensitive ones of naïve Hortons Bay.

Gangster Al Capone may well have been intimidated by Evans parade stopping arrest scenario.

It will be some time before we all are over the fearful psychotic terror that Evans perpetrated over our little community.

Kaiser Bill and his Austrian horde are tyrants terrorizing innocent citizens of Italy and France, but we have our own form of tyrant right here in Emmet County, and his name is Game Warden Evans.

"Well, Aunty Beth, handing out those awards really helped me reenter society after spending a long night in the Petoskey slammer."

"Ernie, I figured we had to do something, because that crazy Game Warden has shook up the whole community."

"Yeah, and I can't help thinking it was my fault."

"Now, you stop thinking that, youngster, because no one blames you... understand? Now please don't blame yourself. That psycho Evans is the one who scared all of us, not you, dear boy. Now wash up for a nice chicken dinner the way you like it. I've got plenty, since the Fourth of July meals all got canceled."

Auntie Beth was doing her best to distract me from blaming myself for the Fourth of July fiasco; however, no matter what she said or did, I still needed to hear it from more citizens of Hortons Bay. Call me thickheaded or maybe too darn guilt ridden from my self-righteous, sanctimonious parents, whichever was, still I needed more convincing of my innocence.

When a community is deprived of their Independence Day parade, and all the rest of its patriotic activities, including its evening fireworks, that lack of celebration has a serious negative psychic effect on the naive citizens of this small hamlet.

Knowing Evans was gunning for me led me at first inclination to lay low. If I had only listened to my first hunch, none of this would've happened, but Darrow and Jennings gave me confidence to ride in Bill's Buick. I guess they were baiting the trap for Evans to make his move, and I was the bait.

Somehow, I feel responsible for Hortons Bay's lack of a Fourth of July celebration. Somehow I have to make it up to them. I will do whatever I can, but it will have to be big to make them forget about the Fourth of July that never was.

So far, nothing has gone as expected. It seems like God is throwing me one curve after another.

But He is the boss. I never lose track of that, so I wonder just how this latest drama will unfold. My last summer up in Michigan sure is unfolding in a most adventuresome way.

Auntie Beth had invited all my friends to my welcome home chicken dinner: of course, Bill and Kate Smith, and YK, Grace Quinlan, plus a number of steady summer people.

Bill started the conversation, "Well, old boy, you've certainly given us quite a start being hauled off right in the middle of our Independence Day."

Kate added, "Indeed, old sport, a bit of the dramatic I did say."

Grace commented, "Ernie, we all are in shock."

Marge stated, "Ernie, you must've been through hell, welcome back, old friend."

"Hey listen, friends, thanks for all those kind words of support. It was my misfortune to be on the Game Warden's doo-doo list, but seriously, 'His Turdness' could have waited at least til after the fireworks; however, I don't mind spending a night in jail if it will mean the end of Evans domination around these parts. By the way, Bill, here's a blue ribbon. You won 'Best Decorated Buick'."

Bill said, "Gee, thanks. Too bad the parade was so abbreviated, yet glad you're back among us again, my friend."

Kate states, "We were all so worried. That arrest shocked the entire community to the core."

Grace adds, "Glad you're back, Ernie. After Evans hauled you off, everyone disbanded to the safety of their own homes."

"Well friends, let me assure you, there's no place like home. Our jail is no place fit for man or beast, but our guest Clarence Darrow got me released. My hearing is tomorrow. That's when we find out how we're going to plead..."

Bill said, "Of course we know... you're not guilty."

Kate adds, "By the way, what is the charge?"

I said, "You know... Evans was so emotional about it, I think he forgot the charge, for I have yet to find out."

Bill asked, "Isn't that against the law to arrest someone without stating the charge?"

I added, "Yup, and that's one of the many mistakes in this case."

YK added, "Evans has been gunning for you for years. Now he's so strung out emotionally, he's going to blow his own case against you."

Kate adds, "Yup... exactly. His better judgment is clouded by his hate for you. Oh, Wemedge, I hope this means the end of Mr. Evans as Game Warden."

I replied, "You know, Kate, that just might be my parting gift for Hortons Bay."

Grace announced, "What fitting justice. This just might be your parting gift to us, Ernie."

Bill says, "Yeah, Wemedge, what a swansong."

Kate adds, "Oh, Stein, I'm so proud of you!"

Everyone says, "Group hug!"

Beth announces, "Okay boys and girls, please be seated. Here comes your belated Fourth of July feast... my famous fried chicken with all the trimmings. Now stop all that hugging and be seated. For heaven sake."

Bill toasts, "Friends of Ernie Hemingway, we are here to welcome him back from the jaws of death, and certain execution at the hands of our local tyrant, the Game Warden... the one and only Turd Face Evans. I propose a toast to our friend's health and reuniting with all of his friends."

"Hip hip hooray, hip hip hooray."

Well we tore into Auntie Beth's chicken as if we hadn't eaten in days. That was true for me, for I got only moldy bread and water at the jail. The townspeople got shorted of their traditional July Fourth meal served by Mrs. Dilworth and the ladies auxiliary.

Nothing unites a group, which has been recently traumatized, like a complete chicken dinner, and with each delicious bite, we were all getting closer knit than ever before... the Hortons Bay gang.

While enjoying the feast, I also chewed on Kate's observation of what my case could do to Evans.

If Judge Jennings could convict him of enough serious charges, my messed up arrest could well be what gives Evans his walking papers out of our county for good. If that were to happen, I would have repaid Hortons Bay for the spoiling of their Fourth of July celebration.

If that would be the end result of all my grief, then all my suffering would be worth it.

Kate's refreshing point of view gave me a new perspective and as a result, hope, to help focus me on the light at the end of the tunnel. Her comment succeeded in giving me an appropriate goal on which I could focus once I stopped feeling sorry for myself. I could now see my way out of the intense courtroom scenes and the anxiety which that brings.

Kate, and her own homespun simplicity had eased my anxious mind from worry about the court proceedings on to the potential grand result of Evans defeat.

Kinda shows my lack of faith in my lawyer and Judge Jennings, two strong legal minds who will put Evans where he belongs.

To quote a phrase, 'I can't see the forest for the trees.' This comes into play here, as I found myself so caught up in my own personal drama that I could not see the bigger picture, and my girl Kate helped me to do just that.

Beth comments, "I hope you all have room for chocolate cake. Joe Bacon dropped this off when he delivered all those chickens you just devoured."

Everyone says, "PIP PIP for Joe Bacon. PIP PIP hooray."

Wes remarked, "Hey, I've been busy cranking homemade vanilla ice cream... anybody want some?"

Everyone says, "PIP PIP for Wes Dilworth... PIP PIP hooray."

So that's the way it was that last summer. Somehow we all sensed the gang was gonna split up with our respective careers taking us off to the four corners of the earth, hence an unspoken spirit de corps brought out our best behavior and Aunty's and the surrounding neighbors best cooking.

We knew Clarence Darrow was spending the night at Red Fox Inn, and sooner or later we would hear Kotesky taxi pull up, and it did, just as we dished into cake and ice cream.

"Greetings, young people," announced Mr. Darrow.

Kate asked, "Mr. Darrow, you're just in time for cake and ice cream. Please join us."

Darrow replied, "Don't mind if I do. Glad to see you finally got a decent meal after your chilly reception at jail, Ernest."

Kate said, "Yes, doesn't he clean up well? We just had his welcome home dinner."

Darrow added, "Well, I'm happy to announce that Judge threw Evans in jail for false arrest and abuse of a minor. Ernest, you can press charges and maybe sue for a nice piece of change to boot. He could also be facing charges for starting a riot. Judge wants to throw the book at him."

I replied, "Well, I never expected this, Mr. Darrow, and what about the Wolverine charge?"

Darrow continued, "Judge threw that out due to a lack of evidence, which prompted him to immediately slap Evans with the other more serious charges unbecoming of the Game Warden who mishandled your dramatic arrest and false imprisonment."

I added, "So I'm in the clear and Evans is in the can?"

Darrow says, "Yes... that's about the size of it. He violated a number of your rights and forgot to treat you like a juvenile. So if you file charges against him, he will do some time, probably lose his job, and owe you money on top of that."

Bill yells, "Let's hear it for Clarence Darrow. PIP PIP, hooray, PIP PIP, hooray."

Another unexpected result of an awful looking episode in my life. At a time when I was in despair, suffering from gloom, and depression with seemingly no positive way out, along comes another unexpected blessing. One that will be enjoyed by everyone in Emmet County for many years to come.

Folks will be talking about this incident for decades. My legacy will hopefully be my writing ability, and not all my girlfriends, and my alcohol consumption.

All this unexpected joy happened during my last summer up in Michigan. I must say I will without any doubt never forget such an eventful time in my young life, nor will anyone else of the summer people who visit enchanted Hortons Bay. I don't care what you say, you just can't make up this stuff. And concerning the monumental visit from Clarence Darrow, most famous for the Scopes monkey trial, and Leopold and Loeb murder trial. One will be hard-pressed to find any mention of the trial of Turd Face Evans, but everyone in Emmet County, Michigan will remember, and if they recall, a kid named Ernest Hemingway was used to bait the trap which triggered an elaborate triumph of justice.

Chapter 31. The Kid Who Saved Hortons Bay

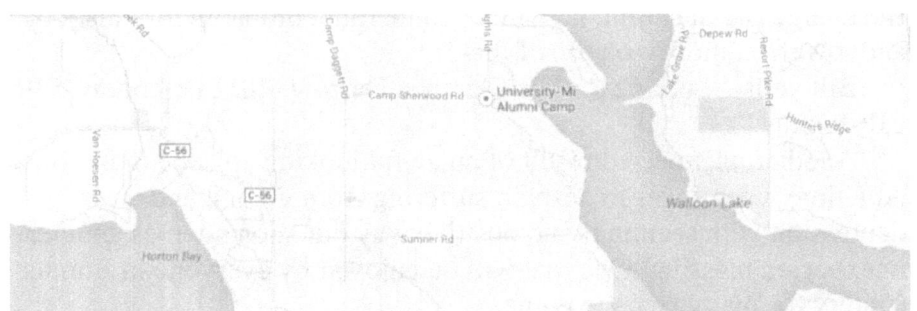

Lake Charlevoix and Horton's Bay is on the left, and Walloon Lake on the right. The Hemingway cabin is near the far right point. Ernest would row across the lake, stow his boat, and take the easy 3 mile trek across to Horton's Bay.

Today is Sunday; a cool, cloudy, Michigan summer morning. A time when the whole family climbs into Pop's Model T Ford and heads toward the little country church on Resort Pike Road.

Being as I had just been sprung from jail by my lawyer, Clarence Darrow, I had plenty for which to thank God.

Tyrant Turd Face Evans now was in jail and peace had finally come to our pleasant little Northern Michigan community. We all had good reason to get on our knees in solemn thankfulness, so this Sunday the church was packed.

After thanking God for my deliverance, my eyes began to wander around the congregation in notice of all my girlfriends, because God's house is always a good place to find chicks.

Today was no exception, for they were all here this morning giving thanks to God for the miraculous removal of that corrupt Game Warden.

It didn't take much to guess they each wanted to thank me personally for being the bait which helped spring the trap that caught that evil Evans.

Glancing down the long, varnished pews, I spotted a bevy of beauties each beaming as Parson passed on the blessed benediction which allowed them to broadcast their communal 'amen'.

At the end of service, Parson must've felt neglected as the line of persons waiting to shake his hand was now waiting in front of me to shake my hand. We were all decked out in our Sunday finest. I in my Brooks Brothers suit, with high starch collar and white shirt. All the girls wore ankle length dresses, high lace collars, tight waist and high button shoes. Most of them wore fancy bonnets with no shortage of lace anywhere, in a variety of pastel shades.

Marge and Pudge Bump both offered me a peck on the cheek, so polite and so discreet.

Marge stated, "Hey Ernie, we are all so darn proud of you. Can we have you over for parlor popcorn sometime?"

"Why absolutely, darling...of course. Does this mean that your mother has forgiven me?"

The girls gave me blank stares as the line moved on.

Grace Quinlan made her usual two deep impressions into my chest with a tight extended hug.

"Golly Gee, Stein. The whole town owes you... big time. How can I thank you?"

"Something will pop up, I'm sure," I said.

Kate cut in line saying, "Hey, can a girl get a hug here from my hero?"

"Absolutely, Kate. Just cut on in here," I stated.

"Wemedge, you are our most amazing summer resident. How can I thank you?"

"Let's see, Kate. Um... since you and Bill raise apples, I guess an apple pie will do okay?"

"You got it, my friend. Come over tonight."

Somehow after feeling the adulation of that church full of my closest fans, my thoughts drifted back to Julius Caesar when he returned victorious to Rome after conquering all his enemies. I could hear echos of trumpets and troubadour welcoming Caesar home.

All my concubines were there offering their praises and heartfelt gifts, although Marge and Pudge's offer of popcorn doesn't sound like much, it meant a peace offering in hopes of clearing things up between me and Mrs. Bump, whom I offended by asking for an amount Marge would stand to inherit of the Bump Hardware fortune.

By being the local hero now, maybe the cranky old gal will begin to see me in a different light.

So that seemingly simple offer of Bump parlor popcorn actually is an invitation to start over on a clean slate with the offended Mrs. Bump. The girls were never offended by my inquiry into their inheritance, but the mother came totally unglued and banned me from their mansion.

When a guy shoots off his big mouth without giving any thought to the repercussions it may have, he spends a lot of time mending fences, so the offer of popcorn at the Bump mansion was seen as a lot more than corn, it must be considered pure gold, fence mending, if Mrs. Bump can forgive and forget.

Parson reacted to the short line waiting to shake his hand, "Gosh, young Hemingway... I'm jealous. I thought my sermon was better than last week."

"It's a gift, Padre. Actually, if you follow local news, I've come up looking like the town hero."

"Well, whatever it was, you sure are a popular young lad. I hope to see you next Sunday, okay... and bring your posse, okay?"

Somehow my enormous ego got in the way while chatting with Parson, and I missed the chance to give God glory for my good fortune.

Seeing how Padre knew nothing about the jailing of Game Warden Evans, I kinda got a glimpse of how safe it must be living in an ivory tower, untouched by the high drama of reality; however, God has seen fit to place me directly into the meat grinder of life... on the street with the common people where I feel their pain and anxiety and fears, when subjected to the evil whims of a tyrant.

If Padre knew nothing of the Evans case, I couldn't cast judgment on the guy's lack of local application of truth, but it was then and there that I made a conscious resolve to always be on top of local and regional news, because it has the power to track and diffuse the evil workings of tyranny.

Knowing that my reporter's job was only a few short months away, I was already being shown how vital my observation skills would be to Kansas City readers, and I like that feeling. In a sense, my Pops would be proud of my community doctoring skills, since a good reporter needs his thumb on the pulse of the nation in order to make diagnoses and prognoses... what's wrong in town and how can we fix it?

So in a sense, I'll be doing my own doctoring with words out of Kansas.

Having read the Bible all the way through twice and eventually memorizing the whole Holy Book, I felt confident I can hold my own in most discussions on doctoring as well as doctrine... Jesus being the great physician and the last word when it comes to doctrine.

Now I find myself in the middle of my own baptism, and immersion into journalism of the highest order, and although it is scary, I find that I wouldn't want it any other way.

By right of consciousness I am perfectly positioned for my choice of work. With my highly competitive nature, I plan to be Kansas City Star's star word jockey, and eventually my novels will knock their socks off.

Kipling, Conrad, and Stevenson can be beat, and I plan to knock them on the canvas soon for the full count.

Riding the crest of the high wave of success in Hortons Bay sure feels good. It comes at a good time and is completely unexpected, for when I first found out that the Game Warden was gunning for me, I must admit the news put me at my lowest in despair, but the good Lord done fetched me from that darkest place, and led me to a high point of which I never knew was possible.

Now my job is to continue to thank and praise Him and ascribe all glory to Him. If I don't, I know my success will fail me. Right now it is hard to see where all the success will lead, because from my vantage point, it's hard to tell, but God sees the big picture, so I have to always yield to His direction and each small step along the path.

After what happened so far this summer, I'll be known as the kid who saved Hortons Bay. My Pops will lose his title as DOC Hemingway, and will now be called father of Ernest Hemingway... a guy can dream, can't he?

Right now I am open to receiving my Hortons Bay laurels for being the bait that brought down corrupt Game Warden Evans. The rewards will be small, but I prefer accolades for superior story writing skill and memorable book titles which would register as big sales at nationwide bookstores.

Being the town hero now has its perks. All of my girlfriends are worshiping me and making sure I get plenty of baked goods, children asking all sorts of interesting questions about my harrowing exploits, especially how life was in jail.

Eventually, I find myself developing a pat answer for most of their queries, making sure to discourage poaching, fishing out of season, and any lawbreaking that lands one in jail. The local jail is about the lousiest, filthiest, vermin infested place on earth and must be avoided at all costs.

Petoskey City Hall and Jail

Chapter 32. The Hero of Hortons Bay

Being the hero of Hortons Bay was a heady role to play. What I liked about it was all the worship I received from teenaged girls and children, the back slaps from men, free chicken dinners from Auntie Beth, and fresh baked pies, cakes, and cookies from the ladies auxiliary; however, most heartfelt and rewarding was the honor and respect shown to me by the local tribe.

Nick Boulton, Billy Tabeshaw, and Prudence walked up to our cabin one morning in July to invite me to help haul a wagon load of Hemlock bark to market.

Skies were cloudy, a steady northeastern breeze cooled my sweaty brow as I was just putting the last split logs on our wood pile.

A dignified native, Nick Boulton, spoke first, "Heap good day. One darn good morning to chop firewood, huh, Ernie. You handle ax good."

"Why thank you, Mr. Bolton. What brings you fine folk to my humble hogan?"

Billy Tabeshaw answered, "We want'um honor you for your work in putting away bad Game Warden."

"Why, thanks. Coming from the tribe, that really means a lot to me, Pal."

"Good. We want'um you lead the team of horses when wagon load of hemlock bark goes down to market," stated Nick Bolton (the halfbreed).

"Ernie, you hold'um high respect among our people since wild fish and game can be taken now for our food," commented pretty Prudence.

"Driving team to market with wagon load of bark is high honor. Please come now," Prudence continued.

"Gosh, Prudence, how nice of you. Let me put on my boots and I will join you all."

"Nothing doing, Ernie. Here, wear'um nice, new moccasins I made for you. You like?"

"Wow, they are beautiful. How did you know my size? Ernie thanks you."

Prudence answered, "It wasn't hard to get your size."

Nick added, "We see you run all summer in bare feet. Your footprints are all over Emmet County. You got'um big feet. Need'um heap good moccasins now for job. Let's go... now."

From my observation of past struggles the tribe had with hauling their overloaded wagon full of bark, they needed expert handling of the team of horses. More specifically, they needed a good break man to keep control as they headed down the sharp incline of hills toward the barge, which waited below at Hortons Bay pier.

With the gift of new moccasins, I knew they would provide the good traction which was needed on the foot brake.

Being their hunting hero meant they now think there are no laws of limits on their hunting and fishing, but somehow I will have to inform them a new Game Warden will expect their renewed respect for the fish and game laws, but since we white men tree stripped their hunting grounds, I doubt if many will care to buy licenses or wait for the opening seasons to hunt or fish.

My Pops and I are friends with the tribe. They come over to Windemere cabin for doctoring; however, today is different.

Today they need help rolling their overstuffed bark wagon down to Lake Charlevoix where a waiting barge will transport the load to Boyne City tannery.

Peeling Hemlock Bark.

Often, a Native American will bring a gift, but the thought behind it usually gets an important need met for them. Not that I ain't honored to help them, but the bark wagon is always way overloaded which causes problems on the way down to the barge, for having extremely good brake work is then required. A team of horses demand special handling, going downhill especially, and it gets compounded if the wagon tends to tip over from having been stacked too high.

Today the situation is the usual, for as we approached the bark wagon it was ready to tip from a soft breeze.

"Hey, Nick, we need a long rope to secure this load. What you think?" I queried.

"Got it. Be right back."

With Nick gone to fetch rope, I saw my chance to thank Prudence for all her work on my new moccasins.

"Gee, Prudy, thanks for the nice moccasins."

Prudence says, "I chewed the leather myself to soften it. Can I get an Indian hug?"

"You bet. Come here, sweetie. I have missed my favorite Redskin girl. Come, I love your strong hugs."

"Prudy miss you too, Ernie. Want to go on squirrel hunt someday?"

"You bet, Ernie love hunting with Prudy. Say, I like your Wolverine claw necklace."

"Got'um claws from Great White Hunter."

"Yeah, that Wolverine got me into heap big trouble, but it's the incident that flushed out Turd Face Evans... that nasty Game Warden, and now he's history in this region."

"He in heap big shit now, hey, Ernie?"

"Yup. It put me in a lot of grief, but it was all worth it."

"Us Indians proud of you, and that attorney, boyfriend."

"Well that's good, 'cause Evans gave the tribe a heck of a rough time, I understand."

"Oh yeah. He hate'um Redskins, big time. He hates you, Ernie, for you like'um Redskin too. He no like anyone who like Redskin."

"Yup, I kinda figured that. This last arrest had more anger in it than the usual arrest, which caused him to make heap big mistakes."

"Now he pay for his mistakes right, Ernie-boyfriend?"

"You got that right, Prudy-girlfriend. Say, girl, you always smell good like sweetgrass and hemlock bark."

"Could be... You know, Ernie, we ate that Wolverine heart. It was good... full of heap big medicine."

"Glad you liked it. Listen, kid, you get prettier every time I see you."

"Well kiss me before my stepfather gets back, mmm... mmm... mmm. Ernie, you good kisser."

"Wow! Prudy, you are incredible... uh, oh, here comes big Nick. Thanks, Prudy."

"Me got'um rope. Now let's tie all this down, Ernie," said a worried Nick Bolton.

"Get it good and tight, Nick, all the way around... that's it. Now do it once more and tie it off. Nice team of mules."

"Yup, Earl's all right. Earl Sumner am good White man. We help'um hauling in his hay. Okay, let's go."

Very slowly, I started out that sturdy mule team across the road toward the tannery barge. The enormous stack of Hemlock bark teetered precariously every step of the way, and just as we figured, the rope kept it from falling off.

After the first hill we began to descend easily. I talked kindly to the mule team to give them confidence for the next descent. If we lost this load, it would be an enormous task to reload. The wagon might tip over and break, also. We wouldn't want to return a broken wagon to Earl.

In the distance, we spotted another mule team pulling an empty wagon. It was Earl Sumner.

Earl shouted, "Hey boys, I figured you would need another wagon."

I reply, "Good idea, Earl. There's a good two loads here for sure. Thanks, Pal."

Earl started in loading his wagon, "I'll pull along side so's we can slide half your stack of bark onto mine."

Nick said, "Ernie, heap good mule skinner hey, Earl?"

Earl added, "Yup, Ernie and I have hauled many a wagon load of hay together, right Ernie?"

Nick called out, "Me got'um rope untied. Now slide top of pile onto wagon two."

Earl comments, "Nick, you boys have done a heckuva job on all this hemlock bark. Must be twice as much as last time... Whoa, mule!"

Eventually, that monstrous load of bark got transferred over to wagon two. So we drove the two mule teams right up to the waiting barge.

The Indians got paid and Earl and I drove our teams back to Sumner farm. While helping Earl unhitch the wagons, I remarked, "You know, Earl, there's got to be a better way for Nick and his tribe to get their hemlock bark to market."

"I agree with you there, Ernie, but the only way better would be to have it skidded down all those hills on a ramp."

"What about rails?"

"Hey, I bet a narrow gauge railroad down to the pier would solve all their problems. All the bark peelers would have to do is load little railcars and with a system of pulleys and ropes they could easily just let gravity roll things down to the pier."

"Yup, that would work, Ernie. Just like the copper mines up north."

I continued, "And since most of the trip is on a decline, we could let gravity run the whole show."

"Yeah, and Boyne City builds railcars, so I bet they already got something to fit the bill," replied Earl. "Dang, Ernie, you got a creative mind on your shoulders. Alls we got to do is contact someone at the tannery, and they can work it out with the railcar company."

With the dawn of the motor car, we had no idea horses would lose popularity and the demand for leather would diminish, but our idea of getting hemlock bark to the tannery by narrow gauge railcar eventually was put into operation and ran well for a number of years. Remnants of the narrow gauged track can still be found.

Bark piled up along the rail tracks to head down to the steamships.

The "Bean House" storage barn, where the hemlock bark was sent down to the Lake Steamers, also the setting of a scene in one of Hemingway's books, *"Up in Michigan"*.

Chapter 33. In Search of Wild

We Hemingways ignored the obvious differences in class that existed between us and our local Native Americans. We naturally felt close to them, my Pops doing the doctoring, and me being in love with Prudy.

Yet somehow I had to remind the tribe that Lansing was going to replace Game Warden Evans at some future date, which meant they still have to hunt and fish only in season. During this period there still were race haters who could not put to rest the violent culture clash of the past, but we did as a family living right next door to their tarpaper shack. We had made our peace with the Redskin.

Pops collected many Indian artifacts from, in, and around Petoskey, as well as along the Des Plains River near our winter residence, Oak Park, near Chicago.

As one searches through Mother's many scrapbooks, pictures of me as a kid can be found wearing an overall outfit fringed at the sides of the arms and legs. I had me an Indian suit.

Daily, I imagined myself an Indian brave while I played with our young Native American neighbor children while sporting my fringed Indian suit. Our family wholeheartedly embraced the Redman philosophy and sympathized with their cultures eventual destruction.

To this very day, I still consider myself a good member of the tribe and for many reasons I have never accepted the white, upper middle class culture into which I was born.

Civilized city life is not for me. I need to roam the wilds in search of fish and game for sustainability unfettered by civilization, and it's crazy demands, which is why my mind prefers to travel back in time now to that last idyllic summer I enjoyed up in Michigan.

As much as one tries to keep the summer scene blissful, there are moments that pull the skids out from under. One such moment occurred when I got the news, months later, that my girl Prudy had committed suicide.

That bit of shocking news caused me deep agony for she must have suffered terribly according to her brother Billy Tabeshaw.

"Yeah, Ernie. Mother Anna tried to keep her away from this white Coast Guard guy named Castle, who they say got her pregnant. Now she can't keep her away. One night she climbed out her bedroom window and escaped. The two of them swallow rat poison. All three died horrible."

"Oh, my God! And the baby? Who did he look like?"

"Baby boy... look a lot like... Like you, Ernie."

"Oh, my God! I am so sorry, Billy. That breaks my heart! You know that."

"Yeah, us three used to hunt squirrel. She sure was some beautiful Indian girl. Now gone. Here, you take Wolverine claw necklace. She would want you to wear it. Might bring'um you good luck."

Billy continued, "Mother Anna and whole tribe all so damn sad. Well, gotta go shave some more hemlock. Sorry, Ernie."

Something told me Billy had no plan to peel Hemlock bark because his breath gave away his real plan... to get drunk on cheap whiskey and pass out somewhere along the road. I ran out of my tent to find a bush where I threw up everything. That bad news about Prudy's suicide was so deep and so devastating I never ate again for two days.

Had that mixed-race baby lived, it would've scandalized both communities for many of the tribe still hate whites, not to mention what my family would say to see a halfbreed Hemingway growing up in high class Oak Park, Illinois. The world is not yet ready for a baby of mixed-race, of anything. Even though Mother Grace was way ahead of her time to know that society would be gossiping about her halfbreed grandson would be too much for her to bear.

It was touching to understand that Prudy's last thoughts were of me and my family's reputation. That idea gave me mixed comfort at best.

In a perfect world, I would've married Prudy and she and I, and our son would have lived as wild Indians in the forest, but lumber companies already had clear cut most of Michigan, removing all good cover and natural habitat for deer and bear and fowl, and their technique for getting logs to the sawmill by floating them down rivers had ruined most good fishing streams, thus making subsistence in the wild a dismal thing of the past.

Tribal sustainability in the wild now was a nightmare-living off the land was a thing of the past in Michigan.

So eventually the cold, harsh facts of reality snapped me out of a sentimental reverie I may have had of Prudy and me, and ever living wild and happily ever after in this present ruined world.

Despite her sudden departure, part of me still yearned for sustaining a life in the wild. Maybe Africa still had areas where this was possible as the persistent reverie had shifted to living a life in the wild somewhere else in the world. Be it ever an unrealistic fantasy, it is still my dream that yearns as an ember that smolders as this Man desires to return to the natural setting of Eden.

Chapter 34. Through the Eyes of Prudy

Meanwhile, the starched, high neck collars of Victorian society in the upper middle class into which I was born once again take a chagrined command of my young life, but it was at this juncture that I resolved to give Prudence a sacrifice for proper honor by focusing my every waking moment on being the best writer that I could be.

Now, carrying my own library card, I determined to read all the famous, well known writers of our time.

By taking careful note of their respective styles, I figured I could master them and beat them at their own game.

By doing so I could create my own unique style that would stand out from the comments there that were being offered as literature presently on the market.

While entertaining such pipe dreams and ambitious desires, the thought of Prudence came to me suggesting that I write as if the narrator were she.

In order to be true to my dearly departed Indian girlfriend, I pursued that train of thought and soon determined it was just the angle from which I was looking.

By writing my stories as if filtered through the mind of an American Indian, it would be a most revolutionary concept. They would be short on adjectives and adverbs, have her unique outlook, brief and to the point, and to be so shocking to the status quo that they would be unforgettable compared to anything on the market today.

This was the most outlandish concept ever imagined and critics would never figure it out.

At that instant, my whole young life flashed before me thus reassuring me that everything that had occurred in my life experiences as a boy will now be coming to the forefront of my mind, and is about to be integrated into my work for the future.

My writing as seen through the eyes of Prudy will impact the literary world as none other, now or ever. My Prudy will be immortalized by my writing and I must say a more fitting tribute could never be conceptualized. No one analyzing the work will ever figure it out. Let them spin their wheels thinking deeply and let them rack their feeble brains about what is being done, but it will never dawn on them what is behind my work; namely, life as seen through the eyes of Prudy, as they analyze what this Hemingway boy has done.

Readers will be shocked to read topics that are totally different in a dialogue of short, cropped, declarative sententious, devoid of adjectives and adverbs, that are most totally different, and which are presented in a style which is also totally different, with topics that are totally different.

When a guy has a breakthrough like this, the news is so uplifting that my feet felt on air. Trying to explain all this to folks who noticed my joy is disconcerting because I'm just not going to reveal a thing. Anyway, it would only have meaning to me.

The big question for me now is...how do I contain my enthusiasm after having such a monumental breakthrough? As usual, I will journal all this good news and eventually write a novel as viewed through Prudy's eyes.

Editor's note: The memory of his Indian girlfriend had such an impact on him, that Hemingway could not shake it from his mind. Prudy and the tribal way of life became an obsession that so persisted, that eventually it became his magnificent obsession.

Putting her on the mental pedestal with daily embellishment through the years eventually ate away at his four marriages and his ability to settle down in one location in an urban setting. He was continually yearning to subsist in a mature forest with a native woman at his side while he hunted and fished for dinner in the wild.

Since he had become an adopted member of the tribe from his youth, this tribal mindset and wilderness living had become his preferred way of life; hence, his many hunting and fishing trips into Michigan's untamed woods as well as the jungles of Africa.

Often he would motor from Key West all the way to Utah or Idaho or Montana in order to hunt deer or bear or mountain goat, so he could shed civilization and recapture these tribal feelings with old pals, and eat fresh caught fish and game.

Chapter 35. Ernie writes: Hemingway's diary...

When I write, it makes me feel good. The simple act of putting words to paper with pencil has a magical way of getting things off my chest. Somehow the writing releases the tension that builds up in my mind.

As long as I can write things down I know I'll never need a guy like Sigmund Freud around.

Having a close pal like Bill Smith to share my troubles with it is important to me also. It's almost as good as having a close girlfriend, but I find that girls think differently which tends to put me on guard and hinder a free flow of ideas, but once I write down what bugs me, I almost always feel lighter for not having to carry those ideas around anymore.

Writing lifts my personal load of burdens and removes them far away from my mind.

Lately, I've been blaming myself for actually creating drama just so I have something to write about. Maybe there is some truth to that since I do tend to stir up trouble... "Stirring the pot" Mother calls it, and believe me, she should know since I call her our family number one instigator of high drama.

She hates it when I shoot her accusations right back at her, but now that I'm the head of the house when Father leaves for Chicago somebody needs to set her straight on reality.

My Pop, the great physician, is a terrific doctor, but when he has to say no to Mother she throws a tantrum and his spine immediately turns to Jell-O. I love the guy, but his backbone got lost during anatomy class or something, for he is supposed to be the head of the house, but he's a scared little mouse around the house.

So it's plain to see that after Game Warden Evans, my next nemesis is my very own mother, because of her treatment of my beloved Pops and me. Plus she's always degrading the writing profession, and her attitude toward me for wanting to be a writer.

Plus, I know there's some hanky panky going on with that live in voice student of hers named Ruth Arnold. I've seen how lovey dovey they are, and I figure that's the reason Mother built herself another cabin across the bay so the two of them can be alone all summer.

My Pops has been so nervous lately. I know this Ruth thing has got to hurt him to the quick. Someday he has to explode and challenge Mother on this. If he doesn't, it will eat him up inside.

So far, we've all given her a free pass on this issue because the topic is just too vile to bring up, but to see her carry on and still maintain her holy Joe, holier than thou attitude, and goody two shoes act is disgusting.

Because my sister Marcy worships Mother, if this vile news hits the kid in the wrong way it could have dangerous results, so I gotta keep it at a low profile.

Sunny and Carol too would be devastated at their young ages to find out that Mother plays with both teams.

Ursa; however, knows what is going on. She and I have this psychic connection always going on. It's hard to explain, but it's like we share the same thoughts and seem to know what the other's thinking at any given time. We share the same mind.

"So, how long have you known Oinbones? About our housekeeper who doesn't keep house?"

"Shh... we don't want Sunny and Carol to find out. Let's go for a walk. Grab a fishing rod, Littless."

"Okay, here's my fishing rod. Where to?"

"Just keep walking."

"But what if Sunny wants to join us? She loves to fish with you."

"Nevermind, just keep walking. I saw her helping Mother work her oil paints."

"Carol too?"

"Uhuh, Carol too. Walk faster."

"We're fishing off the neighbor's dock?"

"No, keep walking!"

"Will you tell me your plan? For heavens sake. Why so secretive?"

"Because this topic should never get out to young ears. Get it?"

"Yeah, I know...just keep walking."

"I can see it doesn't bother you as much as it bothers me?"

"Oh, it bothers me a lot. This is so darned scandalous. We may have to move to River Forest where no one knows us. So when did You know?"

"When did I know? Well, I guess ...when Father blew his stack and banned Ruth from the Oak Park house. I knew there were more than music lessons involved, but then when Grace had the second cabin built, spending my college money on it, that's what really put her over the edge. I knew then that she was addicted to Ruth."

"Hey, I bet there are worms under that big log?"

"Yeah, I bet. Let's check it out."

"Wow, look at them. Big ones!"

"Did you bring a pail, Pal?"

"Here, put those whoppers in my hat."

"But your hat?"

"Nevermind, I got an extra pork pie."

"Oinbones, I ain't never seen such big worms."

"Crawlers, that's what they are... crawlers. We find them at night with flashlights."

"This is so disgusting."

"Yeah, I know Littless, but it's part of fishing, kid."

"No, no, not these worms. I mean...you know what I mean."

"Yeah, and that's how she keeps us silent about it. She knows it's too vile to talk about... too darn friggin vile."

"What do they do? I mean how do they do it?"

"I don't know. I can't picture it. Ruth is just a few years older than Marcy for heaven sake. Mother and Ruth... it's just too darn disgusting. It's too disgusting."

"I don't know either. It's so unnatural. Brrrr... It gives me the willies! Poor Father."

"Yeah. I threw up when the thought first struck me. I puked in my wash basin."

"Hey, Pal, I think your hat has enough worms, Oinbones."

"Yeah, kid sister. Let's go fishing!"

A kid's mind has a natural protection from corruption, consequently they cannot dwell for long upon subjects of a vile nature, but when they do, what follows must be of a blissful nature. Fishing surely was that welcomed relief for us, and we eventually return to hear Sunny and Carol ask to share our giant crawlers.

"Oinbones, Gee thanks for the oversized worms," said Sunny.

"They are crawlers, Sweetie. I bet you are gonna catch a big bass today.

"Gosh, Ernie, I have to double loop these crawlers onto my hook. They sure are huge, thanks," commented Carol.

"Well did Mother finish oil painting?" Ursa queried.

"Nope... but she let us go to see if Ruth could take over our duties," replied Sunny.

"So who is watching Baron?" I asked.

"Oh, he's taking a long nap. He's a big two years old now," said Carol.

"How do you feel about Ruth hanging around Mother so much?" I asked.

"Oh, I guess it makes me jealous that Mother prefers Ruth's company over ours," admitted Sunny.

"Interesting observation, Sis," said Ursa.

"Hey Sunny! Your bobber just disappeared," I whispered.

"Yeah, I think I just got a bite!" replied Sunny. "I know... Set the hook... There... And now let the fight begin!"

I stated, "Sunny, I think you hooked the biggest small-mouth bass of the season. Play him now, kid. I got a net here. Easy... Keep tension on that line... And... Got him. Look at the size of this lunker!"

Sunny said, "Yeah, and he was just waiting for a giant size crawler for his lunch."

"Only his lunch had more iron in it than he expected," Carol cracked.

"Ha, ha, ha... good one Carol," I replied.

Sunny asks, "Do you think Mother will like it?"

"Oh, she will if she knows who caught it, Oinbones," I remarked.

"She's probably tired of clam," Ursa stated.

I say, "Littless, don't try to explain that, okay?"

"Hey... I got a bite!" yelled Carol.

"With a good jerk, set the hook, Beefy, and then keep a tight line," I stated.

"Okay, Ernie. I got this big guy, ready with the net. Yipee, I landed him."

"Magnifico!" yelled Ursa. "He should go over 5 pounds... a lunker!"

"Gee Carol, it's nice to see you're baiting your own hook this year," I says.

Carol asks, "Does this mean I'm now part of the Hemingway fishing club?"

In chorus, we all say, "Yes!"

Throughout the rest of the afternoon everyone landed at least one good size fish, along with dozens of pan fish. All total we caught enough for a Hemingway supper. I cleaned and scaled them.

Ursa and I fried the fish which were first dredged in corn meal, and then rolled in eggwash, with a little salt and pepper... our favorite recipe. While Sunny and Carol set the table, Marcy sliced some fresh-baked bread that Pops had baked before his return to Chicago. It still smelled of all the love Pop's puts into his baking.

Marcy picked water cress and fresh, tender, dandelion greens for a nice big bowl of salad, enhanced with baby carrots, radishes, and leaf lettuce from our garden.

Mother and Ruth appeared from their rowboat which had returned from stress relief cabin number two across the bay.

"Oh! Children, what a nice surprise. You made supper for everyone."

"Yes, Mother," Marcy replied flatly.

"Oh, dear sweet girls. You know, I tried to hire a local cook, but they all want an all year position," Mother said, rather apologetic.

"Yes Mother," replied Marcy, even flatter now.

"Oh, Ruthie, look, a fresh salad," stated Mother.

"I see. How thoughtful, huh? See, they still love you," replied Ruth Arnold.

"Sit down, Mother. You can say the blessing," said Ursa.

"Don't mind if I do. Dear Lord, thank you for this humble meal which we enjoy to our bodies from your bountiful goodness, amen."

"Now, there is plenty of fish. They were biting like crazy today. Carol caught plenty, so she gets to eat two. This summer she baits her own hooks, finally," I added.

"Fried potatoes are coming up next along with green beans. Hope you like Ernie's and my cooking," says Ursa.

"Children, you know I must teach my music lessons which God has called me to do, and young Ruth Arnold here is the recipient of that musical skill, otherwise, I would surely be in your kitchen cooking nice dishes," apologizes Mother.

"Yes, Mother," Marcy replies still flatter in tone than before.

Ursa looks at me and rolls her eyes, and I returned the knowing gesture.

Mother adds, "...and God has made it possible for a cabin at Longfields, so I must follow where He leads me, my darlings."

Stunned by Mother's God directed announcement, we all lay down our forks in unison and with our arms at our sides, we watched as Mother and Ruth marched out of Windemere cabin, climbed into the rowboat, and headed back to Longfields.

Petrified and lock jawed, Ursa broke the silence, "Well, too bad they left, for now we must eat the blueberry pie that father stashed in the pantry. And it is Mother's favorite. Let's hear it for father... PIP PIP."

Everyone says, "Hooray for our Father! PIP PIP hooray!"

Not a word was said regarding Mother's hypocrisy to which we had just been exposed; however, the silent rolling of our eyes kinda said at all.

Even though Father was not present to Mother's lame justification speech, Father's sweet pie (which was baked in love) spoke volumes more than Mother's excuse for never learning to cook.

Then seven years old Carol, in all her innocence, spoke, "We can't eat music, but our tone deaf Father has left us with a mighty tasty symphony in this blueberry pie."

Everyone says, "PIP PIP for Carol Hemingway! PIP PIP hooray."

Ursa and I saw the irony in that statement and we both laughed loudly.

"Ha, ha, ha, ha!"

In the back of my mind smoldered the idea that this musical paragon of virtue had aced me out of my college money through the building of her own private stress relief cabin and Longfields farm.

Now she's rubbing our noses in it by brazenly parading Ruth Arnold around as her live in voice student/housekeeper.

I doubt very much if either label is true for none of us have ever heard Ruth sing and the house is always looking like a pig sty, therefore Ruth must be around for other reasons.

Father had too much of her one day and banned Ruth from his presence; however, as soon as our Pops heads for Chicago, Ruth again slithers onto the scene.

I'm feeling this affair is what's making Father so nervous lately. The emotional strain is getting too much for him. His straight, conservative, religious upbringing did not prepare him for such vile, unnatural, disgusting behavior from his wife, so as a direct result he is a nervous wreck and quite frankly he has me worried. I'm afraid the old boy might do something rash.

So as the drama of my life unfolds, with Turd Face Evans removed as my main nemesis, it appears that my next nemeses challenge is going to be my very own Mother.

From all appearances, the woman may have already done irreparable damage to Father as well as to the rest of the family.

I now understand what is meant by the phrase, "The enemy within," because no matter what I do for her it's never good enough and the son should expect a little acceptance for his chosen field or endeavor... In my case writing.

She has never accepted me or ever once tried to understand me. From her perspective I exist only to satisfy her demands and her demands and various whims will never be met... so eventually she will realize that I have outlived my usefulness and hand me my walking papers.

For the observant, one can deduce from all this that I am living in a no-win situation and you would be right.

To say that I hate my Mother would be putting it mildly, so that brings up the topic of how I deal with strong emotions like hate and rage and anger.

These will eat a person up inside. So far, my best solution is to journal my feelings, for by writing them down I get them away from me, and off my mind.

The Padre tells me that I have to forgive and say a large number of Our Fathers and Hail Marys, but I know he's been trained to say that. Another way of dealing with my troubles is to head for the wild, for when I'm off in the woods away from civilization, that is where I still feel the best.

For some reason, I take all my rage out on the wild critters by killing them, plus it gives me a sense of power or control over what lives and what dies. Shooting is good therapy.

Some wise man once said that thoughts are like boomerangs... they have a way of returning to their source to make you make sure your thoughts are nice and sweet for soon those thoughts you will have to eat.

Folks out East around India advocate meditation is a source of stress relief, or the chanting of a mantra vocalizing so-called holy syllables of their god's names. If it works for them, I say more power to you; but I have a hard time sitting in one spot doing nothing. I need to at least be holding a fishing pole or holding a .30/.30 across my lap in wait for a white tail deer, or a bear, or a bighorn sheep, or a mountain goat, or kudu, or a lion, or a big old water buffalo.

I get a bead on him, take a deep breath, and squeeze off a round. His death would be swift and clean. Then I would gut him, skin him, cut up the meat, and start a campfire where I'd roast the best cuts of meat until tender.

Sitting around a campfire stuffing myself with fresh roasted wild game is about as good as life gets.

To me, this is my form of meditation. Making a ritual of the whole operation is like a form of worship. It makes me feel like a high priest and my church is the cathedral of the wild, and its tall Pines would bring shame to Notre Dame. The sunlight, which filters through its branches also can put stained glass in tall cathedrals to shame.

All this I exclaim in explanation as to how my hatred forces me to behave.

These are ways that I find healing for mind and emotions that are storming inside. Ways that help me let off steam, ways that help me feel good when I can bring home food for my family, ways that keep me from doing something rash.

"Girls, that was some fine meal. I want to think Ursa for helping with cooking, and Marcy for fetching that priceless salad, and Sunny and Carol for setting the table. Any volunteers for washing dishes?... That's what I thought. Okay, Littless, let's clear this table and I ll wash..."

"Okay, Oin'bones, I'll dry."

"Sunny, can you read Baron a story?"

"Yay, Sunny, read me a story, yeah!" said Leichester, a.k.a. Baron.

During summer evenings twilight seems to last forever. Tonight was no exception. With few clouds, the promise of a nice sunset was imminent. After finishing our dish washing, Ursa and I walked out to the dock to have a smoke.

"Geez, Oinbones, you're gonna corrupt your little sister. Where the heck do you find these little brown cigarettes?"

"There's a joint down on Halstead Street. They're imported from Turkey. Too strong?"

"Oh... no, cough! Cough! Just right. I was gonna have one lung removed anyway. We still have two don't we?"

"You're a regular comedian, Littless."

"Cough... so champ, what was your take... puff, puff... on Mother and Ruth tonight?"

"Oh typical... I figured... blinded by love. They're addicted to each other. You can see that."

"Do you figure Marcy knows?"

"She's got to, judging from all those bored, 'Yes mothers'."

"Yeah...I caught that tone also. But Marcy worships mother. Mother could do no wrong. Marcy is in denial I think."

"Did you believe all that sanctimonious, self righteous, B.S. that comes out of Mother's mouth, then she eats and rows off to her private cabin with Ruth."

"Yeah, and she missed dessert... her favorite... blueberry pie. What poetic justice. Ha, ha, ha, ha."

"Yeah, poetic justice all right."

"We won't be able to face our friends back in Oak Park if those two carry on like this at home. Neighbors will be scandalized."

"Father won't allow it. He banned Ruth from the house. He snapped and just yelled at her to never darken our doorstep."

"I might run away from home again."

"Oh yeah. Where to this time?"

"Maybe just hop a train and head West... anywhere and everywhere."

"Well kiddo, you just better think again about that. You are much too pretty to be out by yourself all alone. Egad!"

"Not if'n I dressed like a boy."

"Oh, yeah, sure. You can't hide the fact that you are beautiful. Boys aren't beautiful. Get real, Littless! Look at yourself... your skin, your hair, your eyelashes, your pert little figure... naw. You'd never make it out on the rails."

"Well, I'd never be able to face my friends at Oak Park high this fall. Look what happened to Frank Lloyd Wright."

(Editor's note: Wright's home was three doors down the street from Hemingway's. Wright had an affair with his client's wife, Mrs Martha Cheney. Neither Mrs. Wright nor Mr. Cheney would agree to a divorce, and the news scandalized Oak Park to the point that his architectural business dried up locally, so he with his illicit lover moved to Europe. When they returned, the Oak Park newspaper condemned Wright for bringing scandal to the village. The overly religious community was not able to condone any type of scandal, nor was Clarence Hemingway ever able to deal with his wife's equally scandalous affair with Ruth Arnold, thus causing Ernest to blame his mother for Clarence's eventual suicide.)

"Yeah...I know. You will have to act like Marcy... be in denial. Maybe the old gal will buy a house in River Forest?"

"Maybe... nobody knows us there."

If Al Capone can have a home there, I'm sure they will welcome Mother Grace."

My dialogue with my sister sent me on a bleak outlook for the rest of my summer up in Michigan, but Ursa and I eventually made a pact not to ruin our siblings relationship with Mother, and we both determined to try to tolerate the old girl and put up with her middle-aged dalliances. We pray that this is just a phase that Mother is going through, and she will soon get over it. We continue to pray for our Father who would need all the love and support we could muster.

Meanwhile, I continue to try to meet Mother's demands as she continues to milk the platitude, "Love your mother, just because she is your mother." Meanwhile, our dear Father becomes more nervous, every day because of our Mother's insensitive, unbridled improprieties.

Chapter 36. The Great High Priest of Fishing and Hunting

My wood chopping is finished, fresh ice loaded into the icebox, milk, butter, and bacon has been fetched from Joe Bacon farm, repairs are done on our dock, so I took the liberty to dig up a can of worms and then place them in my bait bottle which hangs around my neck. Being cool and cloudy today should bring the fish around. A slight southerly breeze means that warmer weather is on its way and morning mist will be on our Lake, so I unhitched the boat, rowed across the bay, stashed the boat and oars in a bush, and walked barefoot along the path to Hortons Bay, wearing only a T-shirt and bib overalls.

With fishing rod, reel, and tackle box stashed behind Vollie Fox's Red Fox Inn, I picked up my favorite reel and headed toward Hortons Creek. I heard a voice call my name:

"Well hey, Ernie, come here," yelled Vollie Fox.

I turns to see Vollie standing with a uniformed man sporting a bushy mustache and bright green arm patches.

"I want you to meet somebody. This here is our new Game Warden. He is here to replace our friend, Mr. Evans."

"Our esteemed friend you mean, right?"

"Right... please meet Officer Harold Hodges, just off the train from Lansing."

"Very pleased to meet you, Mr. Hodges. Ernest Hemingway's the name."

"Very pleased, indeed, young Hemingway. Mr. Fox has good reports of you. Hope we can be working together soon."

"Working together?"

"Yes... I hope to gain cooperation from the local tribe, and you could help in this situation."

"Yeah,I suppose we could give you some pointers in that regard. Be glad to help, sir."

"I thought I might pick your brain over a cold drink here at the general store."

"Sure, I could go for an ice cold Vernors, all right. Thanks Officer Hodges."

My first thoughts upon meeting the new Game Warden are numerous: how much like Turd Face Evans will this man be? Is he gonna try to be tough on enforcement of fish and game laws? Will he try to run things strictly by the book? Will he hate the native tribe and their supporters? Just where will his sympathies lie? How much of my past has Vollie Fox divulged?

"What'll it be, gents?" asked Bill O'Donnell, owner of the general store.

"Three Vernors ginger ales please, my good man. Names Harold Hodges. Very pleased to be in Hortons Bay."

"You need a glass for that?" asked Bill O'Donnell.

"Naw, we're okay right from the bottle. Keeps the fizz in that way."

"Well, Ernest, here's to a short war."

"Yeah, right... Short war."

Our bottles clink and we lifted the cold, wet ginger ale soft drinks in a toast regarding our boys over in France and Italy. The bubbles tickled our noses.

"So Ernest, I understand you've had your own wars going on with Officer Evans up here in Emmet County?"

"Oh yeah. We sure did have, but let's hope that's all in the past. A page of ancient history, huh?"

"Part of my job is to help reinstate trust again in the office of Game Warden, so with your help and cooperation, we can get back to being a healthy working state of being. I understand you often hunt and fish with our tribal friends?"

"Yes, Sir, I do. They've adopted me as one of the tribe. My Pops, Dr. Clarence Hemingway, patches them up and gives them free doctoring. He even delivers their babies."

"Fine, fine, so I have heard. You Hemingway's have done a lot to cement good relations with our tribal friends. You're having run with them since childhood is a plus for us. So here's my plan, Ernest. We need you to make good citizens of these folks and convince them to purchase hunting and fishing licenses like the rest of the inhabitants of Emmet County."

"Well Sir, I will do my best with that mission. It won't be easy since us White men invaded their happy hunting grounds, cut down all the habitat trees, as a result scared off their game, then ruined the fishing by floating cut logs along the streams and rivers, destroying the best spawning grounds as a result. The grayling fish have been totally decimated... tragic isn't it? It ain't gonna be easy, Officer."

"Well, I figure you have an in with them and can speak their language. I can't undo the past atrocities which we whites have perpetrated upon them, but I want you to know I'm sympathetic to what they have endured, and I will do whatever it takes to get them hunting and fishing according to the rules. It's for the sake of the future herds of game and schools of fish."

"Officer, I assure you, no one understands conservation like our Native American friends. They rarely over fish or overkill the deer herd so to take that track would not motivate them."

"Well then... What approach should we take to get their compliance?"

"Give me some time on this okay, sir? I've got a few ideas, but I would have to run them by my friends in the tribe."

"Good, real good. I would be very interested in your findings, and Ernest, thank you. I will be staying at Red Fox Inn, so please drop by with the results and all… I thank you, Mr. Hemingway."

"Think nothing of it, Officer Hodges. It's my duty as a citizen to help. Your predecessor almost started another Indian uprising. Actually, I am surprised he wasn't popped by one of the tribe. They hated him."

"Yeah, well, Evans made a lot of mistakes and it is my job to rectify some of those and put things on an even keel. Any input you might have in this regard would be greatly appreciated."

By this time the worms in my bait bottle were getting anxious to go to work, so I shuffled down the dusty road to Hortons Creek and commenced fishing my usual fishing holes… All the while rehashing my meeting with our new Game Warden.

Idea one came into my head that his title has to change to reflect his changing role. Since his concern was protection of the future species, let's call him a Conservation Officer. That takes away the onus of citizens as game violators, but rather ones who share in the preservation of species. Now this next ideal will hear a lot of jaws dropping. I suggest we validate Native Americans as full citizens of this country with full rights and privileges as citizens, which would also include the right to vote in elections, and the privilege to purchase gear and fish licenses to help preserve the species. Knowing these to be very radical ideas... way ahead of their time... still, I was determined to share them with Officer Hodges, whom I felt would be open to all ideas which would come to me.

Not many white folks can say that they have been initiated into the tribe like I have; therefore, he must give a listen to any and all ideas which engender mutual acceptance for many Indians still hate whites and vice versa.

Fishing for me that day seemed automatic, for I had caught my limit of good sized trout without actually giving it too much consideration due to my fixation on how to improve race relations for Officer Hodges.

Hauling that heavy stringer of trout back to Red Fox Inn, I determined to invite Officer Hodges to share a fish fry with me behind Red Fox Inn.

Vollie thought it was a good idea too, so as I cleaned and scaled the fish, and he called Hodges down, they built a nice fire in Vollie's backyard.

"Nothing like a nice fish fry. Thanks Ernest for inviting me down."

"Yeah - you should see when they first hit the hot butter," I commented.

"Vollie added, "Yeah, they turn blue if they are freshly caught."

"Ernest, how do you get them so crunchy?"

"Butter in cornmeal, Mr. Hodges."

"Please call me Harold, men."

"Okay, Harold... more fish? We've got lots."

"Absolutely, Ernest. Load me up."

As Officer Hodges enjoyed the fresh fish, I got to worrying as to where I kept my fishing license. If he demands a showing of my document, I will be up the creek.

Thoughts like that are trouble, and I don't have the license in my wallet. If he challenges me to show it, I'll tell him I left it on my dresser at home. Yeah, that should do it. Can't let negative thoughts throw off my rhythm today, especially as I try to win this Game Warden over to my side and friendship, plus I have some revolutionary ideas to deliver to this old boy from Lansing.

"So, Harold, I've done some more thinking about how we get the tribe on our side regarding hunting and fishing regulation."

"Okay, Ernie, I'm listening. Go ahead. Gosh, these are good fish!"

"Thanks.. all right, first we make them voting citizens of the United States."

"Okay, go on."

"Next, we change your title."

"Radical...I must say. Let me absorb just that first idea. Go on? Go ahead with my new title, then."

"Okay, and you'll like this one: Game Warden... think about it... almost like prison warden... like it implies we are wards of the state to be watched like common criminals... which we ain't. We are citizens, and as good citizens we voluntarily front the state five hard earned bucks in which to improve the herd and plant fingerlings in lakes all around the state. In turn, for our generosity and support we receive a yearly membership, sort of a conservation club to which we join. Get it? And you become the Conservation Officer. Your new title."

"I get it, Ernie. Our present setup now creates an adversarial relationship... makes implied crooks out of all law abiding citizens. The cost of the hunting and fishing licenses like posting bail ahead of time so the warden won't throw you in jail."

"See Harold,I told you he would think of something. Do you like it?"

"Like it? I love it! Now how do you propose we implement all this, since even our women haven't been allowed to vote as yet?"

"Good question, Harold, then Lansing would be open to that title change and the use of license money for building fish hatcheries. All very good ideas. My goodness, you've been thinking about this for some time haven't you?"

"Oh sure, but tribes need to be legitimized by becoming citizens with full voting rights. Right now, we relocate the tribe on reservations just like children, and try to take care of them as if they are all losers who can't take care of themselves. They are a proud nation who have lived here thousands of years subsisting on their skills as hunters, trappers, and fishermen, but since we whites have come through, claimed the land, cut out all the trees, ruined the streams, scattered the deer, bear, fowl, and left the hunting grounds a pile of rubble, and now expect them to pay money for fishing licenses when they deal in barter, horses, and furs, Harold... It makes you wonder why they put up with our foolishness. It breaks my heart the way it is... Officer."

"Yeah, Harold, I gotta agree with Ernie here. We need to re look at this whole picture," replied Vollie Fox.

"Gosh, I'm glad we had this little chat, gentleman. Ernie, you present the problem as well as a solution or two, so I will head down to the capital to present this to our governor on the first train south. You know, maybe we could hire the tribe to run the fish hatcheries."

I said, "See, you're thinking about solutions, Harold. Tell Lansing we said hello."

Well, Officer Hodges seemed like a favorable replacement for Turdface Evans. He at least had an open mind and sat down to listen to solutions. Together with the serving of the fresh trout, it seemed like I was the priest administering Holy Eucharist, which vindicates the sin of Lansing for sending us nasty old Evans.

Native Americans did finally get the vote, just as I suggested. Women got the vote in 1920, but it was several years later in 1924 when Native Americans got the vote. They still needed to get a pass in order to leave the reservation. Washington established the Bureau of Indian Affairs or the B.I.A. and planted a white man called the Indian Agent to run things on each reservation. B.I.A. schools were built and run by church related teachers, who converted young Indian children to Christianity, requiring students to room and board on campus isolated from their respective tribes and parents.

The tribal eight days Sundance was reduced to two days and the use of the peyote was banned due to its addictive quality.

My Prudy came to mind, and I often thought she and Billy Tabeshaw, her brother, would never have survived in such a restrictive atmosphere.

My very own Pops felt he could hunt and fish at any time if he had a hankering. When I asked him about this obvious double standard, this holy Joe stated: "Just don't get caught."

So once again, my expectations were coming along only in the case of Turdface Evans. My view is that his replacement, Officer Hodges, is much more than I had expected. This man is going to overcome Evans damage to the point that once again folks respect the law.

As far as my idea to change his title from Game Warden to that of Conservation Officer, this change did eventually come about, but not until 50 years later.

New fish hatcheries now operate under state mandate and they regularly stock lakes and streams, much to the joy of local anglers.

How could so much drama get packed into a guys last summer up in Michigan? Talk about intense! This excitement is just beginning to mount as one thing after another occurred every day. They got to the point that in my prayers, I began to ask for one old fashioned normal day when nothing happened... at least nothing unusual.

I often ask... what's normal about a fresh new Game Warden coming to a 17 year old? Maybe I look old for my age, or maybe because I'm pals with our local judge and America's finest lawyer, and one of the few whites who have become initiated in the local tribe... Maybe I'm just finally getting some respect around Emmet County.

Maybe, just maybe, I should be writing about hunting and fishing adventures that I have experienced. Would readers find them captivating enough to run out and buy such books?

Before that happens; however, I feel I have a lot to learn about style and delivery. I'm counting on learning at this upcoming newspaper job, for editors and associates are going to give me all sorts of pointers, meanwhile I have 3 months of summer left in which to enjoy myself.

This summer, Longfields farm is producing some lettuce, asparagus, potatoes, beans, early snap peas, and a nice surrounding of marigolds which will keep out certain bugs. Fresh strawberries and raspberries will soon be ready for picking. This stretch of acreage was what mother used to swing father around for an agreement for its purchase. Her construction of the extra cabin on the Hill was an idea which never had Father's Blessing, that she skillfully steamrolled into being by cutting a deal with Mr. Morford who did a masterful job with hand hewn beams hauled in by his hearty team of horses. I tell you what, this guy Morford is incredible. He cuts only prized hardwood logs, hauls them out with his team, and hand shapes the logs promising them to last hundreds of years.

Whomever inherits these cabins will be gifted with Morford skill and choice of lumber. My feeling is they will not be something I will inherit, for daily now I get the feeling Mother knows that I know about her scandalous private life, for which either she will try to discredit me, or try to banish me from our summer cabin. Even now I feel her plotting my exit. Even now I feel her poisoning Father's mind against me, due to jealousy and the need to cast doubt upon any of my testimony, clouding the issues with some religious doubletalk and loose Bible jargon which she is good at.

Sometimes I can't stand her 'holier than thou' sanctimonious, self righteousness and hypocrisy. Say that 10 times fast. The old girl was afraid I will blow the whistle on her behind the scenes, dangerous, dalliances.

Editor's note: Ernest's intuition is eventually proven correct, for soon Grace Hemingway did exactly as he envisioned. In a letter sent to Dr. Clarence, she paints a toxic picture of her oldest son as being lazy, irresponsible, the user of people, and one prone to mooching off his friends. Psychologists analyzing it would call the letter's content a classic case of strategic projection, meaning that the very qualities which she accuses her son of having are very qualities which she possesses.

Clarence, being naïve and browbeaten and the classic enabler of his wife as an addictive personality, enters an agreement with Grace, yet maintains confidence the he did right by his son by arranging a cub reporter's job through his brother Tyler in Kansas City. Ernest will start his writing career within three months.

Most sitting biographies tend to whitewash all negative family dynamics regarding life with the Hemingway's. Each brother and sisters book covering this refers to the mother always in the glowing terms and briefly touches on Clarence's growing nervousness, while never referring that his case of nerves may be caused by Graces outlandish behavior.

What's a kid gonna do? I'm supposed to love my mother, which I do, however, I cannot condone her manipulative behavior and outlandish phoniness together with her lavish misuse of my college funds and her constant milking of the mother diva title, she has ascribed to herself.

I am sure I must've mentioned that when I was a kid she took pleasure in dressing me like a girl together with long curly locks that weren't cut until I was ready for school at the age of five. She ignored the fact that Marcy, my older sister, was over a year my senior, yet she held her out of school until we could both start into kindergarten together, masquerading us as twins.

With her father, Ernest Hall, on the school board, I guess she felt she could get away with it... and she did.

All our teachers thought she was nuts. Oh, did I mention that one-time Marcy decided to give herself a haircut? Mother went ballistic, making Marcy wear a bonnet in school until she grew her hair out. How did Marcy's teachers take to this? Well, you've got an imagination right?

Now you know why I pitched a tent outside beside the cabin and spent most of my private moments out there in my tent, plus, I light a hurricane lantern so's I can read my favorite books late into the night.

Let the record show that I have stated my grievances.

Editor's note: The husband calls the shots in the marriage Bible style. It says the husband is head of house. He loves his wife as Jesus loves the church.

Clarence Hemingway; however, is too shy to stand up for his role. He plays the peacemaker continually digressing to Grace his wishes. The fact that she earns more money than he, plus her father's wealthy estate both give her power over poor Clarence, the unhappy enabler.

Grace has no kitchen skills, so hired cooks and housekeepers handle all domestic chores. Grace focuses her time on her music lessons, choir directing, and singing solos, and shopping the latest fashions, so that she and her children are always well dressed when they go out into conservative Oak Park, where the Hemingway's rank is upper middle class society.

Grace was an organizer for women's right to vote, and she also was active in prohibition of alcohol.

Due to his lack of spine, my father could have avoided all this trouble by taking a firm stand as the man of the house, but since he did not and just gave this crazy woman free reign, all these wacko things began to happen.

Sometimes I feel like she is hiding behind us as her cloak of respectability. Seriously, Oak Park sees us as a well dressed, churchgoing, healthy family of six kids together with a successful doctor husband. What could be more upstanding? No one would ever guess what really goes on within these Hemingway halls.

With fear of overstating my case toward mother, allow me the liberty to post an incident now and then as the thoughts occur to me for many of her atrocities have been repressed by now... very deep in the inner sanctum of my troubled mind. Putting them down on paper helps to get these toxic issues out from the hidden mental corners where the brutal truth can fester, and out into the open air light of day, where we can examine them.

Living with a mother like Grace Hall-Hemingway creates compulsions without any answers as to where they originate, like my quirky idea that every day I have to go out and kill something. Starting with crows, first thing in the morning, at the crack of dawn, I use the 3 .22 cartridges which father rations to me. He thinks nothing of it, for he too has to kill something just like I must.

Being powerless within our family, we two males, and I might add, two frustrated males, must ventilate in our region the best way we can, and that would be by ending the lives of crows, squirrels, rabbits, partridge, ducks, pheasant, quail, snipe, deer, bear, and the list goes on. We are now killers. The power over life and death rests in one little twitch of the trigger finger. Somehow the power we lack over domestic issues usurped by the dominating Mother, we feel compensated for by the power we have over wild game and fish.

I can tell it is a compulsion and not just an innocent hobby and pastime, because I can't stop myself, plus I feel deeply gratified after each kill to the point that I want to immediately go out and pop a bigger one. I break into a cold sweat while I ritualized the preparation of the tools, instruments, and items needed. Sometimes I feel like I am the high priest of death.

Priests are deeply into all the powerful rituals and rubrics, and symbols and important gestures, so too I also go about my prepping and staging for the hunt, just as a good pujori, a Hindu temple priest, trims his wax candles and measures his ceremonial oils and incense utilizing special instruments and tools dedicated for this unique holy purpose.

In a sense, I suppose I'm killing in order to feel powerful, yet the ritual into which I subject myself tends to upgrade the act into a more spiritual dimension, therefore tempering the dastardly deed. To be honest about it though, it is still killing. The innocent are being deprived of life.

Compulsion and devotion are two peas from the same pod, I figure, it's very hard sometimes to tell the difference. Anyway, I find myself devoted to my compulsion.

If one were to look a little deeper, one would find that I have been an alcoholic since age 11 when my pal Bill Smith introduced me to hard cider.

Michigan has banned the sale of alcohol since 1916, way ahead of the nation, so we had to get creative. Apples and raisins placed in a jug atop a warm steam radiator will ferment in a few days. It too, along with fermented dandelion blossoms in the crock of sugar water will drop your bloomers in a few days of fermentation.

Why do I imbibe while my father forbids it... he being a teetotaler? In all honesty, I must state that it is a way that I escape. Alcohol puts me in a different mood, and couple that with my intensely competitive nature, and soon I am trying to out drink everyone.

Because it is in my household forbidden, my rebellious nature wants to engage in it all the more. I tell you, I am a real son of a bitch, but we are dealing with a time when our whole nation is obsessed with homemade alcohol of all kinds, and everyone has a flask on their body somewhere. Women have their flask fastened to the upper thigh with elastic.

During prohibition our whole nation have become outlaws. The banning of alcohol had made hoodlums of us all, and gangsters produced it on a massive scale. America was thirsty. This was a period of the speakeasy, the whiskey smuggled across the border from Canada, and the neighborhood bathtub gin making. I love gin made from Juniper berries. This was a time of radical change at all levels, even women's fashions... hemlines came up above the knee. Dresses were sleeveless. Long hair got Bob short, and parents were outraged, but helpless to stop it.

Our generation was out of control... that's for sure, and on every level.

My older sister Marcy became a smoldering volcano of repressed rage, but she convinced mother to lobby father to allow us to take dance lessons at the Unitarian temple, you know the one designed by her neighbor Frank Lloyd Wright.

Poor girls got their toes crunched as I cut a rug with my number 11 Brogans. My big feet were always causing trouble, but I worked hard to learn because neighborhood dances were good way to meet chicks.

Young college boys were wearing raccoon coats with pork pie hats. It was a time for canoe rides, ukuleles, serenades with megaphones, and everyone danced the Charleston.

In an effort to create a backdrop, I mention all this for the very foundations of society were being drafted at every angle.

Gertrude Stein called us the lost generation, but we were ready for change... change in fashion, dance, art, music, and for me, I wanted change in literature. I was tired of the length of time it took to wade through thousands of unnecessary adjectives, adverbs, and similes. just to get to the good parts.

Victorian literature was way too cluttered with over description and overly sentimental, naive drivel. It reflected the average parlor terribly covered with knickknacks, overly framed paintings housed in homes, covered in gobs of gingerbread. We had endured 100 years of 19th century clutter, and as the new century unfolded in front of us, we were determined not to have any more of it... not in this new century... this age was ours for the taking and we want to set the stage for an age of monumental impact on the arts and society in general. We of all people had paid for this privilege with our lives. We had paid our dues in blood. The war had taken 37 million youth. Millions of our finest young men, and now we felt we had earned the right to set the tone and direction of where we were headed as a planet.

The war had caused something within the youth of our day to snap. All of our old institutions to become suspect. We no longer trusted what previous generations had carved out for us. On some subtle level of awareness, the war had set us all off on a wild, intoxicating new ride without a compass, without an anchor, and also without a rudder. It was change for change's sake. It was art for art's sake. A mad departure from realism, opening up the stage for the world of dreams and psycho drama.

Now, on all levels we needed to break away from the failures which the previous age had perpetrated upon our fresh, young lives. It was time to break away with refreshingly new, yet radically meaningful monumental breakthroughs, and I wanted more than anything to set literature on a new course... call it my competitive nature, but I felt the job had to be done, and I was the man to do it, to redefine what was meant; to put words together.

I was determined to become the jawbone of our new generation, for I have heard the meaningless screams of the millions whose lives were cut certainly short for nothing... absolutely nothing!

After digesting every available novel which is considered great or noteworthy, between hundreds, for example Kipling, Conrad, Stevenson, Tolstoy, the list is vast, my friend, my conclusions are: my work will be shockingly short, sentences are short cropped, adjectives and adverbs will be at a minimum, topics will be unique, visiting areas where no one has ventured before, and written in a style which will stimulate multiple layers of consciousness within the readers mind, utilizing all the five senses as well as the sixth sense, delving into the spiritual, by only hinting at deeper layers, which I call my iceberg effect.

My work will not compete with the great literature, but will be a much yearned for departure and a fast read, must read format which stands out from the crowd in subject matter and representation delivered in a straightforwardness and unsentimental manner.

Easy-to-read, easy to understand due to unsophisticated language tailored for the common man, calling upon uncommon everyday scenes, utilizing common street characters in uncommon adventures. My work will be unmistakable, and as a result ... irresistible, for readers of this century are bored stiff with Victorian literature as we know it. Present institutions that we have inherited are also boring us stiff and need to change. The arts, music, dance, fashion, and mostly, writing.

Using specially chosen words, scenes will be painted like a Cezanne landscape. They will contain a musical rhythm like a ballet held in an art museum.

Ambitious, indeed, but I know lots of good stories, and I'm anxious to share them in a short stack of specially terse words of description and dynamic dialogue.

Having read so many of the last century masters, I feel confident this combination of mine will put most of their backs on the canvas.

But here I am at Windemere during my last summer up in Michigan, basking in my very own heroics, enjoying the teenage adulation of all my girlfriends, as well as all my male friends, and various adults and wondering what can be expected in terms of excitement for the next three months.

June and July action will be hard to beat, but as in the past, something always comes up rather unexpectedly.

Sometimes I get the feeling that we are not in control of anything. Just as my life settles down into a series of mundane habits of daily sameness... an hour by hour ritual dedicated to my personal safety... to break the board of monotony... a monkey wrench notion arises which takes me over the edge.

Often my thoughts drift back to my great-grandfather, the ship captain, whose entire life was filled with adventure as he ventured into the unknown around the tip of South America.

Traveling through uncharted seas, never knowing what he might run into must have been a thrill a minute.

Sailing by the seat of his pants, discovering steamy island nations that were still in the Stone Age, but had never seen an English man, they would just as soon cook your ass for supper, would just as soon shrink your skull down to the size of a softball, oh, that must've been an adventure which never quit.

We used to sit on the edge of our seats listening to Grandmother Hall relay the good times she had when she voyaged out with Great Grandfather Captain Hancock. But alas, sailing ships are dying out now in favor of steam powered vessels, which utilize big boilers fired by coal, no longer at the mercy of free trade wind breezes and propelling ocean currents. We are now propelled through the seven seas with steam powered screws. Guess I was born a few years too late for all that sailing adventure. With all that sensitive adventure streaming through my veins one can only speculate as to how the ship captain Great-Grandfather Hancock's legacy will manifest itself in me, but when life gets way too boring and every day becomes a repeat of every other day in dry, stultifying sameness I hear that wanderlust calling me. No kidding, I really do. Someday I will travel to faraway lands and have me an adventure, however, when no travel plans are on the horizon, I'm the kind of guy who can stir up the local situation until an adventure eventually appears.

Chapter 37. 44 Years Later, back in 1961. Epilogue.

Ernest with his Fourth Wife, Mary.

Since that last good summer of 1917 had so many exciting events, one would think I would cherish every moment and be so buoyed up in spirit that I would be in seventh heaven about the outcome, but because I could get no support for my writing from Mother and Father, I was still stuck in that damning unforgiven relationship.

Granted, while I lived in Paris I got some support for my writing from Gertrude Stein, my substitute mother, and also support from Ezra Pound, who played the role of substitute father; however, every book I sent home to Mom and Pop returned because they rejected them due to the coarse language and repulsive characters.

That parental rejection hurt me so deeply that I never forgave them. This gave me cause to want to end my life. Even though my books were accepted worldwide, even though I was awarded the Pulitzer and the Nobel prizes for literature, but having no recognition from Mother and Pops... being betrayed by my parents... all the awards in the world are meaningless to me. Plus being betrayed by my own body due to diabetes, numerous concussions, post traumatic stress disorder from the war along with my war injuries, the lack of sleep and nightmares, the condemning voices that would not shut up, the destruction by alcohol, plus the paranoia of being tailed constantly by the FBI... as a result, deep depression set in. I felt I had no choice but to do myself in.... end it.

So now I find myself rising up the tube of light, traveling higher, as up to the pearly gates, which I now find being guarded by St. Peter...

"Halt right there," Peter commanded.

"Please," I pleaded, thinking I still wore my press pass in my hat.

"But you're not qualified to go any further. You can't enter the main gate after you have done yourself in. We don't accept suicides," exclaimed Peter.

"Oh, please... I must see Jesus!" I insisted. "You can let me go in, for I really must see Jesus! I gotta see Him!"

Peter comments, "Well this is highly irregular. I guess it won't hurt, just don't blame me if you get into trouble, okay?"

With that unexpected approval, I'm finding myself still moving up the tube of light, which now is getting brighter. Upward into the brighter light, I rose and I spotted a dark silhouette of a person's back. All the light was at His front, which I assumed was His glory emanating forward.

No words were spoken. Telepathic thoughts shot right through me as I came to rest about 10 feet behind him... I'm assuming this is Jesus.

"St. Peter allowed you up here?"

"Oh, yeah, but it's not his fault. He must've seen my press pass?"

"Well... Okay, you made it up this far, so don't expect me to turn and face you, because the glory would be too much for you to bear. Now pilgrim... What have you done with your life?"

Not expecting such a strong and embarrassing telepathic question, Jesus thoughts tore through me like thousands of sharp darts.

Having no excuse for my rotten life, all I could give him was a pathetic shrug of my shoulders. Here I am, a man of letters, known for my strong, profound use of words and nothing comes to mind to share with Jesus... absolutely nothing... zip.

Jesus fired another volley of thoughts my way, even though His back was all I could see.

"All I ever wanted, was to chat with you. We could have been the best of pals. I created you to solve my problems with loneliness… Sounds silly, doesn't it? But God gets lonely too."

With that telepathic comment, His thoughts really rattled my cage, for even though I had memorized His book , the Bible, this concept of God getting lonely had never dawned on me before, never entered my mind.

Jesus continued, "You were all there at the beginning… remember my evening walks with your first parents, Adam and Eve? In the cool of the garden we would talk. We discussed anything, and everything, but since their fall from grace, that changed everything. I even sewed them nice clothing, since the loss of the glory exposed their personal nakedness. They ate from the tree of good and evil, which I forbid."

It all sounded so darned simple now listening to Jesus explain things.

Jesus continues, "Why didn't you ask me to heal you? I was waiting. If you read my book, you saw that I healed many people with worse maladies than yours. All you had to do was ask! Furthermore, your life is so filled with heavy burdens… burdens you could've asked me to carry, like your mother. All you had to do was forgive her, but no… You wouldn't, so you had to drag her around, and as a result that situation ruined every marriage of yours, and just made your life miserable."

Jesus continued nailing me telepathically as I stood watching his hinder parts. Soon I began to realize, he had rescued me from Satan and was qualifying me for purgatory. The prayers of my family and friends at work. They had qualified me for purgatory, but I soon realized how messed up I had made everything by taking my own life. It all could have been avoided had I established a prior personal relationship with Jesus, for He had paid off Satan at Calvary, with His own royal body and blood. Had I established an active prayer life, the way he wanted it, I could've had it all. Jesus was lonesome for me. Taking communion often would have cleared me of sin… mistakes I made where I came short of His glory. I would've honored His body and blood as my redeeming sacrifice, made possible through the sacrament in the blessed bread and wine… the eternal mystery and majesty of the body and blood.

Hemingway's Four Wives: Hadley Richardson, Pauline Pfeiffer, Martha Gellhorn, and Mary Welch

Daily praising and thanking would have made my life a living testimony for others to follow. It would have been a blessing, having Jesus in me and me and Him. It would have made my life so much easier and when at last Jesus wanted to call me home, I could've walked proudly through the Pearly Gates, the main entrance to Paradise, with my head held high and He would've said to me, "Well done, my good and faithful servant. Come in, your mansion is waiting for you." But I now know He really hates suicide.

Since my thoughts were all registering telepathically with Jesus, He was much aware of my regrets and argued wholeheartedly with what I just had self speculated...

Again, Jesus transmitted, "Prayers of your family and friends are recommending leniency, Ernest... But you know you will have to stay in purgatory now for some time, right?"

Wow! That news hit me hard, like the proverbial ton of bricks, but I called it a blessing for I was happy to not be sent to hell.

Being a nominal Catholic had spared me the eternal flames of Satan's hangout. If my family and friends don't forget about me, their prayers will eventually elevate me out of purgatory.

Jesus adds, "Another point you should know about is that after your prayers or after church attendance or Bible reading, I always gave you good ideas for books. You're welcome."

I replies, "Gee thanks... Jesus. This I did not suspect, but it figures. For all intelligence comes from God."

Jesus said, "Plus, here's another item you probably never noticed... since you have considered suicide from an early age, this has been on your mind for quite some time. That is why I sent you Dr. Freud. He was lecturing in Paris while you were there. You almost made an appointment with him, but you got drunk instead... Another sign of suicide."

I said, "Whoops!"

Jesus adds, "Yes, whoops, but who helps you connect with all your Paris writing tutors, like Gertrude, Ezra, Ford, together with all those avant-garde painters like Pablo Picasso, Miro, and Dali?"

I reply, "I guess I should've known... It was You all the way... Every day."

Jesus answers, "Absolutely. Bringing all those key players into your life at the right time and place... That all had to be of divine Providence. It was no easy task bringing together Joyce, T.S. Eliot, Scott Fitzgerald, and so many others, all heavy hitters for you to learn from. By the time you were 25, your work had made you famous. Ernest... You were the high priest of the literary world because of me."

I replied, "Thank you. I am humbled beyond words, my Lord."

Jesus added, "And well you should be, but unfortunately your poor parents never could understand you or your work. Is that correct?"

I adds, "You know me like a book, Sir, and now I'm up here where I should be enjoying eternity... But instead, it's purgatory for me, where I get to closely scrutinize the many ways I messed up my life."

Jesus says, "You learn quickly. That's a correct observation of this, your sad state of affairs, all due to your weak faith in me. You were a nominal believer, a lukewarm, lame Christian... the worst kind, Hemingway... And then to take your own God gifted life... That was the most foolish, cowardly, idiotic action you could have ever perpetrated, my child!"

I stated, "Yeah, well... Satan tricked me... At the time I was in despair, depressed, feeling hopeless, helpless, with no other option. What was I supposed to do?"

Jesus replies, "My child, you must've known it was against my command to kill, and that would include anyone, including your precious self. Ernest, you claimed to have read my Bible twice, and went so far as to memorize it from cover to cover... all 66 books.... yet still you miss that key command, thou shall not kill! My child, you amaze me! Did those Mayo Clinic shock therapies rob you of your common sense? I find your action most uncommon, Mr. Hemingway. Most unlikely, since you considered your father's suicide most cowardly. Most biographers claim he was distraught over bad investments, while your helpful check was placed on his desk, so why do I seek another motive for his self destruction?"

I reply, "Very few are those who would be privy to my devoted father's real motivation to end his life, and it may be too vile for me to air now within this purgatorium."

Jesus replys, "Oh, to the contrary, my son, many a vile topic has been purged among these hallowed clearing grounds. Please feel free to indulge yourself, Ernie, for I have a hunch you need to free your mind of this topic, if it is as vile as you say it is."

I states, "Well okay, then... here goes, for I've been burdened by this far too long... His wife, my mother had carried on a most unnatural love affair with her live in voice student, Ruth. It was Ruth Arnold, young enough to be mother's daughter, whom she was fixated upon, and it drove father out of his mind."

Jesus said, "Go on, my child, please go on, get it all out of your system, purge yourself now, clear your mind of this dark blot."

I continues, "Father, my sensitive, righteous, overly devoted, highly principled person that he was, could not carry on while mother carried on with her villainous, adulterous, fornication with young Ruth."

Jesus says, "Go on, please."

I adds, "My guess is he really wanted to catch them in the act and kill both her and young Ruth, which would have traumatized the children too much, so instead he turned the pistol onto himself... right behind his ear, according to my little brother, Baron. Berry was first to come to his aid, but he was seconds too late, for reaching behind father, his young hand found a hole oozing out blood and brain matter with father moaning out his last earthly sounds. Uncle George said Pops finances were not real bad, at least not worth putting grandfather's Civil War Smith and Wesson to his head."

Jesus reacts, "So am I to assume then that your mother caused your father's suicide?"

I responds, "Hell yes! That's fairly obvious!"

Jesus states, "Good... now we're getting somewhere. You must've carried that grief around for a long time? Did you ever consider giving it to me to carry? I carried the sins of the whole world! I could've carried your mother's lesbian affairs too. Did your mother trigger your alcohol abuse?"

I react, "You mean, I could've given all my burdens for You to carry? Even my alcohol problems? Well I'll be darned. I never knew that. Wow!"

Jesus asks, "Can we discuss your alcohol addiction?"

I concur, "Sure... Why not."

Jesus continues, "Okay... let's see, is it true that you got hooked on hard cider at Bill Smith's, at age 11?"

I reply, "Why, yes. How did you know?"

Jesus adds, "Let's just say a little birdie told me. And then you later graduated to dandelion wine followed by homebrew beer and wine. Followed by your favorite gin... cognac when you can afford it, dry martinis and champagne, all in that order. How am I doing?

And the reason at first was to tell your mind to anesthetize it of pain caused by your mother, her failure to truly understand you, and pain she caused your father."

I retort, "Why yes. At first, but later I got addicted to it. It was automatic, a habit done without thinking, actually.

After a steady intake of the demon rum, my liver and other organs showed signs of serious wear and tear, but I always wrote in the mornings when I was sober."

Jesus added, "And when you were drunk?"

I replied, "I was usually in a bar with my friends, having great food and a great time. I was getting ideas and learning slang for my dialogue writing."

Jesus said, "Not unlike your mother, you would command their attention. Only you use your voice to pontificate, to recite poetry and even lead them in good old time songs into the wee hours."

I retorted, "Yeah, that is true... But gee, why did you say I was like my mother?"

Jesus said, "Well... take a good look at yourself. Because you hate her so much, you had to become her, and act like her, that's how hate works, Ernest. Take a good look. Ironic how life works isn't it?"

I remarks, "Well, I'll be... Funny, I never spotted that, but now that you mention it, it makes sense. Indians got a phrase... 'Walk a mile in someone's moccasins before you cast judgment.' In my case, I was in my mother's shoes because I cast judgment on her."

Jesus remarks, "Now you've got it. But her drive and bravery to buck convention worked to your favor. It made you strive to make your writing standout, like nothing before, which readers enjoyed by the thousands."

I ask, "Do you mean?"

Jesus continues, "Yup... because you unconsciously enacted your mother's panache and desire to break with tradition, this force was what drove you to break away from the pack of literature that had gone before. Your unique style then was the result...something bold and honest and violent, easy to read for the masses, something all writers after you must emulate and try to copy, and see if they can also forge a style which commands attention at the book stands... Do you see it?"

I remark, "Holy cow! I mean, holy crap? I mean, holy Jesus, I never saw it that way before, b-b-but it makes sense, you know."

Jesus adds, "And of course your father's influence was obvious... love of nature, flora and fauna, healing, medicine, detail, accounting, fishing, hunting, camping, cooking, baking. You copied your father consciously because you adored him and wanted to be like him."

I suggest, "And I suppose I copy my mother unconsciously out of hate, the flip side of love?"

Ernest with his son, Gregory Hemingway.

Jesus replies, "Something like that. The very aspects of her which you hated were also active inside you, which is why you can see them so clearly. Your other siblings were not that upset with her, in fact some of them truly adored Mother Grace, but what we resist persists, in other words because you resisted forgiving your Mother, those nasty, even kinky aspects you observed in her, what you called androgyny, would also persist into the next generation through you, and then succeeded to pass them on to the son most like you."

I interject, "You mean, Gregory, right?"

Jesus agrees, "But of course... poor fellow. That is why you never got along with him, you were too much alike. All Gregory needed was your acceptance. He was a very good writer.

He picked up on your gender issues too, so he dressed up as a woman compounded by Pauline's abandonment of the boys Patrick and Gregory.

Dear Ernest, because you likes to play the blame game, never accepting responsibility for your actions, people around you were driven to do crazy things. Patrick eventually retreated to Africa to become a safari guide. He knew you couldn't fault him over there.

Gregory got your attention by becoming a doctor, and he was a good one had your gender kinkiness not gotten in his way, plus he hated Pauline for abandoning him, so he had to become Pauline, what we resist persists, as you know for hating Mother Grace. Your son, Gregory, felt abandoned by Pauline. The nanny who Pauline hired for him was mean and abusive to him, threatening him to never see his mother again, so to feel close to Pauline he invaded her dresser drawer and played with the softness of her nylons and underwear, just to feel close to his mother.

In your case, Dear Ernest, you acted out in the sack by being on the bottom."

I reply, "Yeah, yeah... That's right. Marcy was also abused by her, just as badly as I was, but..."

Jesus adds, "Marcy never let it bother her. They even had money for Marcy's college at Oberon. So all this animosity you had for your Mother about squandering your college funds was unfounded. You could very well have attended any college of your choice."

I interject, "Yeah, I guess I see your point, but that doesn't vindicate her from turning lesbian. That is downright perverted."

Jesus replied, "Indeed! I concur, but was that any reason to end your own life?"

I reply, "In retrospect, I must say no, since I messed up my chances for a grand entrance to the pearly gates, but now I'll spend eternity looking at my failure to have faith in the free redemption plan that you bought for me on the cross. I had a lifetime in which to accept that, but I messed that up too."

Jesus adds, "Yes, indeed... Without faith in my redemption plan ... ha, ha, ha. I like how you put it. Without faith, it's impossible to please me. Many folks get tripped up on that key issue because it is too simple for them. I am the way, the truth, and the light. No man comes to the father except through me.

With Faith your shortcomings are covered, overlooked, though they be as scarlet, I see you as white as snow. My blood and body, the Eucharist, or communion, gives you a free pass at your death of natural causes."

I adds, "Now I see that taking my own life was a huge mistake. Jesus, you could have been my free pass into heaven, carried all my burdens, healed me of alcoholism, healed my body and mind also, and I could have lived to a ripe old age and died gracefully."

Jesus added, "This is true, Ernest. All your troubles would have been over, and I could've lifted you out of darkness and into my marvelous light."

I interrupted, "Yeah, but I was too bullheaded arrogant, thinking that I could handle everything myself; however, all I did was mess things up. My life was out of control, and depression was leading me into a downward spiral, from which there was no pulling out. Mayo Clinic misdiagnosed my case. I needed psychotherapy, not electroshock therapy. I needed a chaplain, not induced convulsions."

Jesus continued, "And the wealthier you got, the harder it was to humble you, and accept the Holy Spirit. My Holy Spirit which paved the way for my gospel, and you would have felt the need for a Savior. You are beyond humbling."

I reply, "Yeah, the wealthy think that they only need their money. I tried to focus my writing on the average Joe."

Jesus interrupted, "But you thought of yourself as their high priest... Pope even, in charge of life-and-death- taking the lives of so many beautiful animals and fish. Your over-the-top macho image was a smokescreen to hide your unconscious need to act and try out Mother Grace's role in bed. You had Pauline cut her own hair short like a man's style haircut. You encouraged her to slip on top during your lovemaking in bed."

I reply, "Wow! You really nailed me on that, Jesus. If one of my critics had said that, I would've broken his jaw. Yet all these gender issues I had were caused by my hate for Mother Grace?"

Jesus adds, "Indeed, dear Ernest... And your sexual perversion would have left you, had you forgiven Grace. Grace actually lead you into an Oedipus relationship with her, another reason to hold her in contempt."

I added, "The woman had no boundaries, plus she used the Bible to cover and validate her twisted lifestyle within the family."

Jesus adds, "Indeed, Ernest. The woman had no shame. And because Clarence, your father, could not put his foot down and pull in the reins to contain her wild behavior, it was allowed to continue from Marcy all the way down to Leichester. Clarence blamed himself so much that he started the bad family habit of suicide."

I react, "Uncle George knew his suicide was not about bad finances; my generous check laid on his desk all the while... so it was

Grace's fault all along. Her unbridled androgyny caused us all to murder ourselves, except Sunny and Carol. How do we explain that?"

Jesus states, "Well, Sunny slipped under the radar by becoming a tomboy, palling around with you, her idol. With the shift of focus she never needed her mother, who had no ambitions for her both academically nor musically, as you know."

Carol and Sunny with the Potato Harvest at Longfields

I adds, "Yeah, by golly, you're right there. Everyone except I never expected much from Sunny. I knew she had potential."

Jesus continues, "Right, she had your love and support and she never needed the others as a result, however much later she developed her musical talent, and she mastered the harp, and she did this for love of music, not for Grace's approval. She eventually played with the Memphis Symphony. Your encouragement spared her."

I reacts, "Well, I'll be! Sunny will escape the suicide like that, by not needing mother's approval."

"Yes, because Grace's love always had strings attached, it was not unconditional."

I recalls, "So Marcy flunks out of college because her motivation was wrong!"

Jesus replies, "Yes, because she craved Grace's love, and she wanted to prove superiority over you, dear boy. She and her husband Sanford bought the Loomis cabin right next to Windemere, just to spite you. Truth was, the place was a shack and later was torn down. She will take her life after her book fails to be successful.

Other siblings of yours murder themselves. Liechester, a.k.a. Baron, who feared diabetes, and Ursula over in Hawaii takes too many sleeping pills due to an illness.

Carol runs off and marries and lives a long and happy life with the man whom you banned. Go figure.

So only your sisters Sunny and Carol humbly live long and happy lives untouched by the family scourge of taking their own lives."

"They both were most humble, not even entertaining desires to be on the world stage; therefore, never having to deal with the tragedy of not attaining global recognition like me, Les, and Marcy. All in my family are stuck in purgatory now, and could've reached heaven had they not taken the cowards way out? Only two made it."

Jesus adds, "That sums it up about right, Ernest. It seems that the key factor in their success spiritually was their devotion to me and my mission as opposed to worldly fame, and self aggrandizement, which you had too,in your early life, but could not maintain.

To achieve real success in the worldly sojourn means to discover me and develop a daily friendship with me through Bible study, meditation, prayer, and right action, by helping others to find me. You had plenty of chances at this.

Do you see how achieving worldly fame as a writer took you off track and got you worshiping your own career rather than me? Hedonism instead of Spiritism.

Being surrounded by religion as a youngster, how is it that you got so sidetracked as you got older?"

I reply, "Damn good question, Jesus (pardon my French). My being surrounded every day by Father and Mother's form of religion began to wear on me as I began to see through Mother's hypocrisy. She became overly sentimental and got her own way by playing the martyred game. She used religion to beat us all emotionally and psychologically.

Father would be called in to inflict the strap and then he made us get on our knees in order to beg God's forgiveness. He was the punisher of sins, instead of the Savior from sin through love... unconditional love of the cross.

As kids, we Hemingway's got inflicted upon us a twisted form of religion. Heavy on judgment and punishment, leaning on the law like the Pharisees. If followed immediately with the gospel and the attraction of forgiveness, this combination might have worked, but I got turned off by too many things and not enough compassion. Plus, I got little support for my writing efforts. We were not free to discover our special gifts, and we never got support for those skills. Mother wanted me to work at the cement plant. Can you imagine that? She claimed I was draining the family provisions. As I got older in my teens, she claimed I was using people and mooching off my friends and neighbors, and she tried her best to convince father of this lie, for none of it was true. She poisoned father's mind against me, putting a wild negative slant on me. Her plan was to have me evicted from my very own home. Eventually, she did just that during my very own birthday party. I was crushed, Jesus. Where was the love? What kind of Christian would kick a guy from his own home on his birthday? This was one cold bitch!"

Jesus replies, "Well how would you like your very own church leaders, whom you saw every day in the Temple, turn on you and have you nailed to planks, and hung out to die outside the city? All based on lies and trumped up charges. Let me tell you, that was painful, but I did it for you because of my great love for you."

I say, "Say Jesus, I always wanted to thank you for that. Seriously, that took a lot of courage, my Lord! And you took on the sins of the whole world! Now that has got to be your greatest miracle, right?"

Jesus adds, "Wait till you see me raise all the dead out of their graves. That's coming soon."

I add, "Yeah, I'll get to see all my pals who died in World War I. There's gonna be millions of them... In World War II, and the Spanish Civil War. I hear Gabriel's gonna play his trumpet."

Jesus adds, "Oh yeah, it'll be a big production. Blessed are they who die in the Lord."

Since time does not exist with Jesus and me in purgatory, we carried on our lengthy discussion until my mind got to aching. I am the chap who usually can pontificate at great length, burdening my friends into the wee hours, but my new friend Jesus has proven to outdo me at my best quality and he has a delightful way of explaining my shortcomings without instilling guilt.

In retrospect, I wish I had made friends with Him long ago. God knows I sure had plenty of chances, and if I had, I would be in heaven, triumphantly strolling through the main gate right now, *instead of on the outskirts looking in and, wishing (another form of regret). Of all my regrets I must admit this is my biggest, not defending Jesus while I had my body.*

Considering I was always on a most diligent search for truth; somehow, I totally missed this, the one highest of all truths. Even I was awarded a writer's highest awards on earth, the Pulitzer and the Nobel, I sadly admit I missed the highest spiritual award honors; namely, heaven at the time of death by natural causes. Entrance into the main gate of heaven is just not awarded to one who cannot wait and commits suicide, for that would be cheating... So one must make the best of the earthly gift of life, and internalize John 3:16.

Jesus states, "I must say, Ernest, when I created you, I had a number of missions that I had for you to do for me. Suicide left those jobs undone, so I cannot say 'well done'... By cutting your life short like you did, you still owe me.

Another big item that did not endear me to you is the fact that I created you in my own image. I lived in you, thus making your body my temple. Your alcoholism, womanism, and accident-prone-ism showed your contempt for this body as Temple idea. You showed a flagrant disrespect for my Temple, which was your body. So let's get clear on that already.

Suicide shows the ultimate disrespect for my temple, and it cuts your time short for all the missions I had in mind for you to perform for me. So there you go friend. You really let me down in two ways.

Ernest... The life I gave you was a gift not to be used or abused by you, but to be pressed into service for me in my mission, not for your personal amusement and frivolity, so the greeting I reserved for you; 'Well done thou good and faithful servant,' can never refer to you."

I reply... "Gosh, I'm awfully sorry, Lord. Dang, I feel so stupid for I knew, too."

"My son... Well... It's too late now. You are just a big disappointment. Had you some faith in me and my mission, and died when and where I wanted you to die, I could've overlooked all your shortcomings, but you never took responsibility for any of your actions, nor did you ever drop your belief in luck and knocking on wood, and rabbits feet and horse chestnuts... It's very pagan, very superstitious.

Now, I want to tell you I got very jealous of that. You had more faith in that crap than in me.

Look here. I created you. I knew you before you were planted in your mother. I created all that is. This is my universe, and I am the boss, and now you, my rebellious servant, sneak up here and expect me to cut you a deal, well the best I can do is purgatory, overlooking the outer realms of heaven, pal.

Although you had achieved high awards on earth, the best I can give you here as a nominal, lukewarm Christian would be a D-."

Having never taken well to criticism of any kind by anyone, in fact if any critic of literary worth ever made a derogatory crack at me in print, he was sure to receive a broken jaw next time I saw the jerk, but here we have Jesus taking charge, literally cutting me down to size.

I have never gotten a D- in my life, but now in purgatory, my life was only worth that, and I knew it. I was not gonna get a free pass into heaven where there was, no bluffing, and definitely no room for BS, and no press pass allowed me in, for nobody ever goes back to earth to report on purgatory or heaven for that matter. My position is to be on the outskirts now looking in, never having had the faith needed to enter like a good and faithful servant.

Such is my fate now having taken my own life without honoring Him who made me, and Who had serious plans for me in His world. I pray now that some poor depressed soul would ask God to help out, for not to do so is the greatest insult to Him and His gift of life. He is always near to help out.

Learning now the hard way, I am finding out that morning I put the double-barreled shotgun to my forehead was the greatest mistake I could've made.

I wasted my life. Instead of learning how to prepare for eternity while on earth, I blew it, for my life on earth was meant to be a launching pad for the afterlife.

The irony in all this, is that I knew all this from reading and actually memorizing God's word, the Bible , so I of all people should have known; however, I guess I never took religion seriously. I thought I could make it on my own. How arrogant of me!

After reading Hebrews 11:6, I discovered now all of my earthly achievements meant nothing to Jesus because only those with faith are able to please him.

Romans 10:9 says it all; namely, Jesus is Lord and Savior. Had I espoused this little truth, I would be in heaven, had I waited for Him to take me at my final hour.

Had I waited for God to call me home, I wouldn't be on the outside of heaven now looking in. Not being allowed to enter paradise is frustrating to me. Had I waited on God's time, I could've renewed my faith. While still in my body, there was always the hope of getting my faith back.

Like in baseball, a team gets three outs. That final out was never made deliberately. Only a damn fool would give up and give up hope. Only a damn fool would give up a chance with there being one more out in which to start a rally or hit a home run, or something, maybe get hit by a wild pitch or player might walk, or hit a bloop single. The point is, anything can happen for a player who never gives up hope and hangs in there.

Mudville never gave up hope as the mighty Casey came to bat. The fans went wild as there still is hope. While a man still has life and breath there is hope, for God can still step in and create His miracles. To end one's own life is to lose courage and fail at faith in the God who created us. While a team has two outs, they still have hope of scoring the win, someone could hit a home run or the next man up could get ahead and start a rally. Many a game has been won in the ninth ending with two outs, but no, I made a conscious decision to end my life on my own, thus ending any last minute rally, thus closing out any intervention by God to enter and perform a miracle. That was a time to ask God for help!

Success in my life had all come from God. He had revealed Himself many times, but due to my getting lost in fame, my arrogance made me forget that.

I was up to bat. There were two outs and I never let God have a chance to lift me up out of depression. All hope is gone because I thought so. Satan had so deluded my mind that thoughts of God never entered in.

By taking my own life, I had forfeited any chance for God to intervene and create a turnaround in the final days of my miserable life.

I was a damn fool to think that the harassing, conflicting voices would stop once the brain was gone.

What a damn fool I was to expect that. Even without my brain the condemning voices continued in my conscience were from Satan, or Satan was amplifying my own chattering conscience, either way there is absolutely no escaping the continual review of all my past mistakes.

Back in Key West when bothered by the condemning voices I always could stroll over to Sloppy Joe's bar, and after a few mojitos or gin gimlets, the alcohol dulled the sting of those chattering condemning courses. During those hours at Joe's bar, I could easily get distracted by my pals storytelling, group songs, or by flirting with the local whores; however, come the dawn of the next morning the voices would return with a vengeance. The splitting headache and hangover were also inescapable.

Reliving that fateful morning when I calmly got up before Mary, slipped on my bathrobe, and unlocked the gun rack, it all seems too easy. Usually there was always someone around to thwart my attempts at suicide.

Going over that methodical loading of my favorite shotgun and slowly shuffling out to the porch, I was certain Mary heard me, but where was she? And why was the gun rack key in the usual place, in plain sight, so easily found. Then the thought struck me! I have an accomplice in my own suicide!

My own loving wife stands to come into about four, maybe $5 million, plus royalties, product endorsements, the entire estate, and probably two or three manuscripts awaiting an editor before publishing. All motive enough to encourage and even grease the skids toward me engaging in my own demise.

I never actually took time to write a farewell or suicide note. Imagine that? A writer who fails to leave a goodbye note. That right there sends up another red flag that possibly I was hoping she again would interrupt yet another of my suicide attempts, but there again, no one came to stop this latest attempt.

I was unprepared in my electric shock mangled brainset, Mary and I had been playing a sick, childish game of cat and mouse; namely, I would attempt suicide and she would thwart my tries each time. Sounds silly, I know, but it gave us an edgy sick thrill each time we engaged in the game, only this day something went wrong. Mary had loaded the gun with real shells, and not the blanks which we usually used. She tricked me!

If she were on serious suicide watch, Mary would have hidden the key and been up for me, making morning coffee. This day was utterly irregular, but I now see her motives for deliberately sleeping in, or faking sleep, that fateful morning, and for leaving the key to my gun rack, and loading the gun with real, live ammo. She had changed the complexion of our little game.

She had won the game, and as a result she had won all my fortune and also the future royalties of a number of my books, published posthumously.

That Mary was a smart cookie. Maybe a jealous one too. She will tell the sheriff it was an unfortunate accident. However my biggest surprise, even bigger than discovering that my shotgun was loaded with live ammo was the fact that there is an afterlife.

When the body dies, the spirit lives on! Now I should've known that from my own earlier death experience back in World War I when a trench mortar blew my spirit right out of my body. It felt like the way a silk handkerchief gets lifted out of one's sport coat, but after 50 years of writing hedonistic novels where the code hero fights hard and plays hard like there is no tomorrow, I guess I forgot. Most of my heroes are macho, hard fighting, hard-boiled bullfighters or hard fishing unlimited characters who fear nothing, with no regard for an afterlife. Taking huge risks with no regard to life or limb. My overlying themes always were: when you're dead you are dead. Death is final; therefore, live hard and courageously for there is no room for a coward, or a weak pansy who faints at one drink, or at the sight of blood, nor at the approach of the thundering herd of Huns, or water buffalo, or angry male lions.

At some point, I myself became that code hero living out my own life as one who had walked out of the pages of my latest novel. All the tabloids and newsreels live off my wild private life as it made for extra sales at the bookstores, and my publisher made no attempt to discourage my larger-than-life lifestyle.

I had a knack for irony. In fact, my writing often played on irony. In fact the shock that occurs when the story takes an unexpected twist is my main tool and plot in most cases. Irony appears in almost every novel.

Upon the very end of my stories I could surprise my readers with an ironic twist. Irony figured big in my stories, so imagine my very own shock when thinking death was actually final, only for me to discover that it ain't.

What a total shock, more than the physical shock of the top of my cranium being blown off. Ironically my mind continues, death is not the end. Death is not as final as I thought it was. I used to believe that when you are dead that's it...you're dead. The end. Irony was at the very end of my miserable life for my existence does go on and will continually remind me of my many regrets and failures during my earthly existence.

Irony let me out of my body and opened the door which ushered in an unending flood of the saddest of memories, and constant rehashing of all my shortcomings.

During this pity party, the thought struck me that since suicide put me in purgatory, I should begin to run into others who also did themselves in.

Wandering down the dreary path which led to the moat which surrounded heaven, I heard water bubbling and upon closer examination I saw what resembled a tub of bubbling water. A dark-haired girl sat in the tub with water up to her brown neck. As I circled around to get a glimpse of her face, I immediately recognized her. It was Prudy.

"Howdy, my Ernie. Prudy happy to see you."

"P-P-Prudy. Happy to see you too. I heard you had killed yourself."

"Oh, Ernie, me have a horrible death. Me ate rat poison. Took long time. Heap big painful way to kill yourself. Hop in tub. Prudy purging out bad mistakes in hot bubbling water. Climb in. Make them get you clean."

Slowly my feet entered the cleansing tub. Before long, I was also up to my neck in hot, foaming waters. Prudy had not changed a bit. Still, she could roll her big brown eyes and melt me with her Woodland Indian bluntness.

"So, Prudy guesses you killum yourself two, huh? How you do that?"

"Oh heck, it was an accident... now that I think about it. Shotgun to the head... Quick and painless."

"Prudy heap big pregnant with your child."

"Oh, I'm sorry. Why didn't you tell me? We could have got married, Prudy."

"Mixed race child not accepted in my tribe, Ernie. Prudy die one heap big disgrace. Little Ernie across the river now, he in heaven."

"Yeah Prudy. I think you are right. The world is not ready for a mixed marriage or a mixed child of any mixture."

"Indian and a white... What a sight, but Little Ernie, he one handsome boy. My Ernie, we made heap nice boy."

"But I guess the time was not right. Oak Park society would have run us three out of town, huh, Prudy, and same with your tribe?"

"My tribe love'um you, Ernie. In few generations may be, but not now. No way, just not now!"

"Oh no! Not now for sure. Sorry you had to end your life in such a darn painful way. Do the hot bubbles help you clear your aura?"

"Some Prudy folk try to speed up cleansing. They run'um through fire. Flame will clean'um you up in a hurry, but Prudy like'um bubble tub. My Ernie, you might like'um too."

Being in purgatory was still quite new to me, I decided to soak with Prudy. The cleansing action of the bubbling waters seemed more pleasant than running through hot flames.

"My Ernie, you should hear little Ernie play the trumpet. Sometimes he comes out to edge of heaven to see his mother. We see him... be proud."

"Let me guess... Gabriel is his instructor?"

"You bet."

Being as my Pops used to play coronet in Mother's band, my mind soon pictured the two of them playing a duet. My guess was such a thing might very well be in the works to give me motivation to desire heaven, because right now I was sure not enjoying purgatory with my old Indian girlfriend in our hot tub together.

Tiring of the hot tub, one can only take so much of it, Prudy offered to show me what she had discovered since her stay in purgatory.

Hand in hand, we old friends strolled along the perimeter of heaven marveling at its beautiful gold and jeweled streets, it's towering vistas of crystal cathedrals, and outdoor amphitheater's connected with numerous overpasses and transparent bridgework, and I wondered if my neighbor Frank Lloyd Wright was up here designing things. All streets lead to an elaborate center throne where Jesus presided. Along side of that beautiful throne was the river of life, and on each side were 12 trees of life which they all ate from.

Each month, the tree produced a new fruit, reminding me of the garden of Eden tree from which Adam and Eve did freely eat.

"Well, Prudy, who are all these men in uniform?"

"That be all your poor pals who die'um in World War I. Must be 1 million. They always have a group sing about this time. They be, what you say, buddies? Spanish Civil War boys join them sometimes."

"Now Prudy, dear, how can we get promoted into heaven?"

"You best have'um friends and family who can pray you out of purgatory, my Ernie."

I then thought of my Pops and wonder if Uncle Willoughby or Uncle Tyler may be praying Pops in right now. Thinking also of my favorite authors now. Had Kipling and Conrad made it? Had Robert Louis Stevenson and Jack London and Samuel Clemons, and did the long list of many other writers of choice actually make it?

Keeping them in mind, my curiosity had me asking Jesus for a test trip to heaven, just to see who had made the long sojourn, and while I was at it, I was wondering if we could cruise by the tree of life which was producing fruit this month. Buildings beckon me with the desire to enter.

Being a nominal Christian was barely keeping me out of hell, yet it was also showing up as a non-benefit as far as heaven was concerned. We purgatorians needed to get unified to negotiate with Jesus as to clarification of steps necessary for future entrance into heaven.

Needing a strong lobby now, it had become obvious as to what purgatorians needed most up here, and yours truly was just the man who could give it a try.

Having experienced reporting on peace conferences at Luazanne, in Geneva, and interviewing heads of state around the world, I have developed courage to probe and present challenging questions to Jesus who appeared to me as one magistrate who might be open to my lobbying for better living conditions, which might give us hope for eventual entrance into heaven. Following this concept to its rightful conclusion meant I would soon be forming a union of dedicated purgatorians... a union with one aim and that would be to negotiate a pact with the son of God and how we could eventually enter heaven, His father's kingdom.

"Say there, sir,... Jesus, please, can I have a word with you?"

"Certainly, what's on your mind, Mr. Hemingway?"

"Well, a couple of the boys and I had a great idea yesterday."

"You've been thinking again, haven't you? You know how that always gets you in trouble, my son."

"Well, yeah, I know, but some of us purgatorians got to feeling kinda low, seeing as all the action that goes on up here always goes on in heaven, on the other side of the river, we feel more needs to be done to clarify what needs to be done on our part to enter there. In heaven that is."

"Mr. Hemingway, that's been on my mind also. We could use your creative mind. Did you know I created you before we found a suitable mom-and-pop for you? I created you like all others... In my image, born to create."

And so it goes on and on, Jesus and I dialogued until I got a standard prayer for all souls in purgatory which is spoken now in the churches at each daily mass.

Continuing to fight for purgatory rights, I plead for all my fans to pray for us, but it became obvious that Jesus was not one to be pressured by political maneuvering by his purgatory subjects. In fact, the only thing getting his attention was acts done in faith by his earthly flock, period!

Faith is the sole factor getting his attention. Any benevolent project done without faith he ignored, as one would consider dirty rags.

I know it doesn't sound democratic, but faith was the common denominator that moved Jesus. Faith moves mountains, was a term I often heard, and without faith it is impossible to please Him.

So it became clear that any good project not done with faith as the motivating factor would get tossed in the garbage. So much for the purgatory union, and so much for my earthly fame if it did not engender faith, nor was motivated by faith.

"Well, Prudy, I'm back. Slide over, make room for your Ernie and his hot tub."

"My Ernie, you will need more so come in bubble tub. How goes it with Jesus?"

"Not good, my Indian Princess. He only accepts faith as the going currency. Now we did get added to the prayers during Catholic communion. That was priceless. Kinda like Job's sacrifice and prayer to God benefited his sons."

"Better than nothing, my Ernie. Hop in."

"Hey! Who turned up the heat?"

You'um, my Ernie. You need'um more purging. Heap big fire walk tonight. Are you'um up for that?"

"Fire walk? Heck yeah! I'll try anything to get out of purgatory. It will be an adventure. You know me, always looking for adventure... white Ernie, brave warrior. Pretty proud. So, will I need anything? Asbestos socks, maybe insulated shoes? Will it be hot as hell?"

"When drums began, you'um will follow leader."

After listening at great length, waiting to hear hypnotic drums, it dawned on me that these folks all were pagans, and at best pantheists, with whom I used to run and hunt and fish. Their vision of heaven was somewhere called their happy hunting ground. Jesus played no part whatsoever in this religion, and it all became apparent to me now, that Jesus death had to be efficient enough to also include the sins of a guy like me, thus canceling the need for purgatory. In fact the establishment of purgatory would seem to me as an insult to the power and efficiency of Jesus' atonement.

With that breakthrough, all of purgatory began to fade from view, as if it had all been a bad dream. As I continue to dwell on the power of Jesus body and blood, I saw a golden bridge appear in front of me, and then Peter walked up to me and placed a shimmering silver robe around my shoulders.

"Your faith has gained you leave into the side entrance of heaven you have desired. Arise, shake off this bad dream and claim your rightful heritage based upon your belief in the power of the body and blood of our Lord."

Tying my sparkling robe at my neck, I stepped into the side door of heaven. The light emanating from everything was almost blinding, and a choir of angels showed me up to the river of life which was flanked on both sides by trees of life, one of which was filled with fruit.

An angel holding a silver tray offered me spiritual fruit and drink from a crystal cup containing living water, from this special river, and I did partake, and I thought to myself that this hero's entrance could have been mine at the main High gate with Jesus and all His glory, with trumpet fanfare's and angel choirs from the start, had I not killed myself, had I waited on God's time to call me.

St. Peter had no 'well done thou good and faithful servant' speech, none of that, but at least I finally made it and even if it wasn't at the main gate.

Entering at the side door of any establishment had never been my style in life, but up here in heaven the front gate is only for those who have cultivated a daily personal relationship with the Lord Jesus, and who had followed His plan for their life, enduring to the end when He calls them home.

That sums up the way I got into heaven, but I would not recommend it for anyone because Jesus doesn't like it. Since suicide shows a lack of faith, and faith is the ticket needed to enter.

Hope is lost when one contemplates ending their own life, and hope comes as a result of faith. Hope brings certainty of future events, a certain confidence of positive things yet to come. Our walk with Jesus gives eternal hope, but we walk a path illuminated each step of the way, each moment of each day until He calls us home, all in His good time.

Now Prudy's faith is in some impersonal God found only in nature which somehow fails to include Jesus.

When she mentioned my joining up with her people at a fire walk, a red light of caution came up for me. At the mention of drums, that kinda did it for me. I knew that I was ready to move on. Purgatory no longer could hold me.

Her tribal drummers can hypnotize a guy; however, that was not something I needed. My mind needed to be clear of tribal ritual so's I could have the breakthrough which Jesus needed me to have regarding the inclusive potency of His whole body blood sacrifice.

Faith in the gospel can propel the dead right out of the grave, as seen at Lazarus's tomb, and at my Lord's tomb Easter morn. Over trumped by my strong desire for heaven, Prudy's tribal magic soon faded from importance for me and so I left her soaking in the hot tub. She couldn't get it through her head how God could come down as baby Jesus and then sacrifice Himself in redemption for our mistakes, but now she has two reasons to figure out how to get into heaven: her son, and me, for Jesus died for all including our Native American Indian folk.

Being as Prudy attended Green Sky Methodist Church in Charlevoix, along with her brother and mother Anna Tabeshaw, I am certain she has heard the gospel message. Now my only hope is that

Jesus powerful truth germinates in her heart and mind, and sprouts into a mature faith, and functions as a giant magnet pulling her spirit out of purgatory and into the marvelous light of His heaven.

One of my many regrets now is that I never pushed Jesus enough among my friends. In fact, as I recall there were many chances to witness to Billy Tabeshaw, Prudy's brother, but we were too busy fishing and shooting, and just being boys in the Michigan woods.

Having parents who are fanatical about religion had become boring, and their hypocrisy gave us Hemingway kids the big turnoff, as we never felt very enthusiastic about religion as we got older. Our parents were too damn strict in the application of the law, so after a half dozen ass whippings, in the name of God, we all kinda lost respect for religion after that.

Had that ass whipping occurred today, my parents would be in jail and they would lose custody of all six of us. Little did I know at the time, but us kids grew up abused, not only physically but mentally as well, by a couple of the most God-fearing, Bible-thumpers of the day...members in good standing at the Third Congregationalist Church of Oak Park, Illinois.

Their brand of Christianity caused four (half) of the Hemingway family to take our own lives: Clarence our father, me, Ernie, Ursula, and little brother Leichester. Kinda scary when I look back at it. Rumor has it, Marcy ended her life later on, after her book came out, so that would bring the tally up to five of eight, and some of my grandkids have also cut their own lives short.

Sunny and Carol were the only ones to live on and die of natural causes. I am sure they went directly through main gate heaven, had the trumpet fanfare, and St. Peter and Jesus saying, 'well done my good and faithful servant.'

I feel the need to pontificate some more about this whole process of making it into heaven, however, it isn't that complicated after all. I think the simplicity of it all tripped me up, but now I get it. All that is required of us is faith and honoring the power of the body and blood of our Lord.

THE END

The Hemingways: Marceline, Sunny, Dr. Clarence, Mother Grace, Ursula, and Ernie.

www.ingramcontent.com/pod-product-compliance
Lightning Source LLC
Chambersburg PA
CBHW050543260626
47157CB00002B/413